Jonathan Kellerman is one of the world's most popular authors. He has brought his expertise as a clinical psychologist to more than two dozen bestselling crime novels, including the Alex Delaware series, *Bones*, *The Butcher's Theatre*, *Billy Straight*, *The Conspiracy Club* and *Twisted*. He is the author of numerous essays, short stories, scientific articles, two children's books and three volumes of psychology, including *Savage Spawn: Reflections On Violent Children*. He has won the Goldwyn, Edgar and Anthony awards, and has been nominated for a Shamus Award. Jonathan lives in California and New Mexico, with his wife, writer Faye Kellerman, and their four children, which include the novelist Jesse Kellerman.

Praise for Jonathan Kellerman's novels:

'When they're this good, it's impossible to get enough'
Mirror

'Kellerman has shaped the psychological mystery novel into an art form'   *Los Angeles Times Book Review*

'An alert eye for detail . . . Engrossing'   *New York Times*

'Plot and sub-plot coalesce satisfyingly in high octane entertainment that never loses its characters' vulnerability'
The Times

'A fast, professional read, with strong insights into the quirks of human   *Guardian*

D1369222

By Jonathan Kellerman

THE BUTCHER'S THEATRE
THE CONSPIRACY CLUB

Alex Delaware Novels
WHEN THE BOUGH BREAKS
BLOOD TEST
OVER THE EDGE
SILENT PARTNER
TIME BOMB
PRIVATE EYES
DEVIL'S WALTZ
BAD LOVE
SELF-DEFENCE
THE WEB
THE CLINIC
SURVIVAL OF THE FITTEST
MONSTER
DOCTOR DEATH
FLESH AND BLOOD
THE MURDER BOOK
A COLD HEART
THERAPY
RAGE
GONE
OBSESSION
COMPULSION
BONES
TRUE DETECTIVES

Novels featuring Petra Connor
BILLY STRAIGHT
TWISTED

With Faye Kellerman
DOUBLE HOMICIDE
CAPITAL CRIMES

JONATHAN KELLERMAN

BILLY STRAIGHT

headline

First published in the United States in 1998
by Random House Inc.

First published in Great Britain in 1998
by Little, Brown and Company

This edition published in 2009
by HEADLINE PUBLISHING GROUP

10 9 8 7 6 5 4 3 2 1

Cataloguing in Publication Data is available from the British Library

ISBN 978 0 7553 4294 5

Typeset in Fournier MT by Palimpsest Book Production Limited,
Grangemouth, Stirlingshire

Printed and bound in Great Britain by CPI Mackays, Chatham ME5 8TD

Headline's policy is to use papers that are natural, renewable and recyclable
products and made from wood grown in sustainable forests.
The logging and manufacturing processes are expected to conform
to the environmental regulations of the country of origin.

HEADLINE PUBLISHING GROUP
An Hachette UK Company
338 Euston Road
London NW1 3BH

www.headline.co.uk
www.hachette.co.uk

To Faye. For Faye. At the core, it's always Faye.

'Unique is she, my constant dove,
My perfect one.'

Song of Songs, VI:9

1

IN THE park you see things.

But not what I saw tonight.

God, God...

I wanted to be dreaming but I was awake, smelling chili-meat and onions and the pine trees.

First, the car drove up to the edge of the parking lot. They got out and talked and he grabbed her, like in a hug. I thought maybe they were going to kiss and I'd watch that.

Then all of a sudden, she made a weird sound – surprised, squeaky, like a cat or dog that gets stepped on.

He let go of her and she fell. Then he bent down next to her and his arm started moving up and down really fast. I thought he was punching her and that was bad enough and I kept thinking should I do something. But then I heard another sound, fast, wet, like the butcher at Stater Brothers back in Watson chopping meat *chuck chuck chuck*.

He kept *doing* it, moving his arm up and down.

I wasn't breathing. My heart was on fire. My legs were cold. Then they turned hot-wet.

Pissing my pants like a stupid baby!

The *chuck chuck* stopped. He stood up, big and wide, wiped his hands on his pants. Something was in his hand and he held it far from his body.

He looked all around. Then in my direction.

Could he see me, hear me – *smell* me?

He kept looking. I wanted to run but knew he'd hear me. But staying here could trap me – how could he see anything behind the rocks? They're like a cave with no roof, just cracks you can look through, which is the reason I picked them as one of my places.

My stomach started to churn around and I wanted to run so badly my leg muscles were jumping under my skin.

A breeze came through the trees, blowing up pine smell and piss stink.

Would it blow against the chili-burger's wrapping paper and make noise? Would he smell me?

He looked around some more. My stomach hurt so bad.

All of a sudden he jumped, ran back to the car, got in, drove away.

I didn't want to see when he passed under the lamp at the corner of the parking lot, didn't want to read the license plate.

PLYR 1.

The letters burned into my mind.

Why did I look?

Why?

I'm still sitting here. My Casio says 1:12 A.M.

I need to get out of here but what if he's just driving around and comes back – no, that would be stupid, why would he do that?

I can't stand it. She's down there and I smell like piss and meat and onions and chili. Real dinner from the Oki-Rama on the Boulevard, that Chinese guy who never smiles or

2

looks at your face. I paid two dollars thirty-eight and now I want to throw it up.

My jeans are starting to get sticky and itchy. Going over to the public bathroom at the other end of the lot is too dangerous . . . that arm going up and down. Like he was just doing a job. He wasn't as big as Moron, but he was big enough. She trusted him, let him hug her . . . what did she do to make him so mad . . . could she still be *alive*?

No way. Impossible.

I listen carefully to see if she's making any sounds. Nothing but the freeway noise from across the east side of the park and traffic from the Boulevard. Not much traffic tonight. Sometimes, when the wind blows north, you hear ambulance sirens, motorcycles, car honks. The city's all around. The park looks like the country but I know the difference.

Who is she? – forget that, I don't want to know.

What I *want* is to put tonight on Rewind.

That squeaky sound – like he took the air right out of her. For sure she's . . . gone. But what if she *isn't*?

Even if she isn't, she will be soon, all that *chucking*. And what could I do for her, anyway? Breathe into her mouth, put my face in her blood?

What if he comes back while I'm doing it?

Would he come back? That would be stupid, but there are always surprises. She sure found that out.

I can't help her. I have to put this all out of my mind.

I'll sit here for ten more minutes – no, fifteen. Twenty. Then I'll get my Place Two stuff together and move.

Where to? Place One, up near the observatory, is too far, and so are Three and Four, even though Three would be

3

good, cause it has a stream for washing. That leaves Five, in the fern tangle behind the zoo, all those trees. A little closer but still a long walk in the dark.

But it's also the hardest one to find.

OK, I'll go to Five. Me and the animals. The way they cry and roar and smash against their cages makes it hard to sleep but tonight I probably won't sleep anyway.

Meantime, I sit here and wait.

Pray.

Our Father in Heaven, how about no more surprises?

Not that praying ever got me anything and sometimes I wonder if there's anyone up there to pray to or just stars — humongous balls of gas in an empty black universe.

Then I get worried that I'm blaspheming.

Maybe some kind of God *is* up there, maybe He's saved me lots of times and I'm just too dumb to know it. Or not a good enough person to appreciate Him.

Maybe God saved me *tonight*, putting me behind the rocks instead of out in the open.

But if he had seen me when he drove up, he probably would've changed his mind and not done anything to her.

So did God *want* her to . . .

No, he just would've gone somewhere else to do it . . . whatever.

In case you saved me, thank you God.

In case you're up there, do you have a plan for me?

2

When the call came into Hollywood Division, Petra Connor was well into overtime but up for more action.

Sunday, she'd enjoyed unusually peaceful sleep from 8 A.M. to 4 P.M., no gnawing dreams, thoughts of ravaged brain tissue, empty wombs, things that would never be. Waking to a nice, warm afternoon, she took advantage of the light and spent an hour at her easel. Then, half a pastrami sandwich and a Coke, a hot shower, and off to the station to finalize the stakeout.

She and Stu Bishop rolled out just after dark, cruising alleys and ignoring minor felonies; they had more important things on their minds. Selecting a spot, they sat watching the apartment building on Cherokee, not talking.

Usually they chatted, managed to turn the boredom into semi-fun. But Stu had been acting weird lately. Remote, tight-lipped, as if the job no longer interested him.

Maybe it was five days on graveyard.

Petra was bugged but what could she do, he was the senior partner. She put it aside, thought about Flemish pictures at the Getty. Amazing pigments, superb use of light.

Two hours of butt-numbing stasis. Their patience paid off just after 2 A.M. and another imbecilic but elusive killer hooked up.

Now she sat at a scabrous metal desk opposite Stu, completing the paperwork, thinking about going back to her apartment, maybe doing some sketching. The five days had energized her. Stu looked half dead as he talked to his wife.

It was a warm June, well before daybreak, and the fact that the two of them were still there at the tail end of a severely understaffed graveyard shift was a fluke.

Petra had been a detective for exactly three years, the first twenty-eight months in Auto Theft, the remaining eight in daytime Homicide with Stu.

Her partner was a nine-year vet and a family man. Dayshift suited his lifestyle and his biorhythms. Petra had been a nighthawk from childhood, before the deep blue midnights of her artist days, when lying awake at night had been inspirational.

Well before her marriage, when listening to Nick's breathing had lulled her to sleep.

She lived alone now, loved the black of night more than ever. Black was her favorite color, as a teenager she'd worn nothing but. So wasn't it odd that she'd never asked for night-time assignments since graduating the academy?

It was adherence to duty that brought about the temporary switch.

Wayne Carlos Freshwater crawled out at night, scoring weed and crack and pills on Hollywood sidestreets, killing prostitutes. No way was he going to be found when the sun shone.

Over a six-month period, he'd strangled four street-girls that Petra and Stu knew about, the last one a sixteen-year-old runaway from Idaho whom he'd tossed in an alley dumpster near Selma and Franklin. No cutting but a pocket

6

knife found at the scene yielded prints and led to a search for Freshwater.

Incredibly stupid, dropping the blade, but no big surprise. Freshwater's file said his IQ had been tested twice by the state: Eighty-three and ninety-one. Not that it had stopped him from eluding them.

Male black, thirty-six years old, five seven, 140, multiple arrests and convictions over the last twenty years, the last for an ag assault/attempted rape which sent him to Soledad for ten years, cut down, of course, to four.

The usual sullen mugshot, bored with the process.

Even when they caught him, he looked bored. No sudden moves, no attempt at escape, just standing there in a rancid hallway, pupils dilated, faking cool. But after the cuffs went on, he switched to wide-eyed surprise.

Whud I do, Officer?

The funny thing was, he *looked* innocent. Knowing his size, Petra had expected some Napoleon full of testosterone, but here was this dainty little twerp with a dainty little Michael Jackson voice. Neatly dressed, too. Preppy, brand-new Gap stuff, probably boosted. Later, the jailer told her Freshwater'd been wearing women's underwear under the pressed khakis.

The ten-year Soledad invitation had been for choking a sixty-year-old grandmother in Watts. Freshwater was released angrier than ever and took a week to get going again, ratcheting up the violence level.

Great system. Petra used the memory of Freshwater's moronic surprise to get herself smiling as she completed the report.

Whud I do?

You were a bad, bad boy.

7

Stu was still on the phone with Kathy: Home soon, honey, kiss the kids for me.

Six kids, lots of kissing. Petra had watched them line up for Stu before dinner, platinum heads, sparkling hands and nails.

It had taken her a long time to be able to look at other people's kids without thinking of her own useless ovaries.

Stu loosened his tie. She caught his eye but he looked away. Going back on days would be good for him.

He was thirty-seven, eight years Petra's senior, looked closer to thirty, a slim, nice-looking man with wavy blond hair and gold-hazel eyes. The two of them had been quickly labeled Ken and Barbie, even though Petra had the dark tresses. Stu had a taste for expensive traditional suits, white French-cuffed shirts, braided leather suspenders and striped silk ties, carried the most frequently oiled 9mm in the department, and a Screen Actors' Guild card from doing bit parts in TV cop shows. Last year he'd made Detective-III.

Smart, ambitious, a devout Mormon, he and pretty Kathy and the half-dozen tykettes lived on a one-acre spread in La Crescenta. He'd been a great teacher for Petra, no sexism or personal garbage, a good listener. Like Petra, a work-fiend, driven to achieve maximal arrests. Match made in heaven. Till a week ago. What was wrong?

Something political? The first day they partnered he informed her he was thinking about shifting to the paper track eventually, going for lieutenant.

Preparing her for goodbye, but he hadn't mentioned it since.

Petra wondered if he was aiming even higher. His father was a successful ophthalmologist and Stu had grown up in a huge house in Flintridge, surfed in Hawaii, skied in Utah, was used to good things.

Captain Bishop. Deputy Chief Bishop. She could imagine him in a few years, with graying temples, Cary Grant crinkles, charming the press, playing the game. But doing a solid job, because he was substance as well as style.

Freshwater was a major bust. So why didn't it matter to him?

Especially because he was the one who'd really solved it. The old-fashioned way. Despite the Joe Clean demeanor, nine years had made him an expert on streetlife, and he'd collected a stable of lowlife confidential informants.

Two separate CI's had come through on Freshwater, each reporting that the hooker-killer had a heavy crack habit, was selling stolen goods on the Boulevard at night and scoring rock at a flop apartment on Cherokee. Two gift-wraps: Precise address, down to the apartment number, and exactly where the dealers' lookouts hung out.

Stu and Petra staked out for three nights. On the third, they grabbed Freshwater as he entered the building from the back, and Petra got to clamp the cuffs.

Delicate wrists. *Whud I do, Officer?* She chuckled out loud and filled the arrest form's inadequate spaces with her elegant draftsman's hand.

Just as Stu hung up his phone, Petra's jangled. She picked up and the sergeant downstairs said, 'Guess what, Barbie? Got a call from the park rangers over at Griffith. Woman down in a parking lot, probable 187. Tag, you're it.'

'Which lot in Griffith?'

'East end, back behind one of the picnic areas. It's supposed to be chained off, but you know how that goes.

Take Los Feliz like you're going to the zoo, instead of continuing on to the freeway, turn off. The blues'll be there along with a ranger car. Do it Code Two.'

'Sure, but why us?'

'Why you?' The sergeant laughed. 'Look around. See anyone else but you and Kenny? Blame the city council.' She hung up.

'What?' said Stu. His Carroll & Company foulard was tightly knotted and his hair was perfectly combed. But tired, definitely tired.

Petra told him.

He stood and buttoned his jacket. 'Let's go.'

No gripe. Stu never complained.

3

I PACK up my Place Two stuff in three layers of dry-cleaner's plastic and begin walking up the hill behind the rocks, into the trees. I trip and fall a lot because I'm afraid to use the penlight until I get deep inside but I don't care, just get me out of here.

The zoo's miles away, it will take a long time.

I walk like a machine that can't be hurt, thinking what he did to her. No good. I have to put it out of my mind.

Back in Watson, after trouble with Moron or any kind of difficult day, I used lists to keep my mind busy. Sometimes it worked.

Here goes: Presidents. In order of election: Washington, Adams, Jefferson, Madison, Monroe, Quincy Adams, Jackson, Martin Van Buren . . . the shortest President.

Oh shit, here I go again, down on my knees. I get up. Keep going.

Back in Watson, I had a book on the Presidents, published by the Library of Congress with heavy paper and excellent photographs and the official Presidential seal on the cover. I got it in fourth grade for winning the President Bee, read it about five hundred times, trying to put myself back in time, imagine what it was like to be George Washington, running a brand-new country, or Thomas Jefferson, an amazing genius, inventing things, writing with five pens at one time.

Even being Martin Van Buren, short but still boss over everyone.

Books became a problem when Moron moved in. He hated when I read, especially when his chopper was busted or Mom had no money for him.

Little fuck with his fuckin' books, thinks he's smarter'n everyone.

After he moved in I had to sit in the kitchen while he and Mom took up my sleeper couch watching TV. One day he came in the trailer totally blasted while I was trying to do homework. I could tell because of his eyes and the way he just kept walking around in circles, making fists and opening them, making that growling noise. The homework was pre-algebra, easy stuff. Mrs Annison didn't believe me the one time I told her I already knew it, and she kept assigning me the same work as the rest of the class. I was speeding through the problems, almost finished, when Moron got a container of bean dip out of the fridge, started eating it with his hands. I looked at him, but just for a second. He reached over and pulled my hair and slammed the math book on my fingers. Then he grabbed up a bunch of notebooks and other text-books and ripped them in half, including the math book *Thinking with Numbers*.

He said, 'Fuck this shit!' and tossed it in the trash. 'Get off your fuckin' ass, you little faggot, do something useful around here . . .'

My hair smelled of beans and the next day my hand was so swollen I couldn't move the fingers and I kept it in my pocket when I told Mrs Annison I'd lost the book. She was eating corn nuts at her desk and grading papers and didn't bother to look up, just said, 'Well, Billy, I guess you'll have to buy another one.'

I couldn't ask Mom for money so I never got another book, couldn't do homework anymore, and my math grades started going down. I kept thinking Mrs Annison or someone would get curious but no one did.

Another time Moron ripped up this magazine collection I'd put together from other people's trash and most of my personal books, including the Presidents book. One of the first things I looked for when I finally located the library on Hillhurst Avenue was another Presidents book. I found one but it was different. Not as heavy paper, only black and white photographs. Still interesting, though. I learned that William Henry Harrison caught a cold right after his election and died.

Bad luck for the first William president.

This is working, my head's clear. But my heart and stomach feel like they're burning up. More: Taylor, Fillmore, Pierce . . . James Buchanan, the only President who never got married, must have been lonely for him in the White House, though I guess he was busy enough. Maybe he liked being alone. I can understand that.

Lincoln, Johnson, Grant, McKinley.

Another *William* president. Did anyone ever call him Billy? From his picture, bald and squinty and angry-looking, I don't think so.

No one ever called me William except teachers on the first day of school, and soon then they switched to Billy, too, because all the kids laughed at *William*.

Billy Goat, Billy the Goat.

William Bradley Straight.

It's a plain name, nothing special about it, but better than some of the other things I've been called.

Chuck chuck . . .

Oops – I stumble but don't fall. Place Five is still far. It's a warm night, I wish I could take off my piss-stink clothes and run through the trees naked, a wild, strong animal who knows where he's going . . . I'll breathe ten times to cool down my heart.

. . . Better. More lists: Tropical fish: Platys, swordtails, neon tetras, guppies, angelfish, oscars, catfish, tinfoil barbs, arowanas. Never had an aquarium but in my magazine collection were old copies of *Tropical Fish Hobbyist* and the pictures filled my head with color.

One point the fish articles kept making was you have to be careful setting up an aquarium, know who you're dealing with. Oscars and arowanas will eat all the others if they're big enough, and if the arowanas get really big they'll try to eat the oscars. Goldfish are the most peaceful, but they're also the slowest and get eaten all the time.

My stomach still burns, like someone's in there, chewing at me . . . breathe . . . animals you see in the park: Birds, lizards, squirrels, snakes once in a while. I ignore them.

Same for people.

At night you sometimes see homeless crazy guys with carts full of garbage but they never stay long. Also Mexicans in low cars, playing loud music. When they stop, it's over by the trains. Junkies, of course, because it's Hollywood. I've seen them drive up, sit at one of the picnic tables like they're ready to have a meal, tie up their arms, jab in needles and stare out at nothing.

14

After the dope really gets into their blood, they sigh and nod and fall asleep and they just look like anyone napping.

Sometimes couples park at the edge of the lot, including gay guys. Talking, making out, smoking – you can see cigarettes in the distance like little orange stars.

Everyone having a good time.

That's what I thought *they* were going to do, tonight.

Someone's always cutting the chain and the rangers take weeks to fix it. The cops don't patrol much because it's ranger territory. The park's huge. In the library I found a book that said it had 4,100 acres. It also said the park got started in a weird way: A crazy guy named Colonel Griffith tried to kill his wife and he had to give the land to the city in return for not going to jail.

So maybe there's something about the place that's unlucky for women . . .

Six hundred forty acres is a square mile so with 4,100 we're talking major humongous. I know, because I've walked most of it.

Sometimes the rangers stop and smoke and talk, too. A few weeks ago, a man and a woman ranger pulled over to the picnic area just after midnight, got out, sat down on their car's hood and started talking and laughing. Then they were kissing. I could hear their breathing get faster, heard her go 'Mmm,' and figured they'd be getting it on pretty soon. Then the woman pulled her head away and said, 'Come on, Burt. All we need is for someone to see us.'

Burt didn't say anything at first. Then: 'Aw, spoilsport.' But he was laughing and she started laughing, too, they kissed some more and felt each other up a little before they got back in their car and drove away. My guess is they didn't forget about having some sex, probably waited until work was over and then went somewhere else to do it. Maybe to one of their homes or one of those motels on the Boulevard where you pay for rooms by the hour and the prosties wait out in front.

Now I stay away from those motels, but when I first got here a prostie – a fat black one wearing bright shorts and a black lace top with nothing underneath – tried to sell herself to me.

She kept saying, 'C'mere, boy-child.' It sounded like '*Me, bocha, me bocha, me bocha.*' Then she pulled up her blouse and showed me a gigantic black tit. Her nipple was lumpy, big and purple like a fresh plum. I ran away and her laughter followed me the way a dog follows a chicken.

In a strange way she made me feel good, that she thought I could do it. Even though I knew she was probably kidding. I remember that nipple, the way she stuck it out at me, like here, take it, suck on it. Her mouth was wide open and her teeth were huge and white.

She was probably joking on me or just needed money bad and was ready to do it with anybody. Most of the prosties are junkies or crackheads.

The way those two rangers laughed was a little like the way the prostie laughed.

Is there such a thing as a sex laugh?

Being treated like a kid can be good or bad. When you go into a store with money, even if you're in line ahead of adults, the adults get served first. A bigger problem is the Boulevard, and all the smaller streets full of weirdos and perverts out to rape kids. Once I found a magazine in an alley and it showed pictures of perverts doing it with kids – putting dicks up their butts or in their mouths. Some kids were crying, others looked sleepy. You don't see the perverts' faces, just their hairy legs and their dicks. For a long time, it gave me nightmares, those kids, the way their eyes looked. But it also made me careful.

I've had guys pull up in cars when I'm walking, even in bright sunlight, waving money or candy bars or even their dicks. I ignore them and if they don't butt out, I run. Used to be when I was in a bad mood because of no dinner or a night full of bad dreams, I'd flip them off before I'd run. But a month ago one of them tried to run me down with his car. I got away from him but now I keep my finger to myself.

There's no telling what'll cause problems. A week ago, two guys got into a car accident on Gower, just a small dent in the front car but the guy got out with a baseball bat and smashed the other's windshield. Then he went for the other guy, who ran away.

You've got maniacs yelling and screaming at everyone and no one, gunshots all the time at night. I've even seen guys walking around during the day with bulges in their pockets that could be guns.

The only dead person I saw was an old shopping-cart guy lying in an alley, his mouth open like he was sleeping, but his skin had turned gray and flies went in and out between his lips. Nearby was the dumpster I was going to dive but I just got out of there, no more appetite. That night, I woke up really hungry thinking I was stupid to let it get to me. He was old, anyway.

17

When I get enough food, I'm full of energy. Super-fast. When I run, I feel jet-propelled, no gravity, no limits.

Sometimes I get into a running rhythm and it's like a music beat in my head, ba-boom, ba-boom, like nothing can stop me. When that happens I *force* myself to slow down because it's dangerous to forget who you are.

I also slow down anytime I'm about to go into the park. Way in advance. I always look around to make sure no one's watching me, then I head in, relaxed, like I live in one of the huge houses at the foot of the park.

One of the books Moron ripped up was by a French scientist named Jacques Cousteau, on octopus and squid. One chapter talked about how octopi can match their colors to their backgrounds. I'm no octopus but I know how to blend in.

I take things but that doesn't make me a thief.

I found the same octopus book in the library, borrowed it, brought it back.

I took the Presidents book and kept it.

But no one had checked it out for nine months, that's what the card in back said.

Back in Watson the library was pathetic, just a store next to the VFW hall that nobody used and it was mostly closed. The lady behind the desk always looked at me like I was going to take something and the funny thing was I never was.

At the Hillhurst library, there's also an old one but she mostly stays in her office and the one who actually checks books out is young, pretty, and Mexican with really long hair. She smiled at me once but I ignored her and the smile dropped from her face like I'd torn it off.

I can't get a library card because I have no address. My

18

technique is I go in there looking like a kid from King Middle School with homework to do, sit down by myself at a table and read and write for a while, usually math problems. Then I go back to the shelves.

I'll return the Presidents book one day.

Even if I kept it forever, no one would miss it. Probably.

An *advantage* of looking like a harmless little kid is sometimes you can go into a store and take stuff without being noticed. I know it's a sin but without food, you die and suicide's a sin, too.

Also: People aren't scared of kids, at least not white kids, so if you ask someone for spare change the worst they usually do is shine you on. I mean what are they going to say to me? Get a job, junior?

One thing I learned back in Watson: Make people nervous and you're the one who gets hurt.

So maybe God helped me by making me small for my age. I would like to grow eventually, though.

Mom, before she got sadder, would sometimes hold me under the chin and say 'Look at this. Like an angel. A damned *cherub*.'

I *hated* that, it sounded so *gay*.

Some of those kids being raped in the magazine looked like angels.

There's no way to know what's safe. I avoid all people and the park's perfect for that, 4,100 acres of mostly peace and quiet.

Thank you, crazy Mr Griffith.

The way he tried to kill his wife was by shooting her in the eye.

4

IN EIGHT months, Petra had worked twenty-one other homicides, some fairly sloppy. But nothing like this. Not even the Hernandez wedding.

This woman looked shredded. Washed in blood. *Dipped* in it, like fruit in chocolate. The front of her dress was a mass of gore, glossy gray tubes of entrail popping out from slashes in the fabric. Silky fabric, not great in terms of latents. The blood would be a good cover, too; try lifting anything from skin. Maybe the jewelry, if the killer had touched it.

She and Stu arrived in darkness, encountering grim faces, radio static, a blinking symphony of red lights. They took reports from the rangers who'd found the body, waited for sunrise to have a careful look at the victim.

The blood had dried red-brown, streaking the skin and the surrounding asphalt, running down the parking lot in rivulets, some of the spatters still tacky.

Petra stood by the corpse, sketching the surrounding terrain and the body, tabulating the wounds she could see. At least seventeen cuts and that was only the front.

Bending and getting as close as she could without messing anything up, she examined torn flesh, the lower lip almost completely severed, the left eye reduced to ruby pulp. All the damage on the left side.

If you could see your squeamish kid now, Dad.

Twenty-one other bodies notwithstanding, viewing this one in sunlight jolted her with nausea. Then something worse hit her: The pain of sympathy.

Poor thing. Poor, poor thing, what led you to this?

Outwardly she maintained. No one watching would have seen anything but trim efficiency. She'd been told she looked efficient. An accusation thrown at her by Nick, implying competence wasn't sexy. Along with all the other garbage he'd dumped on her; why hadn't she realized what was going on?

She liked being thought of as businesslike. Had found a business she liked.

A month ago she'd gone to a Melrose salon and ordered the reluctant stylist to lop off six inches of black hair, ending up with a short, ebony, minimal-care wedge-cut.

Stu had noticed right away. 'Very becoming.'

She thought it framed her lean, pale face pretty well.

Her clothes were picked for nothing but practicality, now. Good pant suits bought on sale at Loehmann's and Robinsons-May that she took home and tailored herself so that they fit her long frame perfectly. Mostly black, like today. A couple of navys, one chocolate brown, one char-coal.

She wore Mac lipstick, deep red with a brown tint, a little eye shadow and mascara. No foundation, her skin was white and smooth as notepaper. No jewelry. Nothing a suspect could yank.

The victim wore foundation.

Petra could see it clearly where the crimson hadn't settled. Traces of blush, powder, mascara applied a little heavier than Petra's, to the eye that remained intact.

21

The damaged eye was a sightless, black-cherry hole, the eyeball collapsed to folded cellophane, some of the jelly-like humor leaking out and specking the nose.

Nice nose, where it hadn't been slashed.

The right eye was wide, blue, filmed over. That dull *dead* look, you couldn't fake it, there was nothing like it.

Flight of the soul? Leaving behind what? A casing, no more alive than a snake's molt?

She continued studying the corpse with an artist's precision, noticed a small but deep cut on the left cheek that she'd missed. Eighteen. She couldn't flip the body till the crime-scene photographer was finished and the coroner gave the OK. The definitive wound count would be the pathologist's, once he had the corpse stretched out on his steel table.

She added the cheek wound to her drawing. Might as well be careful; the coroner's office was a zoo, doctors made mistakes.

Stu was over with the coroner, now – an older man named Leavitt – both of them serious but relaxed. None of that tasteless joke stuff you saw on cop movies. The real detectives she'd met were mostly regular guys, relatively bright, patient, tenacious, very little in common with cinema sleuths.

She tried to look past the blood, get a sense of the person beneath the carnage.

The woman appeared young and Petra was pretty sure she'd been good-looking. Even savaged like that, dumped on the parking lot like refuse, you could see the fineness of her features. Not tall, but her legs were long and shapely, exposed to mid-thigh, her waist narrow in the short, black silk dress. Big bust – maybe silicone. Nowadays when Petra saw a slender woman with a healthy chest, she assumed surgery.

No sign of any bizarre leakage in the torso, though with all that blood, who knew. What would happen to silicone breasts when slashed? What did silicone look like, anyway? Eight months in Homicide, the issue had never come up.

Pantihose ripped but it looked like asphalt wear. No obvious sign of sexual assault or posing, no visible semen around the ruined mouth or the legs.

Big hair. Honey-blond, good dye-job, a few dark roots starting to show, but nice, expertly done. The dress was a jacquard with hand-stitching and the way it was pulled up and bunched around the shoulders, Petra could read the label. Armani Exchange.

The shiny things Petra hoped would yield prints were a diamond tennis bracelet on the left wrist with nice-size cut stones, a sapphire and diamond cocktail ring, a gold Lady Rolex, small diamond studs in the ears.

No wedding band.

No purse, either, so forget instant identification on this one. How'd she end up here? Out on a date? Big hair, minidress – a call-girl lured onto the streets by an extra bonus?

The purse gone, but the jewelry hadn't been taken. The watch alone had to be three grand. So not a mugging. Unless the mugger was an even-stupider-than-usual street fool who'd taken the purse and panicked.

No, that made no sense. All these wounds didn't spell panic or robbery. This piece of dirt had taken his time.

Snatching the purse to fake robbery, not thinking about the jewelry?

She pictured someone ripping away out of rage. Deep wounds, no defense cuts, but defense cuts were rarer than most people thought and a decent-sized man wouldn't have had much trouble subduing a woman this slender.

Still, it might indicate someone she knew.

The wound overkill sure did.

Had the blond woman been caught off-guard?

Petra's brain flooded with fast-motion images. She quelled them. It was too soon to theorize.

God, it looked ferocious. A predator's attack. The massive frontal disemboweling wound was her guess for the fatal one, but most of the punishment had been concentrated on the face.

Gutting the woman then trying to wipe away her beauty? Such intense hatred, an *explosion* of hatred.

Something *personal*, the more Petra thought about it the more that made sense. What kind of relationship had led to *this*? Husband? Boyfriend? Some reasonable facsimile of a *lover*?

A beast let loose.

Petra unclenched her hands, jammed them into the pockets of her pant suit. DKNY, Saks overstock, lightweight crepe, true black. Comfortable, so she'd worn it to the Freshwater stakeout.

The blond woman's dress had just a touch of blue in it. Blue-black rinsed in rusty water.

Two women in black; the mourning had begun.

Stu continued to confer with Leavitt, and Petra stayed by the corpse, a self-appointed guardian.

Protecting a molt?

24

As a little girl in Arizona, on summer digs with her father and her brother Dick, she'd found plenty of shedded skins, the lacy donations of snakes and lizards, collected them, tried to braid them, fashion lanyards. They'd turned to dust in her hands and she'd started to think of reptiles as fragile, too, and somehow less frightening.

But they continued to poison her dreams for years. As did scorpions, wildcats, owls, horned toads, flying beetles, black widows, the seemingly endless stream of creatures that came in off the Interstate.

Poor Dad, sentenced to hour-long nightly routines – stories and dumb jokes and obsessive-compulsive checking rituals – all so his youngest child would sleep and allow him some single-parent quiet time.

When he finally got some solitude, what did he do with it?

Knowing Dad, any spare time was spent grading papers or working on the textbook that never got finished. A tall glass of Chivas for fortification. She knew he kept a bottle in his nightstand and that it was emptied often, though she never saw him really drunk.

Professor Kenneth Connor, physical anthropologist of medium repute, now fossilized himself by Alzheimer's, dead prematurely, twenty months ago. She remembered the day, had been chasing a stolen Mercedes all the way down to Mexico when the station patched through the hospital call. Cerebral accident. Fancy name for stroke. The neurologist suggesting Dad's brain had been weakened by placque.

Dad had specialized in invertebrate genetics but collected shells, skins, skulls, shards, and other bits of organic antiquity, their tiny, highway-bordering house outside of

Phoenix crammed with detritus and relics, smelling like a neglected museum. A kind man, a caring father. Petra's mother had died birthing her but never once had Dad showed any resentment, though she was certain he must have felt something. She'd certainly punished herself, turning into a wild, angry teenager, setting up confrontations till Dad had been forced to send her to boarding school and she could luxuriate as a victim.

His will specified cremation and she and her brothers had complied, tossing his ashes over a mesa in the dead of night.

Each one of them waiting for the other to say something.

Finally, Bruce broke the silence. 'It's over, he's at peace. Let's get the fuck out of here.'

Dad, the tissue collector, reduced to gray particles. Maybe one day, millions of years in the future, some archaeologist would find a Kenneth Connor molecule and hypothesize about what life had been like back in the twentieth century.

Now here was *this* lump of dead flesh, right next to her, fresh and pathetic.

Petra guessed the woman's age at twenty-five to thirty. The tight jawline said not too much older, no tuck scars behind the ears that she could see.

Good cheekbones, judging by the right side. The entire left side was crimson mush. Probably a right-handed killer, the head rolling to the right as he cut her.

Except for Freshwater, her twenty-one previous cases were the typical stuff: Bar shootings, one-jab knifings, beatings. Stupid men killing other stupid men.

The ugliest had been the Hernandez wedding, a Saturday affair in a VFW hall near the border of Rampart Division, the groom killing the bride's father at the reception, using a brand-new, pearloid-handled cake knife to slit the older man from sternum to groin, just *filleting* him as his new eighteen-year-old wife and a hundred other people watched in horror.

Some honeymoon.

Petra and Stu found the groom hiding out in Baldwin Park, served the warrant, brought him in. A nineteen-year-old gardener's assistant, the knife hidden in a fertilizer sack in back of his boss's truck, the idiot.

Look, Dad, I solved it, no heebie-jeebies.

She imagined her father's surprised smile at the trajectory of his shuddering, phobic baby.

Efficient.

She swallowed morning air. Sweet, you could smell the pines. Suddenly she was tired of waiting around, itching to do something, learn something.

Finally Stu walked away from Dr Leavitt and passed behind the tape into the outer region of the parking lot, where the police and coroner vehicles had grouped. Being his usual methodical self, telling the techs what to do, what not to do, what to take back for analysis. The coroner drove away and the morgue attendants stayed behind, listening to rap music in their van, the bass thumping.

Everyone waiting for the photographer and K-9 units to arrive so the body could be taken away and the dogs could check out the wooded area above the parking lot.

Stu talked to a uniform, barely moving his lips, noble profile framed by sunlight.

Chief Bishop. If he didn't get a big movie role first.

Two weeks into their partnership, he'd taken out his wallet

to pay for lunch at Musso and Frank's and she'd seen the SAG card, next to a frequent-flyer Visa.

'You're an actor?'

His Celtic skin reddened and he closed the wallet. 'Purely by accident. They came to the station a few years ago, filming a *Murder Street* on the Boulevard, wanting real cops as extras. They bugged me till I finally agreed.'

Petra couldn't resist. 'So when do your hands and feet go in the cement?'

Stu's swimming-pool aqua eyes softened. 'It's an unbelievably stupid business, Petra. Incredibly self-centered. Do you know how they refer to themselves? The *industry*. As if they're manufacturing steel.' He shook his head.

'What kind of roles have you had?'

'Minor walk-ons. It doesn't even cut into my routine. A lot of the filming goes on at night and if I'm still in town, leaving later makes the freeway ride shorter. So I don't really lose any time.'

He grinned. It was protest-too-much time and they both knew it.

Petra smiled back wickedly. 'Got an agent?'

Stu turned scarlet.

'You do?'

'If you're going to work, you need one, Petra. They're sharks, it's worth the ten percent to have someone else deal with it.'

'Ever get any speaking parts?' Petra was genuinely interested but also fighting back laughter.

'If you call "Freeze, scumbag, or I'll shoot" speaking.'

Petra finished her coffee and Stu worked on his mineral water.

She said, 'So when do you write your screenplay?'

'Come on, give me a break,' he said, opening the wallet again and taking out cash.

But the next week, he took a part as an extra out in Pacoima. Everyone in LA, even a straight guy like Stu, wanted to be something else.

Except her. She'd come to California, after a year of state college in Tucson, to attend the Pacific Art Institute, gotten a fine arts degree with a specialty in painting and entered the workplace with a husband sharing her bed. Nick had a great job designing cars at the new GM future lab. She earned chump change illustrating newspaper ads, sold a few of her paintings out of a co-op gallery in Santa Monica for the price of supplies. One day it hit her: This was it; things were unlikely to change in any big way. But at least she had Nick.

Then her body failed her, Nick showed his real soul, or lack of, leaving her baffled, broken, alone. A week after he walked out, someone broke into her apartment and stole the few valuable things she owned, including her easel and her brushes.

She sank into a two-month depression, finally dragged herself out of bed one November night and drove around the city, limp, deadened, defenseless. Thinking she should eat, her skin looked terrible and her hair was starting to fall out, but she wasn't really hungry, the thought of food made her sick. Finding herself on Wilshire, she turned around, headed for home, spied an LAPD recruitment billboard near Crescent Heights and amazed herself by copying down the 1–800 number.

It took her another two weeks to call. The police

29

commission said the department had to actively recruit women. She got a nice warm welcome.

Entering the academy on whim, thinking it a stupid, incomprehensible *mistake*, she'd surprised herself by liking it, then loving it. Even the physical fitness challenges, learning to use her flexibility rather than brute strength getting over The Wall. Avoiding the turtle squad and learning she had good reflexes, a natural talent for using leverage to floor hand-to-hand opponents.

Even the uniform.

Not the wimpy powder-blue top and navy pants of the cadet, the real one, all navy, all business.

She, who'd bucked so many boarding-school fascists over issues of rank conformity, ended up attached to her uniform.

Lots of the guys in her academy class were buffed jocks and they had their blues tapered to second-skin tautness, emphasizing biceps, deltoids, latissimi.

Boy's version of a push-up bra.

One night, impulsively, she'd customized her own uniform, using the old, chipped Singer sewing machine she'd brought with her from Tucson, one of the few things the burglars had left behind.

She was five seven, 132 pounds, with slim legs, boyish hips, big square shoulders, a butt she thought too flat, and a small but *natural* bust that she'd finally come to appreciate. Growing up with a father and four brothers, she'd found it valuable to learn how to sew.

She worked mostly with the shirt because it bagged around her waist and with those hips she needed *some* shape. The end result had flattered her figure without flaunting it.

After graduation, she was even happier, though she didn't

30

invite anyone to the ceremony, still nervous about what Dad and her brothers would think.

A month into her probationary year she told them, and they were all surprised but no one put her down. By then, she was in the groove.

Everything about police work felt right. Keeping fit, cruising, roll call, shooting on the range. Even the paperwork, because one thing boarding school had taught her was good study habits and proper English and that put her ahead of most of the buff-jocks with their pencil-chewing agony over syntax and punctuation.

Within eighteen months, she made Detective-I.

Earning the right to guard a molt.

A new car joined the others in the parking lot. Subcompact with a department emblem on the door. A woman police photographer came out lugging a professional Polaroid camera. Young, around the victim's age, in sloppy clothes and with long, too-black hair. Four pierces in one ear, two in the other, just holes, no earrings. Plain face, sunken cheeks, a spot of acne on each. Combative Generation-X eyes.

As she approached the body, Petra constructed a hypothetical identity for her: Like Petra, an artistic type gone practical. At night she probably put on black duds, smoked dope and drank stingers at Sunset Strip clubs, hanging out with failed rock musicians who took her for granted.

She opened her camera, looked down and said, 'My God, I know who this is!'

Petra said, 'Who?' as she waved Stu over.

'I don't know her name but I know who she is. Cart Ramsey's wife. Or maybe it's ex-wife by now. I saw her on

TV around a year ago. He hit her. It was one of those tabloid shows, showbiz exposé. She made Ramsey out to be a real asshole.'

'You're sure this is her?'

'Hundred percent,' said the woman, peeved. Her photo badge ID'd her as Susan Rose, Photog-I. 'This is her, believe me. They said she was a beauty queen and Ramsey met her at a pageant – God, look at her, what a sick *fuck*!' The hand holding the camera tightened and the black box swayed.

Stu came over and Petra repeated what Susan Rose had said.

'You're sure,' he said.

'Jesus. Yeah, very.' Susan began to shoot pictures, rapidly, thrusting the camera forward as if it were a weapon. 'On the show she had a black eye and bruises. Fucking *bastard*!'

'Who?' said Petra.

'Ramsey. He's probably the one who did this, right?'

'Cart Ramsey,' Stu said without inflection, and Petra found herself wondering if Stu had ever worked on Ramsey's show, what was it called – *The Adjustor*, some private-eye hero who solved the problems of the downtrodden.

Wouldn't that be cute?

Susan Rose removed a cartridge and dropped it into her case. Petra told her, 'Thanks, we'll get verification. Meanwhile, do your thing.'

'It's her, believe me,' said Susan Rose irritably. 'Can I turn her over? I already got all of the front.'

5

Two hours of walking. I'm not tripping as much.

The way he stabbed her.

PLYR 1. There's a bar on the Boulevard called Players where pimps hang out. Maybe they call themselves that because they fool around, don't do real work.

What he did to her makes me think of something I saw in Watson, out in one of the dry fields behind the orange groves.

These two dogs were passing each other. One was white with brown spots, full of muscles, kind of like a pitbull but not exactly. The other was a big black mutt that didn't walk well. The white dog looked calm, happy with life, had almost a smiley face. Maybe that's why at first the black dog didn't seem afraid of him. Then the white dog just turned, without barking, jumped on the black dog, got his jaws around the black dog's neck, twisted a couple of times and the black dog was dead. That fast. The white dog didn't eat the black dog or lick the blood or anything, he just kicked the dirt with his hind legs and walked away, like he'd done his job.

He *knew* he had the power.

I was wrong. I'm not close yet. My feet weigh a ton and I start to feel stupid for living in the park, tell myself I'm not, it's a smart decision.

What's the choice, something like the Melodie Anne?

That's a building on Selma, just off the Boulevard, burnt out from a fire, with the windows boarded up. Lots of kids crash there and late at night you can see them bringing older guys in. Sometimes you actually see them giving the old guys blowjobs right outside in the alley, boys and girls.

I would rather kill myself than do that. Suicide is a sin, but so is living the wrong life.

I check the Casio. 4:04. I must be close. No matter how many lists I try, my head is filled with terrible pictures. Men hurting women, dogs killing dogs, planes blowing up, kids snatched from their bedrooms, drive-by shootings, blood everywhere.

I think about Mom but see Moron instead and now I'm thinking about the way he called Mom a whore all the time and she took it, just sat there.

On bad days he hit her. I used to close my eyes, grind my teeth, try to beam myself somewhere else. For a long time, I couldn't understand why she took him in. Then I figured out she thinks she's not worth much cause she's got no education and he's what she deserves.

She met him at the Sunnyside, which is where she finds all the losers she brings home. She wasn't working there anymore but she was still going there to drink and watch TV and joke with the guys shooting pool.

The other losers never stayed long and they ignored me. The first night she brought Moran home he stank up the trailer with body odor and motorcycle grease. The two of them got stoned. I was out on the sleeper couch, could smell the joints they lit up, hear them laughing, then the bed squeaking. I put my fingers in my ears and got totally under the blankets.

The next morning he came out into the front room, naked,

holding his shorts in one hand, flaps and folds of tattooed fat all over his body. I pretended to still be sleeping. He opened the door, grunted, put his shorts on and went outside to pee. When he finished he said, '*Yeah*' and cleared his throat and spat.

On the way back to Mom's bed, he tripped and his knee came down on my back. It felt like an elephant crushing me, I couldn't breathe. He came back, went into the kitchen, got a box of Cap'n Crunch and scooped cereal into his mouth, spilling it all over.

I pretended to wake up. He said, 'Oh man, a rug-rat. Hell, Sharla, you didn't say you had onea *them*.'

Mom laughed from the bedroom. 'We wasn't *talking* much, was we, Cowboy?'

Moron laughed too, then he held out a hand for a high five. His nails were black around the edges and his fingers were the size and color of hot dogs.

'Motor Moran, bro. Who're you?' For such a big guy he had a high voice.

'Billy.'

'Billy what?'

'Billy Straight.'

'Ha, same as her – so you got no daddy, little fuckin' accident, huh?'

I lowered my hand but he grabbed it, shook it hard, hurting me, looking to see if I'd show it. I ignored him.

'This your cereal, bro?'

'Kind of.'

'Well too fuckin' bad.' That made him really laugh.

Mom came in and she giggled along with him. But her eyes had that sad look I've seen so many times before.

35

Sorry, honey, what can I do?

I don't protect her, either, so I guess we're even.

He punched my arm hard. 'Don't fuckin' use it up.' Tossing me the cereal box, he went to the fridge and got beer and salsa. 'Got any chips, woman?'

'Sure, Cowboy.'

'Then move your ass and fix me some dip.'

'You got it, Cowboy.'

She calls all the losers she brings home Cowboy.

Moran thought it was all for him. 'Back in the saddle, baby, we goin' gallop!'

Motor Moron. His real name is Buell Erville Moran, so you can see why he'd want a nickname, even a stupid one. I saw it on his driver's license, which was expired and full of lies. Like his height being six four when it's maybe six one. And his weight being 200 when it's at least 280. On the picture he was wearing a huge red beard. By the time Mom brought him home he'd shaved off the chin hairs and the mustache and left humongous sideburns that stick out, really stupid.

He wears the same thing every day: Greasy jeans, smelly black Harley T-shirts and boots. Trying to make like he's a Hells Angel or some big outlaw biker, but he has no gang and his chopper is a rusty hunk of junk, usually broken. All he does is fool with it alongside the trailer, get blasted, watch talk-shows and eat, eat, eat.

And spend the AFDC and the disability checks. The AFDC's are basically mine. Aid to families with *dependent children*. My money.

At least I'm not dependent anymore.

Mom changed when I turned around five. She was never educated but she used to be happier. More interested in how she looked, using a hot comb and makeup and wearing different outfits. Now it's all T-shirts and shorts and even though she's not really fat, she kind of droops and her skin's pale and rough.

She used to work the Sunnyside weeks and only drink and toke on weekends. I don't want to blame her, she's had a hard life, started picking in the fields when she was fourteen, had me when she was sixteen. Now she's twenty-eight and some of her teeth are gone because she has no money to take care of them.

She never had much schooling because her parents picked fruit, too, travelling up and down with the crops, and they were alcoholic and didn't believe in education. She can barely read and write and she doesn't use good grammar, but I never said anything to her about that, it really didn't bother me.

She had me nine months after her parents died in a car crash. Her dad was drunk, coming back to Watson from seeing a movie in Bolsa Chica, and he drove off Route 5 straight into a power pole.

Mom and I passed by the exact spot lots of times on the bus. Every time we did, she'd say, 'There it is, that damned pole,' and start rubbing her eyes.

She didn't die because she was out partying with some grove workers instead of being with her parents at the movies.

She used to tell me the whole story, over and over, especially when she was drunk or stoned. Then she started adding stuff to it: The party was at some fancy restaurant, with bigshots from the farm workers' union. Then it turned from a party into a date, her and some rich union guy and she was all dressed up, 'looking hot.' Then she really got going, saying the rich guy was handsome and smart, a lawyer who was a genius.

One night she got totally blasted and made this big confession: The rich guy was supposed to be my father.

Her version of Cinderella, only she never got to live in the palace.

Having a rich, smart, handsome father would be a cool thing but I know it's bull. If he had money, why wouldn't she go after it?

When she got that way, she sometimes pulled out old pictures of herself, showing me when she was slender and pretty and had thick, dark hair that hung down past her waist.

She has no pictures of the amazing rich guy. Big surprise.

When she told Moron the story, he said, 'Cut that bull-shit, Sharla, you fucked a million assholes, can't remember nonea them.'

Mom didn't answer and Moron's face got dark and he looked over at me and for a minute I thought he was going to come after me, too. Instead, he just laughed and said, 'How you ever gonna know which gleam in the eye produced this little piece a shit?'

Mom smiled and twisted her hair. 'I just know, Buell. A woman *knows*.'

That's when he backhanded her. She fell back against the fridge and her head snapped back like it was going to come off.

I was sitting at the table, eating the little he'd left me of a jumbo can of Hormel Chili and all of a sudden fear and

38

anger were burning through me and I looked for something to grab but the knives were across the kitchen, too far away, and his gun was under his bed with him right in the way.

Mom sat up and started crying.

'Cut the bullshit,' he said. 'Shut the fuck up.' He raised his hand again. This time I did stand up and he saw me and his eyes got really small. He turned red as ketchup, started breathing hard, made a move toward me. Maybe Mom was trying to help me or maybe she was just helping herself but all of a sudden she was in his lap, wrapping her arms around him, saying, 'Yeah, you're right, baby, it is bullshit, total bullshit, I don't know jack, sorry, I'll never lay that bullshit on you again, Cowboy.'

He started to shake her off but changed his mind, said, 'You gotta cool it with that bullshit.'

Mom said, 'I ain't arguin'. C'mon, baby, let's scoot into town and party.'

He didn't answer. Finally he said, 'Fucking A.' Looking over at me, he licked her cheek and slipped his hand under her tank-top.

Moving his hand in slow, slow circles.

'Let's party right *here*, baby,' he said, starting to pull the tank-top off of her.

I ran out of the trailer, hearing him laughing, saying, 'Looks like the rich guy's kid got all *hot*.'

He started off with more hand-squeezes, tripping me, pinching my arm. When he saw he could get away with that, he started slapping me for stupid reasons, like when I didn't get him a pickled egg fast enough. It made my head buzz and I couldn't hear right for hours.

The worst time of the day was when I came home from school. He'd be outside the trailer working on his bike. 'Hey you, Rich Guy's Jizz! Get the fuck over here.'

There was only one door to the trailer and he was in front of it so I had to do it.

Sometimes he bugged me, sometimes he didn't, and that was almost worse cause I kept waiting for it to happen.

Rich man's kid, fuckin' rug-rat snotty-little-asshole think-you're-smarter'n everyone.

Then he started with the tools. Putting a chisel under my chin, sticking my thumb in a lug wrench and tightening it on the bone, watching my eyes to see what I would do.

I worked hard at not moving my eyes or any other part of me. The wrench felt like when you catch your hand in a drawer but at least that's over fast, this kept throbbing and throbbing. I could imagine my bones cracking and breaking and never healing again.

Going through life with broken hands and being called Claw Boy.

Next time was a screwdriver. He tickled my ear with it, pretended to jam it in with the heel of his hand, laughing and saying, 'Shit, I missed.'

A few days later, his hacksaw blade went up against my neck and I could feel its teeth, like an animal biting me.

After that, I couldn't sleep well, would wake up a bunch of times a night and in the morning I'd have a sore face from clenching my teeth.

Why didn't I just sneak over to their bed and get his gun and shoot him?

Part of it was being scared he'd wake up, get to the gun first. And even if I did shoot him, who'd believe I had a good reason? I'd end up in jail, ruined forever, even when I got out I'd be an ex-con, no right to vote.

I started thinking about running away. The thing that decided it for me happened on a Sunday. Sundays were the worst because he sat around all day drinking and smoking weed and popping pills and watching Rambo videos and soon he'd feel like being Rambo.

Mom was in town getting groceries and I was trying to read.

He said, 'Get the fuck over here,' and when I did, he laughed and pulled out a pair of wire cutters, then yanked down my jeans and my shorts and put my dick between the blades. The sac, too.

Billy No-Balls.

I almost peed but forced myself to hold it in because if I wet him I was sure he'd cut it off.

'Rich Guy's Kid got a *little* one, don't he?'

I stood there, trying not to feel, wishing I could be somewhere else. Lists, lists, nothing was working.

He said, 'Snip, snip, go sing in the fuckin' Pope's choir.'

He licked his lips. Then he let me go.

Two days later, when they were both at the Sunnyside, I went through the trailer looking for money. All I found at first was eighty cents in change under the couch cushions and I was getting discouraged and wondering if I could leave without money. Then I came across the Bathroom Miracle. Some money Mom had been hiding in a Tampax box under the sink. I guess she never really trusted Moron, figured he wouldn't look there. Maybe she felt trapped, too, wanted to get out one day. If I messed up her plans, I'm sorry, but she still has the AFDC and it was my balls between the blades

41

of that cutter and if I stayed longer he would've killed me. Which would make her feel terrible and probably get her in trouble for child neglect or something.

So by leaving I was doing her a favor.

The money in the Tampax box came out to a hundred and twenty-six dollars.

I wrapped it in two Ziploc bags, put *them* in a paper bag tied with four rubber bands and stuffed it all in my shorts. I couldn't take books or too many clothes, so I just put my most comfortable stuff in another paper bag, buckled my Casio on my arm, and walked out into the night.

There are no street lamps in the trailer park, just lights from inside the trailers, and at that hour most people were in bed, so it was nice and dark. It's not really a park, just a dirt field next to a grove of old, twisted orange trees cut low by the wind that don't fruit anymore, and one long, curvy, open road that leads to the highway.

I walked the highway all night, staying on the grass, far as I could from the road so cars and trucks couldn't see me. It was mostly trucks, big ones, and they just zoomed by, creating their own storms. I must have walked twelve miles because the sign at Bolsa Chica said it's that far to Watson. But my feet weren't hurting that bad and I felt free.

The station was closed because the first bus to LA was at 6 A.M. I waited around till some old Mexican went behind the counter and he took forty of my Tampax dollars without even looking up. I bought a sweet roll and milk at the station and a *Mad Magazine* from the newsrack, was first on the bus, sitting in the last row.

Everyone else was Mexican, mostly workers and a few

42

women, one of them pregnant and moving around in her seat a lot. The bus was old and hot but pretty clean.

The driver was an old white guy with a crushed face and a hat too big for him. He chewed gum and spit out the window, started off slowly but once he got going, we were rolling along and some of the Mexicans took out food.

We drove by some used car lots on the outskirts of Bolsa Chica, all these windshields reflecting white light like mirrors, then some strawberry fields covered with strips of plastic. When I'd passed them with Mom she'd always say, 'Strawberry fields, just like the song.' I thought about her, then made myself stop. After the fields came nothing but road and mountains.

A little while later we passed the place where Mom's parents drove off the road. I stared at it, watched it disappear through the back window. Then I fell asleep.

6

STU DREW Petra aside. 'Cart Ramsey. If it's true.'

'She seemed sure.'

He glanced at Susan Rose, loading her tripod back in her car. 'She looks like a stoner but she does have a certain conviction.'

'My first thought seeing all that overkill was someone the vic knew.'

Stu frowned. 'I'm calling Schoelkopf right now, get some guidelines. Any idea where Ramsey lives?'

'Nope. Thought you might.'

'Me? Why – oh.' His smile was thin. 'No, never did his show. Have you ever seen it?'

'Never. He plays a PI, right?'

'More like a one-man vigilante squad. Fixing stuff the cops can't.'

'Charming.'

'Bad even for TV. It started out on network, got dropped, went indie, managed to pull some syndication. I think Ramsey owns the show.' He shook his head. 'Thank God I never got called for it. Can't you just see the fun some F. Lee Bombast would have with that?' His lips twisted and he looked ready to spit as he turned his back on Petra.

'What's especially bad about the show?' she said.

He faced her. 'Wooden dialogue, weak story-lines, no character development, Ramsey can't act. Need more? It fills space in a late Sunday time slot, so the station probably picks it up at budget price.'

'Meaning Ramsey's only a minor gazillionaire.'

Stu thumbed a suspender and looked over at Lisa Ramsey's body, now covered. 'Ramsey's ex means media-carrion. While I call Schoelkopf, would you please go over to Ms Rose and ask her to keep her mouth zipped till the bosses have weighed in?'

Before she could reply, he started for their car. A uniform began waving frantically from the far end of the parking lot and they both hurried over.

'Found this right over there.' The cop pointed to some brush near the entry gate. 'Didn't touch it.'

A black ostrich purse.

A tall young tech named Alan Lau gloved up and went through it. Compact, lipstick – also Mac, that made Petra's stomach flutter. Loose change, a black ostrich wallet. Inside the wallet were credit cards, some made out to Lisa Ramsey, others to Lisa Boehlinger. California driver's license with a picture of a gorgeous blonde. Lisa Lee Ramsey. The birth date made her twenty-seven years old. Five five, 115 matched the corpse. Address on Doheny Drive, an apartment, Beverly Hills. No paper money.

'Emptied and tossed,' said Petra. 'A robbery or wanting to make it look like one.'

Stu didn't comment, just headed for the car again as Lau began bagging the contents. Petra returned to the body. Susan Rose was near the feet, capping her camera lens.

'Finished,' she said. 'Want me to shoot something else?'

'Maybe the hills up there,' said Petra. 'We're waiting for the K-9's, depends on what they find.'

Susan shrugged. 'I get paid either way.' She reached under her grubby sweatshirt, drew out a necklace and began playing with it.

Guitar picks on a steel chain. Bingo for Detective Connor's intuition!

'Play music?' said Petra.

Susan looked puzzled. 'Oh, this. No. My boyfriend's in a band.'

'What kind of music?'

'Alternative. You into it?'

Petra kept her smile within bounds and shook her head. 'Tone deaf.'

Susan nodded. 'I can carry a tune, but that's about it.'

'Listen,' said Petra, 'thanks again for the ID. You were right.'

'Course I was. But no big deal, you would've found out soon enough.' The photographer turned to leave.

'One other thing, Susan. Who she is complicates things. So we'd appreciate it if you don't talk to anyone about this until we work out a plan for handling the press.'

Susan fingered the necklace. 'Sure, but someone like this, everyone'll know before you can say "senseless murder."'

'Exactly. We've got a narrow window of opportunity. Detective Bishop's calling the brass right now, trying to get a plan. We're also going to need to inform Cart Ramsey. Any idea where he lives?'

'Calabasas,' said Susan.

Petra stared at her.

The photographer shrugged. 'It was on that tabloid show.

Like *Lifestyles of the Rich and Famous*. Sitting in the Jacuzzi, drinking champagne, a little putting green. Her in some beauty pageant bathing-suit competition or something, then after he beat her up, with a black eye, split lip. You know, before and after.'

'A beauty queen,' said Petra.

'Miss Something. They showed her playing the saxophone. Look where her talent got her – hey, here're the dogs.'

Two K-9 officers, one with a German shepherd, the other with a chocolate Labrador, took instructions from Stu and started up the slope above the parking lot.

Captain Schoelkopf was at a meeting at Parker Center but Stu managed to get patched through. When Schoelkopf found out who the victim was he let out a stream of profanity, ending with a warning not to 'F-up' (Stu's cleansed translation). Doheny Drive was a jurisdictional mess, cutting through LA, Beverly Hills, West Hollywood. A lucky break: Lisa's apartment was LAPD territory and uniforms were dispatched. A maid was working there and she was detained. With no knowledge of other relatives, Stu and Petra's immediate assignment was to notify the ex-husband.

Now they watched as the dogs circled and sniffed and made their way upward methodically, toward a wooded area, thick with cedar and sycamore and pine, fronted by outcroppings of boulders. A stone ridge, midway up the slope, some of the rocks graffitied, most worn smooth and shiny. The Labrador was ahead but both dogs were moving fast, closing in on a particular formation.

Something up there? thought Petra. No big deal, this was

Griffith Park, there had to be tons of human scent all over the place. Pulling tire marks from the parking lot was useless for the same reason. The asphalt was one giant mural of black rubber.

Soon they'd be heading out to Calabasas. Sheriff territory. That edged the whole thing up another notch on the complication scale.

Cart Ramsey. What a name, had to be a fake. His real one was probably something like Ernie Glutz, which would play havoc with the Mr Rockjaw image.

She rarely watched TV but she was vaguely aware Ramsey had knocked around on the tube for years. Never achieving major stardom, but the guy did seem to work pretty steadily.

A bland type, she'd always thought. Was he capable of this kind of brutality? Were all men, given the proper circumstances?

Her dad had once told her it was a lie that only people murdered. Chimpanzees and other primates did, sometimes just to dominate, sometimes for no apparent reason. So was bloody homicide aberrant behaviour or just basic primate impulse taken to an extreme?

Pointless, time-filling conjecture. Headgame horseshit, her brother Bruce used to call it. Though not the oldest of the Connor boys, he was the biggest, the strongest, the most aggressive. Now an electronics engineer for NASA in Florida, he thought anything that couldn't be measured with a machine was voodoo.

When she'd finally confessed her new police status to the family, Dick, Eric, and Glenn had been stunned, muttering congratulations and telling her to be careful. Bruce had said, 'Cool. Go out and kill some bad guys for me.'

The cop with the shepherd came out in front of a boulder pile and said, 'You'd better take a look at this.'

Nature had arranged the rocks in a tight U, like a backless cave. The boulders were high – seven or eight feet tall – and there were cracks where the rocks pressed up against each other, invisible from below, but Petra could look through them and see the parking lot clearly.

Like a bowhole in a castle.

Perfect vantage point for an observer.

And there'd been someone there observing. Recently.

The floor of the U was a soft bed of leaves. Petra was no forest ranger but even she could see the body-shaped compression. Nearby was a piece of wrinkled yellow paper, darkening to brown translucence where grease had saturated it.

Food wrapper. Specks of something that looked like ground beef.

The shepherd had sniffed out bits of shredded lettuce, barely wilted, amid some dry leaves a few inches from the paper.

Petra sniffed the wrapper. Chili sauce. Last night's taco dinner?

Then the dog began nosing frantically at one corner of the U and Stu summoned a tech over to check it out.

'Probably body fluid,' said the shepherd's handler. 'He acts that way when he smells body fluid.'

Alan Lau came over. Petra noticed he had nervous hands.

A few minutes later, the field kit results: 'Urine. On these leaves.'

'Human?'

'Human or ape,' said Lau.

'Well,' said Stu, 'unless some chimp got loose from the zoo and bought himself dinner it's probably safe to say Homo sapiens.'

Lau frowned. 'Probably. Anything else?'

'Any other fluids?'

'Like blood?'

'Like anything, Alan.'

Lau's flinched as if Stu had slapped him. 'Not so far.'

'Check it out. Please.'

Lau returned to swabbing, dusting, probing. Susan Rose was summoned back to take pictures of the rocks. Petra sketched them anyway, then drifted away.

All that scientific work going on but it was she who had the next find.

Twenty feet above the rocks, where she'd gone to explore because there was nothing for her to do and the dogs had moved on.

But they'd missed something, half-concealed by leaves and pine needles. Flash of color beneath the green and brown.

Red. At first she thought: More blood, uh-oh. Then she bent and saw what it was, looked for Stu.

He was back at the car, talking on his cell phone – the minuscule one his father the retired eye surgeon had given him for Christmas. Petra beckoned Lau. He sifted and found nothing around the red object, and Susan snapped away. They left and Petra gloved up and picked it up.

A book. Thick, heavy, hardcovered, re-bound in red leatherette. Library call number on the spine.

Our Presidents: The March of American History.

She flipped it open. LA Public Library, Hillhurst branch, the Los Feliz district.

Check-out card still in the pocket. Not much action on this one. Seven stamps in four years, the most recent nine months ago.

Stolen? De-acquisitioned? She knew the library got rid of stock all the time because back in her starving artist days she'd filled her own bookshelves with some great rejects.

She flipped pages. No de-acquisition stamp, but that didn't prove anything.

Petra's mental camera began snapping. Had some homeless guy with an interest in US history found himself a nice little natural lean-to where he could read and eat a taco and take a leak in the great wide open, only to witness a murder?

But no grease on the book, so maybe it had no connection to the person who sacked out behind the U-shaped rocks.

Or maybe Mr Taco was a neat eater.

Even if the book *was* his, no big deal. There was nothing to say he'd been around precisely when Lisa Ramsey was being butchered.

Except for the fact that the urine *was* fresh. Within twelve hours according to Lau, and Dr Leavitt had estimated the murder at between midnight and four A.M.

A witness, or the murderer himself? The Fiend From The Hills hiding behind the rocks, waiting for the perfect victim.

Susan Rose had made the logical assumption that wife-beater Ramsey was the prime suspect, but other theories had to be considered.

But what would have brought Lisa Boehlinger Ramsey to Griffith Park at night? And where was her car? Jacked? Was robbery the motive after all?

Would someone this vicious *need* a motive?

51

A nut-crime? Then why had the money been taken? Why not the jewelry?

Something didn't mesh. She just couldn't see a woman like Lisa coming alone to the park at that hour, all made up, wearing jewelry, that little black dress.

It spelled date. Out for the evening and she'd detoured. Or had been detoured. Why? By whom? Something hush-hush?

Buying drugs? There were lots of easier ways to score dope in LA.

A date with the murderer? Had he driven her here with intent?

If Lisa had gone out on the town with a man, maybe someone had seen the two of them together.

One thing was sure: If it was a date the lucky guy hadn't been some loner who read old library books and ate tacos and peed behind rocks.

Crashing in the park, no indoor plumbing, spelled homeless.

Modern day caveman staking out his spot behind the rocks and marking it?

A spot from which he had a vantage view of the murder scene.

Or maybe he'd wet himself out of *fear*.

Seeing it.

Looking through that bowhole and *seeing* it.

7

ALMOST THERE for sure, now. The sun is out and I feel uncovered – like a target on a video game, something small that gets eaten.

I can walk forever if I have to. All I've done in LA is walk.

The bus let me off in a station full of people and echoes. Outside, the sky was a strange brownish gray and the air smelled bitter. I had no idea which way to go. In one direction were what looked like factories, power poles, trucks going back and forth. People seemed to be going the other way so I followed them.

So much noise, everyone staring straight ahead. Between each block were alleys full of garbage cans with weird-looking guys sitting against the wall. Some of them watched me pass with cold eyes. I walked three blocks before I realized I was being followed by one of them, a real crazy-looking guy with rags around his head.

He saw me spot him and came at me faster. I ran and slid into the crowd, feeling the eighty-six dollars in my shorts bouncing around but making sure not to touch it or look at it. Everyone was taller than me and I couldn't see too far in front of me. I kept pushing through, saying 'excuse me' and finally, two blocks later, he gave up and turned around.

My heart was going really fast and my mouth was dry. People kept piling onto the sidewalk, mostly Mexicans and a few Chinese. Some of the signs on restaurants were in Spanish and one huge movie theater with gold scrolls over the sign was playing something called *Mi Vida, Mi Amor*. A bunch of guys were selling fruit ices and churros and hot dogs from carts and now my mouth filled with spit. I started to wonder if I was dreaming or in some foreign country.

I walked till I found a street where the buildings were cleaner and newer. The nicest-looking building was something called the College Club, with US and California flags out in front and a pink-faced guy in a gray uniform and hat with his arms folded across his chest. As I walked by he looked down his nose, as if I'd farted or done something rude. Then a long black car pulled up to the curb and all of a sudden he was just a servant, hurrying to open the door and saying, 'How are *you* today, sir?' to a white-haired guy in a blue suit.

I made it to a little park that looked nice, with a fountain and some colorful statues, but when I got closer I saw that the benches were full of more weird guys. Right next door was a place called the Children's Museum but no kids were going in. I was tired and hungry and thirsty, didn't want to spend any more of the Tampax money till I had a plan.

I sat down on a corner of grass and tried to figure it out.

I came to LA because it was the closest real city I knew, but the only neighborhoods I'd heard about were Anaheim, where Disneyland is, Beverly Hills, Hollywood and Malibu. Anaheim was probably far and what else was there besides Disneyland? I'd seen a TV show about Hollywood that said kids still came there looking for movie stars and got into trouble. Beverly Hills was full of rich people and the way the guy in the gray uniform had looked at me told me that wouldn't be safe.

That left Malibu but that was the beach, nowhere to hide.

Maybe something *near* Hollywood would be OK. I wasn't like those other kids, thinking life was a movie. All I wanted was to be left alone, no one putting my dick in a wire cutter.

I sat there for a long time, thinking I'd been crazy to leave. Where would I live? What would I eat, where would I sleep? The weather was good now, but what would happen in the winter?

But too late to go back now. Mom would find out about the money and think of me as a thief. And Moron . . . my stomach started to hurt really bad. I started to think people were looking at me, but when I checked no one was. My lips felt like sandpaper again. Even my eyes felt dry. It hurt to blink.

I stood up, figuring I'd just walk. Then I saw two people coming through the park holding hands, a guy and a girl, maybe twenty or twenty-five, wearing jeans and long hair and looking pretty relaxed.

I said, 'Excuse me,' and smiled, asked them where Hollywood was, and Malibu, just to play it safe.

'Malibu, huh,' said the guy. He had a fuzzy little beard and his hair was longer than the girl's.

'My parents are in there,' I said, pointing to the museum. 'They took my little brother in, but I figured it was boring. They promised to take me to the beach and Hollywood if we can find it.'

'Where're you from?' said the girl.

'Kinderhook, New York.' The first thing that spilled out.

'Oh. Well, Hollyweird's about five, six miles that way — west — and the beach is the same direction, another fifteen miles after that. Kinderhook, huh? That a small town?'

'Uh-huh.' I had no idea. All I knew was it was Martin Van Buren's birthplace.

'You a farm boy?'

'Not really, we live in a house.'

'Oh.' She smiled again, even wider, and looked at the guy. He seemed bored. 'Well, tell your parents Hollyweird *is* weird, all kinds of freaks, be careful, you know? During the day if you're with your parents it should be OK, but not at night. Right, Chuck?'

'Yeah,' said Chuck, touching his little beard. 'If you go, check out the Wax Museum on Hollywood Boulevard, little dude. It's pretty cool. And the Chinese theater, ever hear of that?'

'Sure,' I said. 'Where the movie stars put their hands and feet in the cement.'

'Yeah,' said the guy, laughing. 'And their minds in the gutter.'

They laughed and walked on.

The first bus I got on the driver said I needed exact change, so I had to get off and buy a lime sno-cone and get change. Which was fine, because it took care of my thirst and put a sweet taste in my mouth. Half an hour later, another bus came along and I was ready with the right coins, like someone who belonged.

The bus made a lot of stops and there was so much traffic I could see the sky turning grayish-pink through the tinted bus windows by the time the driver called out, 'Hollywood Boulevard.'

It didn't look that much different than where I'd just been: Old buildings with cheap-looking stores and theaters. Same noise, too. Waves of noise that never stopped. Watson has its sounds – dogs barking, trucks rumbling over the highway, people yelling when they're mad. But each noise is separate, you can make sense of things. Here in LA, everything's one big soup.

At the trailer park, I could walk around at night, look in windows. I've even seen people doing sex – not just young people, old ones, too, with white hair and flabby skin, moving around under a blanket with their eyes closed and their mouths open, holding onto each other like they're drowning. I knew places in the groves where it was always quiet.

Hollywood didn't look like a place where I could find quiet but here I was.

I walked up Hollywood Boulevard, looking out for the freaks Chuck had warned me about, not sure who they really were. I saw a big tall woman with huge hands that I realized was a man and that sure qualified, teenagers with rooster-hair and black lipstick, more drunks, some of them pushing shopping carts, black people, brown people, Chinese, whatever. The restaurants sold stuff I'd never heard of like gyros and shwarma and oki-dogs. The stores sold clothing, costumes and masks, souvenirs, boomboxes, fancy underwear for girls.

Lots of bars. One of them, called The Cave, had a row of Harleys parked in front and guys coming in and out, big and ugly, dressed like Moron, and seeing them made my stomach burn. I went past there really fast.

I saw a hamburger stand that looked normal but the guy inside was Chinese and he didn't look up when I stood there.

One hand kept frying meat, and his face was half hidden by smoke and steam.

Two dollars forty-two for a burger. I couldn't spend anything till I had a plan, but I did manage to take some ketchup packets lying out on the counter. I ducked behind a building, opened them and sucked out the ketchup, then I kept walking, to a street called Western Avenue, and turned right because I saw some mountains in the distance.

To get to them I had to pass a porno theater with XXXXX's all over the front and posters of blond women with big, open mouths, then some really dirty buildings with wood over the windows. I saw women in short shorts talking on payphones and giving each other cigarettes and guys hanging nearby smoking. The mountains were pretty and by now the sun was behind them, with a yellow-orange glow shooting up and spreading on top, like a hat made of melted copper.

A block later I had to cross the street because teenagers were laughing and pointing at me. I passed another alley. No weird drunks here, just lots of garbage dumpsters and the back doors of stores and restaurants. A sweating fat guy wearing a stained white apron came out of a place called La Fiesta holding armfuls of bread wrapped in plastic. He threw them in a dumpster and went back inside.

I waited for him to come back but he didn't, looked around to make sure no one was watching still and went over to the dumpster. To get a look inside, I had to stand on a cardboard box that didn't feel too strong and keep hitting flies away. Once I got up there, the smell was terrible. The bread sat on top of rotten-looking vegetables with brown edges, wet paper, scraps of meat and bones and hunks of uncooked white fat. Little white worms crawled all over the meat, which smelled worse than a dead dog. But the bread looked clean.

Hot dog buns, still totally wrapped. Probably stale – when people go to restaurants they want everything super-fresh. One time – the only time – Mom and Moron and I went to a restaurant, it was a Denny's in Bolsa Chica and Moron sent his fried chicken back because he said it tasted like 'warmed-over shit.' The waitress called the manager who told Moron not to use that language. Moron stood up to show he was taller than the manager, with Mom holding on to his arm, saying, 'Cowboy, c'mon, c'mon.' Finally, the manager agreed to give us our food to go for free, if we left.

I reached in and grabbed two packages of buns, almost falling into the dumpster and getting some crud on my T-shirt.

But I had the buns and they were clean. After looking around some more, I walked a ways into the alley, found a dark spot between two other dumpsters, tore open the first package, bit into a bun.

Stale, all right, but my chewing mushed it up and by the third mouthful it started to taste sweet. Then the smell of the dumpster came back to me and I started to gag.

I got up, walked around, took deep breaths and I told myself it was my imagination, pretend these were home-made buns right out of the oven, baked by some TV commercial mom with a wide-awake smile and a strong interest in nutrition.

It worked a little. The rest of the bun didn't taste great but I got it down. Back to the mountains.

As I climbed, the road got steeper and I started to pass houses. Mowed lawns, and all sorts of trees and plants and flowers, but no people I could see, not a one. Now, after four months in LA I'm used to that. People here like to stay inside, especially at night, and anyone out there after dark is probably prowling for something.

At the top, Western curved and turned into another street called Los Feliz and these houses were *huge,* behind high walls with fancy metal gates and surrounded by pine trees and palms. This must have been what Hollywood was like when the movie stars lived here.

The mountains were still far away but in front of them was a big stretch of clean, green grass, a few people lying on blankets, some of them sleeping, even with all the traffic noise. Behind the grass, tons of trees.

A park.

I waited for traffic to slow down and ran across the street. *Griffith Park*, the sign said.

The only park in Watson is a dry little square in the center of town with one bench, an old cannon and a brass sign saying it's dedicated to men who've died in wars. This was different. Humongous. You could get lost in here.

8

'INTERESTING,' SAID Stu, hearing about the library book, but he sounded distracted.

He'd been on the phone and now it went back in his pocket. 'West LA uniforms are with Lisa Ramsey's maid, it's not Beverly Hills, a few blocks away. Sunday was the maid's day off, she just got back, Lisa hadn't slept in her bed. Lisa's Porsche isn't in the garage, so it looks like she drove herself somewhere, either hooked up with the killer and switched to his vehicle or got jacked. We've got to hustle over to Ramsey's place in Calabasas to do the notification, then return to interview the maid. He wasn't at his studio office and protocol says we make every attempt to notify in person. He lives in one of those gated-estate deals, I've got the address.'

They walked to their white Ford. It was Stu's day to drive and he got behind the wheel.

'Calabasas is tan-shirt territory,' said Petra as he started the engine. He drove slowly. As usual. More slowly than any cop she'd known.

'Tan as an anchorman,' he said. 'Schoelkopf called the boss sheriff out at the Malibu station to define some ground rules but seeing as it's a 187, they punted to their downtown Homicide boys. The jurisdiction's ours but they want to be there when we notify, cause Ramsey's house is their turf, they don't want to be perceived as out of the loop. A couple of their downtown homicide investigators will meet us outside the gates.'

'Big drive from downtown to Calabasas,' said Petra. 'So on some level they *do* think they're investigating it?'

'Who knows. Maybe they can help us.'

'As in getting hold of Ramsey's domestic violence history?'

'That. Anything.'

As they got on the stretch of road that ran between the park and the 5 Freeway, Stu said, 'Schoelkopf gave me the kind of lecture I haven't heard since I rookied. "Don't go in without permission, don't climb any walls, treat him one hundred percent like a grieving ex, not a suspect. No searching of any kind, don't go to the *john* if it can be construed as a search. No asking questions that might incriminate anyone because then you'd have to Mirandize the guy and I don't want even a hint that he's a suspect."'

'What about getting hold of that TV tape?'

'Not even that, yet, because it would show clear signs of suspicion.'

'Come on. It's public domain,' said Petra.

Stu shrugged.

Petra said, 'When do we get to detect?'

'When we know more.'

'But we're not allowed to look for more.'

Stu gave a tight smile.

Petra said, 'All this smoke because Ramsey's VIP?'

'Welcome to Locust-land. I love my job.'

Till recently he had. What was going on?

He entered the freeway heading north. A mile later, Petra said, 'What about the book and that food wrapper? Potential witness?'

'If whoever was eating and/or reading just happened to be there when Lisa was killed. My religion tells me to believe in miracles but . . .'

'And/or?'

'Could be two separate guys. Even if it's one, the scene spells homeless guy – or woman. Lau said the body impression was small.'

'A bag lady,' said Petra.

'Whoever it was didn't call 911, so if he/she was there, it shows a certain lack of civic responsibility. Don't hold your breath waiting for someone to come forward.'

'So many bag ladies are schizophrenic,' said Petra. 'Witnessing a murder would be terrifying to anyone, but someone already over the edge . . .'

Stu didn't answer. Petra let him drive a while before she said, 'I was also thinking – I know it's remote – but what if whoever was behind the rock killed Lisa?'

He thought about that, then rattled off the same objections Petra had come up with.

'Plus,' he added, 'I agree with your first impression: All that facial damage, the overkill, implies passion, someone she knew. If what Susie Shutterbug said about Ramsey beating up Lisa is true, he sure fits that bill.'

'But we can't treat him like a suspect.'

'But we *can* psych him out while playing Sympathetic Public Servant during the notification. Which is why I'm glad you're here. He's an actor. A bad one, but even bad ones are better at hiding their feelings than the average person.'

'What does that have to do with me?' said Petra.

'You're good at reading people.'

Not at reading you, she thought.

Soon after they got on the 134 West, they got stuck in traffic.

Common enough situation and whenever Petra found herself in a jam she fantasized about flying cars of the future – those VW with propeller gizmos predicted in Dad's old *Popular Mechanics*.

Just sitting there drove her crazy and both of them knew it. Stu was a calm driver, sometimes maddeningly so.

'We could take the shoulder,' she said.

He'd heard it a hundred times before and smiled wearily.

'We could at least put on the lights and the howler,' she added.

'Sure,' he said, shifting the car into Park and gunning the engine. 'Let's use our guns, too, shoot our way out . . . so what approach should we take with Ramsey?'

'Sympathetic, like you said. Be there with tissues for his crocodile tears.'

'Crocodile,' he said. 'So you've decided hedunit.'

'If Mormons gambled, where would you put your money?'

He nodded, turned his head in order to suppress a yawn, and they crawled a quarter mile, then stopped again. Rubbing her eyelids, Petra created twin kaleidoscopes behind the thin flesh. A headache was coming on. She had to learn to deal better with frustration.

'All these years working Hollywood,' Stu said, 'and I never had a celebrity murder. Closest I came was this old guy – Alphonse Dortmund. German émigré character actor, used to play Nazis in World War Two movies. Got strangled in his apartment on Gower. Real dump, he hadn't worked in years, drank, let himself go. Uniforms responding to a bad odor call found him all tied up in his bed – hogtied with the rope around his neck, complicated knots.'

'Sexual asphyxia?'

'That was my first impression but I was wrong, he didn't do it to himself. Turns out he picked up a fifteen year old on the Boulevard, showed the kid how to truss him, then the kid decided to take it further, choked him out, ransacked the apartment.'

'How'd you catch the kid?'

'What do you think?'

'He bragged.'

'To anyone he could find. My partner at the time – Chick Reilly – and I went to all the usual places, talked to all the usual people, and *everyone* knew what had happened. It made us feel like rubes just off the farm.' He laughed. 'Thank God most of them are idiots.'

'Wonder how smart Ramsey is,' said Petra. 'Any particular reason he wouldn't be in his office?'

'You're thinking he rabbited already? No, we can't assume that. He's not filming. All this year's shows are already in the can.'

'His show specifically, or all of the shows?'

'All the main ones,' said Stu. 'He could be playing tennis, soaking in the Jacuzzi. Or on a chartered jet to the south of France.'

'Wouldn't that be inopportune.'

'Indeed. Hey, maybe we *should* shoot our way out of this.'

* * *

Forty-five minutes later, they got off the freeway at Calabasas Road and took a curving road north, into the Santa Susanna mountains. Smooth, rolling slopes sported groves of live oaks that had survived progress. The trees were acutely sensitive to over-watering, and irrigation had killed hundreds of them before someone had caught on and designated them protected.

Fires had fun out here, too, Petra knew, racing through dry brush and chaparral, devouring the big, vanilla, retro Spanish houses that seemed to be the thing in upscale, West-Valley neighborhoods. No matter how much money went into them, they never looked anything *but* retro.

They passed several tracts of vanilla, now, some behind gates. Twin-paddock horse setups, small corrals alongside tennis courts and stone-waterfall swimming pools. The air was good, the lots were generous, and once you got away from the freeway it was quiet. But Petra knew it wasn't for her. Too far from bookstores, theaters, museums, LA's meager cultural mix. Too calm, also. Cut off from the *pulse*.

Not to mention the commute, two hours of your life each day spent studying the white lines on the 134, wondering if this was success.

Calabasas was popular with what Petra, secretly a snob, thought of as the non-thinking rich: Athletes, rock stars, overnight entrepreneurs, actors like Ramsey. People with long blocks of leisure and a melanoma-be-damned view of sunshine.

Petra suspected the free time caused problems. A recent Parker Center memo had warned of white Valley teenagers starting to emulate the inner-city gangbangers. What did kids *do* out here except get into trouble?

Back in her artist days, she sometimes fantasized about what her life would be if she ever made it big – twenty thousand a canvas, no need for commercial jobs. Half the year in LA, half in London. It had never come to that, of course. She'd sketched and ziptoned and T-squared twelve hours a day just to pretend she was contributing financially to the marriage, telling Nick what he earned was his. How noble. How stupid.

'Here we are,' said Stu.

RanchHaven sat atop a knoll planted with golden poppies. High, scrolled gates on pink columns. Behind the wrought iron were the biggest haciendas they'd seen so far scattered thinly on multi-acre lots. An unmarked Dodge was parked on the side of the road, twenty yards before the gates. No-frills wheels and multiple antennae made it every bit as obtrusive as Stu and Petra's Ford.

They pulled up behind it and two men got out. One was Hispanic, forty-five, five ten, heavyset, with a gigantic swooping black mustache and a tie full of birds and flowers. His partner was white, much younger, same height, thirty pounds lighter, also with lip hair, but his 'stache was clipped and yellow-gray. Both wore gray sportcoats. Black and navy slacks respectively. The white deputy's tie was narrow and maroon and he had a pleasant boyish face just short of handsome.

They introduced themselves as De la Torre and Banks. Greetings all around, nice and friendly so far.

'What exactly happened?' said De la Torre.

Stu filled them in.

'Ugly,' said Banks.

Petra said, 'Your boss never told you?'

Banks shook his head. 'We were told Ramsey's wife had been killed, but not how. The order was to get here, wait for you. We were also told it wasn't our case, we should just be here so later no one could say we weren't. Where'd it go down?'

'Griffith Park.'

'Just took my kids to the zoo there last Sunday,' said Banks, shaking his head. He looked bothered and Petra wondered how long he'd been in Homicide.

'Think he did it?' said De la Torre.

Stu said, 'Our info is he beat her up last year and they got divorced soon after.'

'There's a couple of high-riskers for you.'

'One thing for sure,' said Stu, 'it was no street-idiot mugging. Mega-wounds, mega-fury, someone took cash out of the purse but left credit cards and her jewelry. We figure someone she knew or, less probably, a sex fiend. Whoever it was either drove off in her car or took her there in his.'

'What did she drive?' said Banks.

'Porsche 911 Targa, four years old, black. We put a want out for it.'

'To some people that's worth killing for.'

'Maybe,' said Stu, 'but stabbing her two dozen times for wheels? Why bother?'

Silence for a few seconds.

'Cash, no jewels,' said De la Torre. 'Attempted fake-out? Ever watch Ramsey's show? I did. Once. Stinks.'

Petra said, 'It would be good to know if he ever caused problems around here.'

'We can check with the locals for you,' said Banks, offering her a brief, puzzling smile.

68

'That would be great.'

'So exactly how do you want to proceed?' said De la Torre. 'I mean, seeing as we're just here for the chorus line, we don't want to screw up your solo.'

'Appreciate it,' said Stu.

'So what's the plan?'

Stu looked at Petra.

'Low profile,' she said. 'No treating him like a suspect, no biasing the case prematurely.'

'Ramsey's an actor, so everyone's got to put on a performance – don't you just love this town?' said Banks. 'OK, we'll just hang behind, be discreet – think you can do that, Hector?'

De la Torre shrugged and said, '*Me no know*,' in a cartoon Mexican voice.

'Hector's an intellectual,' said Banks. 'Earned a Master's degree last summer so now he thinks he's entitled to have opinions.'

'Master's in what?' said Petra.

'Communications.'

'Thinks he's going to do sports on TV one day,' said Banks. 'Or the weather. Do the weather for them, Hector.'

De la Torre smiled good-naturedly and looked up at the sky. 'High pressure hitting a low pressure coming down and encountering a medium pressure. Possibly leading to precipitation. Also, actors beating on their wives, possibly leading to murder.'

Both unmarkeds pulled up to the pink column. The gates had a green pseudo-patina. On the left column was a talk-box and a sign that said *Deliveries*. Twenty feet up was a guardhouse.

Stu leaned out, pushed the button on the box and said, 'Police for Mr Cart Ramsey.'

The uniformed guard stuck his head out and came forward. Stu's badge was out and by the time the gates slid open, Petra could see from the guard's body language that he was ready to cooperate.

'Help you?' he said. Older guy, round gut, deep tan, lots of wrinkles, hair dyed beige. Walkie-talkie and baton but no gun.

'We need to talk to Mr Ramsey,' said Stu. 'Privately. I guess you understand how highly Mr Ramsey and his neighbors value privacy.'

The guard's eyes widened. 'Oh, sure.'

'So we can count on you, Officer . . . Dilbeck, to be discreet?'

'Sure, sure – should I call ahead to tell him you're coming? Usually, that's what we do.'

'No, thanks,' said Stu. 'As a matter of fact, please don't. Tell me, Officer, has Mr Ramsey entered or exited RanchHaven today?'

'Not during my shift – that's from eleven o'clock on.'

The normal thing would be to ask who'd been on night shift. Instead, Stu said, 'Thanks. How do we get up there?'

'Keep going to the top and take the first left which is Rambla Bonita. Go up again, straight to the top and that's his place. Big pink place, just like these columns.'

'Pink,' Petra repeated.

'Pink as it gets. When he bought it, it was white but he and the wife re-painted.'

'Ramsey have any problem with that?'

'Not that he told me. But he don't say much at all. Like that character he plays – Dack whatever-his-name-is.'

'Strong and silent?' said Petra.

'You might say that.' Dilbeck stepped aside.

As they reached the top of the first rise, Petra said, 'Well that clinches it, doesn't it? It's always the quiet ones.'

9

THE PARK took me in like a friend. I learned.

Things like what times the rangers patrolled and how to avoid them. Which restaurants threw out the freshest food and how if you worked in the dark you didn't get bothered while dumpster-diving.

Who people were.

The guys on Western were drug dealers and all they wanted was to do their business without being annoyed, so I stayed on the other side of the street and after about a month, one of them crossed over and said, 'Smart boy,' and gave me five dollars.

I learned how to get stuff.

If you go far enough east on Los Feliz, the fancy houses stop and there are apartments. On Sunday, the people who live in the apartments sell stuff out on their front lawns and if you wait till the end of the day you can pick up things extra-cheap because they don't want to bother packing it up.

I bought a green blanket that smelled of wet dog for one dollar and a sleeping bag for three, and I got the guy who was selling the sleeping bag to throw in a pocket knife with three blades, one of them a screwdriver, for free.

Sometimes the people selling looked at me strangely, like

what's a kid doing buying underwear, but they never turned down my money.

I bought a flashlight, two packets of AA batteries, some old T-shirts and a sweater and a round couch pillow that was hard as rock and rotted, a total waste.

I spent thirty-four more Tampax dollars the first month. Adding the five I got from the dope dealer, that left fifty-seven dollars. I found the Five Places and spread my stuff around them.

I learned when to smile, when not to, who to look at, who to ignore. Found out money is a language.

I made mistakes. Ate bad food and got sick, one time really bad, throwing up for three days straight with fever and chills and sure I was going to die. That time I was in a cave in Three, living with bugs and spiders and not caring. On the third day, I crept out before sunrise and washed my clothes in the brook. My legs were so weak it felt like someone was kicking me in back of my knees. I got better, but since then, my stomach hurts a lot.

I learned about prosties and pimps and saw people doing sex in alleys, mostly women down on their knees sucking on guys who didn't move, just groaned.

I realized that to get enough money so no one would use me, I'd have to be educated, but how was I going to do that living in the park?

The answer I came up with was: Teach yourself. Meaning schoolbooks, meaning a school. A junior high because back in Watson, I was in seventh grade, even though a counselor visiting from Bakersfield once showed me some puzzles and told me I could skip to eighth if Mom signed some forms. She said she would, but she never did, and then she lost the forms and the counselor never asked, so I stayed in seventh, and unless I let my imagination race around I was so bored my mind felt like wood.

I found a Yellow Pages in a phone booth, took it back to the park and looked up *Schools*. There were no junior highs listed and that confused me, so the next day, I called the School Board making my voice as low as possible and saying I'd just moved to Hollywood with my twelve-year-old son and he needed a junior high.

The woman on the other end said, 'One second, ma'am,' and put me on hold for a long time. Then she came back, saying, 'Thomas Starr King Middle School on Fountain Avenue,' and she gave me the address.

I walked over at noon. It turned out to be around two miles away from Place Three in a grungy-looking neighborhood and gigantic – all these pink buildings with bright blue doors, a humongous yard surrounded by high fences. I watched from across the street and learned that school ended at one P.M., with tons of kids flooding out of the yard laughing and punching each other. That gave me a pain in my throat.

One P.M. dismissal meant I could walk around in the afternoon and not get busted.

I made a schedule: Mornings would be for washing up, eating whatever I'd put away the night before for breakfast, reading and studying, checking out the Places to make sure no one had found the stuff I hid. Afternoons would be for getting new food and whatever else I needed.

I went back to King Middle School again, during ten o'clock recess. Kids were out in the yard and the teachers I saw were talking to each other. I slipped in through one of the gates and walked around like I belonged. There were two separate supply rooms where the books were stored.

It took eight visits to get what I needed.

It was easy. Who'd suspect a kid would take books?

I got myself textbooks for seventh, eighth, and ninth grade, some pens and pencils and pads of lined paper. English, history, science, math all the way up to algebra.

Without rowdy kids or Moron distracting me, I could concentrate, and it only took two months to get through all the books. Even algebra, which I'd never had before and looked hard, all those letter symbols that didn't make any sense at first, but the beginning was all review and I just moved ahead page by page.

I liked the idea of variables, something meaning nothing by itself but taking on any identity you wanted.

The all-powerful X. I thought of myself as X-boy, nothing, but also everything.

I took all the books back to King School one night and left them at the fence. Except the algebra text, because I wanted to practice equations. I knew I had to keep my mind busy or it would get weak, but I was tired of schoolbooks, wanted some vacation. Different types of knowledge – encyclopedias, biographies of people who'd succeeded. I missed my Presidents book.

No storybooks, no science fiction, I don't care about things that aren't true.

I found a library right off Los Feliz, just a few blocks down on Hillhurst, a strange-looking place with no windows, stuck in the middle of a shopping center. Inside was one big

75

room with colorful posters of foreign cities trying to imitate windows and just a few old people reading newspapers.

I was dressed neat and had the algebra book, pencil and paper and a backpack. Sitting at a table in a far corner, I pretended to be doing equations and checked the place out.

The woman who seemed to be the boss was old and sour-looking like the librarian back in Watson, but she stayed up front talking on the phone. The young Mexican with the really long hair was in charge of checking out books and she did notice me, came over smiling to ask if I needed help.

I shook my head, and kept doing equations.

'Ah,' she said, in a very soft voice. 'Math homework, huh?'

I shrugged, just ignored her completely, and she stopped smiling and walked away.

The next time I came in, she tried to catch my eye, but I kept shining her on and after that she ignored me, too.

I started to show up once or twice a week, always after one, starting with phony homework, then examining the shelves till I found something, and reading for two hours.

Sometimes I could finish a whole book in that time. On the third week, I came across the *exact* Jacques Cousteau book I'd had back in Watson and thought: I am definitely in the right place.

I found the other Presidents book, soon after. It was the first one I took. It's the only one I kept and I'm still not sure why. I took excellent care of it, wrapping it in dry-cleaner's plastic. So there was no real crime.

Still, I felt bad about it. Kept telling myself that one day, when I was an adult and had money, I'd give books *to* the library. Sometimes I wondered if I'd last long enough to be an adult.

76

Now, after what I've seen, everything seems shaky. Maybe it's time to leave the park. But where would I go?

My foot catches on a rock but I keep my balance – finally, here's Five, the smell of the zoo blowing through the fern tangle. Time to hide, get some rest, do some thinking.

I've got to do some *serious* thinking.

10

SEEING RAMSEY'S house, Petra thought back to her architectural history course and tried to come up with a label. Confused Spanish pseudo-Palladian? Postmodern Mediterranean Eclectic? Hotshot Hacienda?

One big heap of stucco.

The structure sat atop a peak so steep Petra had to crane to see the top. Pink, as the guard had promised, a rosy hue darker than the columns behind another set of columns and gates – cage within a cage. The driveway up to the house was stamped to look like adobe bricks, lined with Mexican fan palms. Through the posts she saw a shiny black Lexus parked in front.

They drove up to the gates and now Petra could see at least an acre of sloping front lawn. The house was two and a half stories tall, the half being a bell tower above limed-oak double entrance doors. A real-life bell looked to be a knockoff of the one in Philadelphia. Wings flared at oblique angles, like those of a turkey that had cooked too long and loosened. Lots of odd-shaped windows, some leaded and stained. Verandas and balconies were fronted by verdigrised iron railings and the roof-tiles had been artificially antiqued rust-gold. To the right of the limed doors was a five-door, extra-deep garage. Room for Ramsey's studio-supplied limo, she supposed.

No other houses nearby. King of the mountain.

More palms rose behind the house, their fringed tops extending above the roofline like some kind of New-Age buzzcut. Petra could smell horses but she couldn't see any. The Santa Susannas were chalky-blue in the distance. No live oaks here. Too many sprinklers.

Stu nosed the Ford close to the box. 'Ready, O ye messenger of doom?'

'Oh, yeah.'

He pushed the button. Nothing for a second, then a woman's voice said, 'Ya?'

'Mr Ramsey, please.'

'Who this?'

'Police.'

Silence. 'Hold on.'

A long minute passed, during which Petra looked back at the sheriff's car. Hector De la Torre was at the wheel, saying something she couldn't read. Banks was listening but he saw her and gave a small wave just as a short, stout Hispanic woman in a pink and white uniform came out through the double doors. She walked halfway down the driveway, stared at them. Fifty to sixty years old and conspicuously bowlegged, she wore her hair tied back tight and had a face as dark and static as a bronze casting. She pressed the remote.

The gates opened and the cars drove onto the property. All four detectives got out. The air was a good ten degrees warmer than in Hollywood, and now Petra spotted a section of posts and stakes to the left of the house – a corral. Brown patches of equine flesh moved in and out of view.

Dry heat; her eyes felt gritty. Off to the north a small plane hovered over the mountains. A cloud of crows burst out of a thicket of sycamore, then dispersed, squawking, as if in fear.

'Ma'am,' said Stu, showing his badge to the maid.

She stared at him.

'I'm Detective Bishop and this is Detective Connor.'

No answer.

'And you are, ma'am?'

'Estrella.'

'Last name, please, ma'am.'

'Flores.'

'Do you work for Mr Ramsey, Ms Flores?'

'Yes.'

'Is Mr Ramsey here, Ms Flores?'

'Playing de golf.'

She looks scared, thought Petra. Immigration anxiety? Unless Ramsey planned on running for office, he didn't need to worry about checking papers, so she could easily be illegal.

Or something else. Did she know something? Problems in the Ramsey household? Ramsey's comings and goings last night? Petra wrote down the woman's name and then an asterisk. Be sure to re-contact.

Closing her pad, she smiled. Estrella Flores didn't notice.

'Mr Ramsey's not here?' said Stu.

If so it was a contradiction of what the guard had said.

'No. Here.'

'He is here?'

'Yes.' The woman frowned.

'He's playing golf here?'

'De golf in back.'

'He's got his own putting green,' said Petra, remembering Susan Rose's recollection of the TV show.

80

'May we speak to him, please, Ms Flores?'

The woman glanced at the two sheriffs a few feet away, then back at the wide open doors to the house. Inside, Petra saw cream walls and floors.

'Wan' come in?' said Estrella Flores.

'Only with Mr Ramsey's permission, ma'am.'

Puzzlement.

'Why don't you go tell Mr Ramsey we're here, Ms Flores.'

Petra smiled at her again. Lot of good it did. Estrella Flores bowlegged herself back to the house.

Not long after, Cart Ramsey came running out, followed by a blond man.

The TV sleuth wore a bright green polo shirt, jeans and running shoes. Good shape for a guy his age, which Petra figured to be forty-five, fifty. Six two, 200, with big shoulders, narrow hips, flat gut, tight waist, no love handles. Black, curly hair, TV tan.

The jaw.

The mustache. What was his character's name – Dack Price.

His companion was about the same age, just as big, the same kind of halfback shoulders, but wider hips. More of the typical middle-aged setup here: Significant swell of belly above the belt, looseness at the jowls, jiggling of the breasts as he ran. The fair hair was thinning, longish at the back, pink skin showing at the crown. He wore little round sunglasses with black lenses. His bright blue silk shirt was long-sleeved and oversized and his pleated black cotton pants were tight around the waist. Ramsey outpaced him easily and reached the car breathing normally.

'Police? What is it?' Deep, TV voice.

Stu showed his badge. 'I'm sorry, sir, but we've got some troubling news.'

Ramsey's blue eyes startled, blinked, froze. Very pale blue, dramatic against the ruddy-tan skin, though up close Petra could see that the hair was too sable to be real and the skin was grainy with open pores in the cheeks and veins spidering the nose. Too many dressing-room vodkas? Or all those years of pancake makeup?

'What kind of news? What are you talking about?' Ramsey's voice had started to thicken with panic.

'Your ex-wife—'

'Lisa? What happened?'

'I'm afraid she's dead, sir.'

'*What!*' Bug-eyed. Ramsey's big hands tightened into huge fists and his biceps swelled. Petra put on a sympathetic look as she looked for cuts and bruises up and down his arms. Nothing. De la Torre and Banks were doing the same thing but the actor didn't realize it. He was bent over and covering his face with one hand.

The big blond man in the blue shirt arrived huffing, shades askew. His hair was too-blond, probably another tint-job. 'What's going on, Cart?'

Ramsey didn't answer.

'Cart?'

Ramsey spoke from behind his hand. 'They . . . Lisa.' His voice choked up between the two words.

'Lisa?' said the blond man. 'What happened to her?'

The hand dropped and Ramsey turned on him. 'She's *dead*, Greg! They're telling me she's *dead*!'

'Oh my God – what – how—!' Greg's mouth gaped as he looked at the detectives.

'She's dead, Greg? This is *real*!' Ramsey roared, and for a moment it looked as if he'd haul off and hit the blond man.

Instead, he turned back suddenly and stared at them. At Petra. 'You're sure it's her?'

'I'm afraid so, Mr Ramsey.'

'How can you – I can't – she – how? This is crazy – where? What happened? What the hell happened? Did she total her car or something?'

'She was murdered, Mr Ramsey,' said Petra. 'Found this morning in Griffith Park.'

'*Murdered?*' Ramsey sagged and covered the bottom of his face, this time with both hands. 'Jesus God – Griffith Par— What the *hell* was she doing *there*?'

'We don't know, sir.'

It was an opening for Ramsey to fill, but the actor just said, 'This morning? Oh God, I can't believe this!'

'Early this morning, sir.'

Ramsey shook his head, over and over. 'Griffith Park? I don't get it. Why would she be there early in the morning? Was she – how was she . . . ?'

Blond Greg came closer and patted Ramsey's shoulder. Ramsey shook him off, but the other man didn't react – used to it?

'Let's go inside, Cart,' he said. 'They can give us the details inside.'

'No, no, I need to know – was she shot?' said Ramsey.

'No, sir,' said Stu. 'Stabbed.'

'Oh, Christ.' Ramsey sank an inch. 'Do you know who *did* it?'

'Not yet, sir.'

Ramsey rubbed his head with one hand. Liver spots, Petra

83

noticed. But a big, strong-looking hand, fingers as thick as hour cigars, with sturdy squared-off nails.

'Oh, shit! *Lisa!* I can't believe it! Oh, Lisa, what the hell did you *do?*' Ramsey turned his back on the detectives, walked a few steps, doubled over as if about to vomit, but just remained in that position. Petra saw a shudder course along his broad back.

The blond man let his hands drop limply. 'I'm Greg Balch, Mr Ramsey's business manager—'

Ramsey wheeled around suddenly. 'Did it have anything to do with drugs?'

A second of silence, then Stu said, 'Did Mrs Ramsey have a drug problem?'

'No, no, just a while back – actually she's not – wasn't Mrs Ramsey anymore. We got divorced six months ago and she took back her maiden name. It was friendly but . . . we didn't see each other.' He shielded his face again and began to cry. Big wracking, baritone sobs. Petra couldn't see if there were any tears.

Balch put his arm around Ramsey and the actor let himself be guided into the house. The detectives followed. A moment later, when Ramsey made eye contact it was with Petra and she saw that his were dry, steady, the whites unblemished, the sky-colored irises clear.

The house smelled of bacon. The first thing Petra noticed once she got past the fifteen-foot ceilings and the junk art and all that endless cream furniture – like being dropped into a vat of buttermilk – was the five-door garage.

Because a wall of plate glass offered a view from inside the house. This was a garage like da Vinci was a cartoonist.

Fifty by twenty with true-white walls, mega-buffed black granite floors, black track lighting. Five spaces but only four were filled. And no limo, these were all collectibles: Tomato-red Ferrari roadster with a predatory nose; charcoal-gray Porsche speedster with racing numbers on the door; black and maroon Rolls-Royce sedan with wonderful, swooping fenders, a gigantic, ostentatious chrome grill, and a crystal hood mascot, probably Lalique; bright blue early Corvette ragtop, probably 1950's – the same blue as business manager Greg Balch's silk shirt.

In the fifth space, just a gravel-filled drip tray.

On the walls were framed racing posters and airbrushed depictions of penile cars.

Stu and the sheriffs had stopped to look. Men and cars. Petra was one woman who actually understood that syndrome. Maybe it was four brothers, maybe her sense of aesthetics, an appreciation of functional art. One of the reasons she'd hit it off with Nick was because she was able to stroke his ego and mean it. No stretch; the bastard had no soul, but he could carve masterpieces. His favorite was the '67 Stingray, the apex of design, he called it. When Petra told him she was pregnant, he looked at her as if she were an Edsel . . .

Greg Balch was a few feet ahead, squiring Ramsey into the next room, as the detectives pulled themselves away from the glass wall. Balch sat Ramsey down on an overstuffed cream silk loveseat and the actor remained hunched as if praying, head down, hands laced together on his right knee, bulky neck muscles tight.

The four detectives took places on a facing nine-foot-long sofa, moving around pastel throw pillows to find space. One cushion ended up in De la Torre's wide lap, and his stumpy, brown fingers drummed the glossy fabric. Banks sat calmly. A coffee table composed of a granite boulder with a slab of glass on top marked the space between Ramsey and the cops. Balch took a side chair.

Petra scanned the room. Grotesquely big – she supposed it was a den. It looked into three equally cavernous spaces, each with the same pale overscale furniture, bleached wood accents, huge, terrible pastel abstractions on the walls. Through glass doors she saw grass and palms, a rock pool with waterfall, a four-hole putting course, the grass mown to the skin, nearly gray.

De golf. Two chrome irons lay on the nubby grass. Behind the green was the corral and a cute little pink barn.

Where was vehicle number five? Hidden so it could be cleaned, scrubbed of blood?

And they couldn't even ask about it. She'd seen how long it took the techs to go over a vehicle carefully. If the investigation ever got to the point where they had a search warrant, just doing all the Ramsey wheels would require a major crew for days.

Her eyes drifted back to the corral. Bales of hay, piled up neatly. Two horses lolling, one brown, one white. She imagined Lisa on the white one, wearing a tailored jacket and custom jodhpurs, honey hair streaming.

Had the woman been a rider? She knew nothing about her.

Two horses. Five cars. And a partridge in a – what belonged in the *empty* spot?

Ramsey remained bowed and silent. De la Torre, Banks,

and Stu were studying him without being obvious. Balch looked uncomfortable, the helping hand not knowing how to help. De la Torre looked back at the cars again. Grim-faced, all business, but managing to take in the chrome, the lacquer paint, the oiled leather, licorice-black tires. Banks saw him, smiled. Made eye contact with Petra and smiled a little wider.

Stu just sat there. The blank tablet look, he called it. Let the interviewee fill in the spaces. Maybe he found it easy with Ramsey because he had no car lust — not that he'd shown to Petra, anyway. His civilian ride was a white Chevy suburban with two child safety seats and toys all over. Petra had been a passenger a few times, the Bishop's dinner guest, if you could call transporting six children to Chuck E. Cheese dinner. The video games were fun, though. She liked kidstuff . . .

She found herself touching her flat belly, stopped and directed her attention back to Ramsey.

Black curls bounced as the actor kept shaking his head, as if telling himself no. Petra had seen that so many times. Denying. Or pretending to. The guy was a TV private eye. Actors did research, he had to know the drill.

Greg Balch patted Ramsey on the back, again. The business manager still wore that helpless-lackey look.

Petra watched Ramsey some more, thought, What if he's clean? What if this is the worst kind of whodunit?

Then she reminded herself that he'd beaten Lisa up. Played parts for a living.

She gazed at the huge, formless rooms. Den One, Den Two, Den Three — how many dens did a wolf need?

Finally, Ramsey straightened and said, 'Thanks for coming

87

over . . . guess I'd better call her folks . . . oh, Jesus . . .' He threw up his hands.

'Where do her folks live?' said Stu.

'Cleveland. A suburb, Chagrin Falls. Her father's a doctor. Dr John Boehlinger. I haven't talked to them since the divorce.'

'I can call them,' said Stu.

'No, no, it should be someone who . . . do you usually do that? I mean as a normal part of procedure?'

'Yes, sir.'

'Oh.' Ramsey breathed in and let the air out, wiped his eye with a pinkie. 'No, it should still be me . . . although . . . the problem is we're not exactly – Lisa's folks and me. Since the divorce. You know how it is.'

'Tension?' said Stu.

'I don't know if my calling will make it worse – I mean I really don't know what my place is in all this.' Ramsey looked miserable. 'Officially, I mean. We're not married anymore, so do I have an official role?'

'In terms of?' said Stu.

'Identifying her, arrangements – you know . . . Lisa and I . . . we loved and respected each other but we were . . . apart.' Up went the hands, again. 'I'm rambling, must sound like an idiot. And who gives a *fuck* about arrangements!' Ramsey's hand slammed into a palm. He turned to the right and flashed a profile.

What a chin, thought Petra. In his world love and respect meant a black eye, split lip. His lower lip began to shake and he bit down on it. *Could* he be posing?

She said, 'If there's anything you could tell us about Lisa, it would be helpful, sir.'

Ramsey swiveled slowly and stared at her, and Petra thought she saw something new in his pale eyes – analysis, cold thought, a hardening. Then, a second later, it vanished and he looked grief-stricken again and she wondered if she'd imagined it.

In the interim, Ramsey's eyes had moistened. He said, 'She was a great girl, we were married for nearly two years.'

'What about the drug situation, sir?' said Petra.

Ramsey looked at Balch and the blond man shrugged.

'No big deal,' said Ramsey. 'I shouldn't have said anything. The last thing I want is for the media to get hold of that and smear her as – Jesus, they *will*, won't they? Oh, *shit*! It's ridiculous, she was no bigtime addict, just . . .'

He looked down at his lap.

'You're right, sir,' said Petra, 'sooner or later it'll be out, so we might as well know the facts. With drugs there's always the possibility of violence, so if you could tell us . . .'

Again, his eyes changed and Petra was certain he was appraising her. Were the other D's noticing? Not overtly: De la Torre was ogling the cars again and both Stu and Banks just sat there, noncommittal.

Petra touched her hair and crossed her legs. Ramsey kept his eyes at face level but he blinked as the black crepe rustled. She let her ankle dangle.

'There's nothing to tell,' he said.

'It really wasn't any big deal,' said Greg Balch. His eyes were blue, too, but an insipid, cloudy shade, suffering by proximity to Ramsey's. 'Lisa had a little coke problem, that's all.'

Ramsey glared at him. 'Goddamit, Greg!'

'They might as well know, Cart.'

Holding on to the glare, Ramsey took a deep breath. 'All right, all right. Coke was basically what finished our marriage. Though to be honest, the age difference was an issue, too. I'm from another generation, when party still meant you went to a party and talked and danced. I drink socially, but that's it. Lisa liked to sniff – Jesus, I can't believe she's *gone*!'

He started to hide his face again and Petra spoke a little louder to stop him.

'How old was Lisa, Mr Ramsey?'

His eyes rose, dropped to her knees, then back to her face. 'Was,' he said. '*Was* . . . I can't believe from now on it's always going to be *was* . . . she was twenty-seven, Detective . . .'

'Connor.'

'Twenty-seven, Detective Connor. I met her four years ago, at the Miss Entertainment pageant. I was MC-ing and she was Miss Ohio. She played sax and had a great voice. We dated for a while, lived together for a year, got married. Got divorced. First time for both of us . . . guess we needed practice . . . is there anything else? Cause this is . . .' He touched his neck. 'I'm feeling lousy, I really need to be *alone*.'

'Guys,' said Balch. 'Can we let Mr Ramsey have some privacy?'

Ramsey continued to stroke his neck. His color had faded and his face had taken on a shell-shocked numbness.

Petra softened her voice. 'I'm sorry, sir, I know this is stressful. But sometimes things that come up during periods of stress are really valuable and I know you want us to find your wife's killer.'

Saying wife, not ex-wife, to see if Ramsey would correct her.

He didn't, just nodded feebly.

Balch started to speak but Petra broke in. 'Any idea who she got her drugs from, Mr Ramsey?'

'No. I don't want to make it sound like she was some kind of addict. She sniffed for fun, that's all. For all I know, she never bought, just borrowed.'

'From who?'

'No idea. It wasn't my world.' Ramsey sat up straight. 'Getting dope in the industry is no big challenge. I'm sure I don't have to tell you folks that. Was there something about – what happened – that makes you suspect drugs?'

'No, sir. We're really starting from scratch.'

Ramsey frowned and stood suddenly, and Balch did a Pete-Repeat, edging right next to the boss.

'Sorry, I've *really* got to rest. Just got back from a location trip to Tahoe, not much rest for two days, read scripts on the plane, then Greg had me signing papers, we both collapsed pretty early. Now this. Jesus.'

Offering a detailed alibi without being asked, thought Petra. Fatigued but bright and bushy-tailed the next morning, playing *de golf*.

All four D's were listening actively. No one spoke. No one was allowed to probe too deeply.

Balch filled the silence. 'It was a long couplea days. We both crashed like test-dummies.'

'You stayed here for the night, Mr Balch?' said Petra, knowing she was treading on dangerous ground. She glanced at Stu. He gave her a tiny nod.

'Yup. I do it from time to time, live in Rolling Hills Estates, don't like making the drive when I'm wiped out.'

Ramsey's eyes were glazed. He stared at the floor.

91

Stu nodded again at Petra and all four detectives stood. Stu held out his card and Ramsey pocketed it without reading. Everyone headed toward the front door. Petra found Ramsey next to her. 'So you'll call Lisa's folks, Detective?'

'Yes, sir.' Even though Stu had made the offer.

'Dr John Everett Boehlinger. Her mother's name is Vivian.' He recited the number and waited as Petra stopped to copy it down. Balch and the other D's were several feet ahead, approaching the glass garage wall.

'Chagrin Falls, Ohio,' she said.

'Funny name, isn't it? As if everyone regretted living there. Lisa sure did, she loved LA.'

Petra smiled. Ramsey smiled back.

Measuring her. But not as a cop. As a woman. The grieving ex-husband was giving her the once-over.

It wasn't a judgment she jumped to easily. She didn't view herself as God's gift to men but she knew when she was being evaluated.

'LA was for Lisa,' said Ramsey as they resumed walking. 'She loved the energy level.'

They made it to the glass. Petra extended her hand. 'Thanks, sir. Sorry you have to go through this.'

Ramsey took it, held it, squeezed. Dry and warm. 'I still don't believe it happened. It's unreal – like a script.' He bit his lip, shook his head, let go of her fingers. 'I probably won't be able to sleep, but I guess I should try before the vultures swoop in.'

'The media?'

'It's just a matter of time – you won't give out my address or number, will you?'

Before Petra could answer, he called out to Balch. 'Tell the gatehouse no one gets close. Call them now.'

'You bet.' Balch hurried off.

Petra touched the glass, raised her eyebrows, made a show of staring at the cars.

Ramsey shrugged. For a middle-aged man he did boyish pretty well. 'You collect toys, then realize they don't mean much.'

'Still,' said Petra, 'nothing wrong with having nice things.'

Ramsey's blue eyes flickered. 'Guess not.'

'What year's the Ferrari?'

''Seventy-three,' said Ramsey. 'Daytona Spider. Used to be owned by an oil sheik, I picked it up at auction. It needs to be tuned every week and an hour behind the wheel kills your back but it's a work of art.'

His voice had picked up enthusiasm. As if realizing it, he grimaced, shook his head again.

Trying to keep her voice light, Petra said, 'What goes over there, in the empty slot?'

'My everyday wheels.'

'The Lexus?'

He looked over at the entry hall where the three other D's had congregated. 'No, that's Greg's car. Mine's a Mercedes – thanks for your kindness, Detectives. And for calling Lisa's folks. Let me see you out.'

Both cop cars left the development and cruised down a quiet side road. Stu drove until houses gave way to fields, then motioned the sheriffs over to the side. When they got out, De la Torre was smoking.

'Gave himself an alibi,' he said. 'Here all night with old

93

Greg. And all that shit about not knowing where he fits in.'

'That,' said Banks, 'could have been trying to dissociate himself from it. Both for our sake and in his own mind.'

Stu said, 'Coulda been,' and looked at Petra.

She said, 'All that's interesting, and so is the way he brought up the subject of drugs, first thing. Then he gets all prissy and reluctant, protecting her reputation when *we* want to discuss it.'

'I think he's dirty as hell,' said De la Torre. 'The alibi especially bugs the hell out of me. I mean, your old lady gets sliced up, you're clean, cops show up to notify, do you feel a need to tell them you went to bed early the night of the murder?'

'I agree,' said Petra. 'Except here we've got a domestic violence thing that's gone public in the post-O.J. era, he knows he'll come under scrutiny, has a reason to protect himself.'

'Still,' said De la Torre, 'too damn cute. The guy does a crime show, probably thinks he knows all the angles.' He grunted and smoked.

Petra thought of the way Ramsey had checked her out. Then sidled next to her. None of them had mentioned it. Should she? No point.

'I hate cop shows,' said De la Torre. 'Bastards catch all the bad guys by the third commercial and damage my self-esteem.'

'He's not a cop on the show,' said Banks. 'He's a PI. This macho do-gooder who protects people when the police can't.'

'Even worse.' De la Torre pulled his mustache.

'Lots of tears, but he turned pretty businesslike when he

ordered Balch to call the guardhouse,' Banks said. 'The wife's not even cold and he's covering his rear with the media.'

'Hey,' said De la Torre, 'he's a big fucking *star*.' He blew smoke at the ground. 'So . . . what can we do for you guys?'

'Check out local files, see if there've been any other domestic violence calls – or anything else on him,' said Stu. 'But quietly, at this point. We can't afford even a hint that he's being investigated.'

'So what was that, a condolence call with four D's?'

'You bet.'

'He'll buy that?'

'Maybe. He's used to special treatment.'

'OK,' said Banks. 'We flip paper quietly. Anything else?'

'Not that I can think of,' said Stu. 'Open to suggestions, though.'

'My *suggestion*,' said De la Torre, 'is we keep the hell outta your hair, go to church and pray for you. Because this ain't gonna be any slam dunk.'

Petra said, 'Pray away. We'll take any help we can get.'

Banks smiled at her. 'I noticed you talking by the glass. He say what the fifth car was?'

Petra studied his eyes for a moment. 'His daily wheels. A Mercedes.'

'Think it's sponge-and-solvent time?'

'Could be,' said Petra. 'With all that blood there'd be a good chance of transfer.'

'What about shoe prints at the scene?'

'Nothing,' said Stu. 'He somehow managed to avoid *stepping* in the blood.'

'Meaning he stepped back. Or pushed her away. Either would mean he was prepared.'

Stu thought about that. His lips compressed. 'I'd like to warrant that Mercedes all right, but we're not even close to that without evidence.'

'What if the guy learned something from his show,' said De la Torre. 'Some ultra-high-tech way to really zap something clean. These celebrities, there's always someone to clean up after them. Some walking-around guy, manager, agent, guest-house bum, whatever — but hey, what am I moanin' about? It's your case. Good luck.'

Handshakes all around, and the sheriffs were gone.

'They seem decent,' said Petra.

They returned to the Ford. As Stu started it up, she said, 'Did I go too far in terms of leaning on Ramsey?'

'Hope not . . . what'd you think about all those other hotrods?'

'Predictable. People in the industry are in an eternal quest for The Best.'

He sounded angry.

'Think he's it?'

'Probably. I'll notify the family when we get back.'

'I can do it,' said Petra, suddenly craving contact with Lisa's family. Contact with *Lisa*.

'No, I don't mind.' He began driving. His starched collar was tinged with grime and his blond beard was coming in like new straw. Neither of them had slept for over twenty-four hours. Petra felt fine.

'No sweat for me, either, Stu. I'll call.'

She expected an argument, but he sagged and said, 'You're sure?'

'Absolutely.'

'You did notification on Gonsalez and Chouinard, and Chouinard was no party.'

Dale Chouinard was a construction worker beaten to death outside a Cahuenga Boulevard tavern. Petra had informed his twenty-four-year-old widow that her four kids under six were orphans. Had thought she'd done OK, comforting the woman, holding her, letting her sob it out. Then, in the kitchen, Mrs Chouinard went berserk, striking out at Petra, nearly clawing out an eye.

She said, 'At least no one can slug me over the phone.'

'I really don't mind doing it, Petra,' he said.

But she knew he did. He'd told her, early in their partnership, that it was the part of the job he hated most. Maybe if she'd go the extra mile, he'd see her for the perfect partner she was, open up about what was bugging him.

'I'm doing it, pard. If it's OK with you, I'll talk to the maid, too.'

'Lisa's?'

'I meant Ramsey's, if I can get her out of the house without being obvious about making Ramsey a suspect. But I can do Lisa's, too.'

'Wait on Ramsey's,' said Stu. 'Too tricky.' He pulled out his notebook and flipped pages. 'Schoelkopf gave me the name: Patricia . . . Kasempitakpong.' He enunciated the unmanageable name very slowly. 'Probably Thai. The blues are holding her but if she asks to leave, they can't stop her from flying back to Bangkok. Or calling the *National Enquirer*.'

'I'll go right after I call the family.'

He gave her the Doheny Drive address.

97

She said, 'Cooperative of the Sheriffs, letting us lead with Ramsey.'

'All the bad press both departments have been getting, maybe someone's finally getting smart.'

'Maybe.' Last month the sheriffs had been exposed for releasing several murderers through clerical error, giving county jail prisoners gourmet food at taxpayer expense, and losing track of millions of dollars. Half a year before that, some deputies had been busted for off-duty armed robbery and a rookie had been found naked and dazed roaming the hills near the Malibu substation.

Stu said, 'The address reminds me. Just a few blocks from Chasens. Which they're tearing down in order to build a shopping center.'

'Aw gee,' said Petra. 'No more celebrity dinners for us, pard.'

'I actually got to go there once,' he said. 'Handled security for a wedding reception, big entertainment lawyer's daughter, major stars all over the place.'

'I didn't know you did that kind of thing.' *Also.*

'Years ago. Mostly it was a drag. That time though, at Chasens, was OK. They fed me. Chili, ribs, steak. Great place, class atmosphere. Reagan's favorite restaurant . . . all right, you'll take the Thai maid and notify the parents, I'll try to figure out a way of discreetly asking some industry types about Ramsey, run DMV on the Mercedes, check back with the coroner and the techs before I go home. If they come up with any good forensics, I'll let you know. So far so good?'

'I'll also call the phone company, pull Lisa's records.'

'Good idea.'

Basic procedure.

'Stu, if Ramsey is the guy how can we touch him?'

No answer.

Petra said, 'I guess what I'm saying is what's the chance of something like this improving the quality of our lives? And how do we do our best by Lisa?'

He fooled with his hair, straightened his rep tie.

'Just take it step by step,' he finally said. 'Do the best we can. Just like what I tell my kids about school.'

'We're just kids on this one?'

'In a way.'

11

THE MONKEYS are the worst screamers. It's only 6 A.M. and they're already complaining.

In four hours the zoo will open. I've been up here when it's full of people, heard mostly noise, but sometimes I catch words, like little kids, whining for something. '*Ice scream!*' '*Lions!*'

When people are in the zoo, the animals get quiet but at night, they really go at it – listen to those monkeys screech – and here's another one, deep, something heavy and tired, maybe a rhino. Like *Let me out of here! We're stuck here cause of people, don't people suck?*

If they did ever get out, the carnivores would go straight for the herbivores, the slow ones, the weak ones, killing and eating them and picking at the bones.

About a month ago, I explored the barbed wire fence around the zoo, found a gate up on top, above *Africa*. A sign said ZOO PERSONNEL ONLY *** GATE TO BE LOCKED AT ALL TIMES, and there was a lock on it but it was left open. I took it off, walked through, put it back, found myself in this parking lot full of little tan dune-buggy things the zoo people drive around in. Across the lot were some buildings that smelled like animal shit with cement floors that had just been hosed down. On the other side were more thick plants and a pathway with another sign: AUTHORIZED ACCESS ONLY.

I made like I belonged and walked right into the zoo, climbed into the big walk-in birdcage with all the people, saw the little kids whining. Then I checked out the whole zoo. I had a pretty good time that day, studying and reading the signs that teach about the natural habitats and diets and endangered species. I saw a two-headed kingsnake in the reptile house. No one looked at me weird. For the first time in a long time I felt relaxed and normal.

I'd brought some of my money roll with me and bought a frozen banana and caramel corn and a Coke. I ate too fast and got a stomach ache but it didn't matter, it was like a clear patch of blue sky had opened up in my brain.

Maybe I'll try to get in today.

Maybe I shouldn't. I need to make sure I'm not an endangered species.

I can't stop thinking of that woman, what the guy did to her.

Horrible, horrible, the way he hugged her, *chuck chuck*. Why would anyone want to do that?

Why would God *allow* it?

My stomach starts to kill and I take five deep breaths to quiet it down.

Walking all night my feet didn't hurt too much but now they do and my sneakers feel tight. I pull them off, also my socks. I must be growing, the shoes have been getting tighter for a while. They're old, the ones I came with, and the soles have thin spots, almost worn through.

I'll give my feet some air, wiggle my toes before I unroll my plastic.

101

Ahh . . . that feels good.

There's no water up in Five for bathing. Wouldn't it be cool to get into the zoo, jump in the sea-lion tank and flip around? The sea lions, freaking out, not knowing what's going on – I have to control myself not to laugh out loud.

I stink from piss. I hate stinking, don't want to turn into one of those shopping-cart guys, you can smell them a block away.

I always loved to shower but after Moron moved in, the hot water was always gone. Not because he used it. Mom wanted to smell good for him so she started taking half an hour in the shower, then putting on perfume spray, the works.

Why would she want to impress him? Why would she want to be with all those *losers*?

I've spent a lot of time wondering about that and the only thing I keep coming back to is she doesn't like herself very much.

I *know* that's true because when she breaks something or makes any kind of mistake, like cutting herself shaving her legs, she cusses herself out, calls herself names. I've heard her crying at night, drunk or stoned, calling herself names. Not so much since Moron moved in, because he threatens to smack her.

I used to go into the bedroom and sit next to her, touch her hair, say, 'What's the matter, Mom?' But she always moved away from me and said, 'Nothing, nothing,' sounding angry, so I stopped trying.

Then one day I realized she was crying about *me*. About having me without planning to, trying to raise me, figuring she wasn't much good at it.

I was her sadness.

I thought about that for a long time, too, decided my best bet was to learn as much as possible so I could get a good career and be able to take care of myself and her. Also, maybe if she saw I was doing OK, she wouldn't feel like such a failure.

The sun is up all the way, hot and orange through the trees. I'm really tired but there's no way I'm going to be able to sleep. Time to unroll the plastic.

I use plastic dry-cleaning bags to wrap and carry things in and to protect them from rain and dirt. Each sheet is printed with a warning that babies can suffocate in it and they're thin, easy to tear. But if you layer them three at a time they're really strong and excellent for protection. Mostly I find them in the trash, keep them rolled up in all five places, under rocks, my cave, wherever.

One good thing about Five is a tree: A huge eucalyptus tree with round, silver-blue leaves that smell like cough drops. I know it's a eucalyptus because that time in the zoo I went to the koala house and it was full of exactly the same species and they were labeled *eucalyptus polyanthemus: Silver dollar gum*. The sign said koalas ate eucalyptus polyanthemus, could live off them, and I wondered what it would be like if I got stuck up in Five with nothing to eat but trees. I asked a zoo-girl and she smiled and said she didn't know but she preferred hamburgers.

This particular tree has a trunk so thick I can barely reach around it, and branches droop down, touch the ground, keep going. Inside, it's like being in a silver-blue cloud, and hidden behind the branches, right next to the trunk is a big, flat, gray rock. It looks heavier than it is and I can lift it and prop something underneath it to keep it partly open, the way you jack up a tire. It didn't take long to scoop out dirt and create a hiding-hole. Once the rock's back down, it works like a trapdoor.

Lifting it, now, is a little harder because my arms are sore from carrying my Place Two stuff all night but I use one of my shoes to prop up the rock and pull out my Five stuff wrapped in plastic: Two pairs of Calvin Klein underwear that I got last month at a Los Feliz yard sale, too big with *Larry R.* inked inside the waistband; after I soaked them in the Fern Dell stream, they came out gray but clean. A spare flashlight and two AA batteries, an unopened package of beef jerky that I took from a Pink Dot on Sunset. A half-gallon bottle of Coke and an unopened box of Honey Nut Cheerios that I bought the next day at the same market cause I felt bad about taking the jerky. Some old magazines I found behind someone's house on Argyle Street – *Westways, People, Reader's Digest* – and the old one percent fat Knudsen milk carton that I use to keep pens and pencils, folders, rolled up notebook paper, and other stuff in.

There's a boy's face on the carton, a black kid named Rudolfo Hawkins who was kidnapped five years ago. The picture is from when he was six years old and it shows him wearing a white shirt and tie and smiling, like at a birthday party or some other special occasion.

It says he was kidnapped by his father in Compton, California but could be in Scranton, Pennsylvania or Detroit, Michigan. I used to look at the picture and wonder what happened to him. After five years he's probably OK . . . at least it was his father and not some pervert.

Maybe he's back in Compton with his mother.

I've thought about Mom looking for me and can't get it straight in my head if she is.

When I was young – five, six – she used to tell me she loved me, we were some pair, just us against the fucking world. Then her drinking and doping got more intense and she paid less and less attention to me. Once Moron moved in, I became invisible.

So would she look for me?

Even if she wanted to, would she know how, not being educated?

Moron would be a problem. He'd say something like, 'Fuck the little prick – he split, Sharla. He didn't give a shit, fuck him – gimme those nachos.'

But even without Moron, I can't get it straight how Mom would feel. Maybe she's sad I left, maybe angry.

Or maybe she's relieved. She never planned to have me. I guess she did the best with what she had.

I know she took good care of me in the beginning because I've seen pictures of when I was a baby that she keeps in an envelope in a drawer in the kitchen and I look healthy and happy. We both do. They're from Christmas, there's a tree full of lights and she's holding me up like some trophy, with a great big smile on her face. Like, Hey, look what *I* got for Christmas.

My birthday's August 10, so that would make me four and a half months old. I have a gross, fat face with pink cheeks and no hair. Mom is pale and skinny and she's got me dressed up in a stupid blue sailor suit. She's wearing the widest smile I've ever seen her wear, so some of her happiness must have been because of me, at least at the beginning.

Because her parents died in that car crash before I was born, what else would make her smile like that?

On the back of the photos are stickers from *Good Shepherd Sanctuary, Modesto, California*. I asked her about it and she said it was a Catholic place and even though we're not Catholic, we lived there when I was a baby. When I tried to ask her more about it, she grabbed the pictures away and said it wasn't important.

That night she cried for a long time and I read my Jacques Cousteau book to block out the sound.

I must have made her happy, back then.

Enough of this stupid stuff, time to unroll the Place Two plastic, here we go, toothbrush and Colgate gel, free samples I got out of someone's mailbox, no name on it, just *Resident*, so it really didn't belong to anyone. Another pair of underpants, out of a garbage can behind one of the huge houses at the foot of the park, a bunch of the ketchup and mustard and mayonnaise packets taken from restaurants. My books—

Only one book. Algebra.

Where's the Presidents book from the library? Got to be somewhere inside the plastic, I used three layers . . . no, not here. Did it fall out when I unpacked – no . . . did I drop it nearby?

I get up, look.

Nothing.

I backtrack for a while.

No Presidents book.

I must have dropped it in the dark.

Oh no. Shit. I was planning to give it back one day.

Now I am a thief.

12

STU DROPPED Petra off behind the station and drove off.

Back at her desk, she called Cleveland information for a backup work number for Dr Boehlinger at Washington University Hospital. The home number was in the book, too. Maybe folks were more trusting in Chagrin Falls.

She dialed, got a woman's recorded voice.

The time difference made it afternoon in Ohio. Was Mrs Boehlinger out shopping? Some surprise Petra would have for her. She visualized Lisa's mother shrieking, sobbing, maybe throwing up.

She remembered Ramsey's show of grief, the dry eyes. Bad actor unable to produce tears?

The Boehlingers' tape machine beeped. Not the time to leave a message. She hung up and tried the hospital. Dr Boehlinger's office was closed and a page produced no response.

Feeling no relief, only an ordeal postponed, she called the phone company and went through a couple of supervisors before finding a sympathetic voice. Lots of paperwork would be necessary for a full year's worth of Lisa's records, but the woman promised to fax over the latest bill when she found it. Petra thanked her, and then she drove to Doheny Drive, ready for Lisa's maid, Patsy Whatever-her-name-was.

Sunset was clogged and she took Cahuenga south to Beverly Boulevard and got a clearer sail. As she drove, she played one of her private games, composing a mental picture of the Thai maid: Young, tiny, cute, barely able to speak English. Sitting in another cream-colored room, terrified of all the cops who were playing strong and silent, not telling her a thing.

The building on Doheny was ten stories tall and shaped like a boomerang. The lobby was small, four walls of gold-streaked mirror, some plants and mock Louis XIV chairs guarded by a nervous-looking young Iranian in a blue blazer nametagged *A. Ramzisadeh*, kept company by a sheriff deputy. Petra showed her badge and inspected the two closed-circuit TVs on the desk. Black and white long view of hallways, nothing moving, the picture shifting every few seconds.

The guard shook her hand limply. 'Terrible. Poor Miss Boehlinger. It would never happen here.'

Petra clucked sympathetically. 'When's the last time you saw her, sir?'

'I think yesterday – she come home from work, six P.M.'

'Not today?'

'No, sorry.'

'How'd she leave without your seeing her?'

'Each floor has two elevator. One to the front, one to the back. The back lead down to garage.'

'Straight down to the garage?'

'Most people call down to have car brought around.'

'But Ms Boehlinger didn't.'

'No, she always drive herself. Go straight to the garage.'

Petra tapped one of the TV monitors. 'Does the closed-circuit scan the garage?'

'Sure, look.' Ramzisadeh indicated a slowly scanning black and white view of parked cars. Murky spaces, glints of grille and bumper.

'There,' he said.

'Do you keep tapes?'

'No, no tapes.'

'So there'd be no way to know exactly when Ms Boehlinger left?'

'No, Officer.'

Petra walked to the elevator and the tan cop tagged along. 'Big help, huh?' He pushed the button. 'Up at the top. Ten-seventeen.'

The door to Lisa Ramsey's apartment was closed but unlocked and when Petra walked in she saw the maid sitting on the edge of a couch. The physical similarity to Petra's mental image threw her so hard she almost lost her balance. Ten points on the ESP-meter.

Patricia Kasempitakpong was five one, tops, maybe a hundred pounds, with a pretty, heart-shaped face under a thick mop of long, layered ebony hair. She wore a beige cotton knit top, blue jeans and black flats. The sofa was as overstuffed as those in Cart Ramsey's house. But not cream – Petra's prophecy-fest ended there.

Lisa Ramsey's apartment was a study in color. Red and blue velvet couches with tasseled skirts, parquet floors stained black, a zebra-skin rug thrown across the wood. A real rug; the animal's head was pointing toward a black glass vase filled with yellow daffodils.

From what Petra could see, the apartment was small, the kitchen just a cubby of white lacquered wood and gray tile counters. The ceilings were low and flat. Basically the place was just another LA box. But the tenth-floor corner location and sliding glass doors gave it fantastic views of the west-side all the way to the ocean. Beyond the door was a skimpy balcony. No furniture, no potted palms. A cigar of smog floated above the horizon.

Two uniforms were enjoying the view and they turned to Petra just long enough to see her flash the badge. On the wall behind Patricia Kasem-whatever was a black metal shelving unit housing black stereo equipment and a twenty-five-inch TV.

No books.

Petra hadn't seen any in Ramsey's place, either. Nothing like common apathy as the basis for a relationship.

The hard-edged color scheme suggested that Lisa had tired of pastels. Or maybe she'd never liked them in the first place.

Had cream and pink been *Ramsey's* idea of tasteful? Interesting.

She smiled at Patricia and Patricia just stared. Petra came over to her and sat down.

'Hi.'

The maid was scared but loosened up after a while. Fluent English, American born. ('Don't even bother with my name, they call me Patsy K.') She'd only worked two months for Lisa, couldn't see how she could help.

A one-hour interview produced nothing juicy.

Lisa had never said why she'd left Ramsey, nor had the domestic violence episode come up. She had mentioned once that he was too old for her, that marrying him had been a mistake. The maid slept in the spare bedroom, kept the place clean, ran errands. Lisa was a great boss, Lisa always paid on time, was neat and tidy herself. A 'real neat person.'

Patsy K had no trouble crying.

On the subject of spousal support, the maid said Lisa received a monthly check from a firm called Players Management.

'The card's there on the fridge.' Petra retrieved it. Address on Ventura Boulevard in Studio City. Gregory Balch's name at the bottom. Financial Manager. Ramsey paying through his company.

'Any idea how much the checks were for?'

Patsy blushed, no doubt recalling an indiscreet peek.

'Anything you can tell us would be really helpful,' said Petra.

'Seven thousand.'

'A month?'

Nod.

Eighty-four thousand a year. Enough to pay the rent and some bills and have some fun but not much of a dent in Ramsey's seven-figure income. Still, things like that chafed. Paying money to someone you resented. Someone who'd humiliated you on national television.

It spelled tension, but was far from probable cause.

So Lisa had thought Ramsey too old for her. He'd alluded to a generational riff, too. 'Did Lisa and Mr Ramsey talk on the phone?'

'Not that I ever saw.'

'Is there anything else you can tell me, Patsy?'

The maid shook her head and began to cry again. The uniforms on the balcony were watching the sunset, didn't even bother to turn. 'She was nice. Sometimes it was like

111

we were more like friends – eating dinner together up here when she wasn't going out. I know how to cook Thai and she liked it.'

'Did Lisa go out a lot?'

'Sometimes two, three times a week, sometimes not for weeks.'

'Where'd she go?'

'She never really said.'

'No idea at all?'

'Movies, I guess. Screenings, she was a film editor.'

'Who'd she work for?'

'Empty Nest Productions – they're over at Argent Studios in Culver City.'

'When she went out, who was it with?'

'Guys, I guess, but since I've been here she never brought them up here.'

'She went down to meet them?'

Patsy nodded and Petra said, 'But you assume they were guys.'

'She was beautiful. Had been a beauty queen.' Patsy eyed the officers out on the patio.

'During the two months you worked here, none of her dates ever came up?'

'One guy came up but I don't know if he was a date. She worked with him. I think his name was Darrell – a black guy.'

'How many times did he come up?'

'Twice, I think. Maybe it was Darren.'

'When was this?'

Patsy thought. 'Maybe a month ago.'

'Can you describe him?'

'Tall, light-skinned – for a black guy, I mean. Short hair, neat dresser.'

'Facial hair?'

'No, I don't think so.'

'How old?'

'I guess around forty.'

Another older man. Patsy had a blank look in her eyes. The irony had eluded her.

Lisa searching for Dad?

'What was Lisa's work schedule?'

'She worked all hours,' said Patsy. 'Whenever they called her she had to be ready.'

'And Mr Ramsey never showed up here.'

'Not when I was here.'

'And no phone calls.'

'Lisa hardly spoke to anyone on the phone – she didn't like the phone, used to disconnect it so she could have peace and quiet.'

'OK,' said Petra. 'So your day off is Sunday?'

'Saturday night till Monday morning. When I got here at eight Lisa was already gone, I thought maybe she got a night call. Then the officers showed up.'

Patsy held herself tight and began to rock, coughed, gagged on her own saliva. Petra got her a Pellegrino water from the miniature white fridge. There were three more bottles in there, and fresh grapes, three cartons of non-fat raspberry yoghurt, cottage cheese. Lean Cuisine in the freezer.

Patsy drank. When she put the bottle down, Petra said, 'You've been very helpful. I appreciate it.'

'Whatever . . . I still can't believe . . .' Patsy swiped at her eyes.

'Now I'm going to ask you something tough, but I have to. Was Lisa into drugs?'

'No – she – not that I saw.' The Pellegrino bottle shook.

'Patsy, the first thing I'm going to do after we finish talking is search this apartment from top to bottom. If there's dope here, I'll find it. Personally, I don't care if Lisa used. I'm Homicide, not Narcotics. But drugs lead to violence and Lisa was murdered very violently.'

'It wasn't like that,' said Patsy. 'She wasn't a head. She used to sniff a little, but that was it.'

'Any other drugs besides cocaine?'

'Just some grass.' Downward glance. Meaning maybe Lisa had shared her cannabis with Patsy? Or the maid had pilfered?

'She hardly used anything,' Patsy insisted. 'It wasn't regular.'

'How often?'

'I don't know – I never actually *saw* it – the coke.'

'What about the grass?'

'Sometimes she'd smoke a joint while watching TV.'

'Where'd she do the coke?'

'Always in her room. With the door closed.'

'How often?'

'Not often – maybe once a week. Every two weeks. The only reason I know is I'd see powder on her dressing table. And sometimes she left a razor blade out and her nose was pink and she acted different.'

'Different, how?'

'Up. Hyper. Nothing crazy, just a little hyper.'

'Grumpy?'

Silence.

114

'Patsy?'

'Sometimes it made her a little moody.' The tiny woman curled up. 'But basically, she was great.'

Petra softened her tone. 'So once a week. In her room.'

'She never did it in front of me. I'm not into *anything* like that.' Patsy licked her lips.

'Any idea where she got her drugs from?'

'No way.'

'She never said?'

'Never.'

'And there were no drug transactions up here?'

'No way, never. I assumed at the studio.'

'Why's that?'

'Because it's all over the industry. Everyone knows that.'

'Did Lisa tell you that?'

'No,' said Patsy. 'You just hear about it. It's on TV all the time, right?'

'OK,' said Petra. 'I'm going to look around now. Please wait a while longer.'

She stood and looked toward the balcony. Beyond the railing, the sky was a strange, deep sapphire-blue streaked with orange, and the two cops were transfixed. Suddenly, Petra heard traffic from Doheny. It had been there all along. She'd been wrapped up in work. Interview hypnosis.

She went into Patsy's bedroom, first. A glorified closet, really, with a single bed, small oak dresser and matching nightstand. Clothes from Target, the Gap, Old Navy. A portable TV sat on the dresser. Two books on cosmetology and an old copy of *People* in the nightstand drawer.

One bathroom, shared by both women, cramped, with black and white tiles, a black whirlpool tub. Petra learned from the medicine cabinet that Patsy K had taken cortisone for a skin rash and Lisa Ramsey suffered from periodic yeast infections for which an anti-fungal had been prescribed. No birth control pills, though maybe they were in a drawer. The rest was all over-the-counter mundanity. She went into Lisa's bedroom.

Twice as big as Patsy's, but still far from generous. All in all a tight little apartment. Maybe Lisa had wanted the refuge of simplicity after the pink hacienda.

The bed was queen-sized with a bright red satin throw and black linens. Black lacquer furniture, a black cross-country ski machine tucked in the corner, perfume bottles – *Gio* and *Poison* – on the dresser. Bare walls. Very tidy, just as Patsy had said.

She found the dope in the bottom drawer of the bedroom dresser. White granules in a glassine envelope and another packet with three small, neatly rolled joints, tucked beneath ski sweaters and pants and other winter clothes. Still no birth control pills, no diaphragm. Maybe Lisa really had wanted peace and quiet.

She tagged and bagged the drugs, called over the cops from the balcony, showed them the cocaine and asked them to get it over to Hollywood Evidence.

Atop the dresser was a jewelry box full of shiny things. Mostly costume pieces along with two strings of cultured pearls. So Lisa had been wearing her best stuff last night. Hot date? Petra moved on to the lower drawers.

They bore Victoria's Secret lingerie – alluring but not trashy – a couple of sensible plaid flannel nightshirts, cotton and silk underwear, T-shirts and shorts, sweaters and vests, and three pairs of crisply laundered made-in-France blue jeans from Fred Segal on Melrose. The wall-length closet was full of Krizia and Versus and Armani Exchange pant suits, dresses, and skirts and blouses, sizes four to six.

Lots of black, some white, some red, a spot of beige, one bright green jacquard wraparound that stood out like a parrot in a dead tree. Thirty pairs of shoes were lined up in three precise rows on the floor of the closet, toes out. The pumps were all Ferragamo, the casual stuff, Kenneth Cole. Two pairs of white New Balance running shoes, one nearly brand new.

In the nightstand drawer, Petra found a Citibank checkbook, a Beverly Hills branch Home Savings passbook, and, tucked into the check register, the business card of a broker at Merrill Lynch in Westwood named Morad Ghadoomian whose name and number she copied down.

Three thousand dollars in the checking account, twenty-three thou plus some change in the savings account, with two conspicuous monthly deposits: The seven thousand spousal support and another thirty-eight hundred – probably film-editing salary checks.

A pair of regular monthly withdrawals, too. Twenty-two hundred – that had to be rent – and twelve hundred, which Petra guessed was Patsy K's salary. Variable expenditures ranged from two to four thousand a month.

Over ten thou in each month, five, six out, leaving a nice sum to play with for a single girl. Taxes on the salary were already withdrawn. Those on the spousal support would probably soak up some of the gravy, and coke and designer duds could consume a lot more. But given the fact that Lisa had managed to stash away twenty-three thousand, Petra was ready to believe her dope habit hadn't been monstrous.

117

Occasional hits at home. Maybe at work, too, supplied by pals from The Industry.

In return for what?

Ramsey was prime suspect, but there were plenty of blanks to fill.

She was finished by 3:30, took down the name of a friend in Alhambra where Patsy K would be staying, had the uniforms watch as the maid packed up her belongings.

The next two hours were spent going door to door on Lisa's floor and the two stories immediately above and below, and on the sidestreets that flanked the building. Of the few people home, no one had seen Lisa leave Sunday night or early Monday morning, nor had they spied the black Porsche.

Five thirty; now she had to try the Boehlingers again.

Why hadn't she let Stu do it? Ms Samaritan. He hadn't shown much gratitude.

The smartest thing to do was return to the Hollywood station and use a department phone for the notification call, but she just didn't feel like seeing the office again and drove to her apartment on Detroit Avenue just east of Park La Brea.

Once inside, she tossed her jacket on a chair and realized she craved a cool drink. But instead of indulging herself, she called the Boehlinger home. Evening in Cleveland, now. Busy signal. She hoped someone else hadn't reached the family first.

Taking a can of root beer out of the fridge, she kicked off her shoes and sat drinking at the dinette table. Contemplating dinner, though she wasn't really hungry. Her father's voice, gently prodding, reverbed in her head. *Nutrition, Pet. Got to keep those amino acids nice and rich.*

He'd raised her since infancy, had a right to mother. When she thought about his cruel, rotting death it hurt so bad. Quickly, she chased his picture from her mind and the resulting blank space felt horrible, too.

Nutrition . . . force down a sandwich. Dry salami on stale ciabatta, mustard and mayo, something green – a kosher pickle, that qualified, there you go, Food Police.

Fixing a plate but not eating, she tried the Boehlingers a third time. Still busy. Could the story have hit the news that fast?

She switched on the TV, channel-surfed. Nothing. The radio, preset to KKGO, offered her someone's symphony while she nibbled the stiff sandwich.

Her own tight little apartment. Less than half the rent of Lisa's.

She and Nick had started out sharing a West LA flat but right after the impulsive Vegas wedding, they'd leased a much bigger place. Up-and-down studio on Fountain near La Cienega, leaded windows, parquet floors, courtyard with fountain, gorgeous Spanish architecture. More than enough space for both their workplaces, Nick claimed he needed room to stretch and claimed the master bedroom for his studio.

They'd never furnished, lived with boxes and crates, slept on a mattress in the smaller bedroom. Petra's easel and paints ended up downstairs in the breakfast room. Eastern exposure. She dealt with morning glare by drawing the blinds.

Now her easel was in the living room and she still had almost no furniture. Why bother, she was seldom here except to sleep, had no visitors.

The triplex she lived in was just south of Sixth Street, a charming old place with thick walls, high ceilings, crown moldings, waxed oak floors, moderate crime in the neighborhood. At eight hundred a month a bargain, because the landlord, a Taiwanese immigrant named Mary Sun, was thrilled to have a cop tenant. Confiding, 'This city, all the blacks, very bad.'

Museum Row was a short stroll as were the galleries on La Brea, though Petra had yet to visit any of them.

When she had Sundays off, she scanned the papers for auctions, flea markets, antique shows. Even garage sales, when they were in good neighborhoods.

Pickings were slim. Most people thought their garbage was treasure, and she was more of a browser than a buyer. But the few things she had bought were good.

Lovely iron headboard, probably French, with an impossible-to-fake patina. Two birch nightstands with floral stenciling and yellow marble tops. The old woman she'd bargained with had claimed they were English, but Petra knew they were Swedish.

A few old bottles on the ledge of the kitchen window, a bronze statue of a little boy with a small dog, also French.

And that was about it.

She got up and put her plate on the counter. The tile was clean but old, and cracked in a few places. The kitchen at Fountain had featured a Euro range and blue granite counters.

Cold counters.

Nick had two ways of making love. Plan A was telling her how much he loved her, caressing her softly, sometimes too softly but she never protested, and eventually he got around to exerting the right pressure. Kissing her neck, her eyes, her fingertips as he kept up the romantic patter, how beautiful she was, how special, what a privilege it was to be inside her.

Plan B was hoisting her up on blue granite, hiking her skirt, sliding off her panties while managing to unzip himself, placing both hands on her shoulders and plunging in like an enemy.

In the beginning, she'd been excited by both A and B.

Later, she lost her taste for B.

Later, all he wanted was B.

Suddenly, the remains of the salami and the bread and mustard and mayo looked like lab supplies. Pushing the plate away, she picked up the phone.

This time, a man with a cultured, middle-aged voice answered.

'Dr Boehlinger.'

Remote but calm. So they hadn't found out.

Petra's heart was racing; would telling the mother have been worse?

'Doctor, this is Detective Connor of the Los Angeles Police De—'

'Lisa.'

'Sir?'

'It's Lisa, right?'

'I'm afraid so, Doctor. She—'

'Dead?'

'Unfortunately, Doc—'

'Dear God – goddamnit, *goddamnit*, that *bastard*, that goddamn bastard, that bastard!'

'Who, Doc—'

'Who else? *Him*, that piece of garbage she *married*. She

121

told us if anything happened it would be him – oh God, my little girl! Oh, *Jesus! No, no, no!*'

'I'm sorry—'

'I'll *kill* him. Oh Jesus, no, my little girl, my poor little girl!'

'Doctor,' she said, but he kept on. Ranting and cursing and pledging vengeance in a voice that managed, eerily, to remain cultured.

Finally, he ran out of breath.

'Dr Boeh—'

'My wife,' he said, incredulously. 'She's out tonight, goddamn Hospital Auxiliary meeting. Usually *I'm* the one who's out and *she's* in. I *knew* Lisa was worried about him, but how could it come to *this*!'

Then, silence.

'Dr Boehlinger.'

No answer.

'Sir? Are you all right?'

More silence, then a very small, strangled '*What?*' and she knew he'd been crying, was trying to hide it.

'What?' he said.

'I know it's a horrible time, Doctor, but if we could talk for a—'

'Yes, yes, let's *talk*. At least until my wife comes home – then ... Jesus ... what time is it – ten forty. Just got home myself. Saving fools' lives while my little—'

Petra nearly recoiled from the loud, terrible laugh on the other end. Needing to reel him in, she said, 'Are you a surgeon, sir?'

'Emergency room surgeon. I run the ER at Washington U hospital. How did he do it?'

122

'Pardon?'

'How? *Method*. Did he strangle her? Usually husbands shoot or strangle their wives. Least that's what I've seen – *how the hell did he do it?!*'

'She was stabbed, sir, but we don't know yet who—'

'Oh yes you do, Miss – I don't remember your name – you certainly do know, I'm *telling* you, so you know. It was him. Don't doubt it for a goddamn minute. Don't waste your time looking anywhere else, just haul in that piece of garbage and you'll have it solved.'

'Sir—'

'Don't you *understand* what I'm telling you?' Boehlinger shouted. 'He *beat* her – she called us and told us he beat her. A goddamned *actor*. One step above a *whore*! Too damned old for her but when he *hit* her, that was the last straw!'

'What did Lisa tell you about the incident?'

'The *incident*!' he roared. 'He went crazy over something and hauled off and hit her. She said it would be on TV, wanted us to know first. She said she was frightened of him – it's the same old story every week in the ER, but to have your own daughter – you said you were a detective, right? Miss . . .'

'Connor. Yes, sir, I am. And I know about domestic violence.'

'Domestic violence,' said Boehlinger. 'More PC crap. All we do is rename things. It's wife-beating! I've been married thirty-four years, never laid a finger on my wife! First he woos her like Prince Charming then it all goes to hell in a handbasket and he's Mr Hyde – she was *frightened* of him, Miss Connor. Scared clean out of her mind. That's why she left him. We begged her to come back to Ohio, not to stay in that psychotic swamp of yours. But she didn't want to, loved the movies, had her goddamned *career*! Now look where it got her – oh, Jesus God, my little baby girl, my baby my baby *my baby*!'

13

SHARLA STRAIGHT, queasy, still half stoned, sat on the couch in the trailer's front room as Buell 'Motor' Moran ate cold beef stew out of the can and finished the last beer. She was still sore, he'd been rough with her, doing her from the back, clawing her buttocks. Her thoughts cleared partially and she pictured Billy's face.

Her sweet little— Motor grunted and destroyed her thoughts.

He liked doing it that way because he could stand, not put weight on his hands or strain his back. The only benefit to her was she didn't have to see his face.

Even from the back, he smelled. Like unwashed clothes.

Her whole *life* smelled like unwashed clothes.

Her head hurt; tequila wasn't good for her, specially the cheap stuff Motor got at the Stop 'n Shop. Beer was better, beer and weed the best of all because it made her feel far away from things, but they were out of weed and he hogged all the beer.

He *was* a hog – one big mean, hairy pig, even bigger than Daddy. Remembering his nails digging into her hips, knowing they were black around the edges, she kept thinking: Dirty, he's dirty, I'm dirty.

Did she have to end up like this or was there some other way . . . ?

She didn't know, she just didn't know.

The hot, dead haze that passed for air in the trailer felt smothering. The piece of cloth she'd nailed up to cover the small window over the bed had fallen half-loose but all she could see was a square of black – everyone in the park was asleep, must be late – what time was it, anyway?

What time was it where Billy was? If he was somewhere and not—

Four months since that terrible day and when she let it, the memory stuck her like a knife.

Worrying about him lying in some ditch.

Or cut up by some sicko.

Or run over by a truck on some lonely road. That small, skinny, white body, so small, he'd always been so small except when he was a baby and had that fat face . . . cause she nursed him, she didn't want to stop nursing him, even when nothing came out and her nipples bled, but the nuns made her stop, one of them, the tall one whose name she forgot ordering her, 'Stop, girl. You'll have plenty of opportunity to sacrifice.'

Billy gone. It had taken her almost two days to realize it was really true.

He wasn't there when she and Motor got home that night, but sometimes he took walks by himself so she just fell asleep, not waking up till ten and she figured he'd gone to school. When it got dark the next day, she knew something was wrong but she was already stoned and couldn't move.

The next morning, no one to bring her instant coffee, she

126

realized it had been *way* too long. Like a big knife, the panic cut through her and she started screaming silently to herself, oh no, can't be – where, why, who, why?!

She never said anything out loud, never showed the way she felt to Motor. To anyone.

That day, after Motor went out, she left the trailer for the first morning in maybe a month, the sun hurting her eyes, aware, now, that her dress was dirty and one of her shoes had a big hole in it.

Looking all around Watson, walking till her feet hurt.

A real hot day, plenty of birds out, people she never really looked at, cats and dogs and more people. She covered every field and grove, the stores, the Stop 'n Shop, the Sunnyside, even the school, because maybe he just spent the night somewhere and went to school by himself even though that made no sense at all, why would he do that?

But lots of times things didn't make sense, she'd learned a long time ago not to wait for things to make sense.

So she kept walking, looking, checking it all out. Buying a Pepsi at the Stop along with a Payday bar, just to keep fueled, those peanuts were good energy.

Not asking anyone if they'd seen him, just looking, because she didn't want anyone to think she was that bad a mother.

Not telling the sheriff, for sure, because he might get suspicious, go through the trailer, find the stash.

That night, she told Motor and he said big deal, it was just a fucking runaway situation, happened all the time, hell, *he'd* run away when he was fifteen after beating the shit out of his old man and hadn't she done it, too? Everyone ran, finally the little shit had developed some balls.

But Billy, only twelve, looking younger, so small, that wasn't the same thing as her running or a big hog like Motor, no way.

The day she looked everywhere, no one asked what she was doing, where Billy was. Not the first day, the second, the third, never. Not once.

Four months now, still no questions. Not the school, the neighbors – for sure no friends because Billy never had friends, probably her fault because when he was little she was living all by herself out in that even-worse trailer with some people she was still trying to forget about, man she'd been wasted, she didn't think anyone had hurt Billy.

He'd always been a quiet kid, even as a baby, so quiet, you'd never know he was even there . . .

Tears flowed from deep inside her head, flooding her closed eyelids, swelling them, and she had to open them a little to let the water out.

When she did, she was almost surprised to find herself back in the trailer, nothing changed, seeing the dim outlines of the kitchenette, Motor sitting there stuffing his face, dirty dishes, sour, more sour, everything sour.

Where was her little man?

The day after he disappeared, she had a nightmare of it being some dark, damp place, a torture chamber, some crazy person finding him walking in the groves, one of those guys you hear about, cruising near schools, other places, snatching kids, doing what they want with 'em, cutting 'em. She woke up shaking and sweating, her stomach burning like she'd swallowed fire.

Motor snored as she watched the sun lighten the cloth over the trailer window. Too afraid to move. Or think. Then thinking about torture chambers and getting sick to her stomach.

Rushing to the john and throwing up, trying to do it quietly, so as not to wake Motor.

Every night for a week she woke up sweating from the dreams.

Sick with guilt and fear, the horrible person she was, the worst mother in the world, never shoulda been a mother, never shoulda been born *herself*, all she caused in the world was misery and sin, she deserved to be pronged from the back by a hog...

The nightmares went away when she found the Tampax money missing and knew what happened.

Escape. A plan.

She'd saved that money for a long time, keeping it from Motor and all the others before him, her own stash.

For what?

Just in case.

In case what?

Nothing.

Better Billy should have it; let's face it, she'd never use it, didn't *deserve* to use it, the worst mother in the whole world.

Maybe not *the* worst — that crazy girl who drove those two babies into a lake, that was worse. And she'd seen on TV about some girl jumping off a building holding her baby. That was worse.

Some people burned their kids or beat 'em — she sure knew about that — but it didn't say much for her that the only worse thing she could compare herself to was stuff like that, did it?

The truth was, she was bad enough.

No wonder Billy'd had to escape.

No escape for her, she wasn't smart enough, good enough, just like Daddy had said: Something missing, tapping his head with one hand.

Trying to say she was stupid or crazy.

She wasn't, but . . .

She could think fine when she wasn't stoned.

OK, reading was hard for her, so were numbers, but she could think, she knew she could think. She herself didn't understand the things she did sometimes, but she wasn't crazy. No way.

Better not to think . . . but where would Billy *escape* to?

So small and skinny.

No surprise, there. Look where he'd come from.

Weird the way it had happened. Because she usually liked the big ones. Big like Daddy. Hogs, like Motor and others. Names and faces she'd forgotten – all those high football players and wrestlers doing to her just what Daddy suspected they were doing, Daddy beating her ass even though he could never prove it.

She'd wanted to explain it to Daddy: *It ain't hotpants, it's the only chance to get close to people with goals.*

You didn't explain to Daddy.

Goals . . . it had been a long time since she'd thought about the future.

Too many years of sour notes.

Mixed in with one solitary sweet night, the prettiest little baby, those nuns had been grumpy but pretty good to her, she appreciated that even though she knew they wanted her to give Billy up.

No way, what was hers was hers.

She fed herself a little candy-drop memory of Billy's fat little baby-face – she deserved a little sugar, didn't she?

That night, the night of—

She'd been so much younger, prettier, skinnier, lying alone in the grove after midnight. Her choice to be alone – maybe that's where Billy got it from!

So maybe they were the same in at least *one* way!

She found herself smiling, remembering that night, how she'd actually *felt* something.

The warmth between her legs, all over her, the hard dirt didn't even hurt her back.

The orange trees green as bottle glass in the moonlight, snowy with flowers because this was the blossom season, the whole grove smelling so creamy and sweet, a beautiful sky, dark with a halo of nice light overhead because the moon was big and fat and gold and dripping with light, like a butter-soaked pancake.

Lying there, after he kissed her and said sorry, have to go, her skirt still up, floating.

Then a vibration – loud, close, as fast-moving clouds blocked out the moon.

Cicadas, millions of them, swarming through the grove.

She'd heard stories about them but had never seen them.

Never seen them since, either.

A one-time thing.

Maybe it had been a dream, that whole night a dream . . .

Huge bugs like that, should have been scary.

Twice as huge as the shiny black wood bees that freaked the hell out of her when they zoomed out of nowhere.

The cicadas were even noisier, so many of them, she should have been all froze up with fear.

But she wasn't, just lay flat on her back, feeling sweet and female, one big package of pollen and honey, watching as the cicadas settled on row after row of orange tree, covering the entire grove, like bunches of gray-brown blanket.

What were they doing? Eating the flowers? Chewing away at the tiny green oranges, bitter and hard as wood?

But no, all at once they were all gone, zipping up into the sky and disappearing like some cartoon tornado, and the trees looked exactly the same.

Night of the cicadas.

Magic, almost like it had never happened.

But it had. She sure had the proof.

Where was *Billy*?

14

LISA, YOU coke-snorting bitch.

Dance with me and this is what happens.

Dance *around* me and this is what happens.

Oh, the joy.

Ode to joy – wasn't that Bach?

He hated Bach. In the hospital where they'd taken his mother when she had to wear a football helmet they played Bach and other classical crap.

Trying to soothe the patients.

Patients. Inmates is what they really were.

Lisa had tried to drive him crazy.

Tried to lead.

Oh, the look on her face . . . dance with me, darling.

15

THE DOMESTIC violence tape played on all the eleven o'clock news broadcasts: Lisa and Cart Ramsey, both smooth and tan, immersed in Jacuzzi bubbles, lining up putts on the home green, doing a Roy Rogers–Dale Evans number on sleek horses, smooching for the paparazzi. Lisa as a beauty queen and a gorgeous bride, cut frantically with closeups of her post-beating face.

Then somber reporters intoning about the brutality of the dead woman's wounds followed by the department spokesman, a photogenic Parker Center captain named Salmagundi, fielding questions without really answering them.

Petra watched it at her dinette table, hunched over another salami sandwich, feeling violated.

After getting off the phone with Dr Boehlinger, she'd tried to paint. A desert landscape she'd been working on for months, swirls of sienna and umber highlighted with acra red, the faintest hints of lavender, nostalgia-flashes of hikes with her dad. As she dabbed she was certain it was working.

But when she stepped away from the canvas, she saw only mud, and when she tried to fix it her strokes felt clumsy, as if her hands had suddenly seized up.

Washing her brushes, she turned on the TV and thought

some more about Dr Boehlinger, and the mother who had yet to come home.

What it was like to lose a child. A real child.

What it would be like to *have* a child – that opened up the gates of hell, as she remembered what pregnancy felt like, the almost crushing sense of *importance*.

Suddenly, she was crying, just gushing tears. Uncontrollably except for one tiny corner of left hemisphere that watched and scolded: What the hell has gotten into you?

What, indeed?

She took several gasping breaths before she was able to stop, gave her eyes a brutal swipe with a paper napkin.

Lord, what a spectacle, disgustingly maudlin, poor John Everett Boehlinger and his wife have lost a human being and you go on like the thing you expelled from your womb was close to human.

A grape-sized piece of pulp in bloody soup.

A mass of bloody *potential*, floating in the toilet as she'd kneeled and retched and cramped in agony, hating Nick enough to kill him, for bringing it on.

Because he *had*, she was sure of it. The stress, the cold disapproval.

Walking out on her – exactly what he promised he'd never do. Because he'd been made to understand that she'd grown up without a mother, that her father was wasting away in a Tucson sanitarium, that being alone would be true hell, he must never, never walk out on her.

Maybe he'd been sincere when he promised.

A fertilized egg changed everything.

I thought we agreed, Petra! We were using birth control, for God's sake!

Ninety percent effective isn't one hundred, honey.

So why didn't you use something more reliable?

I thought it was good enough – apologizing? Was she really apologizing?

Great, Petra. Fuck around with our lives like that. You're an educated woman! How could you do anything so stupid?

Bloody potential. Cramping so badly she felt she was being torn apart, she'd rested her cheek on the cold porcelain rim of the toilet, flushed, listened to it whirlpool away.

Alone, barely able to stand, she drove herself to the hospital. Tests, a D and C, more tests, three days in a semi-private bed next to a woman who'd just birthed her fourth baby. Two boys, two girls, family members all around, cooing and ahing.

The postcard from Nick came two weeks later. Brilliant sunset over sand. Santa Fe. *Taking some time off to think.* She never saw him again.

The hole that opened in Petra's consciousness expanded, hollowing her, lowering her immunity. More cramps, fever, an infection, back to the hospital.

Outpatient follow-up. Feet in stirrups, too drained to feel demeaned.

Dr Franklin's sad sympathy. *Let's talk in my office.* Charts and pictures.

Unable to focus any better than she had during all those mind-numbing boarding-school health classes, she played dumb.

What are you saying? I'm sterile?

Franklin averted his eyes, dropped his glance to the floor. Just like suspects did when they were about to lie.

No one can say that for sure, Petra. We have all sorts of procedures, nowadays.

She'd flushed away life, flushed her marriage.

Gravitated toward a career full of death. Using the grief of others as a constant reminder of how bad it could get, her situation was OK, right? In that sense, the more brutal the better, bring on the bodies.

So why the hell was she *crying*? She hadn't cried in years.

This case? It had barely begun, she had no feel for the victim.

Then she heard Lisa's name and her aching eyes flew to the screen as the story flashed. Feeling stupid for being surprised, how could it be any other way? Now, millions of people were viewing sixty seconds of tape that Stu and she hadn't been allowed to ask for.

Had Stu seen it? She knew he got to sleep as early as possible, especially when making up for lost nights. If he had, he'd want to know. She supposed.

She phoned his house in La Crescenta. Kathy Bishop answered, sounding subdued.

'Did I wake you? Sorry—'

'No, we're up, Petra. We just watched it too. Here's Stu.'

None of the usual smalltalk. Kathy usually liked to chat. Something different with both of them – a marital thing? No, couldn't be, the Bishops were poster children for Marital Solidity, don't disillusion me, Lord.

Stu came on. 'Just got off the phone with Schoelkopf. Quote: "We don't want another f-ing O.J. My office, eight A.M."'

'Something to wake up for.'

'Yeah. How'd the notification go?'

'Spoke to the father. He hates Ramsey's guts, is positive Ramsey did it.'

'He back that up with anything?'

'The beating. And he says Lisa was scared of Ramsey.'

'Scared of what?'

'He didn't say.'

'Aha . . . OK, eight A.M.'

'What do you think about the broadcast?'

Silence. 'I guess it could help us. Make Ramsey a de facto suspect and get the brass worried about looking stupid if we *don't* press him a little.'

'Good point,' she said.

Silence.

'OK, I won't keep you – just one more thing: Dr Boehlinger runs an ER, probably a take-charge kind of guy. I'm sure he and his wife will be coming out ASAP. He hates Ramsey. What if he decides to get proactive?'

'Hmm,' he said, as if it was mildly interesting. Same way he'd reacted to the library book. Was she off her game? 'Share it with the captain. He's such a sharing person.'

Tuesday, 7:57 A.M.

Edmund Schoelkopf looked more Latin than Teutonic. A short, trim man in his early fifties, he had moist black eyes, thick, artificial-looking black hair combed back from a flat, shallow forehead, and delicate lips. His skin was the color of All-Bran. He wore knockoffs of Armani double-breasteds and aggressive ties, looked like a former cop who'd gone on to corporate security. But he'd spent every moment of his work life in LAPD and would probably never leave till mandatory retirement.

His office was unimpressive, the usual mix of city-issue and community donations. He let Stu and Petra right in.

'Coffee?' His bass voice was morning-thick, barely into the human register. On the walls behind him were the usual graphs and pin charts. Tides of crime that could be surfed but never tamed.

The coffee smelled burnt. They were supposed to refuse it and they did. Schoelkopf pushed back his desk chair and crossed his legs, tugging up knife-crease slacks.

'Tell me,' he said, the basso corseted now.

Stu caught him up on the visit to Ramsey's house and Petra summed up her talk with Patsy K, the search of the apartment and the door-to-door, the notification of Dr Boehlinger. Presented that way, it sounded as if she'd done a lot more work than Stu. She had. He didn't seem to care, kept looking around. Schoelkopf seemed distracted, too, even when Petra talked about the discovery of Lisa's dope.

'The father blames it on Ramsey, sir,' she said. 'He really hates Ramsey's guts.'

'Wouldn't you? So . . . you'll follow up with that black guy at the studio – Darrell.'

'Right away. What if Dr Boehlinger tries to get involved?'

Schoelkopf's black eyes fixed on the center of her forehead. 'We'll deal with that if and when it occurs. Let's concentrate on getting some data. I know the lab's got all the stuff but is there anything even remotely resembling physical evidence yet?'

Petra was about to shake her head when Stu said, 'Petra found something interesting. A library book, hundred feet or so above the body. And there are some other indications someone could have been up there recently. There's a rock formation—'

'I've seen the crime-scene photos,' said Schoelkopf. 'What other indications?'

Petra's hands had tightened. She tried to catch Stu's eye but he focused on the captain. *Something interesting?*

Schoelkopf said, 'Tell me about the other indications, Barbie.'

'Food wrappers,' she said. 'Like from a fast-food joint. Specks of ground beef, maybe tacos. And urine on one of the rocks—'

Schoelkopf said, 'Someone eating and peeing and reading? What kind of library book?'

'Presidents of the United States.'

That seemed to annoy him. 'Checked out recently?'

'No, sir. Nine months ago.'

'Oh, c'mon – that sounds like bullshit.' He tossed coffee down his throat. The mug was steaming. It had to hurt. 'What makes you think this person was up there recently?'

'The meat wasn't dried out, sir.'

'A speck of meat?'

'A few specks. Ground beef.'

'How long does it take for ground beef to dry out?'

'I don't know, sir.'

'I don't either, but I'll bet it varies, depending on how much fat in the meat, temperature, humidity, who knows whatever the fuck else. What about the urine?'

'The crime techs thought it was—'

'It's a park,' said Schoelkopf. 'People come up there to eat and relax, maybe they take a leak when no one's watching – there are picnic tables not far from there, right?'

140

'Yes, but not right there, sir. These rocks—'

'Sometimes people don't bother going to the john – is there a john nearby?'

'Just past the picnic tables.'

'People are lazy – OK, I can see you liking the food and the pee, but the book tells me you're barking up the wrong tree. Because it was *dark*, Barbie. Why the hell would anyone be out there reading in the dark?'

'The person could have arrived earlier, stayed till after dark—'

'What, some intellectual with an interest in political science is reading about the presidents – God knows why, they're all scumbags – eats, takes a leak, and lays his head down on a rock and falls asleep and just happens to wake up to see the girl get sliced? Fine, so where is he? Your witness.'

'We're not saying the book was even related to the food,' she said. 'It was found a ways up from the—'

'Hey,' said Schoelkopf, 'you want a gift from Santa Claus, fine. But for all we know it was *Ramsey* behind those rocks, munching a burger and taking a leak – sitting in wait for her. She shows up, he jumps her.'

'The way she was dressed, sir, she seemed to be out on a date.'

'With who?'

'Maybe Ramsey. His everyday car, a Mercedes, was gone when we visited his house. If we're allowed to ask questions, maybe we can find out where it is.'

Schoelkopf shot forward in his chair. 'You don't think you're being *allowed*?'

Petra didn't answer.

Stu said, 'We have been told to be careful.'

141

'And what the fuck's wrong with that? Ever hear of Orenthal James Asshole? Remember what happens when people aren't careful?'

Silence.

Schoelkopf drank more coffee but remained slanted forward. 'You'll proceed appropriately once the evidentiary basis has been established. Let's get back to your scenario, assume she was having some kind of date that ended in a meeting at the park. Ramsey, dope, or she's trysting with some married guy. Or cruising some fucking whips and chains club, who the hell knows. And let's say your *potential* witness *was* behind the rock. What kind of witness bunks out in the park at night and pees on rocks? Sees a brutal murder and doesn't call us. That sound like Joe Citizen?'

Petra said, 'Maybe a homeless person—'

'Exactly,' said Schoelkopf. 'A lowlife, a mental case. No sane person – no *legit* person – would be out at night alone in Griffith Park. Meaning we've got a bum or a wacko or even the bad guy himself. Hell, I'll go for a scumbag who reads about the presidents, but till you get me a lead I'm not gonna authorize any media-release for the info because we are not going to look like idiots on this one.'

'I wouldn't expect you to, sir,' said Petra.

Schoelkopf stroked his upper lip. Had he ever worn a mustache? 'OK, so what you're telling me is we've got fuck-nothing. Run forensics on all of it – food, book, pee – but don't get sidetracked, because it's weak. And find the *vic's* goddamn car. Meanwhile, here's what I did for you in the real world: Made sure the coroner assigned a *competent* pathologist and not one of those slicer-dicers. I asked Romanescu to personally supervise the post, and he agreed, but who the hell trusts him, he used to work for the communists. Same for the crime techs: I've asked Yamada to oversee, we don't want mumblebums screwing everything up, another fucking travesty like you-know-who, and you better believe the media would love to turn it into one. They should have some prelims soon, keep in touch. What I'm saying is: Every bit of fiber and juice gets micro-analyzed up the yin. Don't tell me ninety-nine percent of the time forensics is useless, I know it is, but we've got to cover all bases. Also, there were no defense wounds on the girl's hands but that doesn't mean she offered no resistance at all, so let's pray for transfer, one damned molecule of body fluid with a story to tell.'

He scratched a front tooth with a fingernail. 'No cuts on Ramsey, huh?'

'Nothing visible,' said Stu.

'Well,' said Schoelkopf, 'don't count on getting the guy to take his clothes off any time soon.' The black eyes dropped to the phone messages. 'At least the race thing isn't an issue. So far.'

'So far, sir?'

Picking up the empty cup, Schoelkopf looked into it, meditating on Styrofoam. 'This black guy, Darrell. Wouldn't that be lovely? What else do we know about him?'

'The maid said he worked with Lisa. And that he was older than her. Just like Ramsey.'

'So she wants to fuck her dad. Write a Psych 101 essay.' Schoelkopf put the cup down, stared at both of them, then avoided their eyes. 'Next item: Ramsey called me last night at ten P.M. Himself, not some lawyer; the page operator wisely decided to put him through. First he pours on the grief, says

143

anything he can do to help. Then he tells me about the domestic violence thing, it's going to be on the news tonight, he wants to explain that it only happened once, he wasn't making excuses, but it was only once. He says the true story is she pushed him and he got pissed. He said it was the stupidest thing he ever did, he felt ashamed.'

Schoelkopf waved a finger round and round. 'Et-fucking-cetera.'

'Covering his rear,' said Stu. 'He never mentioned the DV to us.'

'He's a star,' Petra half-muttered. 'Goes straight to the top.'

Schoelkopf's color deepened. 'Yeah, the bastard's obviously trying to finesse, calling with no legal shield. That tells me he thinks he's smarter than he is. So if we do get some physical evidence, maybe there'll be a way to wedge him open. Not that we'd be able to talk turkey without his getting a lawyer mouthpiece faster'n Michael Jackson gets new faces. But, meanwhile, we finesse too. *That's* what I meant by context: No premature hassling, no getting accused of tunnel vision.'

Petra said, 'The news broadcast—'

'Gives you a good reason to talk to him about all sorts of things, but at the same time you need to do an exhaustive check of all similar homicides. I'm talking two years' worth – make it three. All city divisions. Keep *precise* written records.'

Petra was stunned. This was scutwork, hours – days of it. She looked at Stu.

He said, 'How closely related are we talking about?'

'Start with girls cut up with multiple wounds,' said

144

Schoelkopf. 'Girls killed in parks, blondes killed in parks, whatever, you're the D's. And make sure to check if any new slashers have been operating in non-city areas that border the park, like Burbank, Atwater. Maybe Glendale, Pasadena – yeah, definitely Glendale and Pasadena. La Canada, La Crescenta. Start with those.'

Neither Stu nor Petra spoke.

'Don't give me that surly shit,' said Schoelkopf. 'This is insurance for you. "Yes, Mr Puswipe Defense Attorney, we looked into every goddamn nook and cranny before we busted Mr Ramsey's ass." *Think*. About your faces on *Court TV*, old Mark Fuhrman sitting around in Idaho. Because, you're the ones on the line unless the case gets too big and we don't produce and they kick it over to Downtown Robbery-fucking-Homicide.'

'Which they could do anyway,' said Stu.

Schoelkopf's grin was murderous. 'Anything's possible, Ken. That's what makes this job so charming.' He began thumbing through the phone messages.

'What's the procedure with Ramsey?' said Stu. 'Do we wait to look into all those similars before approaching him or are we allowed to start now?'

'*Allowed*, again? You two think this is being *imposed* on you?'

'Just trying to get the rules straight.'

Schoelkopf looked up. 'The only rule is be smart. Goddamn yes, you talk to Ramsey. If you *don't*, we'll be in a sling over *that*. Just do the other stuff, too. That's why God invented overtime.'

He picked up a message slip and the phone but Stu remained seated and Petra followed his cue.

Stu said, 'In terms of Ramsey's background, I've got some sources at the studios—'

'I can see a problem there,' said Schoelkopf, looking up. 'Movie people are loose-lipped assholes. The fact that your sources blab to you means they're not real good at keeping their mouths shut, right?'

'That's true of any case—'

'This isn't any case.'

'What's to stop them from talking to the press anyway, Captain?' said Petra. 'What if the tabloids start throwing around money and a real feeding frenzy develops? Do we keep bird-dogging the nightly news?'

Schoelkopf's top teeth gnashed his bottom lip. 'OK, pick one or two sources, Ken,' he said, as if Petra hadn't spoken. 'But know this: You *will* be graded. Talk to that black guy, see what he's all about. Sooner rather than later. Have a nice day.'

16

MY EYES are closed and I'm thinking when I feel it. Ants are crawling over me, they probably smelled the Honey Nuts. I jump to my feet and slap them off, stomp as many as I can. Someone watching me would think I'm crazy.

After what I saw I don't feel great even being in the park, but what's my choice? For a second I imagine him finding me, chasing me, cornering me. He's got the knife, the same one, grabs me and stabs down. My heart jumps up to meet the blade.

Why would I think that?

It's 11:34 A.M., have to take my mind off it. I open the algebra book, do equations in my head. I'll try to eat — maybe a piece of beef jerky and at 1:00 P.M., I'll go down to that place along the fence, see if the lock's still off.

Made it. Super-quiet up in Africa. Five dollars in my pocket, the rest of my money's wrapped up and buried.

Hot, summer's coming early. Lots of sleepy animals, most of them hiding in their caves. Not a lot of people — some tourists, mostly Japanese, and young moms with babies in strollers. I've got a notebook with me and a pencil, to make it look like some kind of school assignment. My smell isn't too bad out in the open. No one's looking at me weird and someone actually smiled – a couple of tourists – a man and a woman, Americans, old, kind of geeky, with lots of cameras and this zoo map they can't seem to figure out. I probably remind them of their grandson or something.

I keep going to the top of Africa, most of the animals are sleeping, but I don't care, it feels good to walk without having to. One rhino is out but she just gives me a dirty look so I head for the gorillas.

When I get there, it's a scene.

Two of the young moms are there, freaking out, one of them's brushing off her blouse and screaming, 'Oh, God, gross!' and the other's wheeling her stroller backwards fast. Then they both race away toward North America.

I see why right away.

Shit. All over the ground near the fence that blocks off the gorilla exhibit.

Five gorillas are out, four sitting around and scratching and sleeping and one standing the way they do, bent over with his hands almost reaching the ground. A girl. The males have humongous heads and a silver stripe down their backs.

She starts walking around, stops to check out the other gorillas, scratches, walks some more. Then she bends and picks up a giant piece of shit.

And throws it.

It misses my head and lands on the ground right next to me, exploding into nasty-smelling dust. Some of it gets on my shoes. I try to kick it loose and another chunk flies by me. And another.

'You idiot!' I hear myself scream. No one's around.

148

The gorilla folds her arms across her chest and just looks at me and I swear she's smiling, like this is some terrific gorilla joke.

Then she points at me. Then she picks up another hunk. I get out of there. The whole world has gotten crazy.

I buy a lemonade from a vending machine and walk around, drinking, hoping all the shit dust comes off, because I'm really tired of gross things.

Maybe I'll visit the reptile house, it's cool and shaded, and seeing another two-headed kingsnake would be cool.

On the way in I meet those same two grandparent tourists coming out and they smile again, still looking confused. I cruise by the boas and the anaconda, adders and lizards, rattlesnakes, vipers, and cobras. Spend some time looking at an albino python, huge and fat, with pink-white scales and weird red eyes.

Will its ugly pale face get into my dreams tonight?

That wouldn't be bad if I could get it to eat PLYR 1.

I stand there thinking of myself as The Snakemaster, communicating with reptiles through mental power. Calling the Albino Python to wrap itself around PLYR, crushing him, squeezing him like a juice orange.

Knowing what's happening to him. That's worse than just dying. Knowing.

A little while later, near the edge of the zoo, next to a playground that I guess they keep for little kids who get bored with the animals, is a vegetable patch with a rope around it.

Corn and beans and tomatoes and peppers. The sign says it's for the animals, so they'll have fresh food. I've seen chimps eating corn, so gorillas probably do, too, and that gets me thinking.

I also love corn, steamed sweet, but we never had it at home. Once, when I was in sixth grade, the school threw a Thanksgiving brunch out in the play yard, turkey and corn and sweet potatoes with marshmallows for anyone who paid. Everything piled high on long tables, moms in aprons spooning it out. I went into town to have a look even though I had no money to buy anything. I hung around till the end, found a couple of loose quarters and played some ski-bowl, but lunch was out of the question, five dollars.

But one of the PTA ladies saw me looking at the corn and gave me a whole ear, daisy-yellow and shiny with butter, along with a turkey leg big enough for a family. I took it under a tree and ate and that was the best Thanksgiving I ever had.

Now, I move closer to the vegetable patch and look around.

Clear.

Quickly, I hop over the rope, go straight to the corn, break off three ears and stuff them in my pockets. They stick out, so I tuck them under my T-shirt, hop back over like nothing happened and walk slowly till I find a bathroom.

I go into one of the stalls, close the door, sit on the toilet lid and take out one of the corns, peeling off the leaves and that hairy stuff and wondering what it'll taste like raw.

It's pretty good. Hard, crunchy, not nearly as delicious as steamed corn with butter, but it does have a sweet corn taste. I eat two ears quickly, the third more slowly, chewing hard and getting every bit down while reading the cussword graffiti all over the walls. When I'm finished, I lick all the corn taste from the cobs, toss them into the corner of the stall, take a leak, and use the bathroom sink to wash my face and hands. Then I roll up my jeans and wash the sides of my legs, too.

My stomach hurts, but differently.

Too full. I pigged out.

Your lunch is now mine, gorilla.

Revenge is as sweet as corn!

17

WALKING BACK to the squad room, Stu said, 'He only beat her once. What a guy.'

'Going over us, to Schoelkopf,' said Petra. 'Manipulative.' Being collegial, then telling herself to hell with it. Say what was really on her mind.

She stopped and leaned against a locker. 'Why'd you bring up the book?'

Stu leaned, too. 'It was something tangible and I didn't want one of his lectures on wishful thinking versus evidence.'

'We got a lecture anyway.'

He shrugged.

She said, 'He thinks the book's bull. You agree with him, don't you?'

He straightened and with one hand pinched the knot of his tie. 'Do I think it's thunder and lightning? No, but the lab will run prints on the book and if it's a homeless guy there's a chance he's got a file somewhere so maybe we can locate him. If it turns out to be nothing, we're no worse off.'

She didn't answer.

He said, 'What's the matter?'

'It threw me, your bringing it up like that.'

'Hey, even I can be full of surprises.' His eyes didn't yield. He walked away, not looking back to see if she'd followed.

Petra stood there, hands clenched. She recalled Kathy's curtness last night on the phone. If it was a marital thing, she couldn't expect him to let it ride. OK, cool down, concentrate on the job. But she hated surprises.

Of the twenty-five other Hollywood detectives on the morning roster, six were at their desks, sorting mug shots, typing at newly donated and still baffling computers, muttering into phones, reading murder books. All looked up as Petra and Stu entered and shot sympathetic looks.

Any detective who loved mysteries going into the job had a quick change of heart. The Ramsey case was the worst kind of whodunit. The room smelled exactly like what it was: A windowless space seasoned by mostly-male frustration.

A black D-II named Wilson Fournier said, 'Knew you were gonna have fun when the boss came in early, chewing gum but with no gum in his mouth.'

Petra smiled at him and he resumed scanning gangbanger photos. Stu was at his desk facing hers, at the rear. She sat down and waited.

Stu said, 'What do you want to do about looking for similars?'

'Not much.'

He hooked his thumbs under his suspender straps. His 9mm was nestled in a high shoulder holster. Petra was wearing hers the same way. It hurt her arm and she removed it.

'The way I see it,' said Stu, 'we've got two choices. Go over to Parker and pull microfiche all week, then we'd still have to get on the horn in order to check out Burbank and Atwater and Glendale or any county district. Or do it all telephonically with every homicide D we can find. Schoelkopf said two or three years, let's do two. We could get lucky and move through it within the week. Personally, I'd rather talk to real people than deal with the files downtown, but it's up to you.'

'The realer the better,' said Petra. 'How do we prioritize? Do I call around first, or try to reach this Darrell?'

'Let's devote mornings to the scut, do real work in the afternoon.' He glanced at his watch. 'You check out Darrell and I'll start nosing around the studios.'

Petra stared down the length of the room. 'Speaking of real people, we can start with our colleagues here. It's a waste of time but so's the rest of it.'

'Charity begins at home. Go for it.'

She stood, pushed hair back from her face, cleared her throat dramatically. Three of the six detectives looked up.

'Gentlemen,' she announced, and the remaining three stopped what they were doing.

'As you know, Detective Bishop and I have been assigned a fascinating case, one *so* fascinating that word has come from above to be extra-thorough. In order to establish the proper *context*.' Snickers. 'Because we will – quote unquote – be graded.'

Grim looks all around.

'Detective Bishop and I desire a good grade and so we request your help in locating the unknown perpetrator of this nefarious crime. Who, of course, is totally unknown and must be sought out with the utmost care so as not to prejudice the investigation.'

Knowing smiles. She described the crime scene, Lisa's wounds, said, 'Any 187's within the last two years bear any resemblance?'

Headshakes.

A detective named Markus said, 'Where was O.J. at the time?'

Laughter.

'Thank you, gentlemen.' She sat down to light applause. Stu was clapping, too. He looked fine, now, the blue eyes warm again. Maybe he was just sleep-deprived.

'Six down,' he said, 'a few hundred to go – how about we divide up the districts on the vertical. I take east of here and you take west?'

There was lots more crime east of Hollywood, more detectives, more files. He was giving himself the lion's share of the scut. Feeling guilty? Petra said, 'You've got all the studios, I've only got Darrell. I'll take east.'

'No, it's OK,' he said. 'I told Kathy not to expect me soon.' He blinked rapidly, as if his eyes hurt, and picked up the phone.

A divorce after all this time? Petra wanted to reach out to him. She said, 'Noon break before we go our separate ways? Musso and Frank's?'

He hesitated. Then: 'Sure, we deserve it.' Starting to punch numbers, he stopped himself. 'Someone should also call those sheriff guys – De la Torre and Banks – find out if they learned anything about Lisa's DV complaint.'

'The news broadcast said she never filed a formal complaint.'

155

'There you go,' said Stu. 'The news broadcasts always tell the truth.'

She called Downtown Sheriffs Homicide and asked for Hector De la Torre or Detective Banks, not remembering – or knowing – the younger one's first name. Banks came on the line, greeting her with surprising warmth. 'Thought you might call.'

'Why's that?'

'Last night's news. Unfortunately, I've got nothing for you so far. Agoura substation has no previous complaints on file. Not even the one she went public on. So it looks like she never called it in.'

'OK, thanks.'

'My pleasure,' he said, sounding nervous. 'No messy inter-departmental competition here. Our guys beat your guys in boxing last month so we're feeling secure ... anyway, you have my sympathy. They replayed it on the news early this morning, too. Made the house look even fancier than it was. Nothing on his little car museum, though.'

What a gabby guy.

'Just Jacuzzi bubbles and horses and golf.'

'Interesting, isn't it?' said Banks. 'People getting life handed to them on a platter and they still manage to mess it up royal ... anything else you need?'

'Actually,' she said, suddenly inspired, 'if you've got time, we've been directed to do a file-search on similar homicides over a two-year period. Do you have easy access to county data?'

Banks laughed. 'This is LA. Nothing's easy. But sure, we've learned to walk without scraping our knuckles on the sidewalk. Similars? As in the unknown lurking perp? Why?'

'The brass is nervous.'

'Oh. Sure, I'll check for you.'

'Really appreciate it, Detective Banks.'

'Ron.'

'This is scut, Ron. Don't put your schedule out of joint.'

'Do you have a direct number?'

She gave it to him and he said, 'By similar I'm assuming crime-scene layout, wound type and quantity, idiosyncrasies, victim characteristics. Anything unusual about the crime scene I should know about?'

'No,' she said, feeling protective of her information. 'Just your basic butchery.'

'OK, then. Get back to you if anything comes up. Either way.'

'Thanks, Ron.'

'Sure . . . um . . . listen, I know this kind of case here isn't going to give you much spare time, but if some does come up . . . I mean if you want to get together – maybe just for a cup of coffee . . . if I'm out of line, just say so.'

Stumbling like a high-school kid.

The warmth of his greeting made sense now.

He wasn't remotely her type – whatever that was. She could barely remember his face, had been concentrating on Ramsey's . . . had he been wearing a wedding ring? He *had* mentioned taking his kids to the zoo.

At least he *had* kids. Didn't *hate* kids.

157

She must have taken too long because he came back with, 'Listen, I'm sorry, didn't mean to—'

'No, no that's fine,' she heard herself saying. 'Sure, when things ease up a bit. That would be fine.'

God help her.

18

PARAGON STUDIOS took up three blocks of the north side of Melrose, east of Bronson, a confusion of faded tan towers and corrugated steel hangars, all surrounded by fifteen-foot walls, one of the last major film lots actually located in Hollywood.

The rococo front gates were open and Stu Bishop, anxiety polluting his head, tried to look businesslike as he inched the unmarked Ford toward the guardhouse.

Two vans in front of him, one of them taking its time.

Petra had left the station before him, taking her personal car.

Petra trusted him a little less than she had yesterday.

Couldn't blame her, the way he'd tossed the library book thing at Schoelkopf without warning her. Impulsive. Had the noise in his life finally gotten too loud?

Truth was, he didn't think the book was worth a darn, had used Petra to fend off the captain. Schoelkopf had preached anyway.

All the preaching Stu had endured. Teachers, elders. *Father*. Easton Bishop, MD, was never more at home than when declaring absolute truths to a mute audience of eight kids. Stu had avoided that kind of authoritarianism with his children, trusting them to learn by example, knowing Kathy was the main influence. Kathy . . . dear God.

Stu believed in a forgiving God, but he lived his own life as if the Lord were a harsh, unyielding perfectionist. It made him careful, a sin-avoider. So why now, at this point in his life, was everything coming apart?

Stupid question.

The second van passed through and Stu drove right up. The guard, Ernie Robles, was someone he knew from his four weeks as a bit-player ('non-speaking squad room inhabitant, lots of typing and phoning') on *LA Cop*. Decent fellow, relaxed attitude, no police experience, just a rent-a-cop from way back.

He was scribbling on his clipboard as Stu stopped and let the Ford idle.

'Hey, how's it going, Detective Bishop! Beautiful day, huh?'

And it was. Warm and clear, the sky as blue as one of the matte-painting backdrops the film crews used to make LA look heavenly. Stu hadn't noticed.

He said, 'Gorgeous, Ernie.'

Robles picked up the clipboard. 'Got a part? Where?'

'Where do you think?'

'The *Cop* lot? They're not filming.'

'Nope, all wrapped for this year, but there's someone I've got to see – oh, by the way, here's something I picked up for you at the station.'

He handed Robles what looked like a thin, glossy magazine. Bright yellow letters rimmed with red blared THE SENTINEL at the top. Below that was a high-quality photo of a nasty-looking black USP semi-automatic pistol with silencer and black-tipped brass bullets. Promo from Heckler & Koch, stacks of them left at each police station.

Stu'd thumbed through it at a red light. Features on Benelli shotguns, HK Training, the PSGI – 'a $10,000 rifle and worth it!' Stu appreciated what guns did but found them boring.

Robles was already thumbing through, looking at the pictures.

'Hot off the press, Ernie.'

'Look at some of this stuff – hey man, thanks.'

Stu drove through.

He parked and walked to the Element Productions complex, where he found Scott Wembley easily enough. The Assistant Director was stepping out of a low, unimpressive bungalow, long arms dangling, licking his lips.

Lunch hour. Wembley was alone, probably headed for the commissary.

Stu came up from behind him. 'Hi, Scott.'

Wembley turned and stopped and his long, pale face froze. 'Stu. Hey.'

Like most A.D.'s, Wembley was just a kid, a couple of years out of UC Berkeley with a Fine Arts degree, tolerating the low pay and long hours and abuse by those who mattered for the impressive-sounding title and the chance to make connections.

Like many kids, he lacked spine and judgment.

They shook hands. Wembley was wearing film-lot preppy: Baggy Gap jeans and an oversized plaid button-down shirt that looked too warm for the weather and too expensive for his budget. A steel Rolex made Stu wonder even more.

The kid looked even thinner than last year, had a bony,

somewhat androgynous face fit for a Calvin Klein ad. Pimples on his cheeks. That was new.

The palm Stu grasped was soft and cold and wet. Sweat beaded Wembley's unlined forehead. Too-warm shirt. Long-sleeved shirt, buttoned at the cuffs.

And, of course, the eyes. Those pupils. Poor Scotty hadn't learned a thing.

During Stu's month on the set, Wembley had tried to get next to him, asking questions incessantly, wanting to know what the streets were *really* like. Because he was doing a screenplay, like everyone else, even though his real dream was to be Scorsese, directors had all the control.

Stu had answered him patiently, finding the kid a touching combination of Gen-X bravado and utter ignorance.

Then, the last Friday of the shoot, after working hours, he'd stuck around to finish some paperwork, using an empty soundstage as his office. Loud sighs brought him to a corner of the giant room where he discovered Wembley huddled on the floor, half hidden by prop walls, a spike of heroin imbedded in his arm.

The kid didn't hear him approach, had his eyes closed, veins popping like angel-hair pasta on his long, skinny arm. The needle was one of those cheap plastic disposable things.

Stu said, 'Scott!' sharply and the kid's eyes opened on a junkie's worst possible scenario. Yanking out the needle, Wembley tossed it to the ground, where it plunked and spotted the concrete with milky liquid.

'Oh, man,' said Stu.

Wembley burst into tears.

Moral conundrum.

In the end, Stu chose not to bust the kid, even though that was a clear violation of departmental regulations. '*Upon witnessing a felony . . .*'

Pretending to believe Wembley when the kid insisted it was his first time, he was just experimenting. Two other puncture marks on Wembley's arms proved otherwise but both had the sooty look of old tracks, so at least the kid wasn't mainlining regularly, yet. Stu confiscated the dope-kit he found in the pocket of Wembley's bomber jacket and tossed the works in a dumpster on the lot – putting him in greater legal jeopardy than Wembley but thank God the kid wasn't smart enough to know that.

He drove Wembley to Go-Ji's coffee shop on Hollywood Boulevard, plunked him down in a rear booth and filled him full of strong, black coffee – technically as much of a drug, to Stu – then let the stupid kid glance around the putrid restaurant and see what advanced junkies looked like.

The load in the syringe must have been light, because Wembley was rattled and clear-eyed. Or maybe fear had out-adrenalized the opiate.

He ordered the kid a hamburger, forced him to eat while he delivered the requisite stern lecture. Soon Wembley was mumbling sad biography – the horrors of growing up with affluent, multi-married Marin County parents who refused to set limits, post-college loneliness and alienation, and fear of the future. Stu pretended to take it seriously, wondering if his own kids would be like that when they reached the age. By the end of an hour Wembley was taking solemn vows of chastity, charity, and loyalty to the flag.

Stu drove him back to the studio. The kid looked ready

to kiss him, almost girlishly grateful, and Stu wondered if he was gay, on top of everything else.

After that, Wembley avoided him on the set. It didn't matter. Wembley was in his debt bigtime, and if the kid didn't drop out and move back home, he was someone Stu might be able to use, one day.

And now the day had arrived. *Ta dum!*

'Good to see you, Scott.'

'You, too,' the kid lied miserably. His mouth trembled and he sniffed. Red nose. Those eyes. Stupid little idiot.

'How've you been?'

'Great. What can I do for you, Detective?'

Stu put his arm around Wembley's bony shoulder. 'Actually, quite a bit, Scott. Let's find somewhere to talk.'

He ushered Wembley to a bench and said, 'I need information on Cart Ramsey. Discreet information.'

'All I know is what's been on the news.'

'No rumors around the lot?'

'Why would there be?'

'Because no one gossips more than Industry folk.'

'Well, if there is gossip, I haven't heard it.'

'You're telling me no one's said anything about Ramsey?'

Wembley chewed his cheeks. 'Just . . . whatever everyone else is saying.'

'Which is?'

'He did her.'

'Why do they say that, Scott?'

'He beat her up, right? Maybe he wanted to get back together and she said no.'

'That your theory or someone else's?'

'Everyone's. Isn't it yours?' said Wembley. 'Otherwise why would you be here?'

'Does Ramsey have any sort of reputation?'

Wembley snickered. 'Not as an actor – no, I don't know shit about him. The whole thing doesn't interest me.'

'Well,' said Stu, 'now it does, Scott. It interests you a lot.'

19

I HAD a pretty good time today, getting that corn and being left alone. I'll go back to Five, make some plans.

I head back toward the open fence, see someone waving.

The geeky grandparents. Standing right where the road curves off.

The old guy holds up his camera. They're both waving and the woman calls out, 'Young man? Could you help us for a second?'

I don't want to attract attention by running away or acting weird, so I go over to them.

'Hey, big fella,' says the guy. What a dork. He's wearing a Dodgers T-shirt and shorts and socks and shoes and a light blue hat. His skin's pink and he has a big lumpy nose, like the guys at the Sunnyside.

His camera is huge, in a big black case full of buckles and snaps, and his wife's got one just like it.

'Sorry to bother you, my friend, but you seem like a nice guy,' he says, giving me a smile full of yellow teeth.

'Thank you, sir.'

'Polite,' she says, smiling. 'Not everyone we've met is polite. I'm sure he can do it, honey.'

He clears his throat and taps his camera case. 'This is a Nikon camera from Japan. My wife and I were wondering if you could do us a favor and take a picture of us, so we could have one together.'

'Sure.'

'Thanks a lot, son.' He reaches into his shorts and takes out a dollar bill.

'You don't have to pay me,' I say.

'No, dear, we insist,' says the wife, and even though her eyes are hidden behind sunglasses, something changes on her face – just for a second, her mouth turns down. Like she's sad. Full of pity. Like she knows I need the money.

I'm thinking, maybe if I look poor enough, she'll give me more, and I hunch over a little but all she does is pat my hand.

'Take it. Please.'

I pocket the dollar.

'All righty,' he says. 'So now we've got a business deal.' More teeth. 'OK, hon, where's the best spot?'

'Right where we were, the sun's perfect.' She points and walks up the hill a bit, stamps her foot and touches her own camera. Why they need two cameras is a good question, but I guess some people don't trust machines. Or their memory. They probably want to make sure they capture everything they see, maybe to show the grandkids.

She says, 'OK!' Kind of sings it out. She's short, skinny, wears a man's jacket over her Dodgers T-shirt and green pants.

He takes his camera out of his case and gives it to me and goes up next to her. It looks expensive and I'm nervous holding it.

'Don't worry,' she says. 'It's simple and you look like a smart young man.'

I look at them through the viewfinder. They're too far away so I come closer.

'It's preset, son,' he says. 'just push the button.'

I push. Nothing happens. I try again. Still nothing.

'What's the matter?' he says.

I shrug. 'I pushed it.'

She says, 'Oh, no, did it jam again?'

'Let me take a look,' he says, coming down again. I give him the camera and he turns it around, 'Uh-oh. Same problem.'

'Oh, for Pete's sake,' she says, stomping her foot. 'I told you it was a good idea to bring mine along. When we get back home, first thing I'm doing is going straight back to that dealer and tell him to fix it right this time!'

He gives me an embarrassed smile, like he doesn't like her bossing him around.

She joins us, smelling of some kind of soap. He smells of onions.

'Sorry, sweetie, this will just take a minute,' she says, opening her camera case and taking out – something big and black but not a camera, it's a gun. I can't believe it and all of a sudden she's jabbing it really hard into my bellybutton and I can't breathe and she's pushing it there, like she's trying to force it right through me and her other hand's around my neck squeezing hard, she didn't look that strong but she is she's really strong, and he's holding me too pinning my arms to my sides.

They're on both sides of me, like they're my parents and the three of us are a family, only I can't breathe and they're hurting me and she's saying, 'Now just come with us, street-trash, and don't make the wrong move or we'll kill you, we really will.'

Smiling again. Not pity, something else – the same look that was all over Moron's face before he went for the tools.

They lead me toward the open fence. They know about it, too – not a secret place! I'm so stupid!

Her face is like a mask but he's breathing hard, excited, his mouth's open, his skin's pink as a pencil eraser, the onion smell's blowing on my face, and they're dragging me toward Five and he's saying, 'You're gonna get *done*, kid. Like you *never* been done.'

20

PETRA STAYED at her desk, calling her phone company contact about Lisa's records and getting assured they'd arrive today. She began the preliminary paperwork on the court order for the extended records, phoned the coroner and the criminalists. No medical findings yet, no prints retrieved from Lisa's clothes or body or jewelry. Maybe a glove, the tech opined. Fortified by vending-machine coffee, Petra checked all the approved police tow-yards and consulted rosters of found autos. Lisa's Porsche wasn't listed.

Time to go back on Schoelkopf's scut-line. She'd already talked to dozens of detectives, covering the daywatch from Van Nuys to Devonshire, then West LA. Now she started in on Pacific.

Each time the same reaction: *You've got to be kidding*.

Everyone knew who the bad guy was on this one. But they also understood brass-generated busywork and after the laughter died down, she had their immediate sympathy.

The end result: No similars. Meanwhile, Cart Ramsey got to hit golf balls, soak in the hot-tub, enjoy the chrome and polish of his little car museum while his ex-wife was laid out on the coroner's table getting her face peeled off.

The Mercedes probably scrubbed and steamed and vacuumed cleaner than an operating room.

She thought about Lisa's body, that gaping blood-filled hole in the abdomen, protruding entrails, what had been done to the young woman's face, and wondered what it took to turn love to *that*.

Could it happen any time passions ran high or did the guy have to be twisted?

Domestic bliss, domestic blood. There'd been one moment – an eyeblink instant – when she'd been capable of murder.

Why was she thinking about the past?

Deal with it, kid.

She tortured herself with memories.

A twenty-five-year-old art student pretending cool but so blindly, dumbly in love she'd have been willing to shed her skin for Nick. That rush of feeling, passion like she'd never felt before. Lovemaking till she couldn't walk. Postcoital pillow talk, lying flank to flank, her vagina still throbbing.

Nick had seemed such a good listener. It was only later she figured out it was phony. He kept quiet because he refused to give her anything of himself.

She told him everything: Growing up motherless, the irrational guilt she felt about causing her mother's death, driving her father crazy to the point where boarding schools were the only solution, half of her adolescence spent in musty shared rooms, the other girls giggling and smoking, talking about guys, sometimes masturbating, Petra could tell by the rustle of comforters.

Petra, the weird, silent girl from Arizona just lying there, thinking about having killed her mother.

She'd entrusted Nick with the secret because this was true love.

Then one night, she told him a new secret: Guess what, honey? Patting her tummy.

She'd expected surprise, maybe some initial resentment, knew he'd melt eventually because he loved her.

His eyes froze and he turned white. The fury. Glaring at her across the dinner table with contempt she'd never imagined. The special meal she'd prepared just sitting there, his favorites – ostensibly to celebrate but maybe deep down she'd known he wouldn't be pleased, maybe the veal and the gnocchi, the twenty-dollar chianti classico had been nothing more than bribes.

He just sat there, not moving, not talking, those thin lips she'd once thought aristocratic, so bloodless, the hateful mouth of an old, nasty man.

Nick—

How could you, Petra!

Nick, honey—

You of all people! How could you be so stupid – you know what childbirth does!

Nick—

Fuck you!

If she'd had a gun, then . . .

She opened her eyes, realized for the first time that they'd been closed. Squadroom noise blew back at her, the other detectives busy doing their jobs.

What she needed to do.

She got back on the phone, prepared to waste more time.

172

But four Pacific detectives later, something *did* come up.

A three-year-old unsolved cutting of a pretty blond girl on the southern tip of Venice, near the Marina, handled by a D-II named Phil Sorensen who said, 'You know, when I heard about the Ramsey girl, it struck me, but ours was a German girl, Lufthansa stewardess on vacation, and our leads pointed to an Austrian boyfriend, baggage handler, returned to Europe before we could talk to him. We put wants out with the Austrian police, Interpol, all that good stuff, never found him.'

'What made him a suspect?' said Petra.

'The girlfriend the vic was traveling with – another stew – said he showed up unannounced at their hotel all upset because the vic – Ilse Eggermann's her name – had left Vienna without telling him. Ilse told the friend they'd fought a lot, the boyfriend had a bad temper, roughed her up, she dumped him. The last straw was having to work First Class with a black eye. Still, when the boyfriend showed up in LA, he was able to convince her to go out with him. They left at nine P.M. She was found at four A.M., body dumped in a parking lot near Ballona Creek. We traced the boyfriend's flight, he'd come in on Lufthansa the previous morning, employee discount. No checked-in luggage, and he never registered at any hotels or motels here in LA.'

'So he intended it to be a short trip,' said Petra. 'Accomplished what he wanted and split.'

'That's what it looked like.' Sorensen sounded like an older man. Gentle voice, slow talker, slightly hesitant. 'Stew,' not flight attendant.

'How was Ilse dressed when you found her?' said Petra.

'A nice dress, dark – blue or black. Black, I think. Very pretty girl, she looked very nice. Considering.' Sorensen coughed. 'No sexual assault. We didn't need to Sherlock to establish her being with the boyfriend – Karlheinz Lauch – that night. The waiter who served them dinner, Antoine's on the pier at Redondo Beach. He remembered them because they didn't eat or talk much. Or tip. We figured Lauch was angling for reconciliation, it didn't work, he got upset, drove her somewhere, killed her and dumped her. What he drove, I don't know, because we could never trace a rental car and he had no known associates in California.'

Sorensen's voice had risen a bit. Lots of details at his fingertips for a three-year-old crime. This one had stayed with him.

'She was found at four,' said Petra. 'Any idea when she was killed?'

'The guesstimate was two, two-thirty.'

Early morning, just like Lisa. Dumped in a parking lot. And the Ballona Creek marshlands were a county park, like Griffith. 'Lots of stab wounds?'

'Twenty-nine – clear overkill, which would also fit the boyfriend. Add the domestic violence history, and it seemed pretty clear. Sound at all like yours?'

'There are definite points of similarity, Detective Sorensen,' said Petra, keeping her voice steady. Looked at a certain way it was a damned Xerox.

'Well, you know these guys,' he said. 'The woman-haters. Tend to fall into patterns.'

'True,' she said. 'Where did this Lauch handle baggage?'

'Vienna airport, but he had family in Germany. After the

174

crime he didn't return to work or to his home town. We checked with other airlines, too, but no dice. He could have changed his name, or just rabbited to some other country. Would have been nice to go over there and nose around personally, but you know the chance of prying a European trip out of the budget. So we had to rely on the Austrian police and the Germans and they weren't all that interested because the crime took place here.'

'If Lauch is working baggage under another name, he's eligible for an employee discount,' said Petra. 'Maybe he's still flying back and forth.'

'And ended up in LA again and did a repeat?'

'I sure hope not, Phil, but with what you've told me it looks like we're going to have to check him out all over again. Could you please fax me his data?'

'Give me an hour,' said Sorensen. 'Wouldn't that be something, the guy having that kind of nerve. Of course, first you'd have to establish Lauch was here when the Ramsey girl was killed, then you'd have to connect him with her — meanwhile, you've got DV on the husband. Sounds like fun.'

'Big fun. Thanks for your help, Phil.'

'Hey,' he said, 'if by some miracle it ends up helping you, it'll help me, too. It always bothered me, not being able to close that one. She was a nice-looking girl and he turned her into something horrible.'

It was 1 P.M., time to start looking for Darrell/Darren the film editor, but now she wanted to wait around until Karlheinz Lauch's data came through the fax.

The Ilse Eggermann news was a surprise, but Sorensen

175

was right: The points of similarity could be explained by domestic violence patterns, the same old tragedies, all the way back to Othello.

Or statistical fluke – seek and ye shall find something. Over a three-year period, LA saw well over three thousand homicides. One similar in all that time wasn't the stuff of the Guinness Book.

Meanwhile, she'd reach the rest of the Pacific detectives, do follow-up on some Valley D's she'd missed the first time around, maybe pay another telephonic condolence call to Lisa's family in Chagrin Falls, see if Mrs Boehlinger was available, find out when the parents were coming out to see what was left of their daughter.

Did Mrs B feel as strongly about Ramsey as her husband did?

Petra sorted out her own feelings about the guy: Providing an alibi right off, letting them know about Lisa's drug problems, going over their heads to Schoelkopf. The subtle Don Juan stuff he'd thrown her way.

It smelled of ego, real narcissism. Did that make him someone who'd go berserk if a woman angered or rejected him?

Hard to say, but in her mind, Ramsey had done nothing to dispel suspicion. Despite Ilse Eggermann, the actor was clearly the main man.

She played out a scenario in her head: Lisa, like Ilse Eggermann – like so many battered women – had somehow allowed her ex to talk her into a date. Renewal of old passions, or maybe Ramsey'd tossed her the ultimate female-bait: The chance to talk things out.

Because once upon a time there'd been chemistry between

them and chemicals didn't disappear, they just faded. Because memories could be selective, and women kept hoping men would change.

A date . . . where? Not at a restaurant, somewhere private. Romantic. Secluded.

Not the Calabasas house, too risky. Even if Greg Balch was lying for his boss, someone else could have taken note – the guard, a neighbor. The maid.

Petra remembered how squirrelly Estrella Flores had been. Definitely worth a re-contact, but how to do it without alerting Ramsey? And something basic needed to be added to the list: Talk to the night-shift guard at RanchHaven. A glaring omission, the hands-off policy was really mucking things up.

So many things to do . . . she returned to her last-date melodrama. Where would Ramsey have taken Lisa?

Did he have another home, a weekend hideaway? Didn't actors always have weekend places?

The beach? The mountains? Arrowhead, Big Bear? Or up north – Santa Barbara, Santa Ynez. Lots of 'industry' folks had gotten into the ranch thing . . .

The beach would probably be Malibu, waves crashing, smooth sand, what could be more romantic?

She made a note to search records for every real-estate parcel Ramsey owned.

Go with the beach, for the moment. She pictured it: Ramsey and Lisa on an overstuffed sofa in some wood-and-glass thing on the sand. The three c's: Champagne, caviar, coke. Maybe a nicely hissing fireplace. Ramsey turning on the charm.

Lisa responding? That sexy little black dress riding up

on her thighs? Chemistry . . . helped along by fish eggs, Moët & Chandon, and Medellin's finest? Or another kind of incentive: Money; Lisa had a job but Ramsey still provided the bulk of her income.

The purchase of love? Same old story? Petra felt sad, then reminded herself not to judge. If her own phone rang on a particularly lonely and/or horny night and it was Nick on the other end, saying, 'Hey, Pet,' what would *she* do?

Hang up on the selfish fuck and wish she could make his ears bleed.

Back to Malibu. Tides crashing, tender reminiscence, the nudge toward intimacy.

Ramsey makes his move.

But Lisa changes her mind, resists, shuts him down.

Ramsey seethes, feels like slugging her. But remembering the way she went public, he keeps his rage to himself.

Stays cool, drives her home.

Malibu to Doheny Drive Hills would mean Pacific Coast Highway to Sunset or the freeway through the Valley, then down one of the canyons. But instead of hooking south, he continues east, maybe Laurel Canyon down Hollywood Boulevard, up Western to Los Feliz, then over to Griffith Park.

That hour, not much traffic. He drives to the parking lot. Lisa knows something's wrong, tries to escape.

He holds out for one last embrace.

Then a steel kiss.

No sexual assault because he'd had a blood orgasm.

It felt right to Petra.

178

It also depended on Gregory Balch lying straight-facedly about Ramsey's alibi.

She'd have to learn more about Balch, too. Eventually.

Along with Ilse Eggermann and Karlheinz Lauch. A similar – unbelievable. She imagined Schoelkopf's grin. The disgusted look on Stu's face. When she'd left, he hadn't looked up, just muttered a half-hearted goodbye.

The library-book thing, so out-of-the-blue. Stu was compulsive, mega-organized. Maybe it wasn't his marriage, maybe it was career anxiety. The chance to apply for lieutenant suddenly coming up and he found himself stuck with a bigtime loser whodunit? For Petra, just another case. For him, do or die?

Would he bail on her? Sacrifice her if he needed to?

For eight months, they'd ridden together, eaten together, worked side by side, Stu spending as much time with her as he did with Kathy, sometimes more, and he'd never laid a hand on her, never made a suggestive comment, not even the slightest hint of double-entendre.

She'd thought she knew him, but eight months wasn't very long, was it?

She and Nick had been together over two years. About the same as Lisa and Ramsey.

Men and women . . .

Once, when she was fifteen, home for summer vacation, she'd woken up at 1 A.M. on a long night in Arizona, hearing imaginary things, finally realizing it was the hot desert wind scraping the side of the house. Itchy, jumpy, she'd walked out to the hallway, spied the familiar splinter of light under the door of her father's office, knocked, entered the tiny, dim, detritus-clogged room.

Dad was sitting low in his oak chair facing his Royal manual, blank sheet in the roller. He saw her, gave a slack smile, and when she came closer, she smelled the Scotch on his breath, saw the dullness in his eyes, and took advantage of it as only a teenager can. Getting him to talk about what he hated talking about. The woman who'd died birthing her.

Aware that it would cause him pain, but dammit, she had a right to know!

And talk he did, in a low, slurred voice.

Anecdotes, remembrances, how gawky Kenneth Connor and gorgeous Maureen McIlwaine had met on the Long Island Ferry and found true love. The same old stories, but she thirsted for them, could never get enough.

That night, she sat at his feet on the warped hardwood floor, motionless, silent, afraid any distraction would cause him to stop.

Finally, he did grow quiet, staring down at her, then slapping his hands over his face and holding them there.

'Daddy—'

The hands dropped into his lap. He looked so sad. 'That's all I remember, sweetheart. Mother was a wonderful woman, but . . .'

Then he began crying, and had to hide from her again.

Men hid when they cried.

Petra came over and hugged his broad, bony shoulders. 'Oh, Daddy, I'm so—'

'She *was* wonderful, baby. One in a million, but it wasn't perfect, Pet. It was no storybook situation.'

He opened a desk drawer and peered down at what had to be the bottle.

When he turned back to Petra, his eyes were dry and he was smiling, but it wasn't any of the smiles Petra knew – not the warm, protective one or the wry, sarcastic one or even the soft-around-the-edges drunk one that used to bother her but no longer did.

This was different – flat, hollow, frozen as statuary. In her tenth grade English class they had learned about tragedy and she was sure this was it.

Defeated, that smile. As terrifying as a glimpse of eternity.

'Daddy—'

He scratched his scalp, shook his head, hiked a droopy sock up a pale ankle. 'The thing is, Pet, no matter what . . . I guess what I'm saying, sweetheart, is men and women are really two separate species. Maybe that's the anthropology talking, but it's no less true. One little scrap of DNA separates us – here's something funny: The X chromosome's really the one that counts, Petra. The Y doesn't seem to do much but cause problems – aggression – understand what I'm getting at, sweetheart? We men aren't really worth that much.'

'Oh, Daddy—'

'Mom and I had our problems. Most were my fault. You need to know that so you don't romanticize things, expect too much out of . . . demand too much from yourself. Understand, baby? Am I making sense here?'

Taking hold of her shoulders, the light in his eyes almost maniacal.

'You are, Daddy. Yes.'

He let go. Now the smile was OK. Human.

'The point is, Petra, there are big questions out there. Cosmic questions that have nothing to do with stars and galaxies.'

Waiting for her response. She didn't know what to say and he went on:

'Questions like can men and women ever really know each other or is it always going to be one stupid, clumsy dance around the interpersonal ballroom?'

He flinched, suppressed a belch, sprang up and went into his bedroom and closed the door and she could hear the latch turn and knew he'd locked himself in.

The next morning her brother Glenn, the only one still living at home, got to the breakfast table first and said, 'What's with Dad?'

'What do you mean?'

'He's gone, went out on a field trip, must have been before sunrise. Left me this.' Waving a piece of notebook paper that read, *Out to the desert, kids*.

'Just one of his bone-hunts,' said Petra.

Glenn said, 'Well, he took his camping stuff, that means a long one. Did he mention anything to you? Cause yesterday we were talking about going over to the Big Five and getting some hockey stuff.'

'Actually he did,' she lied.

'Great,' said Glenn. 'That's just great. He tells *you* but never mentions it to me.'

'I'm sure he meant to, Glenn.'

'Yeah, right, great – fuck, I really need a new *stick*. Do you have any money I can borrow?'

She phoned seven more detectives, endured seven more you've-got-to-be-kiddings, no more similars.

From the far end of the room, the fax machine started

humming and she jumped up and was there in a second, snatching papers out of the bin. Moving so quickly, a couple of the other D's looked up. But not for long, they were busy, too. This room, this city – the blood never stopped.

Karlheinz Lauch was big – six four, 233 – and ugly. Small, dark, squinty eyes popped like raisins in a pasty, misshappen crepe of a face. The merest comma of a lopsided mouth, a mustache that looked like a grease squirt. Straight, fair hair – the stats called it brown, so probably dishwater – styled in that modified shag some Europeans still wore.

To Petra, he appeared a grubby loser.

The photo was from a four-year-old Vienna mugshot, lots of fifty-letter German words and umlauts. Sorensen's typed note said Lauch had been busted for assault in Austria the year before Ilse Eggermann's murder, barroom brawl, no time served.

In the photos, Lauch looked mean enough for anything. Wouldn't it be something if the bastard *had* come to LA, cruising for good-looking blondes, somehow connected with Lisa?

Wouldn't it be amazing if Lauch stuck around so they could pick him up? A nice easy solve so Stu could get his promotion and she could add brownie points to her file.

Fantasies, kid.

She studied Lauch's face some more and wondered how someone like him could get Lisa to put on a little black dress and diamonds.

On the other hand, he *had* gotten close to Ilse Eggermann,

who, by Phil Sorensen's account, was also a looker. But a stewardess wasn't the ex-wife of a TV star who'd experienced the good life.

Then again, Lisa had opted *out* of the good life. And some women, even beautiful women, liked to bottom-fish, turned on by whatever was crude and brutish, a man below them on the social ladder.

Beauty and the beastly? Lisa taking risks with rough trade and paying for it?

Petra kept staring at Lauch's photo. The thought of allowing his flesh to come into contact with hers turned her stomach.

She liked her men intelligent, considerate, conventionally handsome.

Probably because her father was an intelligent, nice-looking, gentle man. For the most part, a gentleman.

What was Ilse Eggermann's father like?

What was Dr John Everett Boehlinger like when he wasn't crazed with grief?

Enough with the psychoanalysis. She'd taken it as far as she could for the moment.

She inserted the Eggermann-Lauch data in Lisa's murder book, crossed the room to the Nehi-orange lockers, opened hers and took a Snickers bar from the bag she kept on the top shelf, above her gym shoes and sweats and the cheap black sweaters she kept handy for cold nights and messy corpses.

Death-mops, she called them.

Acrylic that looked like acrylic, attention, K Mart shoppers, our full-style cardigans now on sale for $13.95 in a wide range of colors. She bought five at a time, always black, threw them out the moment they got gory.

In eight months, she'd been through ten.

She hadn't worn one to Lisa's crime scene because the call had been a surprise.

She hadn't been stained by Lisa's corpse.

Hadn't gotten close enough.

21

'MOVE, MOVE, move, keep moving, you little bastard.'
Hiss-whispering in my ear, they squeeze me, poke me,
push me.

She's the angry one, he sounds afraid, nervous. He even
trips a couple of times.

'Come on!' She sticks the gun in my ribs and when I cry
out she sticks me harder and says, 'Shut up!' Not nervous at
all.

She's in charge.

As we get closer to where all the buggies are parked, I
start to pray for some zoo person to be there this time, but
there's no one. Should I scream? No, the gun is up against
me, it wouldn't take much for her to pull the trigger and
blow up my insides – now, we're at the fence. The lock is
on – and it's clamped!

'Do it,' she orders as she looks in all directions. She keeps
the gun on me and he takes a key out of his pocket and opens
the lock.

They know this place.

They're prepared. They will rape me.

He comes back, grabs me, breathes into my ear and
suddenly my stomach starts turning over and over, hard,
fast, painful, like I have to go to the bathroom.

They push me forward again. It's like I'm drifting along in some movie, playing a part, and now I realize the fear is gone and something else has taken over my mind – it's like being asleep and awake at the same time – like being in a dream but knowing you're in one, and you can control everything if you just concentrate, make it come out the way you want.

Maybe that's what it's like after you die.

We go through the gate and start climbing up, into the trees. He's making these low wet grunting noises.

'You,' he says, squeezing my arm harder. Like I've done something wrong.

I keep my head down, seeing my shoes, his.

'OK, come on, come on,' she says, waving her hand as we walk into the fern tangle, through the same path I took down, what I used to think was my secret.

They keep pushing me, telling me to move faster, lead me toward a big tree, not my eucalyptus, another one, also with low branches.

We go past it. Walk a ways till we're in front of another tree and it's so quiet, no one's around, even if I scream no one will hear me.

She stands to one side, still aiming the gun, looks at her camera case. Holding on to my arm, he takes out her camera and gives it to her.

'OK,' she tells me.

I don't know what she wants so I don't speak or move.

She walks up and slaps me hard across the face and my head spins around, but it still doesn't hurt as much as it should.

'Do it, you little shit!'

'What?' I say, but it sounds like another kid's voice. Like I'm out of my body, watching myself move around in some robot movie.

She raises her hand to hit me again and I try to protect my face with my arm. He knees me in the back and *that* hurts.

'Off with the pants, Street-smarts – let him pull 'em down, honey.'

He lets go of me as she keeps the gun on me. I touch my pants but don't pull them down. He pulls his down, lets them fall around his legs. He's wearing baggy white boxers and now he reaches into the fly-hole – I turn away.

'What?' she laughs. 'Something you haven't seen before? Yank 'em down, show us your good side.'

I don't move. She slaps me again. If she didn't have the gun, I'd stomp her face, twist her head off.

She laughs again. 'Obey and it'll all be over before you can say ouch. A little owie, that's all.'

She makes kissy noises and he does, too.

'Sure,' that other kid's voice says. 'Sure, I know what you mean. Only . . .'

'Only what?' She moves closer, puts the gun up against my nose. It feels cold and it smells like a gas station.

The corner of my eye sees that his boxers are all the way down, but still around his ankles, like he doesn't want to really take everything off. He's moving his arm back and forth—

'Only,' the kid says, 'I . . . it . . . like I – I can do it. Sure, OK, but you – it – like now – first I've got to . . .'

'Got to what?' The gun waves in front of my eyes.

'You know.'

188

'I don't know! *What!*'

'Got to . . . shit.'

Silence.

'Hear that?' she says to him.

'Yeah,' he says, very quietly, and I'm thinking oh no, does he like that even better, did I just make a big mistake?

She turns and looks at him and for a second I think of running for it, but then her face is back right in front of mine and I don't know why I think this but the way she looks, she could be a teacher, someone's mother or grandma, it's not my fault—

'So?' she asks him.

'Um . . . not today.'

'OK, trash,' she tells me. 'Go ahead and do your thing – use your shirt to wipe your ass, *then* you're gonna show us your good side.'

I pull down my pants and even though it's a warm day, a beautiful day, a lemonade and corn day, my legs feel like stone.

'So white,' he says.

'C'mon, go, go.' Her voice is thick and I understand: His sickness is doing it to kids, hers is being in *charge*. Watching.

'Undies off, goddamn you – off, off, come on, finish up.'

I pull down my shorts. Bending down, I manage to move a little farther away from her, but only inches. All around it's so quiet, so green, even the leaves don't move, it's like the three of us are part of one big photograph or maybe this is the last moment before God destroys the world, and why shouldn't He?

'Get going or I'll kill you!' The gun and the camera are

aimed at me. She's going to take pictures of everything. I'm her souvenir.

The problem is before I had to really badly but now I can't, it's like my organs are blocks of ice jammed up against each other.

'Do it or I'll *shoot* it out of you!'

The sound of her voice, the thought of being shot, gets my stomach going again and I do it.

Then I reach behind with one hand to catch it.

Gross, I hate doing it, but I tell myself it's just digested food, stuff that was already inside me—

'Look at that,' she says. 'You disgusting little animal.'

'Disgusting,' he says. But he means something else.

I look up at her and nod. And smile. She's surprised, wasn't expecting a smile and for a second she looks away.

I reach back and even though I was never good at sports I aim and throw.

Bam! Right in her face and all over her camera, over her blouse.

She's screaming and stumbling back and slapping at herself and he's tripping over his pants, confused. He straightens up and charges me but she's the one to watch because she's got the gun. She's still screaming and slapping. I yank up my shorts and pants and even before they're completely in place, I'm runrunrunning, through branches that scratch my face, through space, through green that never stops, time that never stops, running, tripping, flying.

Floating.

I hear a loud handclap, don't stop, nothing hurts, I'm OK

or maybe I'm not I don't feel it, can't feel anymore, that wouldn't be bad, that wouldn't be bad at all.

I throw myself through green.

Thank you, gorilla. If I could breathe I'd laugh.

22

JUST AS Petra was about to call Empty Nest Productions for Darrell/Darren, another fax came through: Lisa's last phone bill.

Patsy K was right; the woman really had hated the instrument. Fifteen calls the whole month, one long distance, on the first, to Chagrin Falls, three minutes long. Brief chat with Mom? Just once a month. Not a close relationship?

Two toll calls, both to Alhambra. The number matched one in Petra's notes: One of Patsy K's friends. The rest were all locals: Three to Jacopo's in Beverly Hills for takeout pizza, two to the Shanghai Garden, same city, for Chinese, one each to Neiman-Marcus and Saks.

The last four calls were to a Culver City exchange that turned out to be Empty Nest. Petra phoned it and asked for Darrell in Editing. The receptionist said, 'Darrell Breshear?'

'Yes.'

'One moment, I'll connect you.'

Breshear had no receptionist, just a machine. His voice was pleasant. Patsy K had said he was forty but he sounded like a young man. Rather than leave a message, Petra decided to call back later and ran Breshear through a superficial NCIC check. Clean. Laughing to herself because they hadn't run Ramsey.

She phoned the County Assessor, and after hassling with a snotty clerk, managed to learn that H. Carter Ramsey owned over a dozen pieces of property in LA, all in the Valley: The house in Calabasas, commercial buildings on Ventura Boulevard and busy Encino, Sherman Oaks, North Hollywood, and Studio City cross-streets. One in Studio City matched the address she had for Greg Balch's office at Players Management.

Nothing in Malibu or Santa Monica, nothing that sounded like a romantic hideaway, but maybe when Ramsey got away, he really wanted distance. Go north, young woman, and if that didn't work, the eastern mountain resorts.

At the Ventura Assessor's, she got a more cooperative clerk but nothing. Next came Santa Barbara, even more hassles than LA, but bingo: H. Carter Ramsey – what did the H. stand for anyway? – was the deedholder on a house in Montecito.

Copying down the address, she ran his name through DMV.

Full name here: *Herbert*.

Herb. Herbie C. Ramsey – that just wouldn't do for *The Adjustor*.

Tracing vehicle ownerships, she came across all the vintage cars she'd seen in the little museum, plus a Mercedes 500, personalized license plate PLYR 1.

Plus a two-year-old Jeep Wrangler. PLYR 0. That one was registered to the Montecito address.

Players Management. PLYR. The fact that Ramsey used vanity plates was interesting. Most celebrities craved anonymity. Maybe he sensed his fame was fading, felt he needed to advertise.

PLYR . . . fancying himself quite the stud?

Something else: He'd mentioned the Mercedes but not the Jeep. Because the Jeep was stashed in Montecito, or was the omission deliberate?

Was the four-wheel-drive the murder vehicle, the Mercedes a red-herring?

Could the guy be that devious? Devious, but stupid, because that kind of ruse wouldn't work long. He'd have to know they'd run a DMV early on.

But if Petra's last-date scenario was correct, the crime had been semi-impulsive up to a point – the instant where Ramsey packed a knife as he got into the car. So maybe he'd acted out overwhelming rage, was now scrambling to do what he could.

Montecito . . . the neighborhood was ultra-tony, multi-acre estates like Calabasas, older, classier. No cozy little *pied-à-terre* for Ramsey, he craved space. Lord of two manors.

Greedy guy in more ways than one? If I can't have her, no one can?

It brought to mind a Thomas Hart Benton in an art book she'd pored over as a child. *The Jealous Lover of Lone Green Valley*. A rawboned, Stetsoned hick with psychopath eyes stabbing a woman in the breast, country musicians playing a sad score in the foreground, verdant earth dipping and swooping, evoking the victim's vertigo. It had scared the hell out of her, for all she knew had colored her view of men and romance, maybe even her career choice.

The jealous lover of Calabasas/Montecito.

For all the Hollywood angles, this one would probably play out as the same old story, and she realized that if she stayed in Homicide she'd be spending her life inhaling the worst of clichés.

The lunch plan had been to meet Stu at Musso and Frank's but at 1:45 he phoned in and said, 'Sorry, I'm getting hung up, do you mind?'

Relieved, she said, 'No problem. Anything earth-shattering?'

'All I'm getting so far is no one respects Ramsey as an actor. How about you?'

She told him about the Montecito place and the Jeep, then said, 'Guess what, a similar,' and gave him the details of the Ilse Eggermann murder.

'Wonderful,' he said. 'Phil Sorensen's good; if he didn't solve it, it was probably unsolvable. Maybe we *should* let Robbery-Homicide take it.'

Now she *knew* something was wrong. Stu had little use for the downtown hotshot-elite, considered them arrogant, not nearly as good as they thought they were. Losing a big case was always a sore point for all but the laziest divisional detectives and Stu had never occupied the same continent as lazy. Now he was willing to let R–H roll over him? And her.

If it was a career thing, pending promotion, that didn't make sense. Unless he was certain this one was bound to end badly, figured early damage control was better than being the global-village idiot.

'You're kidding,' she said sharply.

'Yeah, I guess I am,' he said wearily. 'I just didn't want to hear about a valid similar, but no big deal, we'll ride with it.' She heard him inhale. 'OK, beep me if you need something. No news yet of Lisa's car?'

'Nope. I'd like to check out Ramsey's Montecito place.'

Silence. 'Before we get that assertive, we should clear it with Schoelkopf.'

'I don't see why we need to,' said Petra. 'What I got from the meeting this morning was once we do the scut, we're free to be real-life detectives. He admitted if we don't talk to Ramsey soon we'll look like boobs. I think we need to arrange another face-to-face, soon. No lackey to run interference. If Ramsey refuses to speak to us without a lawyer, that tells us something. If he doesn't we come on friendly but try to pry him.'

'I think you misunderstood Schoelkopf, Petra. For him it's not about getting things done, it's about self-protection. And we need to think that way, too—'

'Stu—'

'Hear me out. Who got burned on O.J.? D's, not the brass. The moment we ask to get a close look at Ramsey's houses and his cars, even just an informal request, no warrants, Ramsey becomes the prime suspect and it's a whole other game. If someone finds out you *DMV'd* him, it'll be a whole other game.'

'I don't believe this.'

'Believe.'

'Fine,' she said. 'You know better.'

'I don't, Petra,' he said in the most mournful tone she'd ever heard him use. 'I just know we have to be careful.'

She left the station fuming, was three blocks away when she realized she was driving to see Darrell Breshear without setting up the appointment. Using a pay phone, she called again. This time she talked to the taped message, giving her

196

name and title and asking Breshear to call her at the soonest opportuni—

'This is Darrell.'

'Mr Breshear, thank you. I'm working on Lisa Boehlinger Ramsey's murder and would like to talk to you about her.'

'Because we were friends?'

Odd response. 'Exactly.'

'Sure,' he said, sounding anything but certain. 'What would you like to know?'

'If you don't mind, I'd prefer a face-to-face meeting, Mr Breshear.'

'Oh . . . any particular reason?'

Because I want to study your facial expressions, evaluate your eye contact, see whether you're sweating or twitching or looking at your feet too frequently, because that's a clear sign of lying.

'Procedure,' she said.

He didn't answer.

'Mr Breshear?'

'Well,' he said, 'I guess so – could we not do it here, at the lot?'

'May I ask why?'

'It's – I'd prefer to keep a low profile at work and the police stomping in is . . . bound to attract attention.'

'I promise you I don't stomp, sir.'

He didn't think that was funny. 'You know what I mean.'

'I understand, sir,' she said. The guy was antsy. Why? 'Where would you suggest?'

'Um . . . how about a coffee shop or something like that? There are plenty of places around here.'

'Pick one.'

'How about . . . the Pancake Palace on Venice near Overland, let's say tomorrow at ten A.M.?'

'The Pancake Palace is fine, Mr Breshear, but I was thinking sooner. Like in half an hour.'

'Oh. Well . . . the problem is, I'm elbow-deep in a big project. Final cut on a picture, there's a screening—'

'I understand, sir, but Lisa was murdered.'

'Yes, yes, of course – OK, the Pancake Palace, half an hour. May I ask who told you I'd be worth talking to about Lisa?'

'Various people,' said Petra. 'See you there, sir, and thanks for your help.'

She got back in the car and drove as fast as safety would allow down Western to Olympic. Hoping the guy would show and not complicate her life further.

23

BLUE WALLS, brown booths, the too-sweet fumes of fake maple syrup.

Darrell Breshear wasn't hard to spot. At this hour the Pancake Palace was almost empty and he was the only black man in the place, sitting in a corner booth looking miserable.

Young voice, but indeed older. Patsy K had said forty, but Petra pegged him at forty-five to fifty. He'd already started on a cup of coffee; for all his attempts to delay, he'd showed up early. Definitely antsy.

He was thin and sat tall, had close-cropped graying hair, skin almost as pale as Petra's, African features. He wore a black polo shirt under a gray herringbone jacket.

Bags under his eyes made him look weary. When she got closer, she saw the eyes were amber. A few freckles dotted the bridge of his nose.

He saw her and stood. Six one.

'Mr Breshear.'

'Detective.'

They shook hands. His was dry.

'Coffee?' he said, indicating his half-full cup. More like half-empty, judging from his expression.

'Sure.'

Breshear waved for service and ordered for Petra, saying please and thank you and getting the waitress to smile. 'Sorry to play hard-to-get,' he said. 'Lisa's murder shocked me, and then to be part of an investigation.' He shook his head.

'So far you're a very small part of the investigation, Mr Breshear.' She took her pad out, began writing, then sketching his face.

'Good.' His eyes wandered to the left. 'So . . .'

Rather than answer, Petra drank coffee. Breshear's eyes started bouncing around.

'Please tell me about your relationship with Lisa Ramsey, sir.'

'We worked together.'

'You're a film editor, too?'

'I'm a senior editor, Lisa worked on my team.'

'Senior editor,' said Petra. 'So you've been doing it for a while.'

'Twelve years. I did some acting before that.'

'Really.'

'Nothing big. Not film, musical theater, back east.'

'*Guys and Dolls?*'

Breshear smiled. 'Did that one. And others. It taught me one thing.'

'What's that?'

'I wasn't as talented as I thought.'

Petra smiled back. 'Did you hire Lisa?'

'Empty Nest hired her and assigned her to me. She was good. Considering how new she was. She learned fast. Intelligent. What happened to her is unbelievable.'

Breshear's shoulders dropped and now he maintained eye contact.

Petra said, 'Did she have prior experience as a film editor?'

'She was a theater arts major in college, took some editing courses.'

'How long did she work with you, sir?'

'About half a year.' Up with the eyes. He sipped, kept his cup in front of his mouth, blocking it from view.

'Are editing jobs easy to come by?'

'Not at all.'

'But Lisa got one because of her college training?'

'I – not exactly,' said Breshear. The cup continued to shield his mouth. Petra shifted forward and he lowered it. 'She – I was told she got the job through connections.'

'Told by who?'

'My boss – Steve Zamoutis, he's the producer.'

'Connections with who?'

'Ramsey. He made a call and she got hired.'

'Six months ago,' said Petra. 'Right after the divorce.'

Breshear nodded.

Doing favors for the ex. Did it confirm Ramsey's claim of a friendly parting? Or had he carried the torch for Lisa, tried to get back with her?

'Let me get something straight, sir. Was Lisa qualified for the job?'

'Yes,' Breshear answered quickly. 'Considering her inexperience, she was very competent.'

Petra wrote. And sketched.

Breshear said, 'That's not to say there weren't things she needed to learn.'

It took a second for Petra to untangle the double negative. Was Breshear a complex thinker or was he looking for something other than a coffee cup to hide behind?

'And you taught her.'

'Tried my best.'

'So you and she worked together on the same movies.'

'Two pictures,' he said, naming them. Petra had never heard of either.

Breshear added, 'They haven't been put into release yet.'

'What kind of pictures are they?'

'Comedies.'

'No murder mysteries, huh?'

Breshear gave a snorting laugh that he seemed to regret, because he inhaled deeply, tried to compose himself. 'Not hardly.' He looked at his watch.

'What else can you tell me about Lisa?' she said.

'That's about it. She had no problems on the job. When I found out she was murdered it made me sick.'

'Any ideas about who might have killed her?'

'Everyone's saying it was Ramsey, because he beat her up, but I don't know.'

'Did Lisa talk to you about that?'

'Never.'

Petra put the finishing touches on his portrait. She'd drawn him nervous – with haunted eyes. 'Not even once?'

'Not even once, Detective. His name never came up, period.'

'Did you ever see Lisa use drugs?'

Breshear's mouth opened and shut. Out came another snort-laugh. 'I really don't – is it absolutely necessary to get into that?'

'Yes it is, sir.' Petra moved closer again, sliding her hand across the table so it was only inches from his.

He pulled back. 'Let me say this: Lisa wasn't a heavy

202

doper, but in the industry people tend to – yes, I saw her snort a couple of times.'

'A couple meaning two.'

'Maybe more. Three or four. But that's it.'

'And this was at work?'

'No, no.' He was light enough to blush. Good. Down went the eyes. He said, 'Not at work, strictly speaking. I mean, we weren't actually working – I'm her supervisor. Anything that happens on my shift is my responsibility.'

'I understand, Mr Breshear. You'd never have allowed cocaine to interfere with her work. But you saw her snorting three or four times on the lot after work. Where exactly?'

'In the editing room, but it was after hours. May I ask why you want to know this? Do you think what happened was related to dope? Because it's not some kind of crazy scene around here. We're all business, have to be. Without us the picture doesn't get made.'

Long speech. The heightened color remained, lessening the contrast between freckles and background skin.

'Where else, besides the editing room, did you see her snort?'

'At – in my car. *That* took me by surprise. I was driving and she just pulled out this little glass tube, waited till I stopped for a red light and sucked it up through her nose.'

'In your car,' Petra wrote, watching as Breshear's eyes did a little ocular roller-coaster. 'Where were you going?'

'I don't remember.' Breshear snatched up his cup and emptied it. The waitress came by and poured some more and he started drinking.

Petra declined the refill and when she and Breshear were alone again, she sketched some more, inserting shadows and contours, making him look older. 'So you don't recall where you were going. How long ago was this?'

Down went the cup. 'I'd say one, maybe two months ago.'

'Were you two dating, Mr Breshear?'

'No, no – we were working together. Late. That's the way it is in editing. They call you, you cut.'

You cut. The word-choice sailed right by him.

'So you and Lisa were working late, and . . .'

He didn't fill in the blank and Petra said, 'How'd you end up in your car?'

'I was probably taking her home, or maybe out for a bite – may I ask why you're questioning me?'

'We're questioning all the men Lisa knew, Mr Breshear. Someone told us you'd dated Lisa and we're following up.'

'That's wrong. We never dated.'

'So I guess our source is mistaken.' She smiled, guessing that the existence of a 'source' would rattle him.

He colored again and his eyes bounced around. This guy was no smooth psychopath, but he was hiding something.

'Guess so,' he said.

'Can you tell me where you were on the night Lisa was murdered?'

He stared at her. Touched his forehead. Wiping it, though it was dry. Now his eyes were big and frightened – exactly the expression Petra had drawn on her pad. Look, Dad, I'm a prophetess, too!

'I was with another woman.' Saying it just above a whisper.

'Could I have a name, please?'

Breshear smiled. A sick, guilty, dirt-eating, totally unattractive smile. 'That's kind of a problem.'

'Why's that, sir?'

'Because I'm married and the woman wasn't my wife.'

'If she can be discreet, so can I, Mr Breshear.' Petra waved her pen.

'I'd rather not,' he said. 'Look – I'm going to be straightup with you, Detective Connor. Because I don't want you finding out somewhere else and thinking I was hiding anything. Lisa and I had a short-term thing, but it was no big deal.'

'A thing.'

'We slept together. Seven times.'

He'd counted. A scorekeeper?

'Seven times,' she said.

'A one-week thing.'

She wanted to say: Now tell me, Darrell, was it once a day for seven days, or did you double up a few days and take a break? 'A one-week thing.'

'That's it.' The amber eyes bounced. 'Actually, we really didn't even sleep together. Strictly speaking – God, this is embarrassing.'

'What is?'

'Talking about the details – I guess if you were a man it would be easier.'

She grinned. 'Sorry about that.'

He was staring into his coffee cup again and looked ready to slide under the table.

'So,' said Petra, 'how long into Lisa's employment did this thing occur?'

'A month ago, six weeks.'

That matched Patsy K's recollection.

'So you were intimate,' said Petra, softening her voice, trying to keep him on the edge but still willing to talk. 'But you never slept together.'

'Right,' said Breshear. 'I never stayed over at her place and obviously, I couldn't take her to mine.'

'Where'd you go?'

The blush was deeper than ever. A nice rusty mahogany. It gave him some depth, actually made him more appealing.

'Jesus – is this really necessary?'

'If it relates to your relationship with Lisa, and to your whereabouts the night she was murdered, I'm afraid it is, sir.'

'And you have to write this all down?'

'If what you tell me shows you had nothing to do with Lisa's death, there'd be no reason for anyone to find out.' A crock, everything went into the file, but she closed the pad anyway.

He rubbed his temples and studied his coffee some more. 'Man . . . OK, the night Lisa was murdered, I was with a woman named Kelly Sposito. Her place.'

'Address, please?' said Petra, opening the pad.

He recited a number on Fourth Street, in Venice.

'Apartment number?'

That question seemed to bother him even more, as if specificity drove home her seriousness.

'No, it's a house—'

'And you were at Ms Sposito's house from when to when?'

'All night. Ten P.M. to six A.M. Before that, from around five to six, we had dinner at a restaurant – a Mexican place near the studio. The Hacienda, right down the block, on Washington Boulevard.'

'Ms Sposito works with you?'

Nod. 'She's an editor, too.'

Ah, the rub. Lots of rubbing on the job.

'So you never went home and your wife didn't suspect anything?'

'My wife was out of town – she's a salesperson, travels a lot.'

Mr Take-Charge-Politely Darrell was emerging as the editing-room stud. Meaning there were probably plenty of other 'things' he didn't want unearthed.

'Do you have to call Kelly?' he said.

'Yes, sir. Do you know where she is?'

'At work. Is that it?'

'Almost,' said Petra. 'Can you tell me who Lisa's coke source was?'

'No,' he said. 'Absolutely not.'

'No one at the studio?'

'I have no idea. No one at Empty Nest, that's for sure.'

'Because?'

'Because I know everyone and they don't deal drugs.'

'OK,' said Petra. 'But I imagine it probably wouldn't be any big deal finding someone at the studio to supply, would it?'

'Oh, come on,' he said, angry now. 'You think cause it's the industry we're just running around partying all day. It's a business, Detective. We work hard as hell. I've never seen anyone on the lot try to sell anyone else dope and Lisa never talked about her source. In fact, the first time she snorted she offered me some and I told her, "I don't want you doing that in my car."'

'But she continued to snort anyway,' said Petra. 'In your car.'

'Well – yes, she was an adult. I couldn't control her. But I didn't want any part of it – for me.' He held the cup with

207

both hands. 'You want a confession? I'll give you one. I've had my share of problems with alcohol. Been sober for ten years and intend to stay that way.'

The amber eyes were flashing. Righteous indignation that looked real. Or he should have been on film rather than splicing it. Or on *stage* – singing his heart out.

'All right,' said Petra. 'Thanks for your time.'

'Sure,' said Breshear. 'Call Kelly, fine. Just not my wife, OK? Because she was out of town, couldn't help you. Lisa and I were friends, that's all. Why would I hurt her?'

'Just friends, except for that one week.'

'That was nothing,' he said. 'A passing thing. She was lonely, kind of down, and it just so happened things weren't going so well between me and my wife. We worked late, one thing led to another.'

He gave a you-know-how-it-is shrug.

One thing had led to seven others. Petra said, 'But you never stayed together overnight. Unlike the situation with Kelly Sposito.'

'That's because Lisa didn't want to. It was a point of pride with her – she was independent, doing her own thing.'

'Where did the two of you go?'

'Nowhere. Just – we – oh, Jesus. All right, here's the complete picture: It all happened in my car. We went out for a bite and on the way back to the lot, Lisa asked me to take a little drive, toward the beach. We took PCH, ended up near the old Sand Dune Club. She asked me to park, I had no idea what was going on. Then she pulled out that tube and snorted.'

'So it was powdered cocaine, not crack.'

Breshear smiled. 'Only black people use crack, right?'

208

Petra ignored that.

He said, 'It was powder.'

'She snorted, then what?'

'Then she got kind of . . . active. Physical.'

'Then you had sex in your car,' said Petra.

'That's the way it ended up,' he said. New tone of voice. Amused?

'Seven times,' said Petra. 'You'd go out and she'd snort and you'd have sex in the car.'

'Actually, five of the times were that way. Twice – the last two, I followed her home and waited till she got ready, then we went out for dinner. But we never dated – as in a real relationship. Both times she had to go home for something.'

'Dope?'

'I don't know,' said Breshear.

But he did. They both did. So far, his story meshed perfectly with Patsy K's.

Breshear sucked in breath. 'I don't know why I'm telling you this, but you might as well know everything. We never really had intercourse. She just wanted to give to me.'

Looking right at her, now, sitting straighter, challenging her to press for details.

Because sex was his thing, and once he got over the initial shame, talking about it boosted his confidence.

Petra said, 'Oral sex.'

'Yes,' said Breshear, closing his eyes for a second. 'First she'd get high, then she'd do it. Seven nights, once a night, the same routine. The eighth time, she said, "I like you, Darrell, but . . ." I didn't argue because to tell the truth, I thought the whole thing was weird. She wasn't nasty about it. Very nice, just like, time to move on. I got the feeling she'd done it before.'

'Why's that?'

'Just a feeling. She seemed . . . practiced.'

Petra didn't speak and Breshear's eyes saucered again.

'What is it, sir?'

'It's hard to think of her . . . cut up like that. The news said it was brutal.'

Petra gave him more silence and he said, 'She was a beautiful person. I hope to God you catch whoever did it.'

'Hope so, too. Anything else you want to tell me, Mr Breshear?'

'Nope, can't think of anything – please don't call my wife, OK? Everything's going real well between us now. I don't want to mess it up.'

24

AFTER BRESHEAR left she called Empty Nest and asked for Kelly Sposito, the current flame. Things going well with the wife meant only one on the side?

Sposito was in, had a high, unpleasant voice that got shrill when Petra identified herself and explained the nature of the call.

'Darrell? Are you for real?' But a moment later, she verified Breshear's alibi.

'So he was with you all night?'

'That's what I said – listen, you'd better not put this in the paper or anything, I don't need the grief.'

'I'm a detective, not a reporter, Ms Sposito.'

'I see my name in the paper, I sue.'

Paper tigress. What was with her?

'Why are you hassling Darrell? Because he's black?'

'We're talking to people who knew Lisa, Ms Sposito—'

'Everyone knows who did it.'

'Who?'

'Right,' said the woman. 'Like you don't. And he'll get off because he's rich.'

Petra thanked her for her help, hung up and drove the five blocks to the studio, used her badge and a combination of firmness and charm to get in. She got directions to Empty

Nest from a guy with long hair who looked like an actor but wore a tool belt.

The production company occupied several white clapboard, green-shuttered bungalows scattered between whitewashed sound stages and office buildings, the entire place spotless, with that too-perfect Potemkin village look. Billboards for TV shows and movies stood on metal towers. A field of satellite dishes resembled a giant crockery collection.

A woman in Bungalow A told her Breshear worked in D. She walked into a small, empty reception area, brass and glass and black wood floors, three phones, no typewriter or computer. More movie posters, cheapie flicks she didn't recognize, the smell of fish. Through a door she heard voices and she opened it after the merest knock.

Breshear and two women in their twenties were sitting at a long table mounted with several gray machines — products of a mating between a film projector and a microscope. In an open Styrofoam take-out box were three sushi rolls.

One woman wore an oversized black sweater over skin-tight black leggings, had a sharp, pretty face, bronze skin probably from a bottle, and a mane of big, black curls that trailed down her back. The other was arctic-pale and had thin blond hair held in place by a pink sawtooth clip. Pleasant-looking but not the buxom looker Curly was. Breshear, sitting between them, started to shift his body backwards, distancing himself.

'Detective Connor,' he said. Steaming mug in his hand, Gary Larson cartoon silkscreened on the side. The guy claimed he didn't dope but like many ex-alcoholics he had a caffeine jones.

'Hi,' said Petra. 'Ms Sposito?'

Curly said, 'What?' and stood. Tall – five nine – terrific curvy body evident even under the baggy sweater. Her dark eyes were ten years older than the rest of her. She wore so much mascara her lashes resembled miniature wiper blades. Too hard-looking to be a model or an actress, but definitely someone who'd turn heads. A lioness, with that mane.

'Just thought I'd drop by and talk to you in person.'

Breshear's head swiveled fast as he looked at his girlfriend. Trying to figure out what she'd said over the phone that had complicated things.

Sposito glared as she walked toward Petra with big fluid steps.

The blond girl watched the whole thing, baffled.

When she was two steps away, Sposito said, 'Let's talk outside.' To the blonde: 'We're gonna use your office, Cara.'

'Oh, sure,' said the blond girl. 'Should I just stay here?'

'Yeah. It won't take long.'

Out in the front room, Sposito put her hands on her hips. 'Now what?'

Your fault, Jungle Girl, all that out-of-proportion anger.

'You had some pretty strong opinions about Mr Ramsey,' said Petra.

'Oh, for God's sake! Opinions is all they were – everyone's saying the same thing. Because Mr *Ramsey* was abusive. It's nuts to even consider that Darrell had anything to do with Lisa just because the two of them dated a couple times. But OK, you asked where he was, I told you. And that's all there is. I take enough crap for being with Darrell, I don't need this.'

'Crap from who?'

'Everyone. Society.'

'Racism?'

Kelly laughed. 'Just a few weeks ago, we were at the Rose Bowl swap meet and some idiot made a rude comment. You'd think it'd be different, LA, the nineties, I mean who's the richest woman in America – Oprah.' She frowned and lines formed around her mouth. 'What Darrell and I have is good and I don't want anything messing it up.'

If you only knew, honey.

'I understand,' said Petra. 'Any other opinions you'd like to share? About Lisa's murder? Lisa, in general?'

'Nope. Now, can you please let me get back to work? We do work around here.'

Why were movie people so defensive about doing honest labor?

'How long have you been working here, Kelly?' 'Kelly,' not 'Ms Sposito,' because this one would always try to dominate.

The wiper blades opened and shut. 'A year.'

'So you worked with Lisa.'

'Not with her, like on the same project. She needed training, so Darrell worked with her. I've always been on my own.'

'Lisa was inexperienced?'

Kelly snickered. 'She was a rookie, Darrell was always picking up her slack.'

'The whole six months she worked here?'

'No, she learned, she was OK, but to tell the truth – no, forget it, I don't want to put her down.'

Petra smiled and Kelly bared her teeth. Petra supposed it was a return smile.

214

'OK, I opened my big mouth. I was just going to say editing jobs are hard to come by, you pay dues. Lisa was totally green, I figured she had to have connections.'

'What kind of connections?'

'Don't know.'

Something else Darrell hadn't shared with the Lioness. Suddenly, Petra felt sorry for her. 'What'd you think of her as a person, Kelly?'

'She did her job, I did mine, we didn't socialize.'

Petra said, 'Did you like her?'

Kelly blinked. 'Honestly? She wasn't my favorite person. Because I don't think she treated people well, but I really don't want to speak badly about her, now.'

'Didn't treat who well?'

The dark eyes narrowed. 'I'm talking in general. She had a sharp mouth, that's probably what did her in.'

'What do you mean?'

'She was sarcastic. Had a way of saying something without saying it, know what I mean? Looks, tone of voice, the whole body language thing.' She rubbed her hips, bent one leg, ballerina-style, flexing, then straightening. 'Lisa thought a lot of herself, OK? And if someone didn't measure up, she'd be sure to let them know one way or the other. You want my opinion? Maybe Ramsey was trying to get her back and she shut him down. Aren't those abusers always obsessed?'

Out of the mouths of hostile babes. 'They can be,' said Petra, looking as fascinated as she felt.

'So Ramsey could have still been into Lisa in a big way,' said Kelly, 'and let's say they got together and he tried to make it with her but couldn't get it up or whatever, and she

215

let him know what she thought about that in that Lisa way of hers, and he freaked.'

Petra hid her amazement. The woman had gone from hostile resistance to criminological theory in five minutes. Offering a theory that buttressed Petra's final-date scenario.

'What makes you think Ramsey was impotent?'

'Because Lisa said so – at least she hinted at it. It was about three, four months ago. We were eating lunch – all of us. Darrell, Cara, me, Lisa, and another editor who works here, Laurette Benson, she's gay. And the topic came up about actors, how they get all the glory and how so many of them have totally warped personalities, are totally screwed up, but the public never knows it because everything they hear is bullshit created by the media and publicists. Anyway, we started talking about how actors become sex icons, bigger than human – like Madonna having that baby and everyone's treating it like she was the other madonna and this was some kind of sacred birth, right? Like all those idiots still looking for Elvis, or thinking Michael Jackson's gonna stay married. We editors look at these people day after day, scene after scene, through the window of a Movieola. You see enough rough cuts, see how many takes you need to get them to look good and sound smart, you realize how few of them are even talented in the first place. Anyway, we were talking about that and we got into all the sexual fantasies that the public develops about people who probably half the time can't even cut it in bed. Then Laurette started in about how many actors were gay, even the ones who the public thinks are hetero sex gods. How sexuality and reality are like two completely different planets. And Lisa rolled her eyes and said, 'You have no idea, guys. You have no fucking clue.'

216

So we all stare at her and she cracks up and says, 'Take it from me. You go in thinking you're eating at the Hard Rock Café and it turns out to be the Leaning Tower of Overcooked Pasta.' Then she laughs even harder, then her face takes on this whole different expression – really bummed, angry – and she just stomps out and goes to the bathroom and stays there for a while. Laurette says, "Boy, someone's shorts got yanked." Then Lisa comes back and her nose is red and she's in a too-good mood, know what I mean?'

'She got high.'

Kelly pointed a finger-gun. 'You must be a detective.'

'Did she do that a lot?'

'Enough. Not that I paid attention.'

'So the topic of impotence upset her.'

'Wouldn't it upset you?' said Kelly Sposito. 'Life's tough enough, all the crap you get from men when they're at their best. Who has time for limp spaghetti?'

It was after five when Petra left the lot and she wouldn't have minded a long, hot bath and a good meal prepared by someone else, maybe some torture at the easel. But she still needed to trade notes with Stu, and if he suggested they make their move on Ramsey tonight, she wouldn't argue.

She called the station. Stu wasn't back, but Lilian, the civilian receptionist, said, 'Some stuff came for you from the coroner, Barbie.'

'Big envelope?'

'Medium big. I put it on your desk.'

'Thanks.'

She ate a tuna sandwich at the Apple Pan, washed it down with a Coke, scanned the paper – nothing on Lisa – drove back to Hollywood as quickly as the traffic would allow. By the time she arrived, the night-shift had come on but most of the D's were already out serving warrants and looking for bad guys and her desk was clear. Stu still hadn't checked in.

Inside the brown envelope were preliminary post-mortem findings signed by a Dr Wendell Kobayashi. Countersigned as Schoelkopf had promised by the head coroner, Dr Ilie Romanescu.

Quick turnaround; usually even preliminaries took a week.

She sat down and read the two typed sheets. Traces of cocaine and alcohol had been found in Lisa Ramsey's body, not enough to cause stupor but enough to intoxicate. Meaning she'd been easier to take by surprise. No final autopsy report, yet, but the docs were able to provide a wound count and cause of death. Twenty-three cuts – close enough to Ilse Eggermann's twenty-nine. So far the coroner was guessing that the fatal one had been the very deep abdominal slash Petra had tagged. Point of insertion just above the pubic bone, continuing eight inches upward. A vertical wound that had sliced through intestines and stomach and liver, bisecting the diaphragm, cutting off respiration.

A gutting. Street-fighter's move.

As she drops, he hits her twenty-two more times.

Frenzy or fun. Or both.

Dr Kobayashi guessed that he'd been standing close to her for that first, lethal lunge. Meaning blood on him, too, and if they lucked out and got an exchange, something *he'd* left on *her*. But fiber and fluid analysis would take several days. No footprints, as Alan Lau had noted. Either he'd taken off his shoes or gotten lucky.

She thought about what Darrell had told her about Lisa's sexual proclivities: Oral sex in the car. Like a throwback to high school. Had Lisa been fixated at the cheerleader stage? Cheerleaders and older men?

Kelly had described Lisa as full of herself, but she'd ended up ministering to Darrell, wanting nothing for herself.

Sex in a car. The killer *taking* Lisa somewhere in a car.

Mr Macho Ramsey, unable to function?

A chronic problem? The date Ramsey's last-ditch attempt to prove himself?

In the car? Because he and Lisa had done it before in cars?

That damned car museum! Had it been more than just a millionaire's trophy thing? Ramsey's *marital aid*? All that chrome and steel, big engines, reminding him he was rich, handsome, semi-famous – a gazillion dollars' worth of toys all so the blood would remain in his penis?

Breshear had said Lisa seemed practiced. With Ramsey? Others? After the divorce – before?

But the phone records showed no contact with other men, no apparent social life. Maybe she'd used her work phone for personal contact. Getting those records would be a major hassle, she was sure the production company was the legal owner. She'd start the paperwork tomorrow morning.

Back to the murder night. Lisa dolling herself up.

The car, in the car, let's do it in the car.

And Ramsey couldn't cut it—

Cut. There it was again.

Unable to cut it, so Lisa unleashes the sarcasm and he cuts *her*?

After he'd been such a nice guy, forgiving the way she'd

219

blabbed to the tabloid show, getting her the job at the studio, and still sending her seven grand a month.

Twenty-three in cash, a brokerage account at Merrill Lynch – she'd speak to the broker, Ghadoomian, something else for tomorrow.

Sex, money, failure.

Failure in the car, so he'd *used* the car to kill her?

Driving her to her final destination.

Doing her in a *parking lot*.

How LA.

She needed access to PLYR 0 and PLYR 1 and every other vehicle in Ramsey's collection. For all she knew, the death car had been one of the others – that phallic Ferrari, sitting right there in front of them, Stu and the sheriff's guys gawking, unaware they were looking at a slaughterhouse on wheels.

No, too conspicuous, even for LA. One of the others – her phone rang, had to be Stu.

But it was Alan Lau calling from Parker Center, and the criminalist sounded exhausted. 'Got some initial results on those food wrappers and the urine. The food was a mixture of ground beef and ground pork, peppers, onions, a tomato-based sauce, chili powder, garlic powder, some other spices we haven't identified yet. Bread-crumbs, too. Not mixed in, separate. Probably the bun. White bread.'

'Chili-burger.'

'Quite possibly. The urine was definitely human but I hope you don't want any fancy DNA on it, cause we barely had enough to do a presumptive type. Even if we did, it would cost a fortune and take a long time.'

'What else did you get?' said Petra.

'Prints off the wrapping paper and also off that book you found. The book was full of them. Fulls, partials, nice ridge impressions. I'm no expert but it looked like some matches between the wrapper and book. We sent it all to ID and so far no matches to any files. So looks like your reader isn't a big-time criminal or a government employee. Also, from the size of the finger pads, it probably is a woman.'

Bag lady squatting on a rock, thought Petra. Eating furtively, reading some old library book that probably fed some schizo fantasy, who knew what the Presidents meant to her.

Sad. If nothing turned up, it might be worth checking with the park rangers and some Hollywood patrol officers, see if one particular street woman frequented that section of Griffith.

'Thanks, Alan. Anything show up in the vacuum?'

'Just a pile of dirt so far. For all the blood, this was a pretty clean one.'

Stu came into the squad room at 7:34 P.M., looking like prey. Petra was snacking on her second Snickers bar and wondering where Ramsey was at this very moment, what thoughts were going through his head, did he regret what he'd done or was he exulting in the memory of butchering Lisa?

She asked how he was. He said fine and reported on his day with the dutiful tone of a child giving an oral report. Visits to three studios, three wells dug, wait and see. It didn't sound like enough to turn his normally clear irises rosy-pink.

He removed his suit jacket and draped it neatly over the back of his chair. 'No one had anything personal to say about him, he doesn't seem to hang with any particular industry crowd. The fact that he beat Lisa up makes them assume he killed her.'

'I've got something personal.' Petra told him about her talks with Breshear and Sposito, Lisa's hints about impotence.

He said, 'Interesting.' As if all men went through it. Did they?

'It's a motive,' she said.

'Definitely. Too bad it's tough to verify – you trust Sposito on Breshear's alibi?'

'I called her before Breshear got to her and she wasn't the least bit hinky about it, just p.o.'d at being questioned. You don't want to keep working Breshear, do you?'

'No, I just want to make sure we eliminate him cleanly. Let's keep a nice, neat flow-chart on this one.'

He put his palms down on his desk and leaned, stretching his fingers. 'Now, about that German girl—'

Petra gave him the fax on Karlheinz Lauch. He read it and put it down.

She said, 'So where do we go with it?'

'The Austrian police, again. Other countries where they speak German and have airports, which I guess would be Switzerland. Also Interpol, US Immigration, though with a three-year window, good luck finding anything at Passport Control.'

'Sorensen already did all that.'

'Three years' time lapse means we need to do it again. Now that we've found one similar we need to widen the net, make sure we don't miss others. That means Orange County, Ventura, Santa Barbara, even San Francisco. If we find nothing, I'd feel comfortable putting any notion of a local serial killer to rest. But you never know. There was a guy a few years ago, Jack Unterhoffer – an Austrian, as it turns out – moved between Europe and the US, strangling women. Took a long time to see the pattern. If we don't turn up other leads on Lisa, and Schoelkopf gets really paranoid, he'll want us to go national, so let's preempt him, run Lauch through NCIC, whatever else the Feds have to offer.'

Almost as if he *wanted* to do scut. That didn't fit her chance-for-promotion theory. Or did it?

'Fine,' she said, surprised at the impatience in her voice. 'But Ramsey's still clearly our main guy and now we've learned something that adds to his motive. I know the impotence thing is hearsay—'

'Less than hearsay. Lisa hinted in general terms.'

'But if we don't follow up on it, it's beyond malfeasance.'

'No argument,' he said, sitting back and playing with his suspenders. 'We're not arguing here, Petra, we're prioritizing. There are only two of us, so either we ask for reinforcement, which will mean Robbery-Homicide boots us out, or we split the job. How about I take the whole Eggermann/Lauch thing and you talk to Ramsey. The phonework we continue to divide.'

Petra couldn't believe what he was saying. Giving her sirloin and keeping the gristle for himself. 'You want me to do Ramsey alone?'

'It might work to our advantage, Petra.'

'In what way?'

'If Ramsey does have woman problems, your presence could get him antsy, open some cracks.'

Woman problems. Not potency problems. Not *man* problems.

223

She said, 'OK, but I don't mind some scut.'

'Don't worry about it, Petra. Tell the truth—' He started to say something, stopped. Falling into something he'd taught her about when they started working together: Watch out for suspects who say 'truthfully' or 'frankly' or 'to be honest' or 'tell the truth.' They're usually hiding something.

'I really think you're the best one to psych out Ramsey,' he said. 'Not just the gender thing. It'd be better not to overwhelm him, make it obvious that we're interrogating him. One person rather than two could help with that. Also, back at his house, he seemed to focus on you.'

'What do you mean?'

'He wasn't exactly coming on, but there was interest. At least, I thought so. It tells us something about the way his mind works. His ex has just been murdered, he's putting on the grieving husband bit and he's checking you out.'

So he *had* seen it. What else had he kept to himself?

'I'm not talking bait, Petra. If you don't want to do it alone, I understand. But you've got the talent for this one.'

'Thanks.' Why didn't she feel complimented? Was she growing truly paranoid?

She nodded.

'OK, then it's all set.' He picked up his phone.

25

RUNNINGRUNNING RUNNING notbreathing.

No looking back.

Trees jumping in front of me, trying to grab me – change direction.

Tear through the branches, they tear back, my face, my arms, my legs, all on fire.

I want to close my eyes, hurl myself through space, a missile. I try and it's good but then I fall and roll, hitting rocks and branches and sharp things, hurting my head, opening up a hot wet cut on my arm.

It keeps bleeding, I can feel it dripping down, but it doesn't hurt. Nothing hurts, am I made of clay? Of shit?

Don't know where I'm going, don't care, just out of there, the park was a traitor.

Now I can breathe.

I can hear it in my ears, fuzzy, big bursts of fuzz that fill up my head, in air, out air, fuzz air, my chest hurts.

No more Places. Nothing's safe . . . my heart's beating too hard, too fast, suddenly I have to throw up.

I stop, bend over, it shoots out of me like lava, all over the ground, burning my throat.

When will I have a clean life?

No more, empty now, have to be quiet, have to be quiet.

I am quiet.

Everything's quiet.

I taste and smell like something dead.

I run some more, fall, get up, run, walk, start to feel better and stop to breathe but then I start shaking and can't stop.

I'm in a part of the park that I've maybe seen before, but I'm not sure.

Lots of trees, leaves all over the ground, rocks and dirt, could be anywhere in the park. I lie down and hug myself. My throat is still on fire, my teeth start knocking against each other dadadadadadadada.

It stops. I want to sit up, but so tired. The ground is bumpy. I find a rock, a smooth, cold one, hold it in both hands, squeeze hard, then I throw it away and take a deep breath.

The bleeding cut has dried into this purple line with wet spots and gold-colored stuff leaking out. Probably plasma. It helps you clot.

I start to hurt all over and find all the other cuts and marks, on my arms, my face. I scratch, raise some bloody spots, watch them clot too.

My body's working.

A bird cry makes me jump and my heart shoots up into my throat and I feel like vomiting again.

Breathe, breathe, breathe . . . now I'm dizzy.

Breathe. Listen to the birds, they're just birds.

OK. I'm OK.

Time to start moving again.

* * *

Finally, the night comes.

I'm on a high spot, almost a hill, nothing to see but trees and behind them the huge black shadows of real mountains.

Still in the park but not for long. Traitor.

I've got nothing now, my books, my clothes, my plastic bags, my food, it's all back at Five.

All the Tampax money. Except what's left of the five dollars I took to the zoo. I reach down in my pocket and feel three bills and some change.

How did all this happen? How did they know to go for *me*?

The park was their place too.

My fault, stupid thinking I could relax.

Nice and dark now. Darkness covers me, time to move, again.

I walk till I hear cars. Still can't see them, but I must be getting closer to Los Feliz Boulevard. I keep rubbing the hand that held the shit against rocks and dirt and tree trunks and after a while there's no more stink. The cars are really loud now and it *is* Los Feliz and I know where I am.

Hiding myself behind a thick tree, I think about what to do and *she* comes into my head.

The one who got *chucked*.

Why do I keep meeting evil, gross, sick people?

Is there some message I wear on my face like this kid is a loser, he should get messed up? Do I look weak, wimpy, something to be hunted down?

Am I giving off some kind of sign I can't see – the way you can't tickle yourself?

Do I need to be different?

One thing's for sure: I need to be clean.

And gone.

26

AT 7 P.M. Petra called Ramsey's house. The Spanish maid answered with 'Wan min' and put her on hold.

Two minutes, three, five, six.

Was Ramsey figuring out a way to avoid her? Had he shot a call to his lawyer on another line? She prepared herself for a stonewall, would duly note it and try the Boehlingers again.

A voice came on. 'Detective Connor.' The man himself.

'Evening, Mr Ramsey.'

'Have you learned anything?'

'Afraid not, sir, but I thought we might talk again.'

'Fine. When and where?'

'How about your house, as soon as possible?'

'How about right now?'

She caught the tail end of the evening rush back to the Valley. Some idiot had overturned a truckload of garden furniture near the Canoga Park exit and thousands of other-misery voyeurs just had to slow and stare at mangled lounges and shattered faux-cement birdbaths. What's so fascinating about someone else's misfortune? Who was she to talk? She earned a living off it.

Use the time constructively. Psych out Ramsey.

But there was no sophisticated plan, no details to nail down, because planning too precisely when you had no facts could be worse than no preparation at all. One thing was clear: No confrontation. She'd go in friendly, and even if Ramsey gave her a hard time or renewed the Don Juan thing, she'd stay friendly.

That was her strength, anyway. She was able to elicit confessions gently, just as effectively as the bullies, sometimes more so. Stu had built her confidence by letting her take over some serious interrogations. 'Use your inherent personality as a weapon, Petra. The way a therapist does.'

She'd never thought of therapy as warfare but she understood the message: It was all manipulation and the best manipulators didn't over-act.

Stu's interview persona was Kind But Strict Big Brother, a smart, pleasant but essentially tough guy you were a little afraid of but admired and wanted to please.

Hers was Regular Gal, the kind guys liked to talk to.

Not bait. Talent. But Stu knew damn well bait was a significant part of it. Ramsey, a ladies' man – in his own mind – so dangle a lady.

A *player* packing limp spaghetti.

No lawyer's name had been mentioned, yet, but Petra was sure there was one lurking in the background, feeding Ramsey lines. Just like they did when filming – what did they call those guys? – prompters. Machines did it now – teleprompters.

Ramsey had years of practice mouthing words and making them sound right.

Even a bad actor had it over the average suspect. The typical sad soul she interrogated was so full of anxiety, he gave you more than you needed even when he thought he was lying effectively, and the key was to Mirandize him right away, get every last drop legally. The exception was your basic stone-psychopath who had little or no anxiety, but those guys were so boringly self-destructive, they usually managed to trip themselves up being clever.

So where did Ramsey fit in? A calculated killer or just some pathetic, impotent loser who'd freaked out?

Give him lots of rope, sit back, look and listen. A self-hanging was too much to hope for, but maybe he'd at least knot himself up.

She reached RanchHaven at 8:20, got waved through by the guard. Before she drove through she asked him if he'd been on night duty Sunday and he said no, that was someone else. Then he closed the guardhouse door.

She drove up the hill. Artificial lights bleached the pink house off-white, made it appear even bigger, but just as architecturally confused.

A young Hispanic woman, not Estrella Flores, answered her ring, opening the door halfway. What Petra could see of the house was dark.

'Hello,' she said. 'Detective Connor for Mr Ramsey.'

'*Jes?*' The woman was pretty, with a round face, wide eyes the color of concord grapes and black hair tied in a bun. About twenty-five. Same pink and white uniform Estrella Flores had worn.

Petra repeated her name and showed the badge.

The maid stepped back. 'Wan min.' Same voice as over the phone. Where was the older woman?

'Is Estrella Flores here?'

Confusion. The young woman started to turn and Petra tapped her shoulder. '*Donde esta* Estrella?'

Headshake.

'Estrella Flores? *La* . . . housekeeper?'

No answer and Petra's attempt at a warm, sisterly smile failed to alter the maid's stolid expression.

'*Como se llama usted, señorita?*'

'Maria.'

'*Nombre de familia?*'

'Guerrero.'

'Maria Guerrero.'

'*Si.*'

'*Usted no sabe* Estrella Flores?'

'*No.*'

'Estrella *no trabaja aqui?*'

'*No.*'

'*Cuanto tiempo usted trabaja aqui?*'

'*Dos dias.*'

Two days on the job, Estrella gone. Knowing something she didn't want to know and rabbiting? Petra wished she'd tried to reach her sooner.

As Maria Guerrero turned again to leave, a male voice said, 'Detective,' and Ramsey appeared out of the darkness, wearing a white, seriously wrinkled linen shirt, cream silk slacks, cream loafers, no socks.

A vision in pale tones. *I'm a good guy?*

He held the door open for Petra and she walked in. The house smelled stale, and only a table lamp at the rear of the big sitting-room was lit. The car museum was dark, too, the glass wall a sheet of black.

He walked two feet ahead of her, to the lamp, switched

231

on another and winced, as if the wattage hurt his eyes. Had he been sitting in the darkness till now? His sleeves were rolled carelessly to his elbows and his curly hair looked lumpy and uneven.

'Please, have a seat.' Waiting till she'd settled on one of the overstuffeds, he picked his own spot at a right angle to hers, their knees two feet apart.

Placing his hands at his sides, he sat there. His face looked drawn, older. More gray hairs among the curls, but maybe it was just the lighting. Or some dye wearing off.

'Thanks for meeting with me, sir.'

'Of course,' he said, inhaling and rubbing one corner of his mouth.

Petra took out her pad, letting her jacket fall open so he could see the badge on her shirt pocket. Showing him the side of the pad with the blue LAPD stamp. Trying to study his reaction to those small bits of official presence.

He was looking somewhere else. At the big stone fireplace, cold and dark.

'Would you like something to drink, Detective?'

'No, thanks, sir.'

'If you change your mind, let me know.'

'Will do, Mr Ramsey.' She opened the pad. 'How's everything?'

'Rough. Very rough.'

Petra gave her best understanding smile. 'I noticed you have a different maid than when I was here the first time.'

'The other one walked out on me.'

'Estrella Flores?'

He stared at her. 'Yes.'

'How long had she been working for you?'

232

'Two years, I guess. Give or take. She said she wanted to go back to El Salvador but I know it was the – what happened to Lisa. She liked Lisa, I guess all the . . . when you people were here it must have upset her, because that night she was busy packing.' He shrugged. 'Then all the media calls. It's been hard keeping my head clear.'

'Have there been many calls?'

'Tons, all on the business line. The number I gave you was my private line. I had everything forwarded to Greg's office, he's not talking to anyone, so hopefully it'll taper off.' He rubbed his eyes, shook his head.

'So you got a new maid immediately,' said Petra.

'Greg got her.'

She sat there, not writing. Giving Ramsey some silence to fill, but he lowered his head. Wide shoulders rounding as he slumped, your classic grieving posture. Hand in chin, now. The Thinker.

'Estrella Flores liked Lisa,' she finally said, 'but she didn't go with Lisa when Lisa moved out.'

'Nope,' said Ramsey, looking up. 'Why's Estrella so important?'

'She probably isn't, sir. I'm trying to get a feel for Lisa's personality – was there something about her that would have stopped Estrella from going with her? Was she hard to work for?'

'Doubt it,' said Ramsey. 'It was probably the money. I paid her more than Lisa would've wanted to. Social Security, withholding, everything legal. Lisa had a small place, she wouldn't need someone that expensive.'

So Flores's nervousness that first day hadn't been immigration worries. And now she was gone . . .

Ramsey widened his legs a bit. 'No, Lisa wasn't hard to work for. She was bright, full of energy, had a great sense of humor. Sometimes she could get a little . . . sharp with people, but, no, I wouldn't call her hard to live with.'

'Sharp?'

'Sarcastic.'

Exactly what Kelly Sposito had said.

'Not in a mean way,' said Ramsey, 'just a bit of an . . . edge. Part of it was her sense of humor. She told a joke better than any woman I've ever—'

He stopped himself, pressed his legs close together. 'Guess that sounds sexist, but I haven't really known that many women who enjoyed telling jokes. I don't mean your Phyllis Dillers or your Carol Burnetts. Women who aren't pros.'

'And Lisa liked telling jokes.'

'When she was in the mood – you have no idea who killed her?'

'Not yet, sir. We're open to ideas.'

'It just doesn't make sense, Lisa hooking up with some maniac and going to Griffith Park. For the most part she went for older guys – conservative types, not the type to get . . . wild.'

'She went for older guys after your divorce?'

'I wouldn't know about that,' said Ramsey. 'But I do know that before we started dating she'd had two older boyfriends back in Cleveland. A dentist and a high-school principal.'

'How much older?'

'Ancient. Older than me,' he said, smiling. 'She made a crack about going out with me even though I was too young for her. At the time she was twenty-four and I was forty-seven.'

Making him fifty.

'What were the names of these other men?'

'I honestly can't recall – the principal was Pete something, I think the dentist was Hal. Or maybe Hank. She'd been dating Pete right before she met me, broke up with him the day of the pageant – that's where I met her, Miss Ohio Entertainment – I told you that, didn't I?'

Petra nodded.

'Going senile.' He tapped his head. 'One good thing about Alzheimer's, you get to meet new people every day.'

Thinking of her father, wasting away, Petra forced a smile. Onset at sixty, one of the earliest the doctors had seen. One of the quickest progressions, too. Kenneth Connor, dust at sixty-three . . .

'Are you OK?' said Ramsey.

'Pardon?'

'For a second you looked upset – was it the Alzheimer's joke? That was one of Lisa's – if it was too sick for your taste, I'm—'

'No, not at all, Mr Ramsey,' she said, appalled. What had he seen on her face? 'So Lisa liked jokes.'

'Yes – do you have any idea when there might be a funeral?'

'That would depend on the coroner, Mr Ramsey. And Lisa's family's wishes.'

'Are they coming out to LA?'

'I don't know, sir.'

'By the way, I ended up calling them myself, thought it should be me, not some . . . not a stranger. But all I got was a machine.'

'I got through to Dr Boehlinger.'

He frowned. 'Jack. He hates my guts, always did. Probably told you I was a terrible husband, you should be investigating me.'

Rope.

She waited.

'He's a tough guy but not a bad sort,' said Ramsey. 'Lisa marrying me really blew his mind.' He touched his mustache, tracing a vertical line through the center, stroking the left side, then the right, bisecting again.

'He didn't approve,' said Petra.

'He went crazy. Didn't come to the wedding – it was just a small civil thing at their country club – Jack's and Vivian's. Vivian came. And Lisa's brother, John – Jack Junior, he works for Mobil Oil in Saudi Arabia and he came. Not Jack Senior, though. He called me a week before, tried to talk me out of it, said I was robbing Lisa's youth, she deserved better – babies, a family, the whole nine yards.'

'You didn't want children?'

'I wouldn't have minded but Lisa didn't want them. I didn't tell him that, of course. But Lisa made that clear right from the outset. She was the least domesticated girl I've ever met, but Jack thought she should be some high-achieving house-wife. He's a very domineering guy. Surgeon, used to giving orders. He was tough on Lisa when she was growing up.'

'Tough in what way?'

'Perfectionistic – high standards. Lisa had to get straight A's, go out for every extra-curricular activity, excel in every-thing. She told me when she was twelve, Jack bought her a horse, so she had to learn jumping, dressage, compete whether or not she wanted to. Not the pageants, though. Those were Vivian's idea.'

'Sounds like a lot of pressure.'

'On all sides. Lisa said it was hell. That's probably why she married me.'

'What do you mean?'

'When we were together, Lisa could do whatever she wanted. Sometimes . . .' He waved a hand.

'Sometimes what, sir?'

Ramsey sat straighter. 'Sometimes I think I was too easy-going and she thought I didn't care. I don't want to tell you how to do your job but I can't say I see the point of all this . . . biography, Detective Connor. Lisa was murdered by some maniac and we're sitting here talking about her childhood.'

A topic you brought up. 'Sometimes it's hard to know what's relevant, sir.'

'Well,' he said. 'I just don't see the point.'

Petra drew an oval on her pad and placed a horizontal line two-thirds down. A few more penstrokes turned it into Ramsey's tailored mustache. She sketched in his blue eyes, tilted them downward a bit, made him look sad.

'Any other reason for Dr Boehlinger to hate you other than your being too old for Lisa?'

'I don't know,' he said. 'Jack and I never had any hassles, so I honestly don't know.'

'No problems at all?'

'None – why?'

'He mentioned something to me, Mr Ramsey. The incident—'

'That,' said Ramsey sharply, and now she saw something different in his eyes. Wary. Hardened. 'I figured we'd get around to it. Do you know why Lisa went public? In addition to hurting me?'

'Why, sir?'

'Money.'

'The show paid her?'

'Fifteen thousand. She called it adding insult to injury.'

'She must have been pretty mad at you.'

'Beyond mad – Lisa has Jack's temper.'

Present tense, again. On some level, she was still there with him.

'Tell me about the incident, Mr Ramsey.'

'You don't watch TV?'

'I'd like to know what really happened.'

His lower jaw slung forward and he clicked his teeth. 'What can I say? It was sleazy, tawdry, inexcusable, it still makes me sick. We'd been out to dinner, came home, had words – I don't even remember about what.'

Bet you do, thought Petra.

'It heated up, Lisa started shoving me, hitting me. With a closed hand. Not the first time, I put up with it because of the difference in our sizes. This time I didn't. There was no excuse. What can I say? I lost it.'

He looked at his fist, as if unable to believe it had ever caused damage.

Petra remembered the news clip. Lisa's black eye and split lip.

'It only happened once?'

'Once,' he said. 'One single, solitary time, that's it.' He shook his head. 'One stupid moment, you lose control and it's forever.'

As good a description as any of murder.

'I felt like crap, just like absolute filth, seeing her on the floor like that. I tried to help her up but she screamed at me

238

not to touch her. I tried to get her an icepack – she wouldn't have anything to do with me. So I went out to the pond and when I came back, her car was gone. She stayed away for four days. During that time she went to *Inside Story*. But she never told me about it, came back and acted as if everything was fine. Then, a few days later, we were eating dinner and she turned on the TV, and smiled. And there we were in the hot tub and she gives me this grin and says, "Insult to injury, Cart. Don't ever lay a fucking hand on me again."'

Ramsey studied the offending body part again, opened the palm. 'I never did – I'm going to get something to drink. Sure you don't want?'

'Positive.'

He was gone for several minutes, came back with a can of Diet Sprite. Popping the top, he sat back and drank.

Petra said, 'You just mentioned going out to a pond. I don't remember seeing one out back.'

'That's because it was our other house.' *Our*, not my. Another indication he hadn't severed all the ties. Nor had he lapsed into distancing language, the way murderers some-times do in the middle of their chronologies, starting with 'we' and switching to 'she' and 'I.' Petra'd read an FBI report claiming linguistic analysis could offer major clues. She wasn't convinced, but she was open-minded.

Ramsey drank more soda, looked genuinely miserable.

'Your other house?' said Petra.

'We have a weekend place up in Montecito. Actually, a bigger house than this, it's pretty nuts, maintenance-wise. There's a little pond there I used to find peaceful.'

'Used to?'

'Don't go there much anymore. That's the way it is with second houses – I've heard the same thing from other people.'

'They don't get utilized?'

He nodded. 'You think you're getting yourself some refuge and it just becomes another set of obligations – the place was too damn big in the first place. God knows this one is, too.'

'So you don't go up there much.'

'Last time had to be . . .' He looked at the ceiling, '. . . months ago.'

Suddenly his body jerked, an almost seizure-like movement that snapped his head down and brought his attention forward. His eyes met Petra's. Wet; he wiped them quickly.

'The last time Lisa and I were up there together,' he said, 'was *that* time. We never went back together. A few days after the show aired, she moved out again and I got served with papers. I thought everything was patched up.'

Petra kept the poignance at bay and thought: The DV episode had gone down in Montecito. She'd call Ron Banks and save him more searching.

Ramsey rested his chin in his hand again.

'OK,' she said. 'This is helpful. Now if you don't mind, let's talk about the night Lisa was murdered.'

27

MILDRED BOARD would have liked to scrub the kitchen floor.

Years ago, she'd accomplished the task every single day. A one-hour commitment, up to the elbows in soapy water, from six A.M. to seven. Excellent thinking time, no distraction from the slosh or the circular movements of cotton rags on yellow linoleum.

Once the arthritis set in, all that stooping and rubbing became unbearable and she was lucky if she was able to attend to the floor once a week.

The dining-room parquet required attention, as well. The wood was faded, buckling and cracked in spots, long past due for a refinish.

Every inch of wood visible; the dining room was empty, all the Missus's furniture shipped off to those Sotheby's people in New York.

Mildred felt an uncomfortable tightening around her eyes. She breathed in and straightened her back and said, 'One does one's best,' in a firm voice.

Firm and loud. No one to hear her. The Missus was upstairs. So many other rooms between them, all empty and closed off.

The kitchen, with its old cherrywood cabinets, industrial refrigerators and three ovens, was big enough for a hotel.

The pots and pans and cutlery remained, as did the Missus's favorite bone china set and a few sentimental silver pieces in the butler's pantry. And the magnificent linen press the Sotheby's people said they couldn't hope to sell. But the lovely things – the treasures the Missus and Him had acquired in Europe – were all gone. Brought in fine prices, they had, even after the auctioneer's premium and the taxes. Mildred had seen the check, known everything was going to be all right. For a while.

She and the Missus had never discussed the . . . financial situation. The Missus continued to pay her, insisting upon full salary, though Lord knew Mildred didn't deserve it, what use was she in this state?

Destructive thoughts. Banish, banish.

She spotted a water spot on the cabinet below the sink, found a rag, wiped it clean.

Back in the old days, the kitchen had been a bustling place, the Missus and Him entertaining constantly, caterers milling about, waiters rushing, pots steaming, stainless-steel counters blanketed with platters of savories and sweets. Not the least of the latter were Mildred's pies. No matter who the Missus hired for catering, she'd always craved Mildred's pies, most notably the plum, the Dorset apple, and the mixed berry. So had Him. So had . . . everyone.

Mildred had cooked and cleaned in the big house for forty-one years, two years after the Missus and Him moved in. The lodge at Lake Arrowhead, as well, but lakeside week-ends had only been an occasional thing, even when Him was alive, and often the Missus called in a cleaning service to remove the tarpaulins and clear the taps.

The lodge hadn't been used for over a decade. Not since the terrible weekend.

Mildred sighed and tamped her hair. Forty-one years, shining the silver, shampooing the wall-to-walls, cleaning nearly a hundred windows, even the leaded glass panels Him had acquired from a church in Italy. Oh, the Missus always provided another girl to help, but none of them ever managed to keep up.

For the first decade, her workmate had been Anna Joslyn, that dim, skinny girl from Ireland. Not quite focused, mentally speaking, but a good worker and strong as a brood mare. Then the big loud one from Denmark with the vulgar bosoms, that one hadn't worked out at all, what a mistake!

After the Dane, all the agency sent were Mexicans. Good workers most of them, and generally honest, though Mildred kept her eyes open. Some spoke English, some didn't. Either way it was their problem. Mildred refused to learn Spanish – English and French were quite enough, thank you. Miss Hammock's class at the orphanage had emphasized only English and French and eight decades of its graduates had worked in the finest homes of Britain and the continent.

The Mexicans weren't a horrid lot, but they seldom lasted very long. Rushing to some family crisis in Mexico, children, husbands, paramours, saint's days, who could keep score of all those Catholic assignations. Mildred would have preferred young ladies properly churched and educated, straight-backed girls who knew the difference between Royal Crown Derby and Chinese Export. But one accepted.

The problem, she knew, was that there were no more orphanages, all those babies cut from the womb or allowed to remain with unfit Welfare slatterns. One had only to read the paper.

No need anymore for Mexican girls. Or anyone else, for that matter.

Mildred was seventy-three and she wondered if she'd live long enough to witness the final collapse of everything rational and right.

Not that she expected to keel over any day soon. Except for the arthritis, she felt quite fine. But one never knew, look what had happened to the Missus. Such a beautiful woman, the most graceful woman Mildred had ever seen on either side of the ocean. Nothing but kind words ever left her lips, such patience, and Lord knew living with *Him* had often required patience.

Look at her now . . . thinking about it, Mildred's eyes felt weak.

The coffee pot whistled. Right on time. Mildred poured the Missus's coffee into a Victorian pitcher. Clumsy-looking piece, probably a gift from some dinner guest. The lovely pitcher – the Hester Bateman – was gone. George III, a banner year, proper hallmarks and all. Him had brought it back from one of his London trips, a first-class shop on Mount Street. Someone else might have relegated it to a display case. The Missus believed in using the fine things. It had been her breakfast pitcher.

Till four years ago.

Cartons of silver, paintings, even formal gowns, shipped off like . . . vegetables.

When she'd first been hired, Mildred had been afraid to touch any of the Missus's treasures, fearful of marring something. Even back then she could recognize quality.

The Missus, just a girl back then, but so wise, had put her at ease. *This is a home, dear, not a museum.*

And a fine home she'd made for Him.

Light wound its way through the branches of the ancient twisted sycamore on the breakfast patio, filtering through the kitchen window and settling on Mildred's recalcitrant hands.

Gnarled as badly as the tree. But the sycamore sprouted green every year. If only people merited autumn renewal . . .

Mildred shook her head and stared at the floor, in need of mopping. Such an expanse. Such a big room . . . not that the last girl had been any use. What was her name – Rosa? – Rosita. Three months on the job and fooling with one of the gardener's boys. Mildred had been forced to call the agency yet again.

Hello, Mr Sanche\?.

Hello, Miss Board. And what can I do for you today?

Cheerful he was, and why not? Another commission.

Mildred set up three interviews with 'ladies' then the Missus told her.

Do we really need someone else, Mildred? Just you and me, all we really use is the kitchen and our rooms.

Fighting to sound gay, but biting back tears. Mildred understood. She'd packed the silver and the paintings and the evening gowns.

So this is what it had come to. All those years, the Missus putting up with Him and look how he'd left her.

That temper of his. No doubt it had hastened his death. High blood pressure, the stroke, and Him only a young man. Leaving the Missus alone like that, poor dove, though he had provided for her in a financial way, one couldn't fault him there.

Or so Mildred had thought. Then, four years ago, the change.

Rooms purged and locked.

No more Mexican girls.

The gardening crew cut from every day to twice a week, then once. Then one skinny youth attempting to cover two acres with rapidly diminishing success. Gardens were like children, requiring a hawk-eye lest they go delinquent.

The Missus's garden, once a glory, had become a sad, shaggy thing, lawns spotted and burnt and incompletely mowed, untrimmed hedges swelling uncouthly, trees burdened with dead branches, flowerbeds whiskered with weeds, the fish pond drained.

Mildred tried her best but her hands defied her.

Did the Missus realize? She rarely ventured out anymore. Perhaps that was why. Not wanting to see.

Or perhaps she just didn't care. Not because of the . . . financial issue.

Because Mildred was forced to admit that the Missus had changed a long time ago.

The terrible weekend in Lake Arrowhead. Then Him. Tragedy upon tragedy. Not that the Missus had ever complained. Perhaps it would've been better if she had . . .

The German railway clock over the left-hand freezer chimed. Something else those nasal-voiced Sotheby's people had rejected. Not that Mildred could blame them, hideous, it was. And grossly inaccurate. Nine o'clock on its face meant eight fifty-three. In seven minutes, Mildred would be at the Missus's bedroom door knocking gently. Hearing 'Please come in, dear' from the other side of the molded mahogany. Entering, she'd set the tray on a bureau, prop the Missus while chattering encouragingly, fluff the mountain of pillows, fetch the wicker bed table, set it carefully over the Missus's quilt, and arrange the service precisely. Silver-plate toast rack filled with triangles of extra-thin wheat bread, browned lightly, the coffee, freshly ground African blend from that little shop on Huntington Boulevard, one needed *some* luxury, for heaven's sake! Decaffeinated now, but accompanied by real cream, thick enough to clot for the scones, what a job it was finding *that*! The golden marmalade that Mildred still made herself, using fine white cane sugar and the few sour oranges she managed to find out back in the orchard.

The sour orange tree was dying but it managed to produce a bit of lovely fruit. One thing California was good for was fruit. Mildred still loved to stroll the orchard and pick, pretending the ground wasn't hardpacked and lumpy, pretending the herbs were green and fresh, not the tangle of straw thatching the borders.

Pretending she was a girl back in England, out in the Yorkshire country. Shutting out the fact that on certain days – most days – one could hear the Pasadena freeway.

Fruit and weather. Those were the only things to recommend California. Despite living most of her life in San Marino, Mildred considered the place barbaric.

Horrid things in the newspaper. When she deemed them too horrid, she didn't bring the paper up with the Missus's breakfast.

The Missus never asked about it. The Missus never read much anymore, except for those romance paperbacks and art magazines.

The Missus never did much at all.

Nothing wrong with her, the doctors claimed, but what

did they know? The woman was sixty-six but had suffered centuries' worth of tragedy.

The railway clock said eight fifty-six and Mildred had only three minutes to cross the kitchen to the creaky rear elevator that rose up to the Missus's bedroom on the third floor.

She picked a fine yellow rose from the three without mildew on the thorny grandiflora bush out back. She'd snipped them at dawn, trimmed the stems and placed the flowers in sugar-water. Now she laid the blossom next to the covered platter of shirred eggs. The Missus rarely ate the eggs, but one tried.

Lifting the tray, she walked speedily, steadily.

The kitchen didn't look too awful, all things considered. 'Very good,' Mildred said, to no one in particular.

28

I SNEAK out of the park and go down Los Feliz, staying as far from the light as I can. No one walking up here, just cars whizzing by. Los Feliz ends and Western starts and now the junkies and prosties take over. I turn right on Franklin because it's darker, all apartment buildings, I don't want to be on the Boulevard.

Not too many people out tonight and the ones who are don't seem to notice me. Then I see a couple of Mexicans hanging around a corner, in the shadow of an old brick building. Probably doing a drug deal. I cross the street and they look at me but they don't say anything. A block later, a skinny prostie with spiky white hair and bright blue T-shirt and shorts comes out of an apartment carrying a tiny purse. She spots me and her eyes get wild and she says, 'Hey, boy,' in a drunk voice and wiggles her finger. She's short, just a kid, doesn't look that much older than me. 'Fuck and suck, thirty,' she says, and when I keep walking she says, 'Fuck you, faggot.'

For the next few blocks I don't see anyone, then another prostie, older, fatter, who pays no attention to me, just stands around smoking and watching cars. Then three tall black guys wearing baseball caps and baggy pants come out of the shadows, see me, look at each other. I hear them say something and I cross the street again, trying to seem relaxed. I hear laughter and footsteps and I look back and see one of them chasing me, almost reaching me. I speed up and run and he does, too. His legs are long and he's got his hand up, like to grab me. I run across the street and a car's coming and it has to move to the side not to hit me. The driver honks and yells, 'Fucking idiot!' and I'm still running but the black guy isn't.

I think I hear someone laughing. Probably a game for him. If I had a gun . . .

I walk for a long time. At Cahuenga, there's more light and the entrance to the Hollywood Bowl, a long curvy road that climbs up. I'm not going up there. Too much like the park, I don't want anything to do with parks.

So guess what comes next: Another park, Wattles Park, what a weird name. I've never seen it, never been this far. Not a friendly-looking place, high fences all around and gates with big chain locks and a sign saying the city owns it and it's closed at night, keep out. Through the fence all I can see is plants. It looks messy. Probably full of perverts.

Now Franklin ends, here's Hollywood Boulevard again, I can't avoid it; like it's chasing me, this big burst of noise and light, gas stations, cars, buses, fast-food places, worst of all people, and some of them look at me like I'm a meal. I cross La Brea, it gets quiet again, all apartments, some of them pretty nice-looking. I've never thought of the Boulevard as anything but stores and theaters and weirdos, but look at this, people live here in pretty nice places.

Maybe I should have traveled sooner.

The cut on my arm is dry and it doesn't hurt much. The ones on my face itch.

I'm breathing OK, though my chest still hurts. I'm hungry but three dollars isn't going to buy me much and I look for dumpsters to dive. Nothing. Not even a garbage can.

I walk a little bit more and turn off on a real quiet street. All houses, a nice dark street. But no cans here, either, or alleys. Cars are parked bumper to bumper and down a ways I see more light and noise, another Boulevard. I stop and look around. Some of the houses look OK, others are messy, with cars parked on the lawn.

Then I come to one with no car in the driveway or on the lawn. *Totally* dark. Old-looking, made of some kind of dark wood, with a slanted roof that hangs over a really wide porch. No fence, not even across the driveway. But the grass is cut, so someone lives here and maybe they keep their cans in the backyard.

The driveway is just cement with a strip of grass growing in the middle and I can't see what's at the end of it. I look around to make sure no one's watching and walk back there very slowly. As I pass the front porch, I see a big pile of mail in front of the door. All the windows are totally black. Looks like the people have been gone for a while.

No *Beware of Dog* sign, no barking from inside the house.

I keep going and finally make out what's at the end of the driveway. A garage with wooden doors. The yard is small for such a big house, just a little grass and a couple of trees, one of them gigantic but with no fruit.

The cans are out behind the garage, three of them, two metal, one plastic. Empty. Maybe the people don't live here anymore.

I turn around and am heading back to the street when I notice a dot of orange over the back door. A small bulb, so weak it only lights up the top half of the door. A screen door; behind the screen is glass. The screen's held in place by two loop-type things with hooks, and when you twist them it comes right off.

The glass behind the screen is really a bunch of windows – nine squares in a wooden frame. I touch one lightly and it shakes a little but nothing happens. I touch it harder, knock a few times. Still nothing. Same when I knock on the door.

Taking off my T-shirt, I wrap it around my hand and punch a lower square on the left side pretty hard. It just sits there but the second time I hit it, it comes loose and falls into the house and breaks.

Lots of noise now.

Nothing happens.

I reach in and feel around and find the doorknob. In the middle is a button and when I turn the knob it pops out with a click and the door opens.

Back on goes my T-shirt and I'm inside. It takes a few seconds for my eyes to see in the darkness. The room's some kind of laundry place with a washer-dryer, a box of Tide on top of the washer, some washrags. Next comes a kitchen that smells of bug spray, with lots of plants in pots all over the counters. I open the refrigerator and a light goes on inside and even though I see food, I shut it fast because the light makes me feel naked. As the door closes, I notice a peace-sign sticker and one that says *Sisterhood Is All*.

My heart is really beating fast. But a different kind of fear, not all bad.

I walk around, from dark room to dark room, nothing but a bunch of furniture. Then back to the kitchen. A closed door on the way turns out to be a bathroom, with more plants on the toilet tank. I turn the light on, then off. Clear my throat. Nothing happens.

This place is empty.

This is sort of fun.

I go back to the kitchen. The window over the sink is covered by curtains with flowers on them with little fuzzy balls hanging down. *Sisterhood*. Women live here, men wouldn't have all those plants.

OK, let's try the refrigerator again. On the top shelf are two cans of Barq's root beer and a gallon plastic orange-juice container with just a little juice left. Three gulps of juice. It tastes bitter. I put the root beer cans in my pocket. Next is a tub of Mazola margarine and a stick of Philadelphia cream cheese. I open the cream cheese and it's covered with blue-green mold. The margarine looks OK but I don't know what to do with it.

Below that is a container of strawberry yoghurt and three slices of American cheese, stiff and curly around the edges. No mold, I eat all three.

These people have definitely been gone for a long time.

On the bottom shelf are a package of Oscar Mayer low-fat bologna that's never been opened – I put it in my pocket, along with the root beer – and a whole pineapple with the green thing still attached on top and soft in a few places.

Leaving the refrigerator door open for light, I bring the pineapple to a counter and open drawers until I find forks and knives. In there with them are bobby pins and hair bands.

I take out the biggest knife and slice the pineapple in half. The soft spots turn out to be brown spots and they're spreading all over the pineapple like a disease. I cut around them, this is really a good knife, and manage to get some really nice, ripe pieces of delicious, super-sweet pineapple.

That makes me hungrier and I taste the bologna and end up eating every slice, standing at the counter. Then more pineapple, the juice runs all over my chin and my shirt and I feel it burn my face where the cuts are.

Then one of the root beers.

Now my stomach's killing me because it's full.

I go back to the bathroom right off the kitchen, take a leak, wash my hands and face. Then I notice the shower. On a shelf is soap and shampoo and cream rinse and something called De-Tangler.

Plenty of hot water. I add some cold, make it perfect, run it as hard as it goes. Locking the door, I pull off my clothes and step in. The water's like needles, hurting me but in a good way.

I take the longest shower I've ever had, no Mom waiting to get in and spend half the day there getting ready for Moron, no Moron wanting to sit on the toilet for an hour.

I just keep soaping and washing off, soaping and washing off. Making sure every part of me gets attention: My hair and under my nails, inside my nostrils, deep up my butt, I want to get every bit of crud out of me.

Then around front, under my balls.

I've got a hard-on.

That feels good.

I'm sitting there drying off, loving being clean and safe, thinking about far places, imaginary places, huge mountains – purple majesty, like the song, a silver ocean, surfer dudes, jet skis, girls in bikinis dancing the hula, dolphins, Jacques Cousteau, blue tangs, yellow tangs, moray eels, nautilus.

Then I hear sound and for a minute I think I've really spaced out, created a whole tropical-island movie with a soundtrack, then the voices get louder.

Women's voices. Then a bang – someone putting something down.

Light under the door. From the kitchen.

A scream.

A real scream.

RAMSEY SAID, 'I need a bite, do you mind if we go in the kitchen?'

Nerves making him hungry? Petra said, 'Not at all, Mr Ramsey.' Good chance to see more of the house.

She followed him as he switched lights on, illuminating terrible lithos, big furniture. Veering into exactly what Petra expected: Six hundred square feet of pseudo-adobe walls and rustic-beamed ceilings, white Euro-cabinets, gray granite counters, brushed-steel appliances, copper rack full of lethal weapons hanging from the beams. On the counters sat an array of food processors, toasters, microwaves. A green-house window provided a view of stucco wall. The eastern border of the house. A side door.

In the center of the kitchen was a long, narrow wooden table, old heart pine, scarred and buffed to a satin finish, the scars shiny dents. Probably a genuine antique, country French. Petra saw it as a monastery piece. Nice. But the eight chairs around it were chrome Breuer-types with rawhide leather slings, so discordant she wanted to scream. Whose idea of eclectic, his or Lisa's?

Ramsey opened the fridge on the left. Fully stocked. A bachelor who made himself at home. He took out another Diet Sprite and a carton of cottage cheese with chives.

'Gotta watch the tush,' he said, locating a spoon. 'Sure I can't get you anything? A drink, at least?'

'No, thanks.'

He sat down at the head of the pine table and she took a side-chair.

'This must look weird,' he said, lowering the spoon to the cheese. 'Eating. But I haven't eaten all day, could feel my blood sugar drop.'

'Hypoglycemic?'

'There's diabetes in my family, so I'm careful.' He began eating cottage cheese, wiping white flecks from his mustache. Not caring what he looked like in front of her. Maybe she'd been wrong about the Don Juan thing. Or maybe he turned it on and off. She watched him take a swallow of soda, two more spoonfuls of cheese, got his attention by taking out her pad.

'OK, that night,' he said. 'I told you I was in Tahoe, didn't I? The first time you were here.'

Petra nodded.

'Scouting locations for next season,' he went on. 'We've got a double script with some casino episodes, trying to figure out where we want to do it. We'll be shooting in a month or so.'

'Who was with you on the scouting trip?'

'Greg and our locations supervisor, Scott Merkin. We looked at some properties by the lake, visited a few of the casinos, had dinner at Harrah's, did some night-time inspection and flew home.'

'Commercial flight?'

He put the spoon down, drank some more. 'All these details. So I'm a suspect?'

257

No surprise in his voice. The unspoken final word to the sentence: *Finally*.

'It's just routine, Mr Ramsey.'

He smiled. 'Sure it is. I've said the exact same thing tons of times to suspects – in the show. "Just routine" means Dack Price is gonna go after the guy.'

Petra smiled. 'In real life, routine means routine, Mr Ramsey. But if this isn't a good time to talk—'

'No, this is fine.' The pale eyes locked in on Petra's. Ramsey ate more cottage cheese, raised the soda can to his lips, realized it was empty and fetched another.

'I guess it makes sense, my being a suspect. Because of the . . . incident. That was the slant the news put on it.'

Staring at her.

Rope. She could visualize it uncoiling, like a cobra.

'This whole thing,' said Ramsey. 'The way people are thinking about me after those news broadcasts. No, it wasn't a commercial flight; we went by private charter, we always do. Westward Charter, we use them all the time. Our usual pilot, too. Steve Marionfeldt, I like him cause he was a navy fighter pilot – real *Top Gun*. We flew out of Burbank, everything's recorded in Westward's log. Out around eight A.M., back by eight thirty P.M. Scott drove home and Greg brought me back here. He usually drives when it gets late because my night vision isn't all that great.'

'Eye problems?'

Though his mustache was clean, Ramsey wiped it again. 'Early stages of cataracts. My ophthalmologist wants to laser me but I keep putting it off.'

Telling her he couldn't have driven Lisa to the park at night?

'So you don't go out much at night?'

'I do, it's not that bad, lights just bother me.' He smiled. 'Don't give me a ticket, OK?'

Petra smiled back. 'Promise.'

He dug the spoon into the cottage cheese again, looked at it, put it down. Petra noticed looseness around his mouth. Mottling behind the ears and several fine lines that had to be tuck remnants. Gray hair sprouted from an ear. In the bright light of the kitchen, every wrinkle and vein was advertised.

His body starting to fail him. Blood sugar. The eyes.

The penis.

Appealing to her sense of sympathy? Hoping for female tenderness sarcastic Lisa hadn't offered?

'So Greg drove you home,' she said.

'We got here around nine fifteen, nine thirty, did some paperwork, then I just crashed. Next morning, Greg was up before me working out by the time I got to the gym – I've got a home gym. I did a little treadmill, showered, we had some breakfast here, decided to practice some putting then head over to the Agoura Oaks Country Club for eighteen holes. Then you showed up.'

Sorry to spoil your day, Herbert.

'OK,' said Petra. 'Anything else?'

'That's it,' said Ramsey. 'Who knew.'

She closed the pad and they hiked back to the front door.

'How're the cars?' she said, passing the glass wall.

'Haven't thought about them much.'

Petra stopped and peered through the black glass. Was the Mercedes parked in its allotted space? Without light, visibility was zero.

Ramsey flicked a switch. And there it was. A big sedan, gunmetal gray.

'Toys,' said Ramsey, turning off the light.

He walked her to the Ford and when she got behind the wheel, he said, 'Give my regards to Greg.'

Petra's turn to stare. He gave her a small, sad smile. An old man's smile.

'I know you'll be verifying the alibi,' he said. 'Just routine.'

30

FEELING GUILTY and useless but making sure to look calm and sharp, Stu tightened his tie and put on his suit jacket. Five hours of phone calls, no cases resembling Lisa Ramsey's. Or Ilse Eggermann's.

He didn't know what to make of the German girl's murder, wasn't getting any help from the Austrian police or Interpol or the airlines. Tomorrow he'd try US customs and passport control. Asking them what? To keep an eye out for Lauch? Good luck. He stared at the Viennese mugshot. A conspicuous-looking guy, but it was beyond needle-in-the-haystack.

Maybe Petra was having some luck with Ramsey.

Maybe not. It was hard to care . . . he cleared his desk and locked it, walked across the squad room. Wilson Fournier was on the phone but just as Stu passed, the black detective hung up scowling, and reached for his own jacket. Fournier's partner, Cal Baumlitz, was out, recuperating from knee surgery, and Fournier had been working alone all week and showing the strain.

'New call?' said Stu, forcing himself to be social.

'Poor excuse for one.' Fournier was average size and slim, had a shaved head and a bushy mustache that reminded

261

Stu of one of the actors he'd seen on *Sesame Street*, back when he'd worked nights, had mornings to spend with his kids.

Fournier hitched his holster and collected his gear, and the two of them walked out together. 'Life sucks, Ken. You and Barbie get Lisa Ramsey, celebrities up the ying, and I get an end-of-shift, maybe-prowler/rapist/burglar gig with stupid overtones.'

'You want Ramsey?'

Fournier laughed. 'Yeah, yeah, I know fame has its price.'

'What kind of a maybe-prowler/rapist?'

Fournier shook his head. 'The rapist thing is crap – scuse me, deacon, manure. We're supposed to be working Homicide, for God's sake, and on this one, no one got hurt, let alone dead, so why's it my business? Meanwhile I've got four open 187's and pressure from the boss. Goddamn brain-dead chief and his community policing manure.'

A few steps later, just to be polite, Stu said, 'What exactly happened, Wil?'

'House on North Gardner, two lesbians come home from a week in Big Sur, find someone's been in their kitchen, scarfed food, used the shower. They walk in on it – the shower's still going – freak, run screaming out the front door and the perp rabbits out the back.'

'What was burgled?'

'Food. Part of a pineapple, bologna, some soda. Big bad burglary, huh?'

'So where's the rape?'

'Exactly.' Fournier gave a disgusted look. 'Lesbians. A big pile of mail at the front door – gone an entire week, do

262

they think of putting a stop on it? Or leaving some lights on? Or getting an alarm or a Rottweiler or a poison snake or an AK-47 – man, Ken, what kind of folks still think they can count on us to do a damn thing about crime?'

31

ROUTINE. AM I a suspect?

Was he playing with her?

She called Stu at the station. He'd checked out an hour ago and when she tried his house she got no answer. Out with Kathy and the kids? Must be nice to have a life.

Back in LA, she bought some salads at a mom-and-pop grocery on Fairfax, ate them at home while watching the news – no Ramsey info. She tried Stu again just before ten. Still no answer.

Time to simulate a life for herself.

Changing into acrylic-spattered sweats, she put on Mozart and squeezed paint onto her palette. Hunched on a stool, she worked till midnight. First the landscape, which was responding a bit; she felt in the groove, that hypnotic time contraction. Then another canvas, larger, blank and inviting. She laid on two coats of white primer followed by a luxuriant layer of Mars black, and when that dried, began a series of hastily brushed-in gray ovals that became faces.

No composition, just faces, scores of them, some overlapping, like fruit dangling from an invisible tree. Some with mouths parted innocently, all with pupil-less black eyes that could have been empty sockets, ghostly discs, each one portraying a variant of confusion.

Each face younger than the last, a reverse aging, until she was painting nothing but children.

Perplexed children, growing on an invisible child tree . . . her hand cramped and she dropped the brush. Rather than get psychological about that, she laughed out loud, switched off the music, snatched the canvas off the easel and placed it on the floor, face to the wall. Stripping naked and tossing her clothes on the floor, she took a long shower and got into bed. The moment the lights were off, she was playing back the interview with Ramsey.

Almost positive the guy was manipulating.

Not knowing what to do about it.

She woke up Wednesday morning still thinking about it. The way he'd flicked on the garage light, showing her the Mercedes, as if daring her to probe further. All those sympathy ploys – blood sugar, cataracts. Not much night driving.

Poor old guy, falling apart. But there was one health problem he'd never bring up.

One that could motivate some serious rage.

And still no lawyer, at least not out in the open. Some kind of bluff? Ask the wrong question and in come the mouthpieces?

Or was he just feeling confident, because he had the perfect alibi.

Don't get sucked into it, no frontal assault. Go for the flanks. The underlings. Find Estrella Flores, have a chat with the charter pilot, though that wouldn't prove anything, there'd been plenty of time to get home, leave, pick up Lisa, kill her. Last but not least, Greg Balch, faithful lackey and likely perjurer. Petra was certain

Ramsey had phoned the business manager the minute she drove off, but sometimes underlings harbored deep resentment – Petra remembered the way Ramsey had turned on Balch during the notification call. Balch standing there and taking it. Used to being a whipping boy? Put a little pressure on, ignite some long-buried anger, and sometimes the little people turned.

She reached her desk at 8 A.M, found a note from Stu saying he'd be in late, probably the afternoon.

No reason given.

She felt her face go hot, crumpled the note and tossed it.

The flight manager at Westward Charter confirmed Ramsey and Balch's Tahoe trip and the 8.30 P.M. Burbank arrival. Steve Marionfeldt, the pilot, happened to be in and she spoke to him. Pleasant, mellow, he'd done tons of trips with *The Adjustor*, no problems, nothing different this time. Petra didn't want to ask too many questions for fear of making Ramsey prime suspect. Even though he was. She could imagine some defense attorney using Marionfeldt's testimony to illustrate Ramsey's normal mood that day. If it ever got to a trial – dream on.

A phone call to Social Security verified that Estrella Flores was indeed legal, her only registered address Ramsey's Calabasas house.

'So any checks would go there?' she asked a put-upon SSA worker.

'She hasn't filed for benefits, so there are no checks going out.'

'If you get a change of address would you please let me know, Mr . . .'

'Vicks. If it comes to my attention I'll try, but we don't

work with individual petitions unless there's a specific problem—'

'I've got a specific problem, Mr Vicks.'

'I'm sure you do – all right, let me tag this, but I have to tell you things get lost, so you're best off checking in with us from time to time.'

She called Players Management. No one answered, no machine. Maybe Balch was on his way up the coast to Montecito. Taking some down-time to obliterate evidence at the boss's request.

Next came the Merrill Lynch broker. Morad Ghadoomian had a pleasant, unaccented voice, sounded prepared for the call.

'Poor Ms Boehlinger. I suppose you want to know if she had any financial entanglements. Unfortunately, she didn't.'

'Unfortunately?'

'No entanglements,' he said, 'because there was nothing to tangle.'

'No money in the account?'

'Nothing substantial.'

'Could you be a little more specific, sir?'

'I wish I could – suffice it to say I was led to expect things that never materialized.'

'She told you she'd be investing large sums of money but didn't?'

'Well . . . I'm really not sure what the rules are here in terms of disclosure. Neither is my boss, we've never dealt with a murder before. We do get deceased clients all the time, estate lawyers, IRS reporting, but this . . . suffice it to say Ms Boehlinger only came by my office once and that was to fill out forms and seed the account.'

'How much seed did she sow?' said Petra.

'Well . . . I don't want to step out of line, here . . . suffice it to say it was minimal.'

Petra waited.

'A thousand dollars,' said Ghadoomian. 'Just to get things going.'

'In stock?'

The broker chuckled. 'Ms Boehlinger's plans were to build up a sizeable securities account. Her timing couldn't have been better, I'm sure you know how well the market's been doing. But she never followed through with instructions and the thousand remained in a money market fund earning four percent.'

'How much did she say she was going to invest?'

'She never said, she just implied. My impression was that it would be substantial.'

'Six figures?'

'She talked about achieving financial independence.'

'Who referred her to you?'

'Hmm . . . I believe she just called on her own. Yes, I'm sure of it. A reverse cold call.' He chuckled again.

'But she never followed through.'

'Never. I did try to reach her. Suffice it to say, I was disappointed.'

Financial independence – Lisa expecting a windfall? Or just deciding to get serious as she approached thirty by banking Ramsey's monthly support check and living off her editor's salary. A surplus of eighty grand a year could add up.

A reduction in the eighty would have upset Lisa's investment plans.

Had Ramsey balked, after Lisa got a job, threatened to take her back to court, and was that why she hadn't followed through?

Or was it something simple – she'd chosen another broker?

Not likely. Why would she have left the thousand sitting there with Ghadoomian?

Was money another issue between the Ramseys?

Money and thwarted passion, no better setup for murder.

She spent an hour on the phone talking to civil servants at the Hall of Records, finally located the original Ramsey divorce papers. The final decree had been granted a little over five months ago. No obvious complications, no petitions to alter support, so if Ramsey had balked he hadn't made it official.

Then a message came through to call ID Division at Parker Center, no name.

The civilian clerk there said, 'I'll put you through to Officer Portwine.'

She knew the name but not the face. Portwine was one of the prints specialists, she'd seen his signature on reports.

He had a reedy voice and a humorless, rapid delivery. 'Thanks for calling back. This could be either a major-league screw-up or something interesting, hope you can tell me which.'

'What's wrong?' said Petra.

'You sent us some material from the Lisa Boehlinger Ramsey crime scene – food wrapper and a book. We obtained numerous prints, most likely female from the size, but no match in any of our files. I was just about to write you a report to that effect when I got another batch supposedly from another case. Burglary on North Gardner, latents from a kitchen knife and some food containers. I had a spare minute so I looked at them and they matched yours. So what I need to know is was there some kind of mix-up in the batch numbers, the forms getting screwed up? Because it's bizarre, two batches coming from Hollywood, one after the other, and we get the exact same prints. We caught hell about our cataloguing last year. Even though we're careful, you know how much stuff we process. We've been bending over backwards, meaning if there is a problem on this one, it's on your end, not ours.'

How could a guy talk so fast? Enduring the speech, Petra had dug her nails into her palm.

'When was the burglary?' she said.

'Last night. A Six car handled it and referred it to one of your D's – W.B. Fournier.'

Petra looked over at Wil's desk. Gone and checked out.

'What kind of food containers were printed?'

'Plastic orange-juice jug, the prints were on the paper label. And a pineapple – that was interesting, never printed a pineapple before. There're some other samples supposedly coming, says here a Krazy Glue tape from stainless-steel plumbing fixtures, and a bottle of shampoo, also tape from . . . looks like a refrigerator, yes, a refrigerator. Sounds like a kitchen burglary. So what's the story?'

'I don't know a thing about the burglary, all we sent you from Ramsey were the food wrapper and the book and the victim's clothing.'

'You're telling me this other material isn't yours?'

'That's exactly what I'm telling you,' said Petra.

Portwine whistled. 'Two sets of prints from the same person, two different crime scenes.'

'Looks that way,' said Petra. Her heart was racing. 'Do you still have the Ramsey batch – specifically the book?'

'Nope, sent it down to Evidence yesterday at five P.M., but I did keep a copy of the prints. Some pretty distinctive ridges, that's how I noticed the match.'

'OK, thanks.'

'Welcome,' said Portwine, grudgingly. 'At least we don't have a problem.'

She left Wil Fournier a note to get in touch. Still no message from Stu and he didn't pick up his cell phone.

After driving downtown to Parker Center, she smiled her way into the employee parking lot and went up to the third floor Evidence Room, where she filled out a requisition for the library book. The evidence warden was a dyed-blond black woman named Sipes, unimpressed by the fact that the victim was L. Boehlinger Ramsey and pointing out to Petra that she hadn't written in the case number clearly. Petra erased and rewrote and Sipes disappeared behind endless rows of beige metal shelving, returning ten minutes later shaking her head. 'That lot number hasn't been checked in.'

'I'm sure it has,' said Petra. 'Last night. Officer Portwine from ID sent it over yesterday at five P.M.'

'Yesterday? Why didn't you say so? That would be in a different place.'

Another fifteen minutes passed before Petra had the evidence envelope in her hand and Sipes's permission to take it.

Back in the Ford, she removed the book. *Our Presidents: The March of American History*.

Bag lady with an interest in government and burglary. Breaking into homes stealing food? Most likely schizo. She flipped pages, looking for notes in the margin, some over-looked bit of scrap. Nothing. Remarkably, the checkout card was still in the circulation pocket.

The Hillhurst branch. She remembered that. No activity for nine months.

No activity since Bag Lady had lifted it?

Petra tried to imagine her, living on the street, thieving, reading. Stealing food and knowledge. There was a certain crazy romanticism to that.

Squatting to pee on a rock. Schizo Girl-Thoreau.

She drove back to Hollywood, found the Hillhurst branch in a strip mall a few blocks south of Los Feliz. Strange setup, not what Petra thought of as a library. Windowless slab, pure government graythink, right next to a supermarket. Loose shopping carts nearly blocked the front door. A sign said it was a temporary location.

She went in carrying the evidence packet and her busi-ness card. The place was one big room, a gray-haired female librarian at a desk in the corner, talking on the phone, a younger woman at the check-out desk, one patron: A very old guy in a cloth cap reading the morning paper, a furled umbrella on the table near his elbow, though the June sky was baby-blue and rain hadn't fallen in months.

Natural birch bookshelves on rollers, reading tables of the same pale wood. Travel posters trying to take the place of windows, what a pathetic bit of pretense.

The older librarian was engrossed in her phone-chat and

Petra headed for check-out. The young woman was Hispanic, tall, well dressed in a budget gray rayon suit that looked better than it deserved, draped over her slinky form. She had a pleasant face, warm eyes, decent skin, but what caught Petra's attention was her hair – black, thick, straight, hanging below the hem of her mini-skirt. Like that country singer – Crystal Gayle.

'May I help you?'

Petra introduced herself and showed the card.

'Magda Solis,' said the woman, clearly thrown by the Homicide designation.

Petra slipped the red book out and placed it on the counter. Magda Solis's right hand flew to her left bosom. 'Oh no, has something happened to him?'

'Him?'

'The little boy who . . .' Solis looked over at the gray-haired librarian.

'The boy who stole it?' said Petra. Small body impression, small hands, not a woman, a kid – why hadn't she thought of it? Suddenly she thought of the painting she'd begun last night, the tree full of lost children, and fought the shudder that began at her shoulders and snaked its way down to her navel.

Solis scratched her chin. 'Can we talk outside?'

'Sure.'

Solis hurried over to the older woman with a slightly flat-footed gait that managed to be graceful, arms bent tensely, glorious hair flapping. She said something that made the boss librarian frown and returned, gnawing her lip.

'OK, I'm on break.'

*   *   *

273

Out in the strip mall, near Petra's Ford, she said, 'I'm a trainee, didn't want my supervisor to hear. Did something happen to him?'

'Why don't you tell me what you know, Ms Solis?'

'I – he's just a little boy, maybe ten or eleven, at first I wasn't even sure it was him. Taking the books, I mean. But he was the only one who ever read the ones that were missing – this one especially he kept coming to, over and over, and then it was gone.'

'So he took other books, too.'

Solis fidgeted. 'But he always brought them back – such a serious little boy. Pretending to be doing homework, I guess he didn't want to attract attention. I finally saw him do it – sneak something back. One that I'd marked missing. Something about oceanography, I think.'

'Pretending to do homework?'

'That's what it looked like to me. Always the same few pages of math problems – he always did math. Algebra. So maybe he's older. Or just gifted – from the things he read, I'll bet he was gifted.' Solis shook her head. 'He'd do a little math and then head back to the stacks, find something, read for a couple of hours. It was obvious he just loved to read and that's so rare, we're always trying to attract kids and it's a struggle. Even when they do come in they goof around and make noise. He wasn't like that. So well-behaved, a little gentleman.'

'Except for stealing books.'

Solis worried her lip again. 'Yes. Well, I know I should have said something but he returned them, no harm done.'

'Why didn't you suggest he get a library card?'

'For that he'd need ID and an adult's signature and he

was obviously a street kid. I could tell from his clothes – he tried to look nice, damped down his hair and combed it, but his clothes were old and wrinkled, had holes in them, so did his shoes. And he wore the same couple of things over and over again. His hair was long, hanging over his forehead, looked like it hadn't been cut in a long time.' Reaching back, she touched her own locks and smiled. 'I guess we were kindred spirits – please tell me, Detective, has something *happened* to him?'

'He may have been a witness to something. What else can you tell me about him?'

'Small, skinny – Anglo, kind of a pointy chin. Pale complexion, like he's anemic or something. His hair is light brown. Straight. I'm not sure about his eyes. Blue, I think. Sometimes he walks with good posture but other times he hunches over. Like a little old man – he has an old look to him. I'm sure you've seen that on street kids.'

'Did you ever speak to him?'

'One time, in the beginning, I came over to him and asked if there was anything I could help him with. He shook his head and looked down at the table. Got a scared look in his eyes. I left him alone.'

'A street kid.'

'Last year in college I did some volunteer work at a shelter and he reminded me of the kids I saw there. Not that they were into books – the things he read! Biographies, natural history, government – the Presidents, this one, was his favorite. I mean here was a kid society had obviously failed and he still believed in the system. Don't you think that's remarkable? He *must* be gifted. I couldn't turn him in – does my supervisor need to know?'

Petra smiled and shook her head.

Magda Solis said, 'I figured the best way I could help him was let him use the library the way he wanted. He returned everything. Except the Presidents book — where did you find it?'

'Nearby,' said Petra, and Solis didn't press her.

'How long has he been coming to the library?'

'Two, three months.'

'Every week?'

'Two to three times a week. Always in the afternoon. He'd arrive around two P.M., stay till four or five. I wondered if he chose afternoons because most kids are off from school then and he'd be less conspicuous.'

'Good thinking,' said Petra.

The librarian blushed. 'I could be all wrong about him. Maybe he's a rich kid from Los Feliz, just likes to act weird.'

'When's the last time you saw him, Ms Solis?'

'Let's see . . . a few days ago — last week, must have been last Friday. Yes, Friday. He read a big pile of *National Geographics* and *Smithsonians*, didn't take anything.'

Last weekday before Lisa's murder. He hadn't returned since.

A kid. Living in the park. Reading in the dark — how? By penlight? Part of a street kid's survival stash?

From the Griffith Park lot to the North Gardner burglary was a good four, five miles. Traveling west — why? This was a kid who'd settled down, set up a routine, not a wanderer.

Scared? Because he'd seen something?

'I don't want to put him in danger,' said the librarian.

'On the contrary, Ms Solis. If I find him, I can make sure

276

he's kept *out* of danger.' Solis nodded, wanting to believe. The woman had bruised eyes. *Kindred spirit* – had she meant something beyond untrimmed hair?

'Thanks for your help,' said Petra.

'You're sure he's not . . . hurt?'

He was OK last night. Breaking into a house and cutting pineapple. 'He's fine, but I do need to locate him. Maybe you can help me with that.'

'I've told you everything I know.'

Petra took out her pad and a number three pencil. 'I draw a little. Let's see if we can come up with something.'

32

'*RAPIST! POLICE!*'

Why are they screaming that? I throw on my clothes. The screams get far away, I crack open the door, look out, see nothing and run out the back.

It sounds like they're out in front, still screaming 'Rapist!,' which is crazy. I'd never rape anyone, I know what it feels like to be hunted.

I run behind the garage, climb over the wooden fence into the next yard. Lights on in that house – colors, a TV behind the curtains, I hear someone laughing.

I run through the yard to the next street, then back up to Hollywood Boulevard where I turn down another street, then up again, moving back and forth so no one will see me, walking, not running, blend in, blend in . . . no sirens. The cops haven't come yet.

If those women keep lying about rape they might send up helicopters with those big white beams. That could turn me into a bug on paper . . . then I realize they never saw me, why should anyone think I'm the one?

I slow down even more, pretend everything's great. I'm on another quiet street. People locked inside thinking they're safe.

Or maybe worried they're not.

I'll keep going west, away from the park and Hollywood, stupid women with plants all over the place who leave food to rot.

The next busy street is Sunset. Weirdos, lots more kids than Hollywood, even more cars. Lots of restaurants, clubs. Across the street is a place called Body Body Body! with a plastic sign of a naked lady. Then something called The Snake Club with a big line out in front and two big fat guys not letting anyone in.

Is that guy in the red car looking at me weird?

I turn off to the next quiet street, back and forth again, now my feet are hurting, I've been walking all day. West, maybe the beach, the beach is clean, isn't it?

I have no money. No way to protect myself.

Should have taken the pineapple knife.

33

STU STUDIED the drawing of the boy.

He'd blown in just before four P.M., no explanation. Petra burned to have it out with him, but this new development, a potential witness, meant they had to stay on task.

'Good work,' he said. 'Don't show Harold.'

Harold Beatty was a sixty-year-old Rampart narc who sometimes doubled as a sketch artist. All the faces he drew looked exactly the same. The Beatty Family, other D's called them behind his back.

Stu played with his suspenders and the casual gesture angered Petra further. She wanted acknowledgment that this could be something.

Because she wasn't confident it would lead anywhere.

At least the drawing was good. Guiding Magda Solis through every feature, Petra had produced a highly detailed, carefully shaded rendering. The librarian stared at the finished product and whispered, 'Amazing.'

A nice-looking boy with big, wide-set eyes – Petra left them medium-shaded to accommodate either brown or blue – a narrow nose with pinched nostrils, thin mouth, pointy chin with a dimple. Solis wasn't sure of the boy's eye color, but she was sure of the dimple.

Straight hair, light brown, thick, brushed to the right,

sheathing the forehead to the eyebrows, hanging over the ears, fringing wildly at the shoulders. A skinny neck sprouted from a T-shirt. Solis said he was small, well under five feet, eighty-eight pounds tops, wore T-shirts, jeans, tennis shoes with holes in them, sometimes an old ratty sweater.

Oh yeah, and a watch, one of those cheap digital things.

That interested Petra. Was the timepiece an old Christmas present? Something he'd boosted? Where was his home? How long ago had he run away?

A kid. When she applied for detective, she'd been offered the choice of Juvey or Auto Theft, had chosen hot cars. No one asking why . . .

Stu said, 'He looks grim,' and that was true. The boy's expression was beyond hurt, he looked burdened. Solis's phrase was 'crushed by life.'

'He takes food from the fridge, showers,' said Stu. 'Print match to ours. Unbelievable.'

'Maybe it's Providence,' said Petra. 'Maybe God's rewarding you for all that piety and church time.'

'Sure,' said Stu. His voice rasped. She'd never heard him this angry.

What was the big deal? She always kidded him about religion. Before she could say a thing, he stood and buttoned his jacket. 'OK, let's go tell Schoelkopf.'

Turning his back on her, yet again. Since he'd waltzed into the squad room, they hadn't shared a second of eye contact.

'Let's do it later,' said Petra. 'I've got paperwork.'

He wheeled suddenly. 'What's your problem with doing it by the book, Petra? He made it clear he wanted to be informed and now there's something to inform him about.'

He'd made it to the door when Petra caught up with him and stage-whispered, 'What the hell's going on?'

'Nothing's going on. We're going to inform Schoelkopf.'

'Not that. What's with *you*?'

He kept going, didn't answer.

'Goddamn you, Bishop, you're acting like a complete goddamn jerk!'

He stopped, worked his jaws. His hands were fisted. Never had she cursed at him. She prepared herself for an explosion. This would be interesting.

Instead his face slackened. 'God*damn* me? You could be right.'

In Schoelkopf's office, they both clung to frozen calm.

The captain glanced at the drawing and put it down. 'You did this, Barbie? Hidden talent . . . maybe we should retire Harold.'

He sat back and put his feet on his desk. New shoes, Italian, the soles still black. 'It ain't fish and loaves, but maybe it's half of something.' He ripped the drawing out of Petra's pad. 'Talk to Juvey officers, see if anyone knows this kid. Also shelters, church groups, welfare workers, whoever's dealing with runaways nowadays. I'll make copies for PI.'

'Public Information? You're going to the press with it?' said Petra.

'You've got a better way of publicizing it?'

'Are we sure we want to publicize it right away?'

'Why the hell not?'

'When we first found the book, you thought it was weak – pointed out the unlikelihood of anyone reading in the dark. So what's the chance the boy actually saw anything? But if we let the world know what he looks like and he's a Hollywood street kid, we could set off a hunting frenzy. Also, if the killer knows Hollywood, he could get to him first—'

'I don't believe this,' said Schoelkopf. 'Maternal instincts.' The feet returned to the floor. He looked ready to spit. 'You want to solve a crime or mother some runaway?'

A sickle of rage cut through Petra. A serene voice that couldn't possibly be hers said, 'I want to be cautious, sir. All the more so if he is a witness—'

Schoelkopf waved her silent. 'You talk about "the killer" like it's an abstraction. We're dealing with Ram-fucking-sey. You're telling me *he's* gonna find a runaway before we do? Gimme a break. Tell you what, Barb, if you're worried about child welfare, keep an eye on Ramsey – that might even work out to our benefit, he goes after the kid, we nab him, just like on TV.' Schoelkopf's laugh was metallic. 'Yeah, that's definitely part of your assignment. Surveil Ramsey. Who knows, you could be a hero.'

Petra's lungs felt wooden. She tried to breathe, tried not to show the effort.

'So we're using the boy as bait,' said Stu, and now Petra heard the father of six speaking.

'You, too?' said Schoelkopf. 'We're tracking down a potential witness to a homicide – Jesus, I can't believe I'm having this discussion. What the fuck have we talked about since the beginning of this case? Being careful. What the fuck do you think will happen if the kid *is* righteous and we make no effort to find him? Don't waste any more of my time. You two produced the lead, now develop it!'

'Fine,' said Stu, 'but if Petra spends her time on surveillance, our manpower on the rest of the case—'

'Doesn't sound like too much else is going on with the case—'

'Actually, there is something. Those similars you told us to look for.' Stu told him about Ilse Eggermann, the search for Karlheinz Lauch.

Schoelkopf hid his surprise with a satisfied smile. 'So . . . there you go. OK, you need more manpower – scuse me, *person*power – tell Fournier he's on it, too. The kid's already his anyway, big bad burglar. The three of you do some real work. At the very least we'll keep the streets safe from refrigerator bandits.'

Fournier said, 'What do I do with my other 187's?'

'Ask *him*,' said Stu. 'You were the one complaining about no glory. Here's your chance.'

'Yeah, I'm the Pineapple Protector – OK, how do we divide it?'

Petra said, 'I'm supposed to keep an eye on Ramsey. I've already interviewed him so re-contacts are reasonable. But hell if I'm going to sit outside the gates at RanchHaven all day.'

Fournier said, 'Don't blame you.' He palmed his shaven head.

She knew him casually, had nothing against him. Stu said he was bright. Hope so, she needed to educate him quickly.

She began. Fournier took notes. Stu was looking distracted, again.

The final arrangement was Petra would follow up on Estrella Flores and Greg Balch, maybe take another shot at Ramsey, Stu would stay with the Eggermann case, and Fournier would contact Hollywood Juvey, local shelters and crashpads, try to find the boy.

Before the last word was out of Petra's mouth, Stu got up and walked away.

Fournier said, 'He all right?'

'Just a little tired,' said Petra. 'Too much fun.'

Back at her desk, she called Missing Persons at every LAPD substation, found several Floreses but no Estrella. She copied down the two who were similar in age, Imelda, sixty-three, from East LA and Doris, fifty-nine, from Mar Vista, phoned their families, came up negative.

Same for the Sheriffs' bureaus. What now? Had Flores bolted back to the Old Country? Where was that? Mexico? El Salvador? Then she remembered something Ramsey had told her. Greg Balch had hired the new maid, so maybe he'd found Flores, too.

Another reason to chat with ol' Greg.

But first she owed a call to Ron Banks, to let him know the Ramsey DV had gone down out of LA County.

He was at his desk, said, 'Oh, hi! Haven't gotten back to you because I haven't found any complaints yet.'

'You won't,' she said. 'I just found out Ramsey has a second home in Montecito, Ron. The beating happened there.' Something else she hadn't done yet, follow up on that . . .

'Oh, OK,' said Banks. 'That's Carpenteria Sheriffs.' He cleared his throat. 'Listen, about last time. Asking you out. I didn't mean to put you on the spot. The last thing you need is distraction—'

'It's OK, Ron.'

'That's nice of you to say, but—'

'It's fine, Ron. Really.'

'It was unprofessional. My excuse is I've only been divorced a year, not really good at this kind of thing, and—'

'Let's get together,' she said, scarcely believing it.

Silence. 'You're sure – I mean . . . great, I appreciate it – you name it.'

'How about tonight – where do you live?'

'Granada Hills but I'll be coming from Downtown, so it doesn't matter.'

'Do you like deli food?'

'I like anything.'

'How about Katz's on Fairfax? Say eight.'

'Fantastic.' He almost sang the word.

She could do that to someone!

34

A SKY full of stars. The ocean roars louder than the zoo animals.

I'm at the beach, under the pier, smelling tar and salt, cold, even wrapped in the black plastic sheet.

Wet sand all around, but I found a dry patch near these big, thick poles that hold up the pier. I can't sleep, watching and listening to the waves come in and out, but I don't feel tired. The ocean is black as the sheet, little dots of moonlight drawing a slanted line across the water. It's cold, much colder than in the park. If I stay here I'll need to get a real blanket.

A while ago some bent-over guy walked by on the sand, near the edge of the water. Just one guy on the empty beach and the way he walked, clapping his hands together, jumping up and down every few seconds, I knew he was crazy.

When the sun comes out I'll have to leave.

Two nights ago I saw PLYR kill that woman and now I'm here. Weird. And I didn't even try, it just happened.

I was weaving between Sunset and side streets, passing so many restaurants my nose was stuffed with food smells, guys in red jackets parking cars, people laughing. My stomach was still full but my mouth started watering.

I had no idea where I was going to end up, just knew

I couldn't stand still. I came to a part of Sunset that looked fancier – shinier people, huge billboards advertising movies and clothes and liquor. Then more clubs, more big fat guys standing in front of the door, arms folded over their chests.

The club where it happened was called A-Void, on a dark corner next to a liquor store, painted black with all these black rocks glued to the front. The fat guy there smoked and looked bored. No one was trying to get in. A plastic sign over the door advertised the bands who were playing: Meat Members, Elvis Orgasm, the Stick Figures.

The liquor store was open and a guy in a turban was sitting behind the register. I thought about buying some gum, taking other stuff, but he looked suspicious at me when I stepped through the door so I left. Just then, this tall skinny guy with really long fuzzy black hair and pimples came out of A-Void carrying some drums, ran over to a black van parked around the corner, opened the back door and put the drums in. The van was full of dents and scrapes, stickers all over the side. He didn't lock it.

He made two more trips and then he went back inside and stayed there.

He never locked it.

The fat guy had gone inside, too.

I slid around the corner, looked in the van's passenger window. It had only front seats, the rest was storage.

I opened the door. No alarm rang.

All I found on the driver's seat was junk – candy wrappers, empty cans and bottles, pieces of paper. Maybe the radio, if I could sell it – how do you take one out?

Then I heard voices and saw the skinny guy standing on the corner, his back to the van. Talking to a short girl with yellow hair with a pink streak through the middle of it. She might've seen the van if she looked at it but she was paying attention to him. It looked like they were arguing. He turned.

Too late to jump out.

I jumped in, closed the door, threw myself in back and hid behind the drums. They were half-covered by this thick sheet of black plastic and I got under it, knocking my bones against metal, it really hurt, I had to bite my lip not to cry out.

The plastic was cold and smelled like bleach.

The back door opened again and the van shook as something landed near me.

Slam. Another slam.

I heard the girl's voice from up front. 'You guys were hot.'

'Bullshit.'

'No really, I mean it, Wim.'

'We sucked and everyone knows we sucked so don't bullshit me – did you bring my jacket?'

'Uh . . . sorry, I'll go back and get it.'

'Shit! Get in there fast!'

Another open and slam.

Cough. 'Fucking witch . . .' The motor went on and the metal floor beneath me started to vibrate and I tried to hold on to something so I wouldn't roll but the drums were round and I didn't want to make noise so I pressed against the floor like a spider.

The radio went on, he tried a bunch of different channels, said 'Fuck this shit!,' turned it off.

A rubbing sound, then a click, and I smelled something familiar.

Weed. Back in the trailer I went to sleep with my nose full of it, wondering if it would give me brain damage.

Slam. 'Here you go, honey.'

'Do you know what that is? Lambskin from fucking Mongolia or Tibet or some place. And those nailheads are like hammered by hand and put in by blind peasants who say special prayers or something – I gave my fucking blood for that and you leave it in there! Shit!'

'I'm sorry, Wim!'

They both smoked. No one talked. The motor was running, and I was just pressing my fingers to the floor, trying not to move or breathe, wondering where this was going to take me. No way out because the drums blocked the back door.

At least it was warm.

She said, 'Gimme another taste – ah, that's good shit.'

'Hey, don't give it a blowjob – give it back.'

'Where you wanna go, Wim?'

'Where? Europe – where the fuck do you think? Home, I need to crash.'

'You don't wanna go over to the Whiskey?'

'Fuck no, why would I wanna do that?'

'You said – remember?'

'Huh?'

'Before we left we were talking, you know, maybe like afterwards we'd check out the Whiskey, someone you know might be there, maybe you'd jam—'

'That was then, this is now . . . someone I know. Right. Knowing is fucking bullshit. *Doing* is the name of the game and tonight we did fucking *nothing* – man, I can't believe how bad we sucked, Skootch was like brain-dead and that guy in the second row I'm pretty sure was maybe from Geffen and he left early – fuck, I'm gonna die without being famous!'

'You will be fam—'

'Shut the fuck *up*!'

The van started moving, going awhile – south – then turning right, which meant west again. Wim drove angry, speeding, making sharp turns, fast stops.

It took a while for the girl to talk again. 'Hey, Wim?'

Grunt.

'Wim? What you said before?'

'Whu?'

'About not giving head to the joint? But there are other joints, right?' Giggle.

'Yeah, right, I had a triumphant night and now I'm ready to be romantic – just shut up and let me get us home – I can't believe how bad we sucked!'

After that no one talked at all.

I tried to follow each turn, drawing a map in my head but with all those turns I lost track.

Finally, he stopped and I thought, 'I'm cooked, he's going to get his drums, find me, take his anger out on me.'

I felt around under the plastic, wanting something to swing with, touched cold metal but it wouldn't come free. Totally cooked.

Open. Slam. Footsteps. That got softer. Disappeared.

I got out from under the plastic. The van smelled like one big joint.

It was parked on a quiet street full of apartments.

I climbed into the front seat, unrolled the window. This could be anywhere. Maybe he'd even taken me back to Hollywood. The air outside was cold, so I crawled in back again, managed to pull the black plastic sheet loose, folded it, tucked it under my arm, returned to the front and got out.

A new smell.

Salt. A fishy salt.

Once when I was little, Mom took me to the beach, a long bus ride from Watson. I don't know exactly what beach it was and we never went back there, but the sand was smooth and warm and she bought snow-cones for both of us. It was hot and dry and crowded and we stayed there all day, me digging holes in the sand, Mom just sitting there in her bikini listening to the radio. She didn't bring any sunscreen and we both got burned. I'm lighter than her and got it worse, turning blistery, feeling like my whole body was on fire. All the way back on the bus I screamed, Mom telling me to be quiet, but not like she meant it, she was pink as bubblegum, knew the pain was real.

Back in the trailer, she tried to give me wine, but I wouldn't take it, the smell bothered me and even though I must have been only four or five, I'd seen her drunk, was afraid of alcohol. She tried to force me, pushing the bottle up against my lips and holding one of my hands down, but I just kept twisting my head, pretending my mouth was glued shut till finally she left me alone and I just lay there, every inch of my body roasting while she finished the wine herself.

Smelling the salt, I remembered all that.

And more: Mom sitting on a towel, her bikini was black. Maybe she was hoping some guy would notice her but no one did, probably cause of me.

So here I was. The beach.

Nowhere to go after that.

292

35

STILL NO answer at Greg Balch's office. Petra decided to eyeball the place.

At 6 P.M., she drove out of the station lot, picking up Cahuenga at Franklin and taking it over the hill.

Studio City was the Valley, but to her it had always seemed un-Valley-like. North of Ventura Boulevard, the neighborhood was the usual grid of anonymous apartment tracts, but to the south were pretty hills up to Mulholland, winding trails, stilt houses that had survived the quake. The commercial mix along Ventura was a little shabby in spots, some strip-mall development, but also plenty of antique shops, recording studios, sushi bars, jazz clubs, a few gay bars — definitely funkier than the rest of the Valley.

Nothing avant garde about Players Management's home base, though. The company occupied a dreary two-story box the color of chocolate milk, set back from the street and fronted by a parking lot. Weeds whiskered through the asphalt, gutters sagged, stucco corners were chipped. H. Carter Ramsey wasn't much of a landlord.

Balch's black Lexus was the only vehicle in the lot. So he was in, not answering the phone — orders from the boss to discourage the media? She peeked inside the car. Empty.

Two tenants took up the ground floor of the chocolate

cube, a travel agency sporting the green tree flag of Lebanon and advertising discount flights to the Middle East, and a wholesale-to-the-public beauty supply store. Both closed.

Rusting open steps on the right side climbed to a cement walkway and three mustard-colored doors in need of refinishing. Suite A housed Easy Construction, Inc., B was something called La Darcy Hair Removal, and tucked in back was Players Management. No windows on the west wall. Oppressive.

She knocked, got no answer, knocked again, and Balch opened.

He was wearing a black zip-up velvet sweatsuit with white piping and looked genuinely surprised to see her. Odd. Ramsey had to have called him. Maybe he was an actor, too.

'Hi.' He offered a soft hand. 'C'mon in. Detective Conners, was it?'

'Connor.'

He held the door for her. The suite consisted of two low-ceilinged rooms connected by a door, now open. The rear space looked bigger, messy. Piles of paper all over the cheap green carpet, takeout cartons. The front room was furnished with a gold couch and a scruffy oak desk piled with yet more paper. Flagrantly grained fake rosewood walls were covered with photographs, mostly black and whites, the kind you saw in every dry-cleaner's in town – big airbrushed smiles of stars and has-beens, dubious autographs.

But only one celeb in these. Ramsey as cowboy, police officer, soldier, Roman centurion. An especially ludicrous shot of young H. Cart decked out like some kind of space alien – plastic bodysuit armored by exaggerated pecs, rubbery-looking antennae protruding from his puffy sixties moptop. No mustache, wide, white, hire-me smile. A passing resemblance to Sean Connery. The guy had been a looker.

A color photo at the top showed Ramsey decades later dressed in a nifty sport jacket, turtleneck, looking flinty, striking an action pose with a 9mm. *Dack Price: The Adjustor*. She should probably watch the damn show.

She was about to enter the back office when she noticed something that confirmed her guess about Balch as performer: At the bottom of the wall, half hidden by the desk. Low man in the exhibit – not a coincidence, she was willing to bet.

Balch in his twenties. He'd been decent-looking, too. A good fifty pounds lighter, sun-blond, nicely defined muscles, like a hero in one of those beach movies she used to watch for laughs – Tab Hunter or Troy Donahue.

But even in his youth, the business manager had worn a dull, subservient smile that robbed him of star quality.

'Antiques,' said Balch, sounding self-conscious. 'You know you're old when you don't recognize yourself anymore.'

'So you acted, too.'

'Not really. I should take that stuff down.' The sweats were tight around his paunch, baggy in the trousers. New white sneakers. Now that she had a good look, she could see that his thin, waxy hair was a mixture of blond and white. Pink scalp peeked through.

'Can I get you some coffee?' He indicated the rear office, stood by the door, waiting for her to enter.

'No, thanks.' She stepped in. Finally a couple of windows, but they were covered by chenille drapes the color of old newspaper. No natural lighting and the single desk lamp Balch had on didn't do much to pierce the gloom.

The clutter was monumental – papers on the floor, chairs crowding another cheap desk, bigger, L-shaped. Ledgers, tax manuals, corporate prospectuses, government forms. On the shorter arm of the desk was a white plastic coffee maker spotted with brown. Kentucky Fried Chicken box in a corner, grease stains on the underside of the open lid. A glimpse of breaded fowl.

Total slob. Maybe that's why Ramsey maintained him in low-rent circumstances. Or maybe that was the essence of their relationship.

All those years playing lackey. Could she wedge the guy? He did live in Rolling Hills Estates, very pricey. So Ramsey paid well for loyalty.

Balch cleared an armchair for her, tossing papers into a corner, and sat behind the desk, hands laced on his belly. 'So how's it going? The investigation.'

'It's going.' Petra smiled. 'Do you have any information that might help me, Mr Balch?'

'Me? Wish I did, I still can't get over it.' His lower jaw shifted from side to side. 'Lisa was . . . a nice girl. Little hot-tempered, but basically a great person.'

'Hot-tempered?'

'Listen, I know you've heard about Cart hitting her, all that stuff on TV, but it only happened once. Not that I'm excusing it, it was wrong. But Lisa had a temper. She went off on him all the time.'

Trying to blame the victim to excuse the boss? Did he realize he was offering a motive for the boss's rage?

'So she had a tendency to criticize Mr Ramsey?'

Balch touched his mouth. His eyes had gotten small. 'I'm not saying they didn't get along. They loved each other. All

296

I'm saying is Lisa could be . . . that I can see her – forget it, what do I know, I'm just talking.'

'You can see her getting someone pretty angry.'

'Anyone can get anyone angry. That has nothing to do with what happened. This is obviously some kind of maniac.'

'Why do you say that, Mr Balch?'

'The way it – it was done. Totally insane.' Balch's hand rose to his forehead, rubbing, as if trying to erase a headache. 'Cart's devastated.'

'How long have you and Cart known each other?'

'We grew up together, upstate New York, went to high school and college together at Syracuse, played football – he was the quarterback, damn good one. Scouted by the pros, but he tore his hamstring at the end of the senior season.'

'And you?'

'Offensive lineman.'

Protecting the quarterback.

'So you go back a long ways.'

Balch smiled. 'Centuries. Before your time.'

'Did you come out to Hollywood together?'

'Yup. After graduation, one of those last-fling things before we settled down. Also to cheer Cart up, he was pretty upset, about losing out on the NFL. His dad owned a hardware store and wanted Cart to take it over and he thought he'd probably do that.'

'And you?'

'Me?' Surprised that she cared. 'I had a business degree, some offers from accounting firms, figured eventually I'd get a CPA.'

Petra gazed around at the sty he called an office. Weren't bean-counters supposed to be organized?

'So what led you to acting?'

Balch stroked the top of his pale head. 'It was one of those weird things. Not exactly Lana Turner at Schwab's – are you old enough to know about that?'

'Sure,' said Petra. Knowing it from her father. The honeymoon he and his bride had taken to California. Kenneth Connor had loved LA, saw it as an anthropologist's dream. Look at me, now, Dad. Hobnobbing with the never-greats. Working the *Industry*.

'You and Cart were both discovered?' she said.

Balch smiled again. 'No. Cart was. It was right out of a script. We were a few days from going back to Syracuse, having a couple of beers at Trader Vic's – over at the Beverly Hilton, this was before Merv owned it. Anyway, some guy comes over and says, "I've been watching you two finelooking young men, would you like parts in a movie?" And gives us his card. We're thinking it's got to be a scam, or maybe he's a que— some gay guy hustling. But the next morning, Cart pulls out the card and says, "Hey, let's call, for the hell of it." Cause we were gonna go home and get jobs, why not be adventurous? Turns out it was for real, a casting agency. We went down and auditioned, both got parts – not that it was any big deal, not even a B-movie, more like D. A western. Straight to the Dixie drive-in circuit.'

Balch moved papers around atop his desk, making no impact on the clutter. 'Anyway, one thing led to another and we decided to stay in LA, got a few more jobs over the next year, non-union stuff, barely enough to make the rent. Then I didn't get any more calls but Cart started getting lots, better ones, then an agent, and he was making some decent money, mostly in westerns. I decided to go home. It was winter, almost Christmas, I remember thinking my folks were already mad at me for taking the year off, what would Christmas dinner be like.'

'So you lost faith in Hollywood?'

Balch smiled. 'It wasn't a matter of faith. I wasn't qualified, didn't have the talent to make it – never got speaking parts, just crowd fillers, walk-throughs, that kind of thing. Couldn't find any accounting jobs and I'd blown all my job offers back East, but I figured something would turn up. Then Cart asked me to stay, said it would be fun, we could continue to hang out, he'd find me something. And he did. Bookkeeping gig at Warner Brothers.'

He spread his arms, smiled again. 'And that's the whole glamorous story.'

'When did you start managing Cart's business?'

'Soon as he began making serious bucks. He'd seen what unscrupulous managers could do, wanted someone he could trust. By then I was working in Business Affairs at ABC, knew something about the industry.'

'Do you manage anyone else?'

Balch shifted his weight, smoothed out a black velvet fold of sweatshirt. 'I do a few favors for people, facilitate a deal now and then, but Cart's investments keep me busy.'

'So he's done pretty well.'

'He's earned it.'

Spoken like a true lineman.

'So you handle his contracts?'

'He's got an entertainment lawyer, but yeah, I vet things.'

'What else do you do for him?'

'Prepare his taxes, keep track of things. We're diversified, real estate, securities, the usual. There's some property

299

management. It keeps me busy – anything else I can do for you?'

'Just what you're doing,' said Petra. 'Filling in personal details.'

'About Cart?'

'Cart, Lisa, anything.'

As if the matter required great contemplation, Balch closed his eyes. Opened them. The hands were back on his middle. Blond Buddha.

'Cart and Lisa,' he said very softly, 'is a very sad story. He really flipped for her, felt embarrassed about it. The age difference. I told him it didn't matter, he was in better shape than guys half his age. And Lisa was crazy about him, I thought they were the best thing ever happened to each other.' A pained expression crossed his puffy face. 'I really don't know what happened. Marriage is tough.' The eyes opened. 'Been there twice. Who's to say what makes people tick?'

Petra produced her pad and Balch moved back a bit, as if repulsed by that bit of procedure. 'If you could please give me the timetable for Sunday – the trip to Tahoe and after you got back. As precisely as possible.'

'Timetable . . . sure.' His story matched Ramsey's and that of the pilot, Marionfeldt, detail for detail. The Tahoe trip nonstop business, uneventful flight back, both men asleep before 10 P.M., waking up, exercising, showering, eating breakfast, putting golf balls.

Pleasant dreams during the time Lisa had been murdered.

Petra said, 'OK, thanks . . . By the way, I was just curious why you call your company Players Management.'

'Oh, that.' Balch let out a snort-laugh. 'Football days. We

were amateurs, looking for something catchy. And anonymous – no mention of Cart's name. I came up with it.'

Petra wondered if that was all of it. In the Industry, players were those with power. Had he dreamed of that, once?

'So your job,' she said, 'is protecting Cart's interest. What did you do after Lisa went public with the domestic violence incident?'

'What was there to do? The damage was already done.'

'You didn't ask her not to go public again?'

'I wanted to, but Cart said no, it was personal, not business. I disagreed.'

'Why's that?'

'This town, personal and business sometimes can't be separated. But that's what Cart wanted, so I listened.'

Flipping pages, Petra said, 'So you pay all of Cart's bills.'

'They go through me, yes.'

'Including Lisa's spousal support.'

'Yup – there's an example of the kind of guy Cart is. Lisa's lawyer made an outrageous request – they'd only been married for a little over a year. I'd been through it twice, had a pretty good idea what she'd settle for, but Cart said no negotiation, give it to her.'

Frowning, now. Resentful? Jealous?

'So he's pretty generous,' said Petra.

'Exactly.' He stood. 'Now, if you don't mind, it's a little late—'

'Sure,' said Petra, smiling and rising too. He waited by the door again and as she passed close she smelled him. Heavy fruity cologne and sweat.

Out in the front room, she said, 'Oh, one more thing, Cart's maid, Estrella Flores, any idea where she went?'

'Cart told me she quit without notice. How's that for loyalty? I got him a new girl.'

'Through the same agency?'

'Yup.'

'Remember the name?'

'Of the agency? Some place in Beverly Hills – the Nancy Downey Agency.' He shot a cuff and looked at his watch.

'I appreciate your time, Mr Balch.'

Before she left the office, she glanced at the wall of photos. Two young guys striking poses. Players. Next to the pictures, Balch did look old.

36

SHE DROVE to a gas station pay phone, got the number of the Nancy Downey Agency and called it, though it was well past business hours. No machine. Something to wake up for tomorrow.

Taking Laurel Canyon back to the city, she reviewed the interview with Balch.

Nothing dramatic, but he had provided a possible lead to Estrella Flores, and had offered evidence of friction between Lisa and Ramsey.

She went off on him all the time.

Consistent with what Kelly Sposito had said about Lisa's sarcasm.

Impotent ex-hubby, sharp-tongued wife. Ramsey said she had a habit of shoving him. Had she finally pushed him too far?

How much did Balch know? Had he heard Ramsey leave the house during the early morning hours? Go into the car museum and pull out the Mercedes? Or the Jeep?

How far would the lineman go to protect the quarterback?

Players. Actors. What was real, what was scripted?

Time to talk to the night-guard who'd been on shift Sunday night. Then she thought of something. RanchHaven.

A place that big, smack in the fire zone, there'd have to be a second way out for safety. If so, was it guarded too? Or was there some way for residents to exit without tipping off the security staff?

Too many question marks. Not quizzing the guard right away had been amateurish; she felt like a blind painter.

Was it worth a ride out to Calabasas right now? She'd been going all day, and if she didn't let go of it, she wouldn't sleep and wouldn't that be pretty, one groggy, impaired D mucking things up further.

Tomorrow morning her artwork would appear all over the news and leads about the boy in the park would start pouring in, most of them useless. The whole thing was a distraction. And something about the boy's eyes bothered her – he'd already seen plenty, she didn't even want to think about an eleven year old witnessing something like that.

She thought about him. Eating dinner alone in Griffith Park. Reading. Stealing books, pathetic but charming – enough! Go home, E.T. Soak in tub, eat sandwich – oh, Jesus, she couldn't go home. The eight o'clock appointment with Ron Banks! What had possessed her to do *that*?

She zipped across Sunset and checked her watch. Seven forty-six. Barely enough time to get to Katz's, let alone freshen up and change.

The guy would be forced to stare across the table at a hag.

Big deal, this was no real date.

What was it, then?

She made it at three minutes to, paid for parking in a nearby lot and walked into Katz's corned-beef air. Greeted with a wide, false smile by a dyspeptic waitress who remembered her cop tips, she took a booth toward the back, ordered a Coke, headed for the ladies' room to wash up.

In front of a soap-specked mirror, she fluffed her hair and disapproved of her face. Definitely haggard, every bone showing. Paler than usual, too, and something seemed to be tugging her mouth down – some cruel god sketching in the wrinkles that would soon be engraved there? At least the black pant suit of the day was holding up OK, let's hear it for viscose.

When she returned, the drink was there and Banks was walking through the front door. She waved him over.

He smiled and sat down. 'Good to see you again.' His hands settled on the table, fingers drumming. Unfolding the paper napkin, he placed it on his lap. His hands kept moving.

'Hit much traffic coming over?' she said.

'Not bad.' He looked different. A stranger.

As opposed to? She was sitting across from a stranger – an uncomfortable stranger, look at those hands. Straining for conversation when a hot bath would have proved celestial.

The waitress brought a bowl of sour pickle slices and Petra took one. Defining the ground rules right from the start: Garlic on the breath, don't think of getting close. That seemed to relax Banks and he reached for one, too.

'These are great,' he said. 'Never been here.'

'Good place.'

'Sometimes I go to Langer's, on Alvarado. People are getting shot over at MacArthur Park and they're still lining up for pastrami at Langer's.'

'Been there,' said Petra. 'I'm kind of a deli freak.'

305

'No cholesterol worries?'

'Good genetics,' she said. 'Cholesterol-wise, anyway.'

He laughed. Why did he look so different? Younger, even more boyish than at Ramsey's house. Despite being dressed more formally – navy double-breasted suit, pale blue shirt, maroon tie. Nice. Had *he* somehow found time to spruce up?

Then she realized what the difference was. The mustache was gone. She remembered it as a smallish, blond-gray thing, no big soup-strainer like his partner's. But its absence made a difference. No gray in his head hair, losing the 'stache took off years. He had a pleasant face – a little narrow, the nose a little off-center, but the eyes were well-placed. Hazel. Long lashes. The now-exposed mouth yielding, but not in a weak way. Hairless hands. Young skin. She saw him as someone who'd gone through puberty late, would preserve well.

The mouth turned up slightly at the corners, a perpetual smile that might have gotten him into trouble as a schoolboy – *Banks, stop smirking*.

She realized she was staring, touched her upper lip and arched an eyebrow.

'Got rid of it last night,' he said, almost apologetic. 'It was an experiment, my daughters didn't like it, said it tickled. I shaved it off right in front of them, they thought it was hilarious.'

'How many daughters do you have?'

'Two. They're five and six.'

Knowing he'd carry pictures, she asked if he had any.

'As a matter of fact . . .' he said, pulling several from his wallet.

Two pretty little things, both dark-haired but with fair

skin, somewhat Latino-looking. Big brown eyes, long hair styled into ringlets, identical pink, frothy dresses. No obvious resemblance to Banks, though she thought she saw something in the younger one's smile.

'Totally adorable. What are their names?'

'The older one's Alicia and the baby's Beatrix. We call her Bee, or Honeybee.'

A and B. Someone liked order. She handed the photos back to him and he took a peek before slipping them behind his credit cards.

The waitress stomped over and asked if they were ready.

Petra knew what she wanted but she picked up her menu to give him time.

The waitress's foot tapped. 'I can come back—'

'No, I think we're OK. I'll take the pastrami-coleslaw combo. With fries.'

'And you?'

Banks said, 'Smoked turkey on a kaiser roll. Potato salad.'

'Something to drink?'

'Coffee.'

Alone again, she said, 'How often do you get to be with them?'

'They live with me.'

'Oh.'

'Their mom's Spanish – from Spain. She trains horses, teaches riding. She went back to work at a resort in Majorca and gave me custody. She visits every few months, is still trying to figure out where she's going to live.'

'Must be tough,' said Petra.

'It is. I'm trying to tell them Mommy loves them, cares about them, but what they know is she isn't there.

It's been really tough. I just got them in therapy, hopefully it'll help.'

Most cops ran from anything psychiatric unless they were filing for disability. Banks's easy admission interested her.

She watched him eat another pickle. Narrow hands, the free one continued to drum. The fingers long but sturdy. Impeccable nails.

He chewed slowly. Everything about him seemed slow and deliberate. Except the hands. All his tension filtered down to his fingertips. 'She was always after me to grow a mustache. My ex. Said it was *muy macho*.' He laughed. 'So after she's gone, I do it. Guess a therapist would have something to say about *that*. Anyway, she's still trying to find herself, hopefully she will soon.'

'How long's it been?'

'Final decree was just over a year ago. I'm able to feel sorry for her, now, see her as someone with serious problems, but – oh, by the way, I talked to the Carpenteria sheriff and he said Lisa Ramsey never filed any D.V. complaint on Ramsey there, either. They've got no calls to the house, period.'

Whiplash change of subject. He knew it and blushed and Petra groped for a way to rescue him.

The waitress solved that problem, setting down his coffee hard enough to slosh the saucer and barking, 'Your food's coming up.'

She hurried off and Petra said, 'Thanks for checking, Ron.'

'Least I could do.'

The two of them worked on their drinks. The restaurant was almost full, the usual mixture of soup-sipping old folk and Gen-X depressives showing they didn't care about dietary fat. Behind the stocked case, countermen sliced and wrapped and cracked jokes, the briny aromas of herring and cured meat and stuffed derma yielding to sweetness as fresh rye loaves came out of the kitchen on steel trays.

Suddenly, Petra felt hungry, a little more relaxed.

'How about you?' said Banks. 'Been married?'

'Divorced two and a half years ago, no kids.' Getting that out of the way before he could ask. 'So you've got them full-time. Must be challenging.'

'My mom helps out – picks them up from school and babysits when I have to work late. They're great girls, sweet, smart, into sports – Alicia does soccer, gives the boys a run. Bee's not sure if she likes soccer or t-ball, but she's pretty coordinated.'

Sports dad. Her father had gone that route with all five kids. Football for the boys, softball for Petra. Every Sunday, into a hideous uniform. She hated the entire experience, faked enthusiasm to please him, stuck with it for three summers. Years later he told her she'd done him a big favor quitting, he'd yearned for some free time on weekends.

Single father – was that why she'd gotten together with Banks?

He seemed so unguarded. What was he doing as a cop? She asked him how he got into law enforcement.

'My dad was a fireman, it was either that or police work,' he said. 'Always wanted one of the two.'

'I don't want to sound chauvinistic, but why the sheriffs and not LAPD?'

He grinned. 'Wanted to do real police work – seriously, back then Lulu – my ex – was talking about opening up her own equestrian school one day, we figured we'd be living somewhere unincorporated, so I applied to the sheriff. How about you?'

She gave him a very spare version of the artist-to-detective transition.

He said, 'You paint? Beatrix is kind of artistic. Or at least she seems that way to me. Her mom tried to do pottery. I've still got the wheel at home – just sitting there, as a matter of fact. Want it?'

'No, thanks, Ron.'

'You're sure? It seems a waste.'

'I appreciate the offer but I just paint.'

'Oh, OK. What kinds of things do you paint?'

'Anything.'

'And you actually did it professionally.'

'I wasn't exactly Rembrandt.'

'Still, you must be good.'

She gave him a rundown of her ad agency days, her mouth running while her brain thought: How cute, each of us shifting the focus to the other. In her case, defensiveness, but Banks seemed really interested in her. Polar opposite of Nick. All the other men she'd dated since Nick – artists, then cops. Even when they talked about you, it was really just a ploy to get it back to Me Me Me.

This one seemed different. Or was she just flattering herself?

She ended her recitation: 'Like I said, no big deal.'

'Still,' he said, 'it's tough making any kind of living creatively. I had an uncle did some sculpture, could never make a dime – ah, here comes the food, whoa, look at those portions!'

He ate slowly and that prevented Petra from wolfing. Good influence, Detective Banks.

In between bites, they chatted about work. Dry stuff: Benefits, insurance, the usual gripes, comparing blue and tan bureaucracies, good-natured kidding about intramural sports competitions. Finding more common ground than differences. She noticed he wasn't wearing his gun.

When their sandwiches were gone, they each ordered apple pie à la mode. Petra finished hers first, tried idly to pick up crumbs with the tines of her fork.

'You like to eat,' said Banks. 'Thank God.'

The fork paused mid-air. She put it down.

He blushed again. 'I – no offense – what I mean is, I think that's great. Seriously. It sure doesn't show – at least as far as I can—' He shook his head. 'Oh, Lord, I am *not* good at this.'

She found herself laughing. 'It's OK, Ron. Yes, I do have a healthy appetite when I remember to sit down for a meal.'

He continued to shake his head, wiped his mouth with his napkin, folded it neatly and placed it next to his plate. 'Whatever I just gargled out, please take it as a compliment.'

'So taken,' said Petra. 'You're saying love of food's a healthy thing.'

'Exactly. Too many girls these days get crazy about food. I think about that because I have daughters. My ex always bugged them, obsessed with being skinny—' He stopped himself, again. 'Not too cool, bringing her up every minute.'

'Hey, she was a big part of your life. It's normal.' Implying that she'd done the same with Nick. But she hadn't. She'd never talked about him to anyone.

'Was,' he said. 'Past tense.' He raised one hand and sliced air vertically. 'So . . . how's the case coming?'

'Not too brilliantly.' She talked about it without giving

311

him details. Liking him but not forgetting that he was non-LAPD.

He said, 'Situations like that, publicity, no way you can do your job properly.'

'Ever have one like that?'

'Once in a while.' Touching his napkin, he looked away. Wary, too?

'Once in a while?' she echoed.

'You know us country bumpkin lawmen, runnin' down rustlers, protectin' the pony express.'

'Ah,' said Petra. 'Anything I'd have heard about?'

'Well,' he said, 'Hector and I did do some work on the County Gen slasher.'

Mega-case, three years ago. Wacko killer cutting up nurses on the grounds of the county hospital, four victims in three months. The bad guy turned out to be an orderly who'd served time for rape and assault. He'd faked his way through personnel screening, worked the surgical floors, of all things. Before he was caught, the nurses had threatened to strike.

'That was yours?'

'Hector's and mine.'

'Now *I'm* impressed.'

'Believe me, it was no big Sherlock,' he said. 'Everything pointed to an insider, it was just a matter of flipping paper, checking time-cards, eliminating negatives till we found the positive.'

Petra remembered the feminist frustration, media noise – hadn't there been an initial task force? 'Were you on it from the beginning?'

He blushed again. 'No, they called us in after a few months.'

'So you two are rescuers.'

'Sometimes,' he said. 'And sometimes we get rescued. You know how it is.'

What she knew was that the County Gen slasher was a major case and that he was a rescuer, top dog. And that's who the sheriff had sent for the notification call to Ramsey?

Why was he being so cagy about it? Modest? Or sent by the tans to pump her for details?

'Any ideas on Ramsey?' she said.

'Like I said at his house, the guy rang my bell, but I'm not a big one for bells.' He smiled. 'Give me time-cards, any time.'

She smiled back. He drummed the table. Rubbed the spot where his mustache had been. The waitress gave him the check and, over Petra's protests, he insisted on paying for it. 'Hey, you put up with me, you deserve a sandwich.'

'Nothing to put up with,' she heard herself say.

They left the deli and he walked her to her car. A warm night, still a bit of foot traffic on Fairfax and the newsstand across the street was crowded with browsers. The food smells from Katz's followed them. He didn't walk close to her, seemed to be consciously avoiding it.

'So,' he said, when they got to the Ford. 'This was great. I – is there some place you'd like to go? If you're not too tired, I mean – maybe some music. Are you into music?'

'I'm a little bushed, Ron.'

The crushed look on his face said the evening was personal, nothing to do with the case, and she felt bad for suspecting him.

'Sure,' he said, 'you'd have to be.'

He held out his hand and they shook briefly. 'Thanks a lot, Petra, I really appreciate it.'

Had a man ever thanked her before just for spending time with him? 'Thank *you*, Ron.'

He tilted forward, as if ready to kiss her, then rocked back, gave a small, salute-like wave, and turned, hands in pockets.

'What kind of music do you like?' she said. Figuring country, it had to be traditional country.

He stopped, faced her again, shrugged. 'Mostly rock. Old stuff – blues, Steve Miller, Doobie Brothers. Used to play that kind of stuff in a band.'

'Really?' She fought a giggle. 'Did you have long hair?'

'Long enough,' he said, walking back to her. 'Don't get me wrong, we weren't professionals. I mean, we did a few club dates, played the Whiskey way back when. That's where I met my—' Clamping a hand over his mouth.

'Sure,' said Petra, laughing, 'and not just her, right? You met tons of babes, that's why you joined a band in the first place. Don't tell me, drums.' Those active hands.

'You got it.'

'Drummers always get the girls, right?'

'Don't ask *me*,' said Banks. 'I was always too busy trying to keep the beat.'

'Still play?'

'Not for years. My old kit's rusting in the garage.'

Along with the potter's wheel, bikes, probably piles of old toys, kid stuff, heaven knew what else. Petra pictured a small house full of Levitz furniture. Far cry from the horse ranch that had never materialized.

'So where do you go to listen to music?' she said.

'Used to go to the Country Club, in Reseda. It's not a country place, it's rock—'

'I know where it is.'

'Oh. Sorry.'

'What about this side of the hill?' she said.

'Don't know,' he said. 'Don't go out much.' The admission embarrassed him and he looked at his watch.

'Need to get back?' she said.

'No, they're asleep by now, I called them before I left. My mom's staying over, I just want to phone, make sure everything's OK—'

'Call from my place,' she said. 'It's not far from here.'

Thinking: He'd told his mother he'd be late. Big plans or blind optimism?

For some reason, she didn't care.

While he talked to his mother, she fixed her makeup. Thankfully, the apartment was in decent shape. She'd barely lived in it since the case broke. She invited him to take off his jacket and hung it up. Standing in the kitchen, they each had a glass of red wine. He complimented her decor. At his insistence, she showed him her art. Not the works in progress, her old portfolio, color blowups of pictures she'd sold through the co-op gallery.

He was impressed, didn't try to touch her.

They moved to the living-room and went through her small CD collection, trying to find something they both owned, coming up only with Eric Clapton's *Derek and the Dominos*.

Sitting two feet apart on Petra's couch, they listened to half the album, then his hand shifted six inches closer to hers and remained there. She covered her half of the distance and their fingers touched, then entwined.

Sweaty hands but neither of them dared wipe. She found herself gripping his knuckles too hard and reduced the pressure.

He breathed faster but didn't move.

During 'Bell Bottom Blues' he tilted his head toward her and they kissed.

Closed-mouthed, mutual garlic, for what seemed like a long time, then a wide, open exploration full of clicking teeth and swirling tongues, hands on back of neck, soft lips, he had very soft lips, she was glad the mustache was gone. When they broke, they were both robbed of air.

He was ready for more but the hunger in his eyes shook Petra and she pulled away. They listened to the rest of the song sitting still, holding hands again. She was wet, her nipples ached, her body demanded loving but she didn't want it, not with him, not now. One more song and she got up to use the bathroom. When she returned he was standing, jacket on.

She sat down again, an invitation, but he remained on his feet, in front of her, reaching down to touch her hair, her cheek, her chin. She looked up, saw his bottom teeth pinching his upper lip.

She was trembling, now, and had he tried again, who knew what would have happened.

He just stood there.

She got up, put her arm in his and walked him to the door.

He said, 'I'd really like to see you again.'

More confidence in his voice, but still unsure.

'I'd like that, too.'

* * *

A half hour later, alone in her bed, naked, having touched herself and bathed, someone's late-night TV squeaking through the darkness, she thought of everything she needed to do in the morning.

37

THE SUN comes up behind me, orange. Brighter than in the park, no trees to cover it. The ocean is roaring, gray. The black plastic's too thin; I'm cold.

No one's out on the beach yet, so I just lie there watching the sun and the few cars up on the coast highway going back and forth. The thick poles that hold up the pier are black with tar and crusted with barnacles. I see one that's open, reach over and poke it and it closes.

The Jacques Cousteau book had a chapter about barnacles. They stay where they are, eat whatever floats by. They make their own glue and it's as good as Krazy Glue. Sometimes they're impossible to move.

OK, now it's warming up a little and I better move. I get up and shake the sand out of my hair, fold the plastic and tuck it behind one of the poles, using a rock to weigh it down.

Time to get some new stuff. Food, money. A hat; I remember that sunburn. Maybe some sunscreen, too.

Where should I go? Should I leave LA? Not up north, cause that's closer to Watson. Down south, like to San Diego? But what if that doesn't work out? The next stop would be Mexico and there's no way I'm going to any foreign country.

If I stay in LA, where will I hide?

I think about it for a long time and get really scared. Same feeling like when I watched PLYR – I need to stop thinking about that . . .

It's stupid to even be thinking of a plan. I have no future. Even if I survive for a few months, a year, two years, so what? I'd still be a kid, no schooling, no money, no control over anything.

Still no one out on the beach. It looks so tan and peaceful. The ocean, too, gray as steel except where the tide comes rolling in, throwing up spray, like spitting at the sky.

Spitting at God . . .

Wouldn't it be nice to just walk into the water, let yourself be carried away? Maybe you'd drown. Or maybe there'd be a miracle and you'd wash up like one of those bottles with a message in it on some island with palm trees. Girls wearing just grass skirts, long black hair down to their butts, and you'd come out of the ocean like some god and they'd be all thrilled to see you, fight with each other to be your girlfriend, take care of you, feed you some barbecued pig with an apple in its mouth and fruit that they just pick from the trees, no one has to work.

Either way, no worries.

I get up, walk across the beach to the tideline, roll my pants up and stand there, let the waves trickle over my toes.

Cold. My feet get numb and they look like white wax.

How long would it take before you stopped feeling cold? Before your body stopped feeling anything?

I read in a nature book that gazelles and wildebeest chased by lions stop feeling pain so their death becomes easier.

That didn't happen to me with the pervs, so maybe it's just animals.

319

Or maybe I just didn't get . . . close enough.

If you didn't feel or worry, you could just give yourself up like some sacrifice – like Jesus did.

I must have walked because now I'm in the water up to my knees and my pants are getting wet and kind of ballooning and swirling around. Not so cold anymore. It feels clean. I keep going, the water's sloshing against my belt and I stand there and look across the ocean, maybe I'll see a boat or a whale spouting.

A few birds are out there, flying around, diving. I take another step. Just one but it makes a big difference, the ground drops out from under me and all of a sudden *I'm up to my neck, trying to step back but I can't get a hold on anything and now I feel the water moving under me and I'm in over my head, swallowing water, choking – up again, I can see the top of the water, the beach is getting smaller, I start to swim but it doesn't help, something's pushing me forward, I have no control, start kicking, waving my arms around, knowing this is stupid you have to stay calm stay calm but I'm being pushed out, forced, I don't want this! I'm tiny, weaker than a barnacle because I have no glue, why am I thinking about Mom now, how bad she'll feel, so cold, my eyes burn my throat burns, my eyes got to keep them open but ohnocan'tkeepmyheadabov—*

Up in the air again, coughing spitting, eyes burning, throat hurts like a knife scraping it and I'm still being carried out by the – no, the beach is getting closer—

The ocean tosses me up, the sand gets even closer. Releasing me, like Jonah? No, no, here I go under again, swallowing so much water I think I'll explode, then up, coughing, vomiting, rocks in the water, hitting me, stinging.

The ocean playing with me. Which way will it throw me now?

Stones scraping the bottom of my body. The ground. Sand.

Back on shore.

Sand sticks to my soaked clothes. Salt in the scratches makes them burn. I roll away from the water.

Safe.

Another chance.

God?

Or did even the ocean think I was trash, spit me back like bad food?

I hurry back toward the pier, still coughing and spitting up saltwater, collapse, stay there trying to get a little sun, dry out. A few people are out on the beach now. I just mind my own business, after an hour I'm drier, but still wet, my chest hurts and I'm scratched up by the sand but . . . I'm here.

I need to concentrate. Money and a hat. Some food. Sunscreen.

Mostly dry, I take a walk up to the pier. There's a Ferris wheel, some bumper cars and a merry-go-round but they're all shut and locked and there's nothing to take there. A few restaurants, but they're closed too, and the only food around are dry bits of popcorn stuck to the floor.

All the way at the end of the pier is a bait shack that's open, some dirty-looking guy behind a counter and big white bathtub-type tanks full of anchovies, some of them already dead and floating to the top. A few people are fishing, mostly old Chinese guys and a few black guys. No one's catching anything, everyone looks bored.

The two garbage cans I find are full of fish guts and they stink so bad I almost puke. I leave the pier.

Up above the beach is a street full of fancy-looking restaurants and hotels, nothing there for me. North is a small park with some old people and homeless guys, and if you keep looking, the street just seems to disappear. All those trees, too much like you-know-where.

So I walk south and things start to look a little more familiar – motels and apartment buildings, weirdos who could be from the Boulevard. I find half a donut on the street and it looks OK so I eat it. Next block I see part of a Twix bar left on the sidewalk but it's too melted and gross-looking and I only eat a small bit of it.

A while later, a sign says I'm in Venice. Small houses, people, lots of Mexicans. I walk down a street, at the end is the ocean again, and soon I'm on this big wide path called Ocean Front Walk, like a giant sidewalk, the ocean on one side, stores on the other, all sorts of people – punks, blacks, beautiful bikini-girls on roller skates, their butt-cheeks hanging out, guys looking at them. Young guys – like college students, old people sitting on benches, bikers with tattoos, lots of big, mean-looking dogs. Some Arnold Schwarzenegger-type guys are exercising in these fenced-off areas, their bodies all greased up so the muscles look like grapefruit trying to burst through the skin. Lifting weights, rubbing chalk on their hands, being huge and cool, showing off.

The stores here are mostly small and cheap-looking. Fast food, stands selling ice cream, cold drinks, sunglasses, souvenirs, postcards, T-shirts, bathing suits.

Hats that say *California!* or *Malibu!* or *Venice!* I'd love

322

some dry clothing but there are too many people around to take something.

Still, this might be a good place to hang out, see what happens later.

I decide to walk from one end of Ocean Front to the other, see what turns up.

Halfway down, I see a little gray building with a six-pointed star over the door. A Jewish star, I know that from my history book, the chapter 'The Middle East: Birth of Civilization.'

A Jewish church – what do they call them, synagons? I go over. Jewish letters next to the door, then English ones. Over the door it says *Congregation Beth Torah*.

This might be good. The Jews always have money. At least that's what Moron used to say, he'd go off on how they were all fucking bankers, sucking the blood out of the country, killing Jesus and now they wanted to take our money, too.

Like he ever had money.

Then I think: Why would he be right, he was wrong about everything else. But still . . . what's a church doing in the middle of all these businesses unless they're out to make money?

It wasn't just Moron, Mom used to agree with him, say Cowboy, they really got a talent for making money, must be in the blood.

'You stupid bitch,' he laughed. 'It ain't talent, it's cause they cheat us. Fucking ZOG – know what that is? Zionist Occupation Government, they want to take us over, not even human – come from the devil fucking a snake, didja know that? The Aryan race is the bona fide chosen people.'

323

That night I was sitting at the kitchen table trying to study The Civil War. But then Mom started telling a story and I listened. About some rich Jewish family who owned a big strawberry farm down near Oxnard, her parents and her used to pick there when she was a kid. How the Jews had a big white two-story house, and a Cadillac.

'Fucking bloodsuckers,' Moron said.

'Actually, they was OK, kinda nice—' she started. But he looked at her and she said, 'Except they sure loved their money, the wife always dressed like she was going out to dinner and she was just a farm wife. And here was this big house, maybe it was even three stories, buncha TV antennas all over the roof, but we slept in these little migrant shacks, kerosene heaters.'

'Fucking A.'

Even if it's mostly lies, sometimes lies have some truth. And I don't need thousands of Jewish dollars, just some spare change.

A sign next to the synagon door says prayers will be held on Friday night and that the time for lighting candles is 7:34 P.M., whatever that means.

No one's looking. I try the door. Locked. The next place over is called Cafe Eats and it's closed, too.

There's a space between the church and Cafe Eats. I slip around to the back, where there's an alley, parked cars, but none driving. Two spaces behind the synagon but no cars. They're praying Friday night. That's tomorrow.

I check out the back door. Plain wood, with some little wooden thing nailed to the frame on the right side, also with a Jewish star. Probably some kind of good luck charm, maybe asking God for money.

The back door's locked, too. Right next to it is a window, a small one, too small for a man to fit through, but not for me. A screen over it, just like at the pineapple house. Also like that one, it comes right off.

I don't have to break this window, it's loose — when I push up on it it jiggles. So I shove harder and feel it give some more, then something pops and it slams open and I look up and down the alley.

Still no one. I'm in.

I'm getting good at this.

The room I land in is a bathroom, small but clean, a toilet, a sink, and a mirror. No shower. The mirror tells me I don't look as bad as I thought, just the scratches on my face and some white crust around my ears and my lips. I wash it off, use the toilet.

Considering I almost drowned, I look pretty good.

I thank God, in case it *was* Him, wash my hands.

Now let's find some Jewish money.

38

PETRA AWOKE confused, at 6:30, her head crowded with Ron Banks, Estrella Flores, Ramsey, the boy with the Presidents book – she wrapped herself in a robe and collected the morning paper.

There it was, page three, the drawing smack in the center of the article, no credit given to the artist.

The gist of the article was no progress, the implication, those bumbling police. Salmagundi, the department spokesman, careful not to make too big a deal of the witness angle. The boy was 'just one of several leads we're looking into.'

The last paragraph made her inhale sharply.

Twenty-five-thousand-dollar reward to anyone providing information about the boy or anything else that led to the arrest of a suspect. Money put up by Dr and Mrs John Everett Boehlinger, all calls to be directed to Hollywood Detectives.

Her extension. Blindsided. They must have gone through Schoelkopf, goddamn him. She couldn't work this way.

All day fielding crank calls – had Stu seen it yet?

Normally she'd call him. Nothing was normal anymore.

She got dressed in the first thing she pulled out of the closet, took the paper with her and drove much too fast to the station.

There were already ten messages on her desk. Nine sightings of the boy and a psychic from Fontana claiming to know who'd murdered Lisa. What would the afternoon bring?

Stu hadn't come in yet. To hell with him. Fournier was checked out, too.

She stormed into Schoelkopf's office waving the article. He was sitting at his desk, jumped up and jabbed a finger at her.

'Don't get all pissy with me. The parents blew into town yesterday, went straight to Deputy Chief Lazara, he calls me at ten P.M., I have to come down here to deal with them. The father's an obvious asshole, used to having his way. Who knows what he'll try to do next.'

I tried to warn you, idiot, and you brushed me off.

'You could've called me,' said Petra.

'I could've bought Microsoft at ten bucks, what's the point, Barbie?'

The nickname had never bothered her. Now it was a razor scraping raw nerve fiber. 'The point is—'

'The point is I've been running interference on this for you from day one and you've produced squat. I get yanked out of bed, get dirty looks from Lazara because *he's* working late, he cuts out, leaves me with Mommy boo-hooing, Daddy delivering these fucking speeches: After Menendez and O.J. everyone knows LAPD can't find a felon in the penitentiary. So I give him what I've got, which is this artwork of yours, figuring maybe it'll calm him down. He says OK, what are you doing about it, and I say we're looking for him, Mr Boehlinger. And he says *Doctor* Boehlinger, then he tells me it's not enough, he wants some incentives here – post a reward. I try to explain that rewards bring in mostly nuts and even if we wanted to do that, it would take time. He picks up my phone, calls some lawyer named Hack and says, talk to your buddy at the *Times* and your other buddies at the TV stations. Showing me this Hack's connected. Which he obviously is, it was already eleven and he got the picture in. So sue me, I didn't wake you up at midnight. You think you've got a grievance, file a complaint. Meanwhile, go do your job.'

He waved her out.

A TV cop would have handed in the badge and gun.

A real cop kept her mouth shut. She liked the job and the department was paramilitary, would always be, meaning lockstep rhythm, death of the individual, hierarchies. You pissed down, not up.

Look at Milo Sturgis – she'd worked with the gay detective on one case, had seen him as the ace he was. But before that she'd heard only curses affixed to his name. The highest solve-rate in West LA. To the department, that didn't make up for sleeping with a man.

She returned to her desk, put aside the ten message slips and phoned the Nancy Downey Agency in Beverly Hills. A woman with a Latin accent said, 'You should talk to Mr Sanchez. He's at our other office in San Marino.'

San Marino and BH. Covering the high-priced spreads, east and west.

A man answered there, similar accent.

'Mr Sanchez?'

'Yes.'

She identified herself, told him she was looking for Estrella Flores.

'I am, too.'

'Pardon?'

328

'I just got a call from her son in El Salvador. He's worried, hasn't heard from her since Sunday. Is this about Mrs Ramsey's murder?'

'We'd just like to talk to her, sir. Why's the son worried?'

'Usually she calls him two, three times a week. He said he phoned the Ramsey house but got only a machine. I tried, the same thing happened to me. I left a message but no one's called me back.'

'Mrs Flores quit working for Mr Ramsey, sir.'

'When?'

'The day after the murder.'

'Oh.'

'So she didn't call you about another placement.'

'No.' Sanchez sounded concerned.

'Any ideas where she might be, sir?'

'No, I'm sorry. She worked for the Ramseys for . . . hold on, let me look . . . here it is. Two years. Never complained.'

'Where did she work before that?'

'Before that . . . I couldn't tell you.' Wariness had crept into his voice.

'She wasn't legal?'

'When she came to us she was legal. At least she presented papers. We do our best to—'

'Mr Sanchez, I have no interest in immigration issues—'

'Even if you did, Detective, we have nothing to hide. Our women are all legal, we place them in the finest homes and there must never be a hint of—'

'Of course,' said Petra. 'Please give me Mrs Flores's son's name and number.'

'Javier,' he said, reciting an address on Santa Cristina in San Salvador and a number. 'He's a lawyer.'

'You don't know of any other places she worked?'

'She told us she worked for a family in Brentwood but only for three months. No name, she didn't want to use them as references because they were "immoral."'

'Immoral in what way, sir?'

'I think it was something to do with drinking. Mrs Flores is a very . . . moral woman.'

She hung up, thought about the maid's disappearance. If Flores had left of her own accord, why hadn't she contacted her son? It didn't take much morality to be repulsed by murder. Had she seen something? Or been seen?

Where to go with it . . . more calls to substations, to see if Flores had turned up somewhere as a victim? Unlikely. If she'd been eliminated by Ramsey because she could blow his alibi, he'd have made sure to conceal the body.

Better to scope out RanchHaven, talk to the guard service, ask long-overdue questions. While she was there, she could drop in on Ramsey again, slip in some hints about Flores, see how he reacted.

Wil Fournier appeared in the squad room door, beckoning her with a wiggling finger. He looked angry. Something to do with the boy? She hurried over.

'What's up?'

'Got some people can't wait to meet you.' He angled his head down the hall. Petra looked out and saw a couple in their fifties standing at the far end. Well-dressed, backs to each other.

'The parents?'

'None other,' said Fournier. 'Schoelkopf snagged me as I came in, said they wanted a first-hand report from all three of us. Where's Ken?'

330

'Don't know.' Her tone made him stare. 'What exactly do they want?'

'Info. Got any?'

'Nope, how about you?'

'Talked to a few shelters, churches, some of our Juvey people. No one knows the kid, a couple of social workers thought they might've seen him around but he hasn't checked in anywhere.'

'Outdoor kid,' said Petra. Thinking what guts it took for an eleven year old to go it alone in the park.

'Let's go do some hand-holding,' said Fournier. 'Female D and a coal-colored one. These people look like the type who still think lawn jockeys are funny.'

Mrs Boehlinger was everything Petra expected – petite, perfectly groomed, handsome – long-suffering, Pat Nixon handsomeness. A puff of cold-waved hair the color of dry champagne crowned a roundish face. Contoured eyebrows. Trim figure in a conservatively cut, black St John's knit suit. Black suede pumps and purse. Red eyes.

Her husband defeated expectation. Petra had pictured a big man, hearty, someone like Ramsey. Dr John Everett Boehlinger was five five, 140 pounds tops, with narrow shoulders and a homely face full of homely features: Fat nose, small dark eyes, rubber-mask looseness around the jowls. Bald on top, thin fringe of gray at the sides. A clipped stainless-steel goatee – he could have played Freud in the country club Halloween bash.

He wore a black vested suit, white shirt, gray tie printed with tiny black dots. White silk hankie in the breast pocket. Onyx cufflinks. Cap-tip shoes were polished shiny as motor oil.

331

Two small people in funeral garb. Mrs Boehlinger remained focused on the wall in front of her, clenching and unclenching one hand. The other gripped her purse. Her French nails were glossy but chipped. She still had her back to her husband, didn't look up as Petra and Fournier approached.

Dr Boehlinger had focused on them immediately, body canted forward, as if ready to spar. When they were ten feet away, he said to Petra, 'You're the one I spoke to on the phone.'

'Yes, sir. Detective Connor.' She extended her hand and he submitted to a half-second of skin contact before withdrawing. Wiping his hand on his suit – oh, for God's sake.

Then she reminded herself: The poor man's lost his child. Nothing worse than that.

Nothing.

He said, 'Vivian?' and his wife turned slowly. Ravaged eyes, the corneas a scramble of ruptured capillaries. The irises bright blue – like Lisa's. There was more than a suggestion of Lisa in the fine facial structure. Would Lisa have ended up like this – a fashionable matron, buttoned to the neck, all propriety?

'Detective Connor, Vivian,' the doctor singsonged scoldingly.

Vivian Boehlinger's expression said, 'So what the hell am I supposed to do about it?'

She said, 'Pleased to meet you,' and proffered an icy hand.

Petra smiled. 'And this is Detective Fournier—'

'We've already met Detective Fournier,' said Dr Boehlinger. 'Where's the third one – Bishop?'

'Out in the field,' said Petra.

'Out in the field – sounds like he's planting vegetables.'

'Actually, sir,' said Fournier, 'it's kind of like that. We cultivate leads—'

'Wonderful,' said Boehlinger. 'You know what a metaphor is. Now eliminate the chatter and tell us what you've cultivated about Ramsey.'

Mrs Boehlinger stared, turned, showed him her back once more. He didn't notice. 'Well?'

A detective named Bernstein stepped into the hall, coffee cup in hand, started forward, returned to the squad room.

'Let's talk somewhere private,' said Petra.

All three interrogation rooms were horrible – smaller than jail cells, no windows, the obvious wall of two-way mirror that most of the idiots brought in for questioning took early note of, then promptly forgot.

Bad smell in all three. Sweat, pomade, cheap perfume, tobacco, hormones.

She chose Interrogation One because it had three chairs instead of two. Fournier fetched a fourth and they crowded around a tiny metal table. Forced intimacy. Mrs Boehlinger kept looking at her nails, her knees, her shoes, anywhere but at another human being. The surgeon looked ready to slice flesh.

Petra shut the door and let in some claustrophobia. Mrs B was picking at her knit skirt. Boehlinger was trying to stare down Fournier.

Trying to dominate. To what end? Force of habit?

She remembered what Ramsey had told her about both parents trying to run Lisa's life. 'Let me start by saying how sorry we are for your loss. We're doing everything in our power to find Lisa's killer—'

Mention of her daughter made Mrs B weep. The doctor made no effort to comfort her. 'We know who the *killer* is.'

333

'If there's anything you can tell us to substantiate that, sir—'

'He beat her up, she left him. What more do you need?'

'Unfortunately—'

'This boy, the potential witness,' said Boehlinger, 'I'm sure there've been responses to our reward.'

'A few calls have come in,' said Petra.

'And?'

'We haven't gotten to them yet, sir, been following up other leads.'

'For Christ's sake!' Boehlinger's hand slammed the table. His wife jumped but she didn't look at him. 'I dip into my own damned pocket, do your job for you, and you don't have the decency to follow up—'

'We will, sir,' said Petra. 'Soon as we're free to do so.'

'Why aren't you free?'

'We're here, sir,' said Fournier.

Boehlinger's hand rose again and for a second Petra thought he'd try to strike Wil. But the fist froze in mid-air. Slight tremor. Surgeon past his prime or the stress?

'*We're* delaying you? *We're* the problem—'

'No, sir,' said Fournier. 'We appreciate all your—'

The hand slammed again. 'You,' he said very softly, 'are a very rude man. You're both rude.'

'John!'

'Typical,' said Boehlinger, glaring at Petra and Fournier in turn. 'Civil servants. So you know nothing about this boy. Priceless, just priceless. Affirmative action at its finest – I believe we're going to have to take this one step further, Vivian. Hire our own—'

'Stop it, John. *Please*.'

Boehlinger laughed derisively. 'We will most definitely hire our own investigator, because these two obviously aren't—'

'*Shut up, John!*'

The shriek filled the room. Boehlinger turned white and clawed the table-top. His fingers failed to find purchase and his hands flattened. Without facing his wife, he said, 'Vivian, I'd appreciate it if you—'

'Just shut *up*, John! *Shutup shutup shut up!*'

Now it was her turn to raise a hand. It sailed through the air like a flesh airplane, landed on her bosom, over her heart. She ran out of the room, swinging the door open, not bothering to close it.

Fournier's eyes begged for Petra to follow. Even Dr Bile was preferable to a grieving mother.

Petra caught up with her at the end of the hall, in the stairwell, sitting on the top step, forehead to the wall, the champagne puff bobbing with each sob.

'Ma'am—'

'I'm sorry!'

'No need to apologize, ma'am.'

'I'm very sorry, very very very *sorry*!'

Petra sat down next to the woman and chanced putting her arm around the heaving shoulders. Beneath the knit fabric were small bones. Petra smelled makeup, breath mints, Chanel No. 5. 'Let's find somewhere to go.'

Vivian Boehlinger straightened and pointed at the interrogation rooms. 'Not with him!'

'No,' said Petra. 'By ourselves.'

No one was in the vending-machine room, so she guided

the woman in and closed the door. No lock; she placed a chair against it, sat down, motioning for Vivian Boehlinger to choose one near the folding table that served as the D's' snack center.

'Coffee?'

'No, thank you.' Subdued voice now, that post-tantrum shame/fatigue. Small hands folded in a black-knit lap. Under the fluorescence, Petra could see hints of deep facial lines, muted expertly by makeup. The eyes were tormented, devoid of hope. So disturbing in contrast: Everything else about the woman was so well put together.

'I'm sorry,' she repeated.

'It's really OK, ma'am. Situations like this—'

'When all this is over, I'm going to leave him.'

Petra didn't speak.

Vivian Boehlinger said, 'I was going to do it this year. Now I'll have to wait. Thirty-six years of marriage, what a joke.' She shook her head, made a terrible sound, more parrot squawk than laugh.

'He has affairs with sluts,' she went on. 'Thinks I'm stupid and don't know.' Another bird-sound. It made Petra's flesh crawl. 'Cheap slutty affairs. And now Lisa's gone.'

Odd juxtaposition, but maybe not. Tabulating her miseries. Petra waited for her to take it further, but all she said was, 'My Lisa, my pretty Lisa.'

Several more minutes of silence, then: 'Ma'am, do you think Cart Ramsey did it?'

'I don't know.' Quick answer. She'd thought about it. She gave a pitiful shrug and sniffed. Petra fetched a paper napkin. Dab, dab.

'Thank you. You're very sweet. I don't know what to

think.' She sat up straighter, higher. 'John thinks he can buy everything. He offered Lisa money not to marry Carter, and when that didn't work, even more money to divorce him. So idiotic – Lisa was going to divorce Carter anyway. She told me. If John had ever communicated with her he could have saved himself the offer. Which is all it was. Lisa divorced Carter but did John keep his end of the bargain?'

A scary smile spread across the thin lips. Lipstick and liner had been used to extend the coral borders and radically change the mouth's contours. Without her morning routine, this woman would be unrecognizable.

'He didn't pay up?' said Petra.

'Of course not. He didn't give Lisa one dime. Said he hadn't been serious, it was for Lisa's own good anyway, she had nothing to complain about. Lisa didn't care, she knew who she was dealing with. But still. Don't you think that's terrible?'

'How much did he offer Lisa?'

'Fifty thousand dollars. So now he comes up with half?' She shook her head. 'Don't expect him to pay any reward, Detective. I feel sorry for anyone who thinks they're going to get paid by John – do I think Carter did it? I don't know. To me, he always seemed civil. Then Lisa told me he hit her, so I don't know.'

'How many times did she say he hit her, ma'am?'

'Just the once. They had a tiff, Carter lost control and hit her. More than a slap, her eye was blackened and her lip was split.'

'Just once,' said Petra.

'Once was too much for Lisa.' That sounded boastful. Daughter asserting herself in a way mother never could?

'She told me she wouldn't tolerate it. And I agreed with her. For all the things her father did over thirty-six years, he never laid a hand on me. If he had, who knows what I'd have done.' She lifted her purse, hefted it like a weapon. 'Of course, I didn't know Lisa was going to go on television. If she'd told me about that, I probably would have advised against it.'

'Too public?'

'Tasteless. But I'd have been wrong. Why keep it all inside? What's the point of being quiet and pretty and tasteful?'

She cried some more, dabbed. 'Do I think Carter did it? Why not? He's a man. They're responsible for all the violence in the world, aren't they? Am I as sure as John? No. Because no one's ever as sure as *John*.'

She got up. 'I know you're trying your best, Detective. John wants blood but I only want . . . something I'll never get. My little girl back. Now, if you'd be so kind as to call me a cab.'

'Certainly, ma'am.' Petra stayed with her, holding the door. 'Here's my card. If you think of something, anything, please let me know.'

The two of them returned to the hallway. The door to Interrogation One was still closed.

'Your poor black friend,' said Vivian Boehlinger. 'John's prejudiced – I really despise him.'

'I'll call that cab,' said Petra. 'Where to?'

'The Beverly Wilshire. *He's* staying at the Biltmore.'

Barely after 9 A.M. and she was exhausted; the time spent with the Boehlingers had sapped her energies. Poor Wil was still in there.

338

What a pair, even allowing for tragedy. No marital role-model for Lisa. How much free will did any of us have?

The message stack had grown; four more tips on the boy. She dreaded Dr B's follow-up calls.

In some cases, you bonded with the victim's family. Here she was, wanting to punch Dr B's lights out, creeped-out by Mrs B's avian laugh. Not good at all. And Stu still hadn't arrived. Obviously he didn't give a damn anymore. Which didn't fit a career-opportunity thing. So maybe it *was* marital.

She did some fruitless follow-up with Missing Persons on Flores, was putting down the phone when Stu said, 'Good morning.'

Freshly shaved, every hair in place. He wore a beautiful slate-gray gabardine suit, pearl-gray shirt, smoke and red paisley tie. So perfectly composed.

It pissed her off.

'Is it?' she said.

He turned around and left the squad room.

39

SAM GANZER didn't park the Lincoln carefully. The twenty-year-old land yacht was too wide for each of the spaces behind the *shul* so he used both of them.

Who was there to complain? The synagogue, once a social center for Venice's Jews, had been reduced to a weekend facility, Sam's maintenance calls the only thing that opened its doors before Friday night.

Even on the weekend it was sometimes hard to get ten men together for a *minyan*. Beth Torah wasn't orthodox enough for the yarmulke-clad yuppies who'd gentrified Venice, so they started their own congregation a few blocks away, brought a bearded fanatic rabbi from New York, installed a partition between the men and the women. The old, mostly left-wing crowd who patronized the *shul* wouldn't hear of it.

That had been five years ago. Now most of the regulars had died off. Eventually, Sam knew, Beth Torah would close down, the property be sold. Maybe the yuppies would reclaim it, which would be better than yet another cheap business added to the dozens that lined Ocean Front Walk. Sam didn't mind the yuppies as much as some of the old socialists did. He had a deep-rooted distrust of authority but was, at heart, a businessman. Meanwhile, he'd park any damn way he pleased.

He felt he'd live forever. For seventy-one, his body was working OK. His brother Emil, living down in Irvine, not religious at all, was seventy-six. Good stock: Generations of thickset, robust metalsmiths and carpenters honed by bone-numbing Ukrainian winters.

It had taken pure evil to cut down most of the Ganzer tree.

Mother, father, three younger brothers, two sisters shipped off to Sobibor, never seen again. Avram, Mottel, Baruch, Malkah, Sheindel. Had they made it to America, what would their names have been? Sam's best guess was Abe, Mort, Bernie, Marilyn, Shirley. Last week, he'd raised the question with Emil, who didn't want to talk about it.

All in all, forty-five Ganzers and Leibovics had been rounded up by the Ukrainian police and handed over to the occupying Nazi scum. Sam and Emil, muscular young men – Emil a lightweight boxing champ at the Kovol gymnasium – were spared and enslaved as forced laborers. Eighteen-hour work days on thin soup and sawdust bread. Midnight escape through the snow, living in the forest on leaves and nuts, nearly starving till they'd been taken in by a saintly Catholic woman. When her son had come back from the war, he wanted to turn them over, so the Ganzer brothers ran again, walking till the brink of death, finally making it to Shanghai. The Chinese had been decent; Sam sometimes wondered what it would have been like to stay, marry one of those gorgeous, porcelain girls. Instead, liberation, Canada, Detroit, LA.

For years he hadn't thought about any of that crap. Lately, the memories had been returning, uninvited. Probably some kind of brain damage. His body was strong, but names, places were fading, he'd walk into a room, forget why. The ancient stuff, though, was as clear as day, all that anger, he could feel it pounding in his ears, bad for the blood pressure.

He turned off the Lincoln's engine and got out. On Friday night and Saturday, he assumed sexton's duties, had since Mr Ginzburg died. With the unpaid position came maintenance obligations. Why not? What else did he have to do besides play the mandolin and sit outside his house getting too much sun, he'd already had four pre-cancerous lesions cut off his face and one on his bald spot, had to wear a stupid cap, like an old guy.

He took the hat off, tossed it in the Lincoln and locked the big white car, enjoyed another look at how he'd parked. Better than leaving room for some drug addict to slump in a stolen car and inject himself. That had happened more than once, this neighborhood, always a little nuts, had become a crazy mix of gawking tourists on weekends, lowlifes crawling out of the woodwork at night.

Most of Ocean Front was one big gyp-joint, now. Fly-by-nights selling cheap junk, weekends so jammed you couldn't take two steps without bumping into some yutz.

For forty years Sam and Emil sold hardware and plumbing fixtures from their store on Lincoln Boulevard, things you could use. Both of them knowing how to install as well as sell, pipe a house from scratch. You got to be handy, living on your own, never depending on anyone else. Leaving Shanghai, he'd vowed never to depend on anyone else. Maybe that's why he'd never married. Though the ladies loved him, he'd had his good times, even now he once in a while got between the covers with soft-skinned grandmothers

342

ashamed of what age had done to their bodies. Sam knew how to make them feel young and gorgeous.

He felt for the *shul* key in his pocket, found it, opened the back door. Not noticing the screen from the bathroom window lying on the ground because it was partially blocked by his right front tire.

Moments after he got inside he knew someone had broken in.

The silverplated *pushke* was sitting atop the platform where the Torah was read, shiny against the blue velvet coverlet, right out in the open. The charity box hadn't been used since Friday night, when it was passed around before services. Sam had put it away personally, in a cabinet beneath the bookcases. Just a cheap combination lock, no reason to make a big deal, all it contained was a few dollars in coins.

But someone had tried anyway. And look, food had been taken out of the same cabinet. Snack stuff for the handful of Saturday-morning regulars. Tam Tam crackers and a pink box from a bakery on Fairfax – sugar-coated *kichlen* shaped like bowties. Sam had bought them last week. No preservatives, had to be stale, he'd forgotten to get rid of them.

Crumbs on blue velvet. A quarter and a dime had fallen out of the *pushke*. Hungry thief. What else had he taken?

The only things of value to a junkie were the silver finials and breastplates that graced the three Torahs in the ark. Sam started toward the carved walnut case, ready to draw back the blue velvet curtain, afraid of what he'd find.

Then he stopped himself, raised his heavy arms instinctively. Maybe the crook was still here. All he needed was some junkie jumping out at him.

No one did. Silence, no movement at all.

He stood there and looked around.

The *shul* was four rooms – small entry hall in front, gents'
and ladies' lavs at the back, in between, the main sanctuary:
Rows of walnut pews, seating for 150.

A double-sided dead bolt protected the front door – you
couldn't get in or out without a key. Same for the back. So
how . . . ?

He waited a few more minutes, convinced himself he was
alone, but made sure by inspecting. Then out to the front
room. Still locked, no damage to the door.

In back was where he found it, the window in the ladies'
lav. Closed, but the screen was off – there it was, down near
his tire. Some white chips on the sill where dry paint had
flaked off.

Closing the window after he'd left? Considerate thief?

He returned to the sanctuary, opened the ark, examined
the Torahs. All the silver in place. The bottle-shaped *pushke*
hadn't been emptied either, and the lock didn't show a
scratch. Only Sam and Mr Kravitz knew the combination
and they took turns emptying the weekly take and delivering it to the Hadassah thrift shop on Broadway. Once upon
a time Congregation Beth Torah had proudly contributed
fifty dollars a week to the poor, now it was down to ten,
twelve. Embarrassing, so Sam augmented it with twenty of
his own – what Kravitz did, he had no idea, the guy was a
bit of a cheapskate.

He inspected the *pushke*, rattled it. Still full. Except for
the quarter and the dime. Strange.

Several *kichlen* were gone, and from what Sam could see,
quite a few crackers.

Hungry *gonif*. Probably some bum, too doped up to know

344

what he was doing, one of those nuts who lurched up and down the walkway. Sometimes Sam gave them money, other times he wanted nothing to do with them.

A skinny nut, because the lav window was small. Junkies got skinny. And weren't they always hungry for sweets? OK, no big loss. He dropped the coins back in the *pushke*, brushed crumbs from the velvet, closed the cracker box and the bakery box and carried them over to the bookcase. Opening the lower cabinet where the food went, he saw something else the *gonif* hadn't touched: Schnapps for the regulars. A nearly full bottle of Crown Royal, and a half-empty Smirnoff's vodka.

A junkie with one vice only, no taste for booze?

Next to the bottles were some folded prayer shawls. A bunch of small silk ones, striped blue, but also the big black-striped woolen *tallis* worn by the prayer leader. That one belonged in the compartment under the platform, how had it gotten there?

Had he put it there? Had Kravitz? He strained to remember, damn his memory . . . last *shabbos* . . . yeah, yeah, Mrs Rosen hadn't felt good and Sam had left early to take her home, he'd left Kravitz in charge. The guy had no eye for details.

Removing the woolen shawl, he saw that Kravitz hadn't folded it properly, either. A klutz. He'd clerked for the Water Department all his life, what could you expect from a desk jockey.

Refolding the shawl, caressing the thick wool, Sam carried it to the platform, bent down and opened the compartment door.

Inside was a boy.

A small, skinny kid, curled up into a corner, looking scared as hell.

Breathing hard. Sam could see his chest moving, and now he could hear it, fast, raspy, like he had asthma or something.

Such a look on the face.

Sam knew that look. His siblings; faces through train windows.

Laborers in the camp who didn't make it.

Even tough Emil's face the time he got pneumonia, thought this was it.

Sam's own face when, in the dead of winter, he found a piece of broken glass in the snow, used it for a mirror, saw what he'd become.

This boy looked exactly like that.

'It's OK,' he said.

The boy shivered. Hugging himself like he was cold, and even though this was June, Venice, California, a beautiful sunny day, Sam felt a Ukrainian freeze pass over his own body.

'It's OK,' he repeated. 'Come on out, I don't bite.'

The boy didn't budge.

'Come on, you can't stay in there all day – still hungry? Crackers aren't enough, let's get you some real food.'

It took a long time to coax the boy out, standing far back so the kid could crawl free. When he was finally out, he looked like he wanted to run.

Sam held him by the arm – skin and bones. More memories.

The boy struggled, tried to kick. Sam, knowing what it

346

felt like to be restrained, let go and the boy dashed toward the front of the *shul*.

Rattling the door, but locked in.

Returning to the sanctuary, he gave Sam a wide berth. Wild-eyed, looking from side to side, trying to figure out how to escape.

Sam was sitting in a front pew holding a box of donuts the boy had missed, real *chazerei*, Entenmann's chocolate-covered cake donuts, still unopened, hidden behind some old prayer-books. Kravitz's secret lode, who did he think he was kidding? Next to the donuts was also a sealed jar of gefilte fish balls in jelly, Sam couldn't imagine the boy going for it.

'Here,' he said, holding up the donuts. 'Take it with you.'

The boy stood there and stared. Despite being dirty and ragged and skinny, a scratched-up face, he was a nice-looking kid. Maybe eleven, twelve, what was he doing out here so young? There were plenty of runaways in Venice but they were mostly teenagers, bigshot rebels, with needles and rings stuck into their bodies all over, crazy haircuts, tattoos, a bad attitude. This one just looked like a kid, undernourished and scared.

Definitely *goyische*, look at that upturned nose, that dirty blond hair. Sometimes the goyim beat their kids, abused them, God knows what else, maybe this one had run away. Jews, too, he supposed, though he'd never encountered that personally.

What did he know about kids, anyway?

Emil had one son, a lawyer, lived in Encino – drove a German car! – never talked to his parents or Sam.

'Here,' he said, shaking the donut box. 'Take it.'

No response. The kid, distrustful, thinking Sam was up to something. Dirt stains all over his jeans and that T-shirt was full of holes. He was making fists, a tough little pisher.

Sam put the donuts on the floor, got up, said, 'Fine, I'll open the door for you, you don't have to crawl out the window. But if you ask me, you should get some clean clothes, eat some real food with vitamins.'

Dipping into his trouser pocket, he took some bills out of his wallet. Two twenties, way too generous for someone he didn't know, but what the hell.

He placed the money on the floor next to the donuts, walked to the back of the *shul* and unlocked the rear door. Then he went into the gents' lav, to give the kid a chance to make a graceful exit, and because his bladder was killing him.

40

PETRA STARED at the doorway through which Stu had just passed, then she went after him.

He reappeared in the doorway before she got there. Cocking his head.

C'mere.

Oh yeah, faithful little junior partner will jump up on cue.

They locked eyes. His face was stone, no apologies. Deciding to maintain her dignity, she followed him down the stairs and out of the building to the rear lot where his Suburban was parked. The truck, usually spotless, had dirty windows. Crusted bird droppings freckled the white hood.

She said, 'What the hell's going on, Stu?'

He unlocked the passenger door, motioned for her to get in, came around and sat behind the wheel.

'We're not going anywhere,' she said, remaining outside. 'Some of us have work to do.'

He stared through the windshield. Sun from the east traced the contours of his profile in orange. A paperback book model couldn't have posed for greater effect. Everyone a goddamned actor.

Petra got in and slammed the door so hard the truck shook.

Stu said, 'I owe you an explanation.'

'OK.'

'Kathy has cancer.'

Petra's throat seized and closed and for a moment she couldn't breathe. 'Oh, Stu—'

He held up a finger. 'She's going in for surgery tomorrow. She's been taking tests, we weren't sure. Now we are.'

'I'm so sorry, Stu.' Why didn't you tell me? Obviously, not close enough. Eight months of chasing bad guys doth not a deep relationship make.

'One breast,' he said. 'Her doctor found it on routine checkup. They think it's just a single tumor.'

'What can I do to help?'

'Nothing thanks, we're covered. Mother's taking the kids and Father's dealing with the hospital.'

His right arm rested on the center console. Petra put her hand on his sleeve. 'Go home, Stu. Wil and I will handle everything.'

'No, that's the thing, I was going to take leave of absence but Kathy insisted I shouldn't. She wants me home tonight to take her to the hospital, told me I can stay until she falls asleep. And tomorrow, when she comes out of surgery, I'll be there. But in between she insists I keep working. Even when she gets radiation . . . maybe they can do just a lumpectomy, they're not sure.'

'You're planning to stay on the job?' said Petra.

'Kathy wants it. You know Kathy.'

Petra knew very little about Kathy. Gracious, pretty, efficient, super-mom, never without makeup. High-school prom queen with a teaching credential she'd never used. During the family outings, Petra had observed a super-organizer.

A bit reserved – let's be honest, more than reserved.

Despite superficial friendliness, the woman had always maintained distance and Petra had thought of her as an ice queen.

Thirty-six years old. Six kids.

Petra thought of her own father, raising five children by himself. And all the while, Stu'd been fighting to maintain.

'She's so strong,' Stu said. 'I've never slept with anyone else.'

Saying it with wonderment. Petra patted his arm.

'Most guys get tired of being with the same woman. All I ever wanted was Kathy. I really love her, Petra.'

'I know you do.'

'You try to do the right thing, live a certain way – I know there are no deals with God, He's got His own plan, but still . . .'

'She'll be fine,' said Petra. 'It'll work out, you'll see.'

'Look at Ramsey,' he went on. 'Has a healthy wife, does that to her. The Eggermann woman, all the things we see.'

He put his head down on the steering wheel, broke into startling, phlegmy sobs.

Vivian Boehlinger, now this.

This was different. This was part of her.

Petra reached over and held him.

41

As she approached the elevator, Mildred Board heard footsteps from above. Then a toilet flush, the bath water running. The big house was built beautifully but if you stood in certain places, sound traveled freely through the rafters.

Missus drawing the bath herself. There was something new.

Perhaps it would be a good day.

She returned to the kitchen, ate the shirred eggs and drank the coffee at the old yew-wood table, dumped the coffee, made a fresh pot and waited, allowing the Missus a nice long time to soak. By 8:45 she was riding up with the second batch of breakfast.

No newspaper on the tray. But not because she'd screened it for nastiness. The delivery service had skipped the house this morning. Again. Such a slipshod world.

She'd take care of it after serving, get right on the phone with the newspaper subscription office, give them what for.

Sometimes she wished the Missus would allow the subscription to lapse. There was no need to read the kinds of things they printed.

The lift let her out on the carpeted top landing. She walked past the space where the upstairs Steinway grand had stood, past the ghosts of the Regency chest with its intricate tortoiseshell front, the pair of monumental Kang Xi vases, blue as the sky, white as milk, sitting high on Carrara pedestals. A patch of dust in an alcove made her stop and swipe with the hem of her apron.

The walk to the Missus's suite took her past the echoes of Chinese porcelain, the gilded cases, one filled with animalier bronzes, the other teeming with Japanese inro, jade, ivory, mixed-metal vases.

All irreplaceable. Like the boule chest. It was illegal to kill tortoises now. Unborn babies, yes, but not reptiles.

She knocked on the Missus's door, received the expected faint reply and went in.

The Missus was in bed, wearing the cream satin bedjacket with the covered buttons – what a quest it had been finding a proper dry-cleaner for that – hair wrapped in a white French towel, no makeup but still beautiful. Rosewater scent sweetened the enormous room. The only items on the nightstand were a Limoges tissue-box holder and a black satin eye mask. The bedcovers were barely mussed; even in sleep the woman was genteel.

But the Missus was acting strange – staring straight ahead, not smiling at Mildred.

Bad dreams again?

The room was still dark, both sets of drapes drawn. Mildred stood there, not wanting to intrude, and a second later the Missus turned to her. 'Good morning, dear.'

'Morning, ma'am.'

Her face so thin, so white. Tired, very tired. So it probably *wouldn't* be a good day.

Mildred resolved to try to get her out of the house a bit – a drive to Huntington Gardens? Last month the two of them had spent a glorious hour strolling at the Missus's snail-pace. A week later Mildred had suggested they repeat it, perhaps the art gallery, but the Missus demurred. *Maybe another time, dear.*

Once upon a time, a driver had wheeled the Cadillac and the Lincoln. The Cadillac was gone; Mildred wrestled with the Lincoln . . . how much petrol was in the tank?

If not a drive, at least a stroll out in back, some fresh air. Maybe after lunch.

'Here's some breakfast for you, ma'am.'

'Thank you, Mildred.' Saying it automatically, so politely, that Mildred knew the Missus wasn't hungry, probably wouldn't touch a thing.

The body needed sustenance. That was simple logic. Yet, despite all her education, the college degree from Wellesley – the finest women's school in America – the Missus sometimes seemed unaware of the basics. During those moments, Mildred felt she was the older sister, caring for a child.

'You do need to eat, ma'am.'

'Thank you, Mildred. I'll do my best.'

Mildred put the food down, drew the drapes, fetched the bed-tray and set it up. She noticed a kink in the drapery pleats, straightened it and looked out the window. The blue-tiled pool that Him had modeled after Mr Hearst's at San Simeon was empty and streaked with brown. The boxwood knot garden – too painful to see. Mildred looked away but not before being assaulted by a distant view of downtown Los Angeles. All that steel and glass, hideous from up close, but this far perhaps it did have a certain . . . stature.

When she turned fully, the Missus was wiping her eyes.

Crying? Mildred hadn't heard a sniffle.

The Missus pulled a tissue out of the porcelain box and blew her nose inaudibly. Another cold? Or *had* she been crying?

'Here you go, ma'am, toast just the way you like it.'

'Forgive me, Mildred, it's a beautiful breakfast but . . . maybe in a bit, please leave it.'

'Some coffee to stimulate the appetite, ma'am?'

The Missus started to refuse, then said, 'Yes, please.'

Mildred took hold of the cozy-wrapped pitcher and directed an ebony stream into the Royal Worcester cup. The Missus lifted the coffee. Her hands were shaking so, she needed both to keep it steady.

'What's the matter, ma'am?'

'Nothing. Everything's fine, Mildred – what a beautiful rose.'

'Giant blossoms this year, ma'am. It's going to be a good year for roses.'

'Yes, I'm sure it will . . . thank you for going to the trouble.'

'No trouble at all, ma'am.'

The same dialogue they exchanged every morning. Hundreds of mornings. A ritual but not a formality, because the Missus's gratitude was genuine, she was gracious as royalty – more gracious, look what royalty had become! It was hard to think of her as an American. More of an . . . international.

The Missus reached for another tissue and patted her eyes. Mildred picked up the first tissue, dropping it in the Venetian wastebasket beneath the end table, noticed something in there.

A newspaper. Today's!

'I got up very early and brought it up, Mildred – don't be cross.'

'Early, ma'am?' Mildred had been up at six, taking her own bath, ten minutes of secret bubbles, ten minutes later. She hadn't heard a thing – the Missus's escape concealed by running water!

'I went outside to check the trees. All those winds – the Santa Annas we had last night.'

'I see, ma'am.'

'Oh, Mildred, it's fine.' The soft eyes blinked.

Mildred crossed her arms over her apron. 'How early is early, ma'am?'

'I don't really know, dear – six, six thirty. I suppose I went to sleep too early and my rhythm was off.'

'Very well,' said Mildred. 'Would you be wanting anything else, ma'am?'

'No, thank you, dear.' Now the Missus's hands were shaking again. Holding tight to the covers. Smiling, but it looked forced. Mildred prayed it wasn't another downturn. She looked down at the newspaper.

'You can take it,' said the Missus. 'If you want to read it.'

Mildred folded the horrid thing under her arm. Read it, indeed! She'd throw it out with the kitchen trash.

42

WHEN THE lock clicked on the back door to the Jewish church my brain froze and I couldn't move.

What would the Jews do to me? Now I was finished.

As the back door opened I jumped under the big table, crawled into the cabinet and closed the door quietly. I could hear footsteps from inside.

Just one person walking – yes, just one.

The cabinet was empty and smelled of wood and old clothes. My mouth tasted of crackers and fear. I pushed myself into a corner and didn't move. Praying whoever was in here wouldn't open the doors.

The sign said no prayers till tomorrow; did the Jews have secret prayers?

Whoever it was out there walked around, stopped, walked some more.

Now he was close to me. If he did open the cabinet, I'd jump out, I'd scream like a maniac, surprise him and escape.

Escape, how? Not through the back door, unless he'd left it unlocked.

The front – could you open it from inside? The bathroom window again – that would take time. My stomach started to hurt really bad. I felt like I was being suffocated.

I didn't even do anything really wrong, just ate some of their food and it wasn't that good – crackers with an onion taste, some butterfly-shaped cookies that were stale.

I didn't even mess with the silver bottle with the Jewish star on it, just shook it to see what would fall out. Even though the lock looked dinky. I thought about breaking it but the bottle looked nice and I didn't want to damage it.

This was a Jewish place but it was still a church, so maybe God was here, too.

I'd tell him all that if he caught me.

No I wouldn't, I'd yell and scream and run to the bathroom, lock myself in, get that window up.

I remembered what Moron said about Jews being out to kill Christians . . . that's got to be crazy, but what if . . .

Now he's farther away. Back and forth, back and forth – what's he doing?

Uh-oh, he's coming closer again. I hear rattling – he's shaking the silver bottle, now it sounds like he's scraping the top of the table – probably cleaning up the cracker crumbs . . . now he walks away. Maybe he'll see no one stole anything and just leave—

Now he's walking back—

The door opens.

I don't jump out and yell.

I just push myself harder into the corner.

A face stares at me. An old face, kind of fat. Glasses with thick black frames, a big nose, red, kind of big ears.

A funny-looking old guy. He steps back. He's wearing old guy's clothes: A white shirt and baggy light blue pants and one of those zippered tan jackets. His fingers are really thick and his hands look too big for the rest of him.

358

He doesn't look mad. More surprised. I keep pushing myself into the corner, the wood is hard against my back and my butt but I can't stop pushing.

He steps back some more, says, 'It's OK,' in a deep grumbly voice.

I just sit there.

'It's OK, come on out, I don't bite.'

Then he peeks in closer, smiling, showing me his teeth, like trying to prove they're not for biting kids. The pervert grandpa smiled that way, too.

He's giving me room to get out but I can't move, I just can't move.

He starts saying it's OK, if I'm hungry I should eat right, not junk.

I figure if he gives me troubles I can just push him down. Even with those big, thick hands, he's an old guy.

Finally, my body relaxes and I crawl out. He grabs my arm and he's pretty strong and I try to kick him and he lets go and I run to the front of the synagon but the door's locked with one of those locks you need a key for so now I'm stuck.

I go back. He's sitting down on a church bench. He laughs, holds out a box of chocolate donuts, tries to give it to me but no way will I get close enough to him to take it.

Not just because he's Jewish, because he's a person and you can't trust anyone.

He starts talking again, telling me he'll unlock the back door for me, I don't have to crawl through the window.

Then he pulls out money! Two twenty-dollar bills – forty dollars!

What's he trying to buy?

I don't take it and he puts it down on the floor along with the donuts and gets up and unlocks the door and goes to the bathroom.

I grab up everything and race out of there.

Outside, I breathe again. Inside my pocket the money weighs a ton and the first donut I eat, walking through the alley, tastes fantastic. I eat another one. Then my stomach starts to hurt and I decide to save the rest for later.

Stores are opening and more people are walking and skating and the first thing I do is buy a hat, a Dodgers cap with an adjustable band in back. I fit it to my head and bend the brim over my face so it'll keep the sun off, and also to hide it.

Because buying it is a strange experience. The place I find it is this little shack a ways up from the synagon. The guy who sells it to me is ugly with bad skin, mirrored sunglasses, and long greasy blond-and-gray hair. He looks at me funny. Like he knows me.

I guess he could be from Hollywood, but I never saw him before. He's got a weird accent, like a bad guy from a spy movie – Russian, he sounds like a Russian spy.

So why's he looking at me like that? I mean, I can't be sure he really is, because of the mirrored sunglasses. But it seems like he is – the way he turns his head toward me and just keeps it there. Taking a long time to give me my change.

As I turn away, he says, 'Hey you, kid,' but I leave anyway, pushing the hat down over my face. When I turn around a few moments later, he's in front of the shack, still looking in my direction, so I duck between a building and walk through the alley a little, then back to Ocean Front, too far for him to see me.

The ocean has turned pure blue and my bones finally feel warm. I smell corndogs and popcorn, know I have money to buy them but I'm still full from the crackers and the donuts. All these people and I'm walking along with them, like it's a moving sidewalk and we're all together, doing some dance, no one's bothering anyone.

The corndog smell makes me feel I'm at a carnival. I was at a school carnival, once. Had no money to buy corndogs or anything. This feels like a warm bright dream.

I reach the end of the walkway and there's no place to go but sand.

The whole beach is like the end of the world.

I figure I'll try the other end, turn around, walk for a while until I spot the ugly Russian guy coming my way. He's in the crowd, but he's not part of it. Everyone else seems to be having a good time. He looks angry. And his eyes are all over the place. Looking for something – me?

Another perv?

I don't want to find out. Slipping back over to the alley, I walk back in the direction I came from, checking over my shoulder a few times. I see a couple of people, but not him. Then the alley's empty again and here's the synagon. There's a huge old white Lincoln Continental with a brown top parked there, I realize it was there before, must be the old guy's.

Jew-canoes, Moron called them. Cadillacs and Lincoln Continentals.

Soft cars, he used to say, for soft people.

But the old guy had a strong grip.

The way he just gave me all that money — forty dollars, like it was nothing. So the Jews are rich. But he didn't want anything from me.

Maybe I can get some more money from him.

I'm still out in the alley, thinking about it, when he comes out, sees me and gives a surprised smile. He's really short. This time I notice that his teeth are too white, they have to be false.

Mom had some false teeth made up for the back of her mouth where the rotten ones fell out, but she never put them in and her face started to get saggy.

He holds out his hands, like he's confused.

'What?' he says. 'You already spent it all?'

43

STU LET her comfort him, then, abrupt as a power failure, he broke the embrace. It was the first time they'd ever touched.

'Back to work,' he said.

Back at their desks, he told her, 'I heard from one of my studio sources.'

Scott Wembley had called last night. He gave her the basics, leaving out the whining in the AD's voice:

'It's no big deal, Detective, but you said call for anything.'

'What do you have, Scott?'

'A few of us were sitting around schmoozing and Ramsey's name came up and someone said they thought his show sometimes shot in Griffith Park. Mountain areas, the horse trails – it's just across the freeway from Burbank.'

'Recent shoot?'

'I don't know. That's all I know.'

'Who brought it up?'

'Another AD, and don't ask me where she heard it from cause I didn't pump her – you said be subtle, right?'

'Did she know this for a fact or was she guessing?'

'She said she thought so. Thought she'd heard it somewhere. It was like . . . casual talk. People giving their opinions.'

'What kinds of opinions?'

'One, really: Ramsey's the white man's answer to O.J.'

'OK, Scott. Thanks.'

'Thank me by leaving me alone.'

Petra said, 'So maybe Ramsey knows Griffith.'

'But then why wouldn't he pick a more secluded area of the park?'

'Because then he'd have to drag Lisa along on foot. Using the parking lot meant he could drive in, ostensibly to talk, then stab her by surprise.'

'You think he planned it.'

'I think at some time during their time together he planned it. Also, the car may have had some significance. Psychologically. Ramsey collects cars, Lisa liked to have sex in them. Where better to end their relationship than in a parking lot?'

'The perfect LA couple . . . good point. I like that.' He put his hands on the steering wheel. He'd shaved carelessly, missing a tiny waffle of blond hair below his right ear. 'Be interesting to know if any *Adjustor* episodes match the murder.'

'Life imitating bad TV?' said Petra.

'These people have no imagination. Getting the actual scripts would take time, but I can scan a few years' worth of *TV Guides*, see what comes up in the plot summaries.'

'Fine,' said Petra. More busywork. He looked grateful to do it.

Fournier entered the squad room, picked up a stack of message slips and came over. 'Hey,' he said.

'Hey,' said Stu. Nothing on his face to indicate this wasn't just another day.

Fournier waved the stack. 'Took the liberty of burglarizing your desktop, Barbie.'

'I'll pay you later,' she said. 'Anything new?'

'Still nothing on the kid from shelters, do-gooders or Juvey, but he didn't just blow into town, I've got one nice lead, Korean guy runs the Oki-Rama on Western, says the kid bought food from him once in a while over a three-, four-month period. Always at night, he noticed because the kid looked young to be alone at that hour, never talked except to order, never made eye contact, real careful about counting his change, every penny. "A little banker," the Korean guy called him. Said the kid also came by and swiped ketchup, mustard, mayo, thought he never noticed. And guess what: Last time the kid came in was Sunday night around nine. Bought a chili-burger.'

'There you go,' said Petra, thinking about the boy on his own for three months. Managing his finances. Where'd he get the money? Where did he come from? 'Let's check the national runaway lines.'

'Already faxed the picture,' said Fournier. 'They've got tons of files, it'll take time. Meanwhile, the Korean wants the reward.' He laughed. 'Along with everyone else. Along with the greedy types are a few just-plain wackos. I got an alleged clair*voyant* from Chula Vista claiming some satanic cult murdered Lisa for her thymus gland. Seems there's a new rage for thymus glands among the horned crowd.'

'Lisa's thymus was intact at the time of autopsy,' said Petra.

'I told the lady she hadn't won the jackpot. Didn't know clairvoyants could cuss like that. One last thing: Schoelkopf blew in. They're leaning on him from the top and we are instructed to inform him immediately about anything remotely resembling a lead. Do we have one?'

Stu told him the rumor about Ramsey's show filming in Griffith.

Fournier thought. 'Nah, he can't take that to the press.'

'He actually made it to the squad room?' said Petra. 'Among the great unwashed?'

'For a whole five minutes, Barb. Turn up the heat and the grease spatters.'

44

A WITNESS.

How was it possible?

He'd awoken this morning feeling pretty good about things. Stretched, yawned, made coffee, poured some juice. Opened the paper.

And there it was.

His bowels started churning.

A *kid*?

The article said *maybe* he'd been there, the police were developing other leads.

Meaning the police didn't know a damn thing or they were double-bluffing, trying to draw him out.

He didn't do well with uncertainty.

A *kid*? In the park at that hour?

Maybe it was a bogus clue, a plant to flush someone out.

No, not with a reward. If a false clue got some innocent kid picked up by some money-hungry idiot and the parents sued, there'd be bigtime legal problems.

So probably a real lead . . . but how would anyone know about the kid if he hadn't come forward?

Unless . . . some sort of physical evidence . . . had he left something behind?

Funny thing was, while he was doing Lisa, he'd thought

he heard something. Up behind those rocks. A rustle, a scraping, above the sound of his pumping arm.

He allowed himself a moment of bliss: The look on Lisa's face. Even in the darkness, he'd seen it. Or maybe he'd just imagined it.

He'd convinced himself that he'd imagined the scraping. Had stopped, stood still, heard nothing, returned his attention to Lisa.

So nice and inert.

He had blood on his shirt but was careful to keep his shoes clean because shoe prints could cause problems. Asphalt was good for that, too. Stay off the dirt. Before returning to the car he took the shoes off.

So careful, and yet . . . a kid up there that late . . . it made no sense. He stared at the picture again. White, looked to be eleven or twelve. Could be any of a thousand kids. If he existed.

Even if they found him, what could he have seen in the darkness?

No way his face had been visible in the darkness.

Right?

What about the car? A flash of license plate . . . there were some lights on the edge of the lot. Had he passed under them?

He hadn't worried about it, had assumed no one was there.

If the kid did exist, why hadn't he come forward? So maybe it was bogus . . .

On the other hand, this could be a problem. Not a huge one, certainly nothing compared to Estrella, the evil-eyed bitch.

Throwaway people, LA was full of them.

A kid . . . consciously he didn't feel worried but Christ, his heart was hammering away like a bastard!

He ripped the page out of the paper, squeezed it into a tight sweaty ball. Thought better of it and unfolded the picture. Tried to drink coffee, but it wouldn't go down.

Tried to cheer himself up by thinking of Lisa on the ground.

True love never dies, but she had.

So easily.

The best part had been her surprise.

Bygones be bygones, let's hug. Then wham!

Something quite different from a hug.

'Quite different,' he said aloud, in a cultured British accent. David Niven voice – one of a thousand parts he'd never gotten to play.

No one appreciated his talent.

Lisa had, though, during the last second of her life. The look on her face: Finally seeing him in a new light.

You're capable of this?

He'd made sure to look in her eyes as he jammed the knife in and yanked up.

One of those beautiful moments when everything came together. Best role he'd ever played. Just the two of them, dancing in the dark.

The two of them and a *kid*?

What could he have done to avoid it? Gone traipsing up in those hills, scattering blood and who knew what other kinds of forensic evidence all over the place? Even the LAPD nitwits might have found something.

They'd found out about the kid. *How?*

And now the reward. The old man throwing his weight around.

Maybe the kid *had* been there earlier but left before he and Lisa showed up.

Maybe, maybe, maybe – an old song, one of the doowop ones he loved. Some girl group, the Chantelles or the Shirelles.

All that money would probably bring in nut-cases. Bottom line was, LAPD didn't have a clue.

'Not a bloody clue,' he said in his David Niven voice.

Not the sheriff clowns who'd showed up the first day or that pair from the police department. Bishop, strong and silent, yielding center stage to Connor.

Ms Detective. Those long legs. No chest, but still, that was some piece of poon. What was she, twenty-six, -seven? That dark hair and pale skin. The kind of long, lean body that might look too bony naked but was OK with clothes on. He imagined her, white and smooth, not a scrap of fat on her, stretched out on a poolside lounge as she yielded to his hands, his mouth, his . . .

Another time, another place . . .

He laughed, stretched big arms.

Not a clue, any of them.

Except for this alleged *kid*?

Who wasn't coming forward.

Because he didn't exist?

Out there that late, he had to be a street punk, a runaway – maybe his mind was blown from drugs or AIDS.

Probably nothing to worry about.

He sat there for a long time, trying to convince himself. Finally reaching the ugly conclusion: It needed to be taken seriously.

He'd research it. Unlike the cops, he wasn't bound by rules. Life had taught him to make his own rules.

After all these years it all boiled down to one: Take what you want.

Like that night in Redondo, the German stewardess, sitting in that restaurant, arguing with that plug-ugly boyfriend.

He studied them from the bar across the room, nursing a Heineken, wiping suds from his false beard, wondering what a girl like that saw in someone that repulsive.

Noticing the girl because of her resemblance to Lisa. That boyfriend, a face like pigshit.

He watched them, conjuring up beauty-and-the-beast sexual fantasies that failed to arouse him. Because it was clear that they weren't getting along, glaring at each other, not eating much.

Finally the girl got up and stomped out of the restaurant. Looking so much like Lisa – a bit taller, bigger tits, the lush body in that short, blue dress, those tight, muscular legs as she marched off-screen.

Pigshit tossed bills down and followed. Big guy, but soft, a sack of fertilizer.

He watched them leave, paid for the Heineken, made sure no one was watching and climbed down to the parking lot behind the restaurant, finding a vantage point behind his car. Pigshit was trying to get Blondie into his car, lots of hand gestures on both sides. Every time she moved those tits bounced – from the way they responded, not an ounce of plastic. Chest like that on a skinny girl, you didn't see it very often.

They kept arguing, then Pigshit grabbed her, she pulled away, he grabbed again, she slapped him, he slapped her, she fell, got up.

This was fun.

Now Pigshit looked like he was apologizing – the big idiot actually got down on his knees.

And what did Blondie do?

Spit on him.

Watching from behind his car, he almost laughed out loud. Uh-oh, here comes payback: Pigshit sprang up, swung at her, a giant roundhouse, but clumsy, too many drinks, he missed. Blondie ran across the lot, those wonderful tits heaving-ho, Pigshit shaking his fist but not following.

Blondie stopped at the edge of the lot, folded her hands across the wonder-chest. Pigshit shook his head, got in a compact car, drove away.

Alone, she let her hands drop helplessly. Realizing it was dark, no one's around, the pier has emptied out, try finding a cab in Redondo Beach at this hour.

The smart thing would have been to return to the restaurant. Instead, she just stood there. Crying.

Well, *Fräulein*, stupidity has its rewards.

His turn.

Wonderful. His second time. First had been little Sally Tosk, back in Syracuse, tenth grade, well-developed since eighth. He'd watched her chest grow, almost alarmingly. Not a true blonde, a strawberry blonde, still wearing braces on her top teeth. She'd come on to him all through football season, finally he'd graced her with a date. Secret date, she had a boyfriend but wanted to slut around with him, too.

He'd driven to her house in his father's new Buick, her parents out till late, some kind of Rotary dinner. The Tosks lived on a big piece of land beyond the city limits, used to be a farm. Sally was ready at the door, little nightie, nothing else. Gave him tongue in the living-room, tit in the kitchen, they moved up to her bedroom then she got all hysterical when he refused to say he loved her and tried to push him

372

away and he had to put a hand over her mouth to stop her from screaming.

Covering her mouth and her nose and all of a sudden, she was blue. He panicked. Then he started to see her in a different light and fooled with her body, just exploring. Careful not to leave anything behind, he drove home throbbing with terror and pleasure.

The Tosks came home two hours later. Big scare in town, rumors of a stalking sex-maniac.

He lost sleep for weeks because what if Sally had told someone she was meeting him? Lost weight and told his mother he had the flu.

But she hadn't told anyone, worried about the boyfriend.

The cops talked to the boyfriend.

No leads. He attended Sally's funeral, cried along with everyone else.

Nothing like young lust.

Sally. The German girl. Lisa.

Not that he was a serial killer. He had no compulsion.

But when the opportunity came up . . .

At Sally's funeral, he really lost it when the dirt hit the coffin. One of Sally's girlfriends, another cheerleader, took his hand and dried his eyes, told him later how sensitive he was.

'Dearly beloved,' he intoned in a melodious voice. Not Niven – John Houseman, someone like that.

And the Oscar goes to . . .

45

I TELL the old guy, 'No, I've still got it but I wouldn't mind some more. Have any work I can do?'

He pushes his glasses up his nose. 'So you *can* talk. Want to work, eh? How old are you?'

'Old enough.'

He comes closer. 'Listen, if you're in trouble, running away from something, maybe I can help you. Because a fellow your age shouldn't be out here all alone.'

I back away. 'I don't need help. Just work.'

'Got a work permit?'

I don't answer. He says, 'A work permit. It's the law. To protect kids. They used to force kids to work, not anymore. Not in the United States.'

So he's not going to help me. I start to leave.

'Hold on – you want work? Fine.'

I stop. 'What do you have? How much do you pay?'

He smiles again. 'A businessman. OK, listen, the *shul* here – the synagogue – ' he points over his shoulder – 'is not used much during the week but it would be good to have someone to clean the place up before Friday services. Keep an eye on things, know what I mean?'

'A watchman?'

'Not a night watchman, a day watchman, because there's nowhere to sleep – you have someplace to sleep?'

'Sure.'

'It's dangerous around here at night,' he says, coming even closer. 'You been on the streets a while, haven't you?'

I don't answer.

'I'm not trying to be nosy, sonny, but maybe I can help. Cause I been there, believe me.'

The way he says that, the change that comes over his face – like something I learned in science – metamorphosis. I know he's telling the truth.

'That must have been a long time ago,' I say.

He stares at me. Cracks up. 'Yeah, a real long time. Back in the Stone Age.'

His laugh is funny – deep, like it comes from way down in his belly. I can't help myself. My mouth turns up.

'Ah, he can smile, too. So maybe life's not so bad after all, ay?'

That wipes the smile from my face.

'It is?' he said. 'Someone hurt you that bad?'

Inside the *shul* he shows me a little closet in the men's bathroom where the cleaning stuff is kept. A broom, a dustpan, a mop and pail, Windex for the glass, Lemon Pledge for the wood. Some silver polish, too, but he leaves that there. Sees me looking at it.

'C'mere, sonny – do you have a name, by the way? I'm Sam Ganzer.'

'Sonny is fine.'

He shrugs, holds out his hand and we shake. His hand feels like a hunk of dried meat.

'Nice to meet you,' he says.

'Same here.'

He brings me into the main room of the *shul*. At the front is this big carved wood cabinet that I never had a chance to open, reaching to the ceiling and covered by a blue velvet curtain. He pulls a cord and the curtain opens. Behind it are these doors with twelve little carved scenes – Bible scenes, I recognize Noah's Ark, Moses in the cradle, some other stuff that doesn't mean anything to me.

Nothing about Jesus. Of course. I think: This is weird, what am I doing here?

Behind the carved doors are three things also covered in blue velvet with Jewish writing and wooden handles sticking out on top and bottom and silver handles, just on top. The closest one says, 'Dedicated by Saul and Isidore Levine in memory of their father, Hyman.' Hanging over the front are silver plates.

'Know what these are?' Sam asks.

'No.'

'Torahs. The Jewish Bible – you believe in the Bible, don't you?'

I don't know what I believe in but I nod.

'So you understand these are holy, right?'

'Don't worry, I won't steal the silver,' I say.

He turns red as a tomato. 'That's not what I was implying, sonny. I just want you to know that this is important stuff we're dealing with. So when I ask you to polish the silver you'll be extra-careful. Got it?'

'Got it.' Even though I know what he was really saying.

* * *

We arrange it this way: I'll sweep and mop the entire *shul*, including the bathrooms, Windex the windows, and Lemon Pledge the wood. The last job will be polishing the silver, because he needs to bring me more rags.

'Also,' he says, 'the silver polish is pretty strong, so don't breathe it in too close, got it?'

'Got it.'

'I'm serious,' he says. 'You don't sniff stuff, do you? Glue, paint – you don't do that, right? No drugs?'

'Never,' I said. 'Not once.'

'I believe you,' he said. 'You seem like a nice kid. I'd like to know what you're doing out on the streets, living on crackers, but it's your business.'

I say nothing.

He says, 'I just don't want to come in here, find you knocked out by silver polish fumes. Believe me, I know about these things, owned a plumbing supply business for forty years. At the end junkies and lowlifes were coming in buying all the glue and fixative, it was pretty obvious none of them ever installed a commode.'

Boy, he can really talk.

'I'll be careful,' I say.

'Another thing: Today is Thursday, tomorrow night we have services. Saturday, too, so I can't use you at all on Saturday.'

'Fine. After today, I don't think there'll be anything to do.'

He puts his hands in his pockets. 'So now the important part: How much do you want?'

'Whatever you think is fair.'

'Whatever *I* think? Meaning if I say two pennies an hour, you'll be happy?'

'I think you'll be fair.'

'Flattered, sonny, but if you're gonna be a businessman, learn to set a price.'

I think for a while. How much do they pay kids to flip burgers at McDonald's? I don't know. I really don't know. 'Two dollars an hour.'

'Two dollars an hour? Minimum wage is over four. You don't think you're minimum wage?'

'OK, five.'

'Four fifty.'

'Fine!' I shout and it surprises me.

'I'm not deaf,' he says. 'Four fifty an hour and I figure you've got, what, eight, nine hours, let's say forty bucks total. Here's an advance.'

Out comes his wallet and suddenly there're two ten-dollar bills in my hand and, not believing my good luck, I stick them in my pocket.

'The rest you'll get when you finish – I'll come by in a few hours to check.'

He moves closer again, stops. 'One more thing: This is a cash deal, no withholding for taxes, social security. So don't report me to the government, OK?'

46

THE WAY Motor Moran figured it, if he'd had a good scoot he'd nevera noticed it.

He was thirty years old and, except for those four months guarding that junkyard in Salinas, had never worked a real job. Arts-and-crafts prison shit didn't count, he'd never been in a real pen, anyway, just local shitholes, DUI, drunk and disorderly, a month here, a month there.

Life owed him something before he died. This could be it.

The kind of scoot his dick was quiverin' for cost. Like a '72 Shovelhead, Zenith carbs, nuclear displacement, polished cases – *everything* polished, *satin* chrome. Somethin' chopped, Paughco Fishtails, unleaded valve seats, powder-coated frame with a lot of flake in it. Give the whole thing a nice big stretch with some Kennedy long forks, or just some wide-glides if you didn't want to hard-on that much. Skirted seat with a backrest, because his back hurt, specially in the mornin'.

A double seat. Chromed passenger pegs, cause you had to have a chick in back, holding on for dear life as you took her on a face-blasting putt.

Not Sharla, that stoned-out skank. One of those wenches you saw in *Easy Rider*. The putt would turn her on and, pulling over at some reststop, he'd serve her some Motorized pork for lunch.

Oh, man, if he had the dough, he could have it all.

His current scoot was an Abomination Before the Lord, thrown together from corroded spare parts, fastened with Bondo and re-welds and prayer. He'd even snuck some Jap parts in places you couldn't see. HD emblem on the frame but for all the Harley parts in there, the fucking thing might've said Slant-Special.

At least it made noise. The Jap stuff never made noise.

The day he took the bus into Bakersfield, the bucket o' bolts hadn't started for three days straight. He found the trouble quickly enough. *Troubles*: Starter gear so rotted there was a fucking hole in it, spark coil stone-dead, plugs wasted. The worst thing, the voltage regulator had wires that were coming apart, rattier than Sharla's hair. A hundred bucks minimum, so far, and the belt assembly looked ready to go, another two C's.

All he had left of Sharla's FDIC was sixty bucks and he took it, left her snoring, and began the painful walk to the Bolsa Chica bus station.

Knowing sixty wouldn't get him far with Spanky, but maybe he could haul trash outta the shop, do some construction work over at Spanky's house, his bitch was always remodeling.

Anything to be rollin' again.

Riding the fuckin' bus, all those greasers staring at him. Those drippy brown eyes askin' the question any retardo would ask: Where's your scoot, man?

Cause he was a putter, you could tell by lookin' at him he didn't take no bus. If there was a roof on a ride, it sucked.

He *looked* like a putter, goddamit. Independent jeans – so oil-soaked they stood by themselves, black XXXL T-shirt with the death's head Angel insignia – when no Angels were around. Nailheads, steel boots, leather, leather, leather.

Nice bandanna-style ripper cap, fuck the helmet law!

The bus ride ate twelve of the sixty bucks, came late, made stops along the way to drop greasers off at orchards. Half the day to get to Bandit Cycles and when he arrived at the store it was crowded, weekend warriors glomming the new stuff Spanky had customized. Guys in suits drooling over outrageous '95 Rigids, coupla Softtails, a few antiques that tightened his ball-sac. Lookat that Knuckle/Pan – black-cherry lacquer with a dancing chick in pink.

Rich pussies checking out the merchandise like they knew what it was. Spanky pointing out details, kissing ass.

And if a pussy bought one, what would he be? A pussy on a scoot.

Motor cruised around the showroom, examining parts, leafing through the latest *Rider* – the Fox of the Month was a greaser but look at them brown nipples!

Then back to the grease room behind the store, where two mechanics were working on bikes. Bolting away, two assholes he'd never seen before.

More Mexicans! What got into the Spankster?

Finally, the pussies left with brochures and Spanky went back behind the counter, untied his pony tail and shook out two feeta hair – shit, the guy had gotten gray. No meat on him, face like a skeleton, those rotten teeth, asshole looked like a death-head. When did he start wearing glasses?

Motor walked up to the counter. Spanky had a bottlea Bud in one hand, his right arm was covered with tattoos from shoulder to fingertips. Not the left one, though, that just had Spanky's old lady's name, Tara, on the bicep. Once

Motor had asked him about it and Spanky had said, 'Use the left one to wipe my ass. Like the Hindus.'

Weird.

'Hey, man,' said Motor.

Spanky didn't look up. Draining half the Bud, he picked up a flyer about the Chillicothe meet, pretended to read. Motor read the back. Primo putt, Labor Day, all the way to Ohio. Lord, that was one he woulda loved to do, cruise in formation by the penitentiary, brothers behind the fence lifting their fists in solidarity.

Spanky kept reading, paying him no attention.

'Chillicothe,' said Motor. 'Only thing better would be Sturgis, right? Or maybe Memorial Day at Laconia, hey?'

Spanky continued to ignore him.

Motor coughed and finally the skinny bastard looked up.

'Hey, man,' he said. 'What's happening?'

Spanky waited a while before he muttered, 'Buell.'

Using the name Motor hated.

'Hey, Spank.' Motor raised his hand for a high five. Spanky didn't move. Then he slipped a ring through his beard, turned it into a gray horsetail. Finishing the rest of the beer, he tossed the bottle over his shoulder onto a pile of trash.

'No credit, Buell. You're still into me for those switch-blade wheels.'

'I paid you, man.'

'Yeah, right – took you two years. Wheels like that, coulda moved 'em in two days, you take two years.'

Which was bullshit, the wheels were used, pulled off a wreck and re-shaped, onea them totally skanked where kick-back gravel had knocked out a chunka rim.

'Spank—'

'Forget it, Buell.'

'Listen, it's only a few small ones. And I got dough.'

'How much dough?'

Motor peeled off a twenty and a ten. Spanky looked at the money like it was dogshit.

'C'mon, man, you know I'm good for it.'

Spanky sighed and his chest sucked in like a ho's cheeks givin' head. No hair on his chest or his arms, but that gray beard growing up to his eyes was thicker'n Santa's.

'It's a down payment,' said Motor.

'Yeah, sure – tell you one thing, you ain't gettin' no virgin pieces, if I let you have anything it'll be off the spares pile.'

'Fine,' said Motor. 'Lemme scrounge.'

'Scrounge? You think for thirty bucks you can scrounge?'

'Thirty down, man. Old lady's got a check comin' in next week.' Total lie; Sharla had no income till the enda the month. 'First thing the check comes in, you get it – I'll bring it in person.'

'In person?' Spanky smiled and the ringed beard moved around like ten pounds of lint. 'Why don't you FedEx it to me, Buell? Everything comes FedEx now – ever use FedEx, Buell?'

'Yeah, sure.' Total lie.

'Got your own FedEx account, do you? We got one. Got a computer, too.' Spanky slapped the register. 'Everything's computerized, Buell. Got another computer in back for ordering parts. Got e-mail, too. Know what e-mail is, Buell?'

Motor didn't answer. What an asshole. It dawned on him that Spanky looked . . . Jewish. Like onea them rabbis with that beard, put a hat on him, send him back to fuckin' Israel.

'E-mail, Buell. You send messages through the computer,

383

phone calls, doesn't cost. You can get dirty pictures on the computer, too, Buell. Amateurs, anals, facials, anything. Or just use your e-mail to write fuck you to some asshole – anything you want. What I'm saying, Buell, is it's a new world out there, dude's gotta change with the times. Once upon a time a dude could sit on his ass, scrounge himself a scoot, live free. Now you got to have more than gas money.'

Spanky looked at him with a mixture of pity and contempt. What was the asshole getting at?

'Nowadays you gotta produce something, Buell. Goods and services – like making a scoot or tuning it. I get doctors, lawyers, already have the Mercedes, but they're heavy into the putt. People *producing* something.'

'Lawyers,' said Motor, 'produce more shit than a bear with the runs.'

Spanky didn't laugh. Not even a smile. 'Right, Buell. That's why they can pay for their parts and you're trying to give me thirty bucks.'

'Hey, man—'

'Yeah, yeah, you wanna scrounge the parts pile, awright, but this is the last time, man. And first you gotta go over to the Bell and get me some grub.' Spanky scratched the interior of his left nostril. 'Three tacos – get me the soft ones and a beef burrito, extra guac, extra sauce. And a cheese enchilada. And a jumbo Coke. You pay for my dinner, maybe I'll let you scrounge. At least you're producing something – no goods, but at least it's a service. It's all about *economics*, Buell.'

The Taco Bell was three blocks away and Motor's heels hurt with each step, all that weight pounding down, the worn-down boots not helping. His thighs chafed through filthy denim. When he got there, he was sweating from exertion. He ordered Spanky's food, scowling at the beaner kid who said, 'Yes, sir?' and stopped smiling when he saw Motor's face.

He was about to leave when he saw it, on one of the tables.

LA newspaper. He didn't read newspapers, who gave a shit. But this one, the picture, made him notice.

Fuck if it didn't look like Sharla's rug-rat.

He picked it up. It took him a long time to finish the article and he had to go over it twice to be sure. He'd always had trouble reading, words not making sense, some letters upside down. His old man called him a retard, look who's talkin', fucking unemployed janitor, dead at forty-five from a fucked-up liver. Mom not much better in the booze-slave department, but at least she didn't bug him. She couldn't read good either.

Finally, he got through it. Was this for real? Witness to a murder? Hollywood?

He studied the picture some more. Looked *exactly* like the little rat.

Had to be the rat – he'd split what, four months ago?

And kids always split to Hollywood. Motor had ended up there himself, Old Brain Fry kicking his ass after he flunked tenth grade for the third time, finally telling himself, Fuck it, I'm gone.

He took the Greyhound that time, too, stealing bucks out of Brain Fry's jeans. Scared when he got there, the place was huge, but walking tall, letting people know he wouldn't take shit.

Full grown, he looked older than his age, had few problems on the streets of Hollywood where he strongarmed money from smaller kids, mugged old farts, ripped off a Jap bike from the Roosevelt Hotel parking lot, stripped it, sold the parts, got himself an old hybrid HD Shovelnose from one of the bikers who drank at The Cave.

Best scoot he'd ever owned. Someone had stolen it from right under him.

He bunked in an abandoned building on – where was it? – Argyle. Yeah, Argyle, big empty apartment fulla junkies, place smelled of puke and shit and he never slept good, always looking out in case someone was out to get him. His size helped, so did beatin' the shit out of anyone smaller who crossed his path. And the nigger he knifed for looking at him the wrong way, that got around, he got himself a street rep.

The black leather jacket he bought at a Van Nuys swapmeet got him tight with the bikers at The Cave. Onea them sold him fake ID so he could go inside and drink. Gettin' nice and thick with them, thinking he'd be able to join some club, then they just stopped actin' friendly, he never really understood why.

So kids split to Hollywood for sure.

The rat, too? Why not? The little shit was too small to fight for himself so he was probably whorin' that skinny little bod, catchin' it backdoor, probably had AIDS.

Gone four months, Sharla still cried once in a while and he had to yell at her to shut the fuck up. Cryin' but not doin' a damned thing to find the rat. Pretendin' to givea shit, whata stupid whore, once she sat up in bed, middle of the night, shoutin' about sick-eydas, sick-eydas, over and over, him shaking her, saying what the hell is a sick-eydas. Her looking at him, saying nuthin', Cowboy, I had a bad dream.

It was time to move on, get a real chick.

Twenty-five grand; *this* could be the way.

He was already ahead of the pack: Knew Hollywood, knew the rat.

If he had to fill his scoot with blood, he'd get down there.

It was well after dark by the time he made it back to the trailer.

Sharla was in the kitchen, popping a beer. 'Hey, Cowboy, whereya been?'

Ignoring her, he found a flashlight, went outside, taped the light to his handlebars and began installing the scrounged parts. The plugs were brand-new, he'd lifted them when Spanky wasn't watching. Latest *Rider*, too, the Fox of the Month was Jody from El Paso, Texas, those black nipples. She said she liked to putt without any panties on.

He was doin' good when the trailer door opened, Sharla stood there, T-shirt and shorts, no shoes. Hands on hips, onea those kiss-me smiles.

He said, 'Go inside, make me somethin' to eat.'

'How 'bout a kiss?'

'Get me somethin' to eat. Move it.'

She gave that hurt-little-baby look. 'What do ya wanna eat?'

'What I want I can't get, so cook me up twoa those TV dinners. Macaroni and cheese, Salisbury steak – go on, move!'

She obeyed. At least one thing the bitch did good.

By 11 P.M., he'd gotten the scoot humming, filled his gut, had three beers.

Twenty-five g's! Like onea them bounty hunters.

Sharla waited for him to finish, then tried to get romantic. He pushed her head into his lap and finished quickly.

Hoovered, zipped, ready to roll!

She was in the bathroom washing her mouth out when he pawed through her purse, found five more bucks in change.

He was at the door when she came after him, said, 'Hey.'

He ignored her, checked his pocket for his keys.

'Where ya goin, Cowboy?'

'Out.'

'Again?' That tone of voice he hated – like a trannie about to fail.

She took hold of his arm. 'C'mon, Cowboy, you just got here.'

'And now I'm splittin'.'

'C'mon, I don't wanna be *alone*.'

'Watch TV.'

'I don't *wanna* watch TV, I want *company*. And hey.' Battin' her lashes, puttin' his hand on her tit. 'I made *you* happy, how 'bout me?'

The feel of her – the way she looked and sounded – made him wanna puke. It was always that way. He'd get horny for her, then he'd finish with her and he'd think she was maggoty meat.

He shook her hand off. She grabbed him again, got into that whining thing.

'You want it so bad,' he said, 'go fuck onea them sick-eydas.'

'Huh?' she said. 'What're you talkin' about. Bugs?'

That confused Motor and when he was confused he got

388

mad. He backhanded her across the face and she fell back against the kitchen counter and lay there, didn't move, didn't argue anymore.

He opened the door – the night was warm – kicked it closed.

Seconds later, he was cruising along the access road to the trailer park. When he got to the highway, he remembered to switch on his headlights.

47

THURSDAY, AT 6:30 P.M., after spending more fruitless time on the Eggermann murder, Stu got ready to leave. Petra was in the ladies' room, he supposed he should wait to say goodbye to her.

Tomorrow, he'd go through *TV Guides*. Any decent-sized library would have them. He'd find one near the hospital.

He locked his desk, tried to free his mind of The Worry. Bad margins on the tumor. Lymph nodes full of cancer.

When he was with her, he was Mr Positive. She'd let him know right away that's the way she wanted it.

We've got to keep everything normal for their sakes, honey.

The children came first. He agreed with that, family was everything, but what kind of family would there be tomorrow?

Mommy's going to the hospital for a little checkup, guys. Just a couple of days, everything's fine.

She hadn't shed a tear, spent every day since the problem began the exact same way: Car-pooling, cooking, church auxiliary. Even lovemaking. Stu'd been reluctant, but she'd insisted and he hadn't wanted her to feel damaged.

Nineteen years ago, she'd been Homecoming Queen at Hoover High, Miss Glendale the following, then a sorority sweetheart at Occidental, a 4.0 history major.

Just one tumor, Drizak assured him, relatively small. The family history wasn't terrible: Kathy's mom was healthy, but an aunt had died of breast cancer.

All in all, a decent prognosis, Drizak claimed. But Stu was a doctor's son, knew how imprecise medicine could be.

Bad surprises, Father had told him more than once, are part of a surgeon's life. That's why we all have to trust in the Lord.

Stu *ached* to trust, and for the past few days he'd been praying with the conspicuous fervor of a missionary. Inside, he was hollow as an atheist.

All those please Gods, dear Jesuses. What right did he have to petition?

For the sake of the children. Always the children.

A hand on his shoulder made him jump.

'Sorry,' said Petra.

'Thought I'd shove off.'

Her hand remained there. 'Look, if there's anything I can do . . .'

'Thanks, but we're fine, Petra. I'm sure it'll all go smoothly.'

'What time's the surgery?'

'Six A.M.'

'Don't rush back,' she said. 'Wil and I will handle everything.'

'OK,' he said, wondering if she'd try to hug him again. He hoped not. Not here, in front of all the others.

'What are your plans?' he asked.

'Thought I'd mosey over to Ramsey's place, talk to security, see if there's any other way out of RanchHaven.'

'Good idea,' he said. Petra had pointed out that they'd

391

neglected to question the night guard immediately and he'd been appalled . . . *what would he do without Kathy?*

He told Petra she was doing a great job and left.

Walk steady: One foot in front of the other. But his knees were weak and it felt as if someone were shoving him.

48

El Salvador time was an hour later than LA and Petra doubted Estrella Flores's son would still be in his law office. She tried anyway, got no answer, connected with an international operator, found three more listings for Javier Floreses and lucked out on number two.

'I'm worried about my mother,' said the attorney in heavily accented but sound English. 'Your city is dangerous. My mother doesn't drive. Where would she go? I phoned Ramsey, but he didn't call back. My mother told me he lives out in the country. How could she just walk out of there? She didn't drive, where would she go? This isn't right!'

Flores talked like an interrogator. Articulate, educated. So what was his mother doing cleaning houses?

As if he was used to the question, he said, 'I've been after her to come back and live with us, but she's very independent. But still, she didn't drive. Where would she go? It can't be related to Mrs Ramsey – is it?'

'Your mother told you about Mrs Ramsey?'

'No, the last time I spoke to her was Sunday. The day before it happened. I read about it in the papers, I read American papers – what are you doing to find her, Detective?'

'I've contacted every missing persons bureau, sir. I called

393

you to make sure there was no place your mother could have gone. A relative, a—'

'No, no one,' said Flores. 'She knows no one. So you don't think it had anything to do with Mrs Ramsey?'

'We have no evidence of that, sir—'

'Please!' Flores exploded. 'I'm not stupid! Could she have learned something that put her in danger?'

'I honestly don't know, Mr Flores. So far, there's no evidence of that. Did your mother ever say anything about the Ramseys that could be relevant? Especially last Sunday?'

'No, they didn't come up. She asked how her bank account was doing, that's all. She wires me her money, I deposit it. She's saving up for her own house.'

'All her money goes to El Salvador?'

'Except what's taken out for American taxes.'

'What about past conversations?' said Petra. 'What was her opinion of the Ramseys?'

'She said the wife was young, nice, not too picky.'

'Was Mr Ramsey picky?'

'A little – he had these cars he wanted polished all the time. But it was a good job, better than the one she worked before. Very picky people, they always criticized.'

'Do you remember their names?'

'People in another part of town – Brentwood. Hooper. Mr and Mrs Hooper. The man always ran his finger along the furniture, looking for dust. The woman drank too much, and they didn't pay her well.'

'First names?'

'I don't – wait, the address is here in my book, unless I threw it out when she . . . no, here it is, Hooper – here's the number.'

Petra copied it down. 'I'll call them, Mr Flores.'

'I'll call them, too,' he said. 'But I don't think my mother would have returned to them.'

'Anything more you can tell me about the Ramseys?'

'The one she didn't like was the business manager – he was in charge of paying her, was always late with the check. Finally she complained to Mrs Ramsey and that helped.'

'Mr Balch?'

'She never mentioned his name, said he was a . . . snob. Out to show he was important. Him she didn't like.'

'What about Mr Ramsey?'

'She didn't talk about him much. Do you think he killed the wife?'

'Mr Flores, at this point, I—'

'OK, OK, all I care about is my mother.'

'I'll do everything I can to find her, sir. So as far as you know, there were no conflicts with Mr Ramsey? No reason for your mother to suddenly quit?'

'He wasn't home that often. It was a big house, she didn't like being alone so much.' His voice broke. 'I know there's something wrong.'

The moment Petra hung up the phone, it rang. The civilian clerk on duty said, 'A Dr Boehlinger called.'

'Did he leave a message?'

'Just to call him back. Telling, not asking.'

Just what she needed. Clenching her jaw, she dialed Boehlinger's hotel. He was out. Thank God for small victories.

She phoned the Hoopers in Bel Air. Busy. Maybe Javier Flores was already on the line.

She tried again, connected to a husky-voiced woman. 'Oh,

Jesus, I just spoke to her son. No, I haven't seen her.' Snorting laugh. 'So now the police are trying to bring illegals *back*?'

'Thank you, Mrs Hooper.' You're the one who hired her when she was illegal, Mrs Hooper. Click.

Wil Fournier came over and showed her a piece of paper. Forty or so names, all but three checked off. 'Tipsters. Our little burglar's been spotted all up and down the state but it's mostly garbage – who unlocked the asylum?' He loosened his tie. The tan pad of his hand was inkstained. 'One sweet-heart from Frisco claims he's the son she gave up at birth, she was just about to call *Unsolved Mysteries*, the money would sure come in handy because she wants to become a psychologist. One guy claims the kid's not a kid, he's some kind of mystic guru – an apparition, appears in times of crisis and "renders deliverance." The world may be coming to an end.'

'He might have something there,' said Petra.

'Long as I get my pension,' said Fournier. He tapped off each of the three unchecked names. 'These are possibles. Two come from the same place, some farm town called Watson, between Bakersfield and Fresno. Neither of the callers knows the kid by name but they both think they've seen him around. They didn't sound wacko or greedy and two tips from a small place like that is interesting. I put in a call to the local law. Must be a real hick place because it's a two-man sheriff outfit and both guys were out. I talked to some woman at the desk who sounded about a hundred years old. This last one probably is greed, Russian accent, but at least the guy sounded sane. Insisted he'd seen the kid in Venice this morning, described his clothes – T-shirt, jeans, said the kid looked like he'd been sleeping on the street, had crusted salt on his face, like he'd washed with ocean water. Scratched up, too.'

'Good eye for detail.'

'That's why I'm not dismissing him. He runs a souvenir-stand down on Ocean Front in Venice, claims he sold the kid a hat this morning. Then the kid took off north. The guy thought it was weird, a kid being out by himself, middle of the day. And buying a hat, he never sells hats to kids.'

'Trying to hide his face?' said Petra.

Fournier shrugged. 'Could be, if the kid read today's paper, and we know he's a reader. On the other hand, you're homeless, broke, a runaway, someone's offering twenty-five g's for your presence, wouldn't you turn yourself in, try to collect?'

'He's a child, Wil. Probably an abused child. Why should he trust anyone? Feel enough in control to scheme? And if he saw the murder he could be too scared to think about profit.'

'Guess so. Or maybe the kid was there but not during the murder, figures why bother. Anyway, this Russian is definitely after the money.'

Petra read the man's name out loud. 'Vladimir Zhukanov.'

'That's another thing,' said Fournier. 'His being Russian. I don't want to be prejudiced but you know the scams those guys have been pulling off.' He folded and pocketed the list. 'I'll stop by to see him, have a date in Santa Monica tonight, dinner at Loew's – ever been there?'

Petra shook her head.

'Zhukanov said he'd stay late to talk to me. One last thing: Schoelkopf called me into the office again, pumping for details. I may have to give him something, Barb. And then, boom, right in to the media and we run around like little windup toys.'

'If you have to, you have to,' said Petra. 'It's already out of our hands.'

She was ready to leave at seven when the phone blared again.

A young woman said, 'Hold please for Lawrence Schick.' Ten seconds of bad music, then a sleepy male voice said, 'To which detective do I have the pleasure of speaking?'

'Detective Connor.'

'Evening, Detective Connor, this is Larry Schick.'

Meaningful pause. She was supposed to know who he was. And she did. Six-hundred-bucks-an-hour lawyer, criminal defense, mostly celebrity drunk drivers, actors' kids playing with guns, other delicate felonies. She'd seen him doing soundbites but had never met him. Her typical perp couldn't even afford a Western Avenue hack.

'Evening, Mr Schick.'

'Evening, Detective. How're things on the Ramsey case?'

Finally, the wall goes up. 'Are you asking as a concerned citizen, sir?'

Schick laughed. 'I'm always concerned, but no, Detective Connor, I've been retained by Mr Ramsey to represent him in this matter. So please channel all future communications through my offices.'

Offices, plural. *Look, Ma, I'm important!*

'Communications,' said Petra.

'Anything pertaining to the case,' said Schick.

'Are you saying we can't talk to Mr Ramsey without clearing it with you first, Mr Schick?'

398

'At this point in time,' said the lawyer, 'that would be advisable, Detective. Good night.'

'Same to you,' Petra said to a dead phone. Yesterday she'd chatted with Ramsey in the kitchen. Now this. From Ramsey's point of view, two things had transpired: The reinterview and the talk with Balch. Had she raised something with either of them that worried him?

Grabbing her notepad, she reviewed her notes. The talk with Ramsey had covered nothing earth-shattering . . . he had mentioned being a suspect – scratch that, one new topic: Estrella Flores.

She flipped to the Balch interview. His and Ramsey's Hollywood 'discovery,' Lisa's temperament, the DV episode. Estrella Flores.

Was the maid the hot button?

What had Flores seen that night?

Or did it have something to do with the boy in the paper? Ramsey thinking he'd pulled off the perfect crime only to encounter every bad guy's worst nightmare: A mystery witness.

She would have loved to stare into those baby blues right now, probing for fear.

So, of course, she couldn't.

But no one, not even an overpaid BH lawyer, could stop her from just happening to be in Ramsey's neighborhood and dropping in.

Stopping for a roast beef sandwich at an Arby's on Sunset, she ate in the car, chewing on meat and suspicion, watching night-creatures emerge from the dark, knowing years ago she'd have been scared to get this close. At 7:40 she set out for Calabasas. Post rush-hour, she sailed, arriving at the RanchHaven guardhouse by 8:33.

The guard on duty was a young man, weak-chinned, with discouraged posture. Thin everywhere except around his middle, where the uniform shirt strained. When she drove up, he folded his arms across his chest. Grim watchfulness – ludicrous in the absence of threat – faded when he saw her up close. A crooked smile split his bland pie of a face. Flirtatious. Great. The guy's eyebrows were very faint, nearly invisible. His badge said D. Simkins.

He came out, looked at her, opened the gate. She drove up to him.

'How's it going?' No 'ma'am.' Easy tone coming into play because she was driving a Honda, not a Porsche, not one of the locals.

Petra showed him her badge.

'Oh,' he said, stepping back and hitching his trousers. 'It's about time, Detective.'

'For what?'

'I was on shift the night Lisa Ramsey was killed. Kept wondering when you were gonna come by.' Wagging a finger in mock disapproval.

Petra's turn to smile. 'Well, here I am, Officer Simkins.'

She parked, got out, entered the guardhouse without asking permission. He followed. The booth was a glass closet, barely enough room for both of them. Simkins leaned against a counter, looking her up and down, no shame.

Not much inside: Small cabinet for supplies, a single wheeled chair that Simkins offered her. She stayed on her feet.

She extricated her pad while checking out the security

400

hardware. Multi-line telephone, two-way radio setup, hand-held walkie-talkie. Two closed-circuit TV screens suspended above the counter, one highlighting the mouth of the main road, the other so dark she could barely tell it was switched on. Next to the phone, a greasy paper bag and a copy of *Rolling Stone*. Some rock star instant-emperor on the cover, pierced eyebrows, a silver stud through his tongue.

Simkins said, 'So what can I do for a fellow officer?'

Petra dredged up another smile. 'So you were on all that night, Officer Simkins?'

'Doug. Yes, I was. It was real quiet, but I don't know, I had a feeling, like it was too quiet. Like something could happen.'

'Did anything happen?'

Simkins shook his head. 'But you know, I just felt it was a weird night. Then the next morning when I heard what happened I said, oh man. Like one of them psychic things.'

Lord deliver me from dunderheads. 'This place seems like it must be pretty quiet in general.'

'You'd be surprised,' he said, suddenly defensive. 'You get stuff. Like fires. Like the last time, that big one in Thousand Oaks, thousand acres went down, we called a first-stage alert.'

'Which is?'

'Letting people know we might have to evacuate.'

'Scary,' said Petra.

'That's why we're here.' Touching his own badge. Stainless steel replica of LAPD's – could the department sue?

'So, Doug, what time were you on duty that night?'

'Seven to three's my regular shift, then the morning guy called in sick, so I did double duty.'

'Till when?'

'Eleven, when daywatch starts.'

'Daywatch being Officer . . . Dilbeck.' Retrieving the old guard's name from her memory banks.

'Yeah, Oliver,' said Simkins, frowning. Probably miffed that Dilbeck had already been interviewed.

Petra said, 'Did anyone from the Ramsey house come in or out during that time?'

'He did. Mr Ramsey. He and his friend, a blond guy I always see him with. They came in that night.'

'What time?'

'Nine or so.'

Or so. They didn't log entries and exits?

'Do you have a written record of that?'

'No, we don't hassle with that.' Defensive again.

'Who drove, Doug?'

'The friend.'

'Did either Mr Ramsey or his friend go out again that night?'

'Nope,' said Simkins, decisively, smugly. Delivering the punchline: 'No one from the entire development left after that, though a few more people came home. Like I said, it was a quiet night.'

'What about Mr Ramsey's maid?'

'Nope. Never left. It's real quiet around here. Too quiet. I like action.'

Petra suppressed laughter. 'Know what you mean, Doug. Anything else you can tell me about the Ramseys?'

'Well,' Simkins said, pondering, 'I've only been working here three weeks, just see him going in and out. Same for that friend of his. You think he did it?'

'Don't think much of anything yet, Doug.' Three weeks on duty. He'd never known Lisa. Even with a brain, the guy would've been useless to her. 'Is Mr Ramsey home right now?'

'Hasn't come in or out on my shift.'

'Are there any other ways in and out of RanchHaven?'

'Nope.'

'What about that second screen there?'

Simkins' eyes flashed to the console. 'Oh, that. That's just a fire road, way back at the rear of the property, but no one uses it. Even when we were on evac alert, the plan was to get everyone out through the front.'

'The screen looks pretty dark.'

'It's dark back there.'

Petra bent close to the monitor. 'No officer there?'

'Nope, just one of them cardkey doohickies. The residents get issued cards. But no one uses it, no reason to.'

'I'd like to go over there myself, Doug. Just to take a look.'

'I dunno . . .'

'You can come with me if you want.' She stepped closer to Simkins. Their chests nearly touched. The guard was perspiring heavily.

'Well . . .'

'Just a quick look, Doug. I promise not to steal any dirt.' She winked. It made Simkins flinch.

'Yeah, OK, just don't disturb any of the residents, OK? Because that would be my butt. They like their peace and quiet. That's what they pay me for.'

'How do I get there?'

'Up the main road, to the top.' He gestured, managed to

move closer, their shoulders touching. 'On the way to Ramsey's house, matter of fact. But instead of turning right, you bear left and after a while you'll see this big empty lot that was supposed to be a nine-hole golf course but it never got built, probably cause the residents all play at clubs, anyway. Keep bearing left, all the way around it, and the road'll curve up, suddenly switch directions. Just keep going till you can't go anymore.'

She thanked him, patted his shoulder. He flinched again.

She drove very slowly, pausing when Ramsey's house came into view. The outdoor lighting was on full blast. Weaker illumination leaked from inside. No cars in front. Damn that museum, impossible to know if the guy was home.

She stared at the house. Static. So were the nearby structures. The more expensive neighborhoods got, the deader they looked.

Simkins's directions led her on a ten-minute loop past the would-be golf course, now just a flat gray table planted with young junipers and surrounded by wrought-iron fencing. The road compressed to barely one lane and the brush along both sides thickened to high dark walls. Above them, she could see the kinked and coiled branches of oak trees, dwarfed by a black dome of sky. A few stars struggled through haze. The moon was oversized, gray-white, streaked with fog.

The smell of horse manure and dry dirt.

Her headlights created an amber tunnel through the gloom. She switched her high-beams on, continued at ten miles per. Suddenly the fire exit was there. A single gate, twelve feet high, electric, same iron motif as the main portals.

Stout brick posts, warning signs. The card slot topped a steel post.

She stopped ten yards in, pulled her flashlight from the glove compartment, let the car idle and got out.

The horse aroma was stronger up here. Quiet, not even a bird. But she could hear the freeway baritone, insistent, remote.

She swept her flashlight across the road. Poorly maintained, dusted with soil. Simkins claimed no one used the back exit but she could see the faint corrugation of tire tracks. A few horseprints, smaller ones that could be dog or coyote, she was no gung-ho tracker.

Dad could have helped her with prints.

Keeping to the side of the road, she walked to the gate, then back. Repeated it. The dirt was so compacted it didn't granulate under her feet. Some rust around the card slot. Another slot on the other side of the fence.

Easy entry and exit.

And Ramsey's house was at the upper edge of the development, meaning he wouldn't have to pass many neighbors to sneak out.

She thought about how he'd do it.

Wait till Balch was asleep – or put something in Balch's drink to help sleep along. Then roll the Mercedes out of the mega-garage. Or the Jeep if it had been brought back from Montecito. Headlights off, cruising slowly, with houses so far from the road, all those fences, gates, high foliage, there'd be no reason for anyone to notice. People with pools and Jacuzzis and home theaters and putting greens didn't sit by their front windows.

People who craved that level of privacy often pretended nothing existed beyond their four walls.

She took a closer look at the tire tracks. Degraded, no tread-marks, she doubted they'd be of much use. But still, she'd have loved to get a cast. No way to do it without a warrant and no grounds for a warrant. And now Larry Schick, Esq. was on the scene, forget approaching Ramsey about anything.

Even if they pulled a match to one of Ramsey's cars, it had been four days since the murder, Ramsey could admit being up there, claim he'd taken a cruise in the hills, trying to mellow out, deal with his grief.

The hills . . . great place to get rid of a body.

Was Estrella Flores buried somewhere out there?

Did the fire road lead anywhere other than out to the Santa Susannas?

She backed down till the nearest shoulder, turned around and returned to the guard house. Simkins saw her coming, put down his *Rolling Stone* and opened the exit gate. His window was closed, no desire to talk. Petra stopped alongside the booth. He screwed up his mouth and came over. His big moment over, feeling down, he wanted her gone.

'Find anything?'

'Nope, just like you said, Doug. Tell me, where does the fire road go?'

'Out into the mountains.'

'And then?'

'It connects to a bunch of little side roads.'

'Doesn't it merge with the 101?'

'It kinda hooks back toward it but doesn't actually merge.' He managed to make the last word sound dirty.

'But if I wanted to reach the freeway through the back-roads, I could.'

'Yeah, sure. Everything reaches the freeway. I grew up in West Hills, we used to come out here, hunt rabbits before they built this place. Sometimes they'd run onto the freeway, get turned to freeway butter.'

'The good old days,' said Petra.

Simkins's weak face firmed with recollection, and a resentful frown captured his features. Rich folk moving in on his childhood memories?

'It can get beautiful out there,' he said. Real emotion. Longing. At that moment, she liked him a little better. But not much.

49

SAM SAYS, 'Hey, not bad.'

I've been working all day, going over and over the windows until there are no streaks, mopping the wood floors, using the Pledge to shine them up. I've done only half the seats, but what I finished looks pretty good and the room has a nice lemon smell.

Sam tries to give me the rest of the money.

'I'm not finished yet.'

'I trust you, sonny – by the way, now that you work for me are you ready to give me your name?'

That catches me by surprise and 'Bill' pops out.

'Nice to meet you, Bill.'

It's been so long since anyone's called me by my name. Since I've *talked* to anyone.

Sam shows me a paper bag. 'I got you some dinner – Noah's Bagel, just a plain one cause I didn't know if you liked onions or one a those fancy bagels. Also cream cheese – do you like cream cheese?'

'Sure. Thanks.'

'Hey, you're a working man now, need your nutrition.' He hands me the bag and walks around the *shul*. 'You like the Pledge, huh? Running out of the stuff?'

'Almost.'

'I'll buy some more tomorrow – that is if you want to work tomorrow.'

'Sure.'

'Go ahead, take the money.'

I do. He looks at his watch. 'Time to quit, Bill. We don't want to be accused of exploiting the working man.'

We walk outside and he locks the *shul*. The alley is empty but I can hear the ocean through the space on the side of the building, people talking on the walkway. That big Lincoln of his is parked crazy, the front bumper almost touching the building. He opens the driver's door. 'So.'

'Bye,' I say.

'See you tomorrow, Bill.' He gets in the car and I start to walk away – south, away from that Russian perv. I'm liking the feel of all that money in my pocket but wondering where to go. Back to the pier? But it was so cold. And now I have money . . .

I hear a loud squeak, turn and see Sam backing the Lincoln out of the alley. He has plenty of room but he keeps backing up and stopping, jerking the car, the brakes are squeaking.

Uh-oh, he's gonna hit the fence – no, he misses it. I figure I should direct him before he hurts himself but he makes it, turning the steering wheel with both hands, his head kind of pushed forward, like he's struggling to see through the windshield.

Instead of driving forward, he backs up, stops next to me. 'Hey, Bill. You really got somewhere to go for the night?'

'Sure.'

'Where? The street?'

'I'll be fine.' I start walking. He stays next to me, driving really slowly.

'I'd give you money for a hotel, but no one's gonna rent to a kid, and if you show all that cash, someone's gonna take it from you.'

'I'm fine,' I repeat.

'Sure, sure . . . I can't let you sleep in the *shul* because what if you slip and fall, we got a liability problem – you might sue us.'

'I wouldn't do that.'

He laughs. 'No, you probably wouldn't, but I still can't – listen, I got a house, not far from here. Plenty of room, I live alone. You wanna stay for a day or two, fine. Till you figure out what to do.'

'No, thanks.' That comes out kind of cold and I don't turn to see his face because I know he's going to look insulted.

'Suit yourself, Bill. Don't blame you. Someone probably hurt you, you don't trust no one, for all you know I could be some crazy person.'

'I'm sure you're not crazy.' Why did I say that?

'How can you be sure, Bill? How can you ever be sure? Listen, when I was your age – a little older – people came and took away my family. Killed all of them, except me and my brother. Nazis. Ever hear of them? Only when I knew them, they weren't Nazis, they were my neighbors, people I lived with. My family lived in their country for five hundred years and they did that to me – I'm talking the Second World War. Goddamn Nazis. Ever hear about any of that?'

'Sure,' I said. 'Learned about it in history.'

'History.' He laughs – but not a funny laugh. 'So who am I to tell you to trust people – you're right, plenty of schmucks out there.' He stops driving and I stop walking. More money lands in my hand. Two tens.

'You don't have to, Mr Ganzer.'

'I don't have to but I want to – oh, hell, sleep in the *shul* tonight. Only don't fall and break your neck. And if you do, don't sue us.'

Then he jams his car in reverse and backs up all the way to the *shul*. It's scary, the way he weaves and swerves all over the place. It's a miracle he doesn't smash into anything.

50

PETRA OPENED her front door exhausted, not feeling like a night owl anymore. Thought of Kathy Bishop's ordeal tomorrow. Real problems. No self-pity allowed for you, kid.

She popped a can of Coke, checked the phone machine. A long-distance phone service promised to be her slave if she signed up, Ron Banks had called at seven, leaving an 818 number, probably home, please get back to him. Adele, one of the civilian clerks at the station, requesting the same thing at 8:15.

She would have loved to talk to Ron first. To be with him, the two of them talking, making out on the couch, wherever that led. Business first: She called Adele.

'Hi, Detective Connor. Got a message for you from Pacific Division, a Detective Grauberg. Here's his number.'

Pacific was Ilse Eggermann territory. Had something new come up? Grauberg was out but a D named Salant came on. 'Already spoke to you guys.'

'To who?'

'Hold on – says here Captain Schoelkopf. Guess Grauberg couldn't reach to notify, got kicked upward.'

'Notify what?'

'Got an auto-carcass you were interested in. Black Porsche, registered to Lisa Boehlinger Ramsey.'

'A carcass? Gutted?'

'Gutted and left for the vultures. Probably a Tijuana taxi by now. Got a witness says it was parked there for at least four days.'

'Where?'

'Behind the bus lot near Pacific Avenue. The witness is one of the drivers.'

'Gutted right from the beginning?'

'Progressively gutted. Someone set fire to it last night. That's how we got called in.'

Four days and not a single report.

'You can't see it from the street,' Salant added. 'Blocked by storage buildings. We get hot cars stashed there all the time.'

'Where is it now?' said Petra.

'Downtown. Have fun.'

She talked to several criminalists before locating a female named Wilkerson who was working on the Porsche. The car was a charred shell, no wheels, seats, engine, front windshield.

'Like locusts swept in,' said Wilkerson.

'What about prints?'

'Nothing so far. I'll let you know.'

She drank Coke and tried to put together Lisa's journey from Doheny Drive to Griffith Park. Where did Venice fit in? Just a dumping ground for the Porsche, or had Lisa driven it behind the bus yard? Meeting up with her date on a deserted street in a high-crime neighborhood?

Was the last-date scenario totally wrong? Had Lisa indeed been carjacked and abducted, forced to drive to Venice by a stranger?

Or by someone she knew? Setting out from Doheny for a date with someone else. The murderer watching, stalking, following, pulling off the snatch.

Ramsey would fit that picture.

Venice . . . Kelly Sposito, Darrell Breshear's current flame, lived on Fourth Street, walking distance from the bus yard.

Where was Breshear's home base? She looked him up in her pad. The DMV data had him on Ashland, Ocean Park, the border between Santa Monica and Venice. Very close.

Everything gravitating toward the beach. Including the boy, if Wil's Russian tipster could be believed.

Breshear. Another former actor. Everyone performing . . . news of the recovered car would be in the paper tomorrow. She had to get to Breshear before he had time to construct a story.

It was nearly 10 P.M. Was he with his wife or with Kelly? Betting on the former, she got dressed again, and drove west.

Ashland was a pretty sloping street in the best part of Ocean Park, houses of all sizes, every conceivable architectural style. Breshear's place was at the top, a small, well-maintained craftsman's cottage with lots of cactus in the front, thatches of sword plant instead of lawn. White BMW ragtop in the driveway, behind an iron gate. Bright lights over the gate hinted at a fantastic backyard view. She rang the bell and Breshear answered, wearing a black T-shirt and baggy green shorts, holding a bottle of Heineken. When he saw her, his eyes bulged.

'This is a bad time,' he said. 'My wife . . .'

'It could get worse,' she said. 'I think you lied to me. We

found Lisa's car today. Right here in Venice. Did you have a date with her Sunday night? If you did, we'll find out.'

He looked over his shoulder. Closed the door and came out and said, 'Can we move out to the sidewalk?'

'Won't your wife get curious?'

'She's in the bath.'

Petra accompanied him to the parkway.

'It wasn't really a date,' he said. 'She just said she wanted to talk.'

'About what?'

'I don't know – oh, hell, yeah, she wanted to get it on.'

'So you'd continued your relationship past those glorious seven days.'

'Not really,' he said. 'Just once in a while, maybe once a month.'

'Your idea?'

'Definitely not. Lisa's, one hundred percent.'

'My, my,' said Petra. 'Lisa, Kelly, your wife – what's her name, by the way?'

'Marcia.' Breshear looked back at the house. 'Look—'

'Busy guy,' said Petra.

'It's no crime.'

'Obstructing justice is.'

'I didn't obstruct anything. It – I had nothing to say that would help you because by the time I got there, she was gone. What would it look like, saying I went to meet up with her that night.' Staring at Petra. 'A black man, we know what that's all about.'

'Cut the racial crap,' said Petra. 'The only civil rights that were violated were Lisa's. What time were you supposed to meet her?'

415

'Ten thirty.'

'When did you set it up?'

'She set it up. That day. She called me at work around seven.'

'You were working Sunday?'

'Doing a final cut. Check with the lot guard, I signed in.'

'I will,' said Petra. 'So Lisa called you to get together.'

'She said she was lonely, down, had been sleeping all day, took some coke, now she was wired, couldn't sit still, how about a cruise.'

The car, always in the car.

'A cruise,' said Petra.

'She wanted to get together at nine but I told her I'd be working till then, had a date at Kelly's place right afterward, but I'd see if I could slip out around ten thirty, meet her behind the bus yard.'

'Why there?'

'We'd met there before. It's . . .'

'Clandestine?'

'I didn't like it, too much crime around there, but Lisa did. The risk turned her on.' He shrugged.

Petra said, 'Go on.'

'I had trouble getting out, Kelly . . . kept me busy till after eleven. Finally, I told her I needed to get some air, was going to take a little drive. I made it by eleven-oh-five or so and Lisa's car was there but she wasn't. I waited around till eleven-fifteen, figured she'd showed up and left.'

'The car was there but she wasn't,' said Petra. 'That didn't worry you?'

'Like I said, Lisa liked to take risks. Doing it at traffic lights, a cop car right next to us. Coldwater Canyon, that kind of thing. I figured maybe she'd met up with someone else, was having a good time. Which was OK with me. I really didn't want to see her that night. Didn't want to see her at all, but . . .'

'But what?'

'You know how it is. I have trouble telling women no.'

'When did you get back to Kelly's?'

'Had to be eleven twenty-five, eleven thirty.'

'And you spent the night there.'

'That's the absolute truth.'

'The perfect alibi Kelly gave you wasn't.'

'Come on,' he said. 'I was only out for half an hour max. No way could I have made it to Griffith—'

'You and Kelly are both liable for perjury and obstruction,' said Petra.

'Come on. Please! You're making a big deal out of nothing!'

Petra walked up close to him, pointed at his chest, but didn't touch it. 'At the very least, you cost me a lot of hours, Mr Breshear. If there's anything else you know, spill it now.'

'I don't, that's it.'

She stared him down. He repeated, 'I don't.'

'Listen to me,' she said, pointing again. 'I'm not arresting you. Yet. But don't even come close to thinking about going anywhere. There'll be police officers watching your house and the studio. Surveillance on Kelly, too. You guys make the wrong move, it all hits the fan. Including a nice long chat with Marcia.'

Breshear blinked convulsively.

This feels good, Petra admitted to herself. Finally, someone she could intimidate on this damn case.

As she walked away, the front door opened and a woman's voice said, 'Darrell, honey? Who was that?'

She drove back to her apartment, head suddenly clear, the basic structure of Lisa's last night alive taking form. If Breshear was finally being straight.

A meet at 10:30, abducted between then and 11:15, taken to Griffith Park, at least a half-hour ride, probably longer. Murdered between midnight and four A.M.

The car. Which one? PLYR 1? PLYR 0? Some other set of wheels? Ramsey, with his multiple vehicles, multiple houses, fences, gates, Larry Schick, was a nightmare suspect. Crime paid if you started out rich.

It was nearly eleven when she walked through the door. Too late to call Ron? She did, anyway. Four rings, then a little girl's munchkin voice said, 'When you hear the beep, leave a message. Beep. And beep and beep and—'

Ron broke in. 'Banks.'

'Hi, it's Petra.'

'Petra.' Saying her name with pleasure. She could use some adulation. 'How's it going?'

She told him about the Porsche, Breshear's revised story, the new time-frame.

'Think he's dirty?'

'Unless his girlfriend's lying bigtime about his alibi, he didn't have the time, but who knows? What's up?'

'I phoned Carpenteria Sheriffs again, asked if they could keep an eye on Ramsey's house. They said they'd upped patrols already and today at six forty-five, I got a call-back, tried to reach you at your office but they said you'd already left. Turns out Ramsey hasn't been spotted there for a while but Greg

Balch showed up this morning, left his Lexus and drove back in a Jeep that belongs to Ramsey, license plate—'

'PLYR 0,' said Petra.

'So you know already.'

'I knew Ramsey owned the Jeep, didn't know Balch picked it up.'

'Didn't want to step on your toes – calling Carpenteria – but I'd already made contact with them, figured it would be efficient. A deputy stopped Balch driving off the property around noon. Balch showed him ID, a business card, snapshot of him and Ramsey, keys to the house. Said he was there to pick up the car, bring it down for service. Which seems odd, there are plenty of mechanics in Santa Barbara.'

'An extra-careful cleaning?' said Petra. Or Ramsey wanted a four-wheeler because he was planning to do some heavy-terrain driving? Those hills . . .

'Maybe Ramsey's spooked, now that you've got a potential witness.'

'Maybe.' She told him about Larry Schick's call.

'There you go,' he said. 'Anyway . . .'

'Thanks again, Ron. Your daughter has a cute voice.'

'Wha— oh, that's Bee, she loves to perform. They're both asleep now. Finally.'

'Have your hands full?'

'It takes a while to get them tucked in. My mom says they run rings around me. Tomorrow, though, I get to sleep in. Day off, Mom's driving them to school.'

'Good for you,' said Petra. 'I may just drive up to Montecito tomorrow. Care to join me?'

'Sure,' he said quickly. 'It's a pretty drive.'

* * *

Lying in bed, in darkness so total she felt suspended, she thought about Lisa being abducted and butchered, Balch's picking up the Jeep.

Ramsey edgy because of a little boy who stole books ... wherever he was.

The fact that no one on the street knew him intrigued her. He hadn't taken up with other runaways, hadn't sought help from any agency. A loner. Made sense. A kid who loved to read wouldn't fit in. He'd probably been an outcast back home, too. So why hadn't he been reported missing? Where were the parents?

Had to be abuse. An eleven-year-old intellectual ... running from God knew what. A kid like that witnessing a murder. No reason for him to trust anyone.

A survivor. And now the police had turned him into quarry. *She* had.

She'd just fallen asleep when the phone rang. It was well after midnight and her heart pounded as for one horrible, irrational moment she panicked about her father's condition, then realized he was beyond worry. One of her brothers in trouble – Kathy?

A nervous-sounding woman said, 'Detective Connor? This is Adele again, from the station. I'm really sorry to bother you this late but a call came in for Detective Bishop, long distance, international and no one answers at his house. You're his partner and seeing as it's international, I—'

'International from where?'

'Vienna. A police inspector named Tauber. I guess he didn't figure out the time difference.'

'Thanks, put him on.'

A scratchy voice said, 'Detective Bishop?'

'This is his partner, Detective Connor.'

'Ah. Yes, yes, this is Inspector Ottemar Tauber from Vienna.' Clear connection; the scratchiness was the Austrian's vocal quality. He coughed, cleared his throat a couple of times.

'Hello, Inspector. Is this about Karlheinz Lauch?'

'Two days ago, Detective Bishop submitted an inquiry concerning Herr Lauch,' said Tauber. 'We have located Herr Lauch for you. Unfortunately, he is unavailable to you for questioning, as he is deceased.'

'When did he die?'

'It appears to have occurred fifteen months ago.'

'What was the cause of death, Inspector?'

'It appears to have been cirrhosis of the liver.'

'A young man like that,' said Petra.

Tauber clucked his tongue. 'These things happen.'

Lauch eliminated as a suspect for Lisa. Meaning the similarities between Lisa and Ilse Eggermann weren't worth a damn.

Or were they?

Ramsey a multiple killer? No, too weird.

Tauber's call had burned away any drowsiness. She was wired. Going into the kitchen, she drank ice water, paced, sat down at the table, got up and put on the stereo. *Derek and the Dominos*. There'd been no music in the apartment since Ron's visit.

Think, think . . . Lauch eliminated for Lisa meant concentrate on Ramsey. Stalking Lisa, following her. DV offenders were often obsessive, it made sense.

Did his dispatching Balch to get the Jeep mean the four-wheeler was the murder vehicle? The Mercedes a distraction, just as she'd wondered? She recalled the way Ramsey had flicked on the lights in the car museum. Showing her the gray sedan – probably hoping she'd ask for a look, because he knew she'd learn nothing.

Balch doing the dirty work.

All at once – maybe it was the dark room, her fried nerves – her mind took a hairpin turn.

What if Balch was an active part of it?

Or working for himself?

She sat there, tight as a fiddle-string, viewing the case through a whole new prism.

Just a slight shift of angle and everything changed.

Balch as bad guy. Flashing back to all her hypotheses, she inserted Balch's name in Ramsey's slot.

Everything fit.

Lisa and Balch . . . yet another older man. Romantic *and* financial relationship?

Because Balch wrote the checks, managed Ramsey's finances, probably understood them better than the boss. You heard about that all the time, business managers soaking celebrities.

Balch colluding with *Lisa* to soak Ramsey? Ex-wife and long-suffering lackey finding common ground in their resentment of the man with the dough.

Lisa had talked to Ghadoomian the broker about setting up investments, being financially independent, soon. But she'd never followed through.

Daddy reneging on the fifty thou? Or other plans laid to waste?

Had Lisa gotten greedy, leaned on Balch, caused their partnership to disintegrate?

Petra thought about it for a long time. Balch was no prize, but Lisa was no conventional girl. Balch's motivation was no big puzzle: Bedding the quarterback's ex – the woman Ramsey had failed to satisfy – would be the ultimate thrill for an underachiever like him.

All those years protecting Ramsey on the football field and in real life, watching his own screen dreams fade as Ramsey earned millions. For all Balch's adoration of his buddy, the payback had been limited: Ramsey hadn't helped Balch progress past those first few grade-D flicks. Balch said he had no talent but the same was true for plenty of small-time players, surely Ramsey could have gotten him something in The Industry. Instead, he'd stuck Balch in that dingy office, shuffling papers, while he lived a star's life. Why not a better office, at least?

Ramsey telling Balch: You don't deserve better.

What if Balch finally decided he did?

With Lisa's help. *She* liked taking risks. Had she stepped too far over the edge?

Then something else hit her: Balch lived in Rolling Hills Estates, near Palos Verdes. Ilse Eggermann's body had been dumped near Marina del Rey but her date with Lauch had taken place in Redondo Beach, just a few freeway stops away from the peninsula.

She pictured Balch stopping off at the Redondo pier for dinner or drinks. Watching Ilse and Lauch quarrel, Ilse walking out on Lauch. Allowing Balch to move in.

Noticing Ilse because she reminded him of Lisa?

Picking her up wouldn't have been that tough. Kindly older guy, chivalrous. Ilse would have been vulnerable, alone at night, a foreigner.

423

After a pig like Lauch, Balch might have even seemed suave.

The resemblance between Lisa and Ilse not a coincidence! Because Balch had been lusting for Lisa for years.

The underling, always the underling . . . Balch rescues Ilse, tries for sexual payback, gets shut down.

In a rage, he butchers her. Gets away with it.

Years later, blackmailed, up against the wall, why not do it again?

She ran it through again. Balch managing to get out of the house while Ramsey sleeps. Using the fire road, driving one of Ramsey's cars. But Estrella Flores spots him. She'd never liked Balch in the first place, might have viewed anything he did with suspicion.

He eliminates her.

One more time: It still fit.

Maybe in the morning it would seem ludicrous. Right now, she liked it.

51

WIL FOURNIER had changed into his best suit for the date with Leanna the Macy's model from Ethiopia. He didn't want to get close to the Russian; the guy oozed sleaze.

Selling T-shirts, tourist crap, the outward trappings of a legit business, but those eyes, that demeanor. Wil had worked Wilshire Bunco and Fraud for two years, collaborated with West Hollywood Sheriffs on lots of Russian scams. The weirdest case was five years ago, an immigration racket, strongarming new arrivals. Wil and a sheriff's D making a call to the apartment of one of the suspects, the guy opening the door, covered with blood, holding a carving knife. He'd just dismembered another Russian. What had he been thinking, answering the door like that?

Sharing the bust, Wil found out he liked Homicide, transferred.

He was sure the souvenir vendor had run angles.

The way Zhukanov had leaned over his counter giving him the eye, all that junk hanging from every inch of the stall. Trying to stay cool, like the whole thing didn't matter to him, he was just a citizen trying to do his civic duty. But Wil's mention of the twenty-five grand raised sweat on the Russian's pitted nose.

Absolutely certain he'd seen the kid. It sounded to Wil

like he'd practiced all day convincing himself. Because how could he be that sure? Petra's drawing was good but to Wil the kid didn't look *that* distinctive.

He smiled to himself. All white kids looked the same, right?

He was noncommittal with the Russian, took notes as Zhukanov pointed north, up Ocean Front, where the kid had supposedly disappeared. But when Wil traipsed there, showing the picture to café owners, none of them knew a thing. Most of the other businesses were closed for the evening, so he supposed a re-visit was called for. But he doubted it would produce anything. This whole case had a futile smell to it.

He retraced his steps and the Russian was still there, way past closing time, waving as Wil passed him and headed toward his car. Leanna was due at Loew's in twenty minutes, five-course dinner, wine. He'd met her at a club, those huge brown eyes—

'Sir!' Zhukanov called out.

'Yes, Mr Zhukanov?'

'I will keep my eyes open for you. I call you when I see him again.'

Just what Wil needed, some Moscow mafioso playing junior detective.

Now here it was, the next morning, and all he could think about was the sun on Leanna's shoulders. Beautiful morning.

He'd arrived at seven on the dot, energized. A bunch more crank tipster messages on his desk but the Russian hadn't called, so maybe the kid was gone from Venice, or, more likely, he'd never been there.

426

Those two tips from Watson interested him a lot more. Two righteous-sounding old women, both thought they might have seen the boy in town. He was still waiting for a callback from the Watson sheriff.

His phone rang. A new day dawns.

'Hey, Dubba-yew, it's Vee.'

'Vee, long time.'

Val Vronek was a D-II Wil had worked Narcotics with at Wilshire, now handling hush-hush major crime stuff from downtown. Vronek loved undercover, his favorite thing, posing as a biker meth dealer. Big and heavy, he'd grown his hair shoulder-length, raised a beard that looked like a health hazard.

'Guess what, Wil, I'm in your neighborhood.'

'Oh?'

'Can't discuss details but if you guessed outlaw biker crank-empire I wouldn't contradict you. Just happened to be spending time in some shithole called The Cave.'

'Right up your alley, Vee, white-trash roots and all that.'

'You bet. Daddy rode high, Mama ate bugs,' sang Vronek. 'That's an old country tune. *Blue-eyed soul*.'

'*Blue-eyed soul* is the Righteous Brothers.'

Vronek laughed. 'The reason I'm calling is, in the course of said assignment to said shithole, something happened I thought you should know about. Late last night some guy came in showing around the picture of that kid you've been looking for, implying anyone who could help him would get a cut of the reward.'

'Why would anyone do that?' said Fournier. 'Least of all leather-scum. If they knew where the kid was they'd turn him in themselves, take the whole twenty-five.'

427

'Didn't say the guy was smart, Wil. Just there. And none of the assembled patrons jumped on the offer. It was like, "All those who give a shit step forward." No big boot ballet. I pretended to be one-quarter fascinated, tried to get a feel for the guy. He came across bigtime-stupid.'

'Got a name?'

'Nope, the situation didn't call for that level of intimacy. Here're the vitals: White male, twenty-eight to thirty-five, brown and blue, wavy hair, reddish muttonchop sideburns, my height, add at least fifty pounds.'

'A big boy,' said Fournier.

'He came on like some heavy-duty Angel but no one knew him. I told him I'd look out for the kid, where could I reach him? He said he'd be stopping by again tonight, around eight. You want me to, I'll come out to the sidewalk when he shows and let you know.'

'Deal, Vee. Thanks.'

'Any time. Too bad I won't be able to buy you a drink. They don't like colored folk.'

Just as Fournier hung up, Schoelkopf called. 'You're there. At least someone on Ramsey is.'

'What can I do for you, sir?'

'You don't read the paper?'

'Not yet—'

'You should, this is a public case. They found the girl's car. Burned out in Venice, I had to learn it from the damned paper. Read it, then get in here.'

52

Nigger.

Not taking him seriously. Vladimir Zhukanov pulled a troll doll down from the rack and squeezed its belly. Blond-haired troll, *Surf Dude!* printed on the shirt. He hated the way the damn thing smiled. Some Swede or Dane had invented the original one. This one was made in Korea, pirated, Zhukanov had bought ten gross from an old Moscow friend of his who worked the docks down in Long Beach, a hundred bucks, no questions asked.

A Georgian named Makoshvilli, they'd busted heads together while in the army, breaking up protests near the Kremlin, braining Yids, assorted cosmopolitan dirt.

He brought the trolls in a few at a time, pocketed the cash, fuck the boss.

Vladimir Zhukanov, sergeant in the Moscow police, reduced to trafficking in toys!

America, land of dreams. He'd claimed to be a Yid to get over here, paid a fortune to some immigration lawyer to lie for him, bunked down in some West Hollywood hovel full of Yids while he tried to find a niche for himself in LA. A few months later, Yeltsin opened the gates to anyone, the bastard.

The city was all niggers and brownies. He had yet to find

his niche. He'd driven a cab, tried unsuccessfully to sell his head-busting services to a Van Nuys forgery ring, managed to get into a West Hollywood car-theft ring but couldn't hotwire fast enough so they fired him. He worked nights for a while, bouncing at a Russian club on Third Street till some punks broke his nose – five against one, stupid club owners insisting no weapons, how could they claim it was his fault?

Now, this. Five bucks an hour from the Yid who owned the souvenir stand. Zhukanov skimmed at least five percent regularly, the Yid knew it, didn't care, he was raking it in from twenty other stands all around the city, living in Hancock Park, buying that hook-nosed wife of his diamonds.

One day, Zhukanov figured, he'd break into the house, get those diamonds.

Meanwhile, he sold toys. Till now: Salvation in the form of the kid.

Had to be him. Zhukanov had done his share of hunting, knew what prey smelled like.

Handing it to the nigger cop but the black bastard wasn't taking him seriously. No wonder this multicultural shithole had so much crime – nigger cops. Like having foxes guard chickens.

No way would he let that screw up his plans. Twenty-five grand meant out of here, maybe a quick grab for the boss's diamonds, fly to New York, Brighton Beach, Coney Island, no shortage of outfits there who'd welcome his talents, but with that kind of money he'd start his own business.

He was already self-employed: Personal hunter of the kid.

How far could the little bastard have gone? He was sure to turn up again and Sergeant Zhukanov would grab him.

A flash of optimism lightened his mood. A little vodka, maybe stop off somewhere for a nice meal.

Starting tomorrow, he'd be on full alert.

53

FRIDAY MORNING, Petra woke thinking about Balch as suspect. It still made sense, but so did Ramsey.

Which one of them? Both of them? Neither of them — a horrible thought.

The report of Lisa's burned-out car was on page five, along with a smaller reprint of her drawing, but nothing about the Venice tip or those from Watson. So Wil hadn't been forced to report, yet.

As she showered and soaped her body, she realized Kathy Bishop's body was under the knife right now. She'd call Stu later. When things had settled. Meanwhile, there were some details to take care of before she set out for Montecito.

Dr Boehlinger's hotel room didn't answer — out already, doing who knew what. A re-check of missing persons brought no clue to Estrella Flores's whereabouts and by 9 A.M. she was on her way to Granada Hills to pick up Ron.

When she drove up, he was standing at the curb, holding a cell phone.

His house was a tiny Tudor on a sunsplashed sidestreet, one story, the sharply pitched shake roof and half-timbers and pseudo-gables silly, but somehow touching: Someone had cared enough to lay in details. The grass was mown and edged, but pale, two rose bushes flanking the stone walkway were knobby with dead-heads, and half the oranges on a fifteen-foot Valencia had browned.

He was at the car door before she shifted into park. His hair was shower-moist, cowlicks sprouting like new wheat. A blue V-neck sweater, yellow button-down shirt and off-white Dockers made him look younger – grad-student, business administration. Oxblood penny-loafers. Somewhere along the trajectory from rock drummer to cop he'd touched upon preppy. Dressed casually, he looked *much* younger, maybe younger than she did.

'Hi,' she said.

He got in. 'Hi.' Lime-scented aftershave. He hadn't worn that the first time. That seemed like years ago. He made no move toward her now, locked the door and put the phone in his lap, explaining, 'Just in case my mom needs to call.'

'I should move into the twentieth century, finally get one of those.'

'Get one of those hands-off deals,' he said. 'Talk in the car, make everyone think you're psychotic and they'll leave you alone.'

Laughing, she pulled away from the curb, wondering if she should mention the theory-jolt about Balch. No, too speculative at this point. He had years on her. He was a rescuer. She wanted to look smart in front of him.

As she drove, they chatted. Small talk, but intelligent. He gave off an air of stability. Too boring for the Spanish equestrienne? Or would he reveal some grub-under-the-rock dark side if she waited long enough?

You are one untrusting broad. Thank you, Nick.

'Beautiful day,' she heard him say. His hands were quiet

now. No gripping of the door handle or other signs of anxiety about her driving. The loafers looked freshly polished. Sharp crease in the Dockers – wasn't that sort of an anti-Dockers thing? Petra smiled at the thought of *his* wanting to impress *her*.

By the time they reached the 101 on-ramp, they were really talking.

She sped through the west Valley – past RanchHaven – into Thousand Oaks, Newbury Park, Camarillo, the produce fields and fertilizer stink of Oxnard. At Ventura, Ron pointed out a Golf 'n Stuff on the east side of the freeway, telling her he sometimes took his girls there, they also had U-bump cars and mini-boats, the latter a lot of fun if you don't mind getting wet. Getting all enthusiastic but the bounce went out of his voice when Petra, thinking about Balch again, said, 'Sounds cute.'

'If you're into that kind of thing,' he added, embarrassed.

'I am,' she said, hastening to salvage the conversation. 'Grew up in Arizona, didn't see too many boats, mini or otherwise. After we solve the case, let's stop off on the way back and get wet.'

He didn't answer. She turned her head far enough to catch the blush on his neck.

Oh, jeez. How could a size nine shoe fit completely in a mouth?

'Or,' she said, 'we could golf. But only after we solve Lisa. We're gonna wrap the whole thing up today, right?'

'Sure,' he said, grinning. 'Arizona. Didn't they move London Bridge there?'

* * *

She exited at Santa Ynez, asking him, 'Do you know Montecito?'

'Only by reputation.'

'Which is?'

'Rich.'

Pulling to the side of the grove-bordered road, she consulted her *Thomas Guide*, located Ramsey's street two miles in, a pair of right turns and a left, and resumed driving. Montecito was ten degrees cooler than LA, a perfect sixty-eight. Private groves bordered Santa Ynez Road. Rich, indeed.

Petra had been up to Santa Barbara a few times with Nick, Sunday outings, eating seafood on the pier, scorning the sidewalk art. They'd passed Montecito on the freeway, Nick rhapsodizing about the estates, great Spanish architecture, old money, real class, it made Beverly Hills look like crap. Getting one of his blind ambition grooves, going on about how one day they'd have enough money to get a place there. But he'd never pulled off to show her.

She picked up speed. No town in sight yet, just the clean stretch of asphalt cutting through the umber fudge and chlorophyll of old trees, coral bursts of bougainvillea, oranges and lemons sparkling like gems. The sky was blue, the clouds were white, a clean yellow sun rose from behind the mountains, die-cut sharp, black, dabbed with lavender. What a place.

Ramsey had all this *and* the place in Calabasas, the cars, the real estate. Money wasn't everything but it sure made things nice. What led rich people to screw things up so badly? She looked over at Ron and from his expression, she guessed he was asking himself the same thing.

435

Montecito's business district was four corners of earth-tone lowrise, upscale shops. Then more road. Ramsey's street was skinny, darkened by shaggy eucalyptus, his property at a dead end, announced by blue-gray stone posts and a high black scrollwork gate, wide open. A Carpenteria sheriff car blocked the entrance, one deputy standing near the driver's door, hand on holster, another facing the vehicle, hands on hips.

'Welcoming party?' Petra asked Ron. 'Did you tell them we were coming?'

'No.'

As they got closer, the deputy at the front of the squad car walked into the center of the road and halted them with his palm. Petra stopped. By the time the deputy reached them, she had her badge out.

He studied it. A kid. Tall, husky, red crewcut, two weeks of rusty mustache, swollen biceps. He looked over at Ron.

'Banks, LA Sheriffs. I spoke to Captain Sepulveda.'

'Yeah, he told us. Since the murder, we've been upping our patrols anyway. Good thing. Just caught a trespasser.' He hooked a thumb.

'Right now?' said Petra.

'He made it easy, left the gates open. Looks like a nut-case, verbally abusive. Claims he's Ramsey's father-in-law.'

Petra squinted at the cruiser. Through the rear window Dr Boehlinger's goateed face seethed. She watched Boehlinger slap the glass, then retract his hand, clearly in pain. A surgeon. Brilliant. The deputy watching him must have said something because Boehlinger started screaming. Too far away to hear, but his mouth was wide open. The window glass gave him a preserved look. Rage in a jar.

436

She said, 'He is Ramsey's father-in-law.'

'Come on,' said the red-haired cop. His name was Forbes.

'Dr John Everett Boehlinger. Didn't he have ID?'

'Yeah, that's what his ID said, but that didn't mean anything to us.' Forbes grimaced. 'He sure doesn't act like a doctor – got a toilet mouth.'

'What'd you catch him doing?'

'Coming out of a toolshed out back. The door was smashed, he obviously kicked it in, was carrying a shovel. Looked to us like he was planning to break a window in the house, do an unlawful entry. So he's really her father? Come on.'

Petra nodded.

'Shit.' Forbes cracked massive knuckles. 'His demeanor, we figured a loony for sure. And he was *talking* crazy, bodies buried out here, he was gonna dig them up. We had to restrain him. Hands *and* feet. Kind of tough, hogtying an old guy like that, but he tried to bite us.' Forbes looked at his hand, smooth and tan at the end of the buffed arm. The thought of bodily injury was a narcissistic insult. Working in a rich, quiet town, he'd actually manage to keep himself smooth.

'Small guy,' he added, 'but incredibly feisty. Finally we got him quiet enough to untie his feet. Didn't want a heart attack or anything.' He shook his head. 'Her father – *shit!*'

'Where does he say bodies are buried?' said Petra.

'We didn't ask. We figured him for a loony-tunes star-fucker – we get them from time to time, all the Hollywood types with second homes up here. Tabloid reporters, too. We've been preparing ourselves for problems with Ramsey.'

'Had any?'

'Not till now. Maybe no one knows he's got a weekend place here, yet.'

'Does Ramsey come up here much?'

'I've never seen him, but maybe he comes up at night. Lots of the Hollywood types do. Flying up at night to Santa B in copters or private planes, or they just limo straight up from LA. The whole thing with them is *not* to be spotted. It's like a game, you know? I'm famous but you can't see me. They never come into town to shop, have people doing things for them. And with the size of these properties, it's not like they've got real neighbors.'

Petra took in the surroundings. Long stretches of ten-foot wall on both sides. Through Ramsey's gate was a winding stone motorpath flanked by palms. The guy loved palms.

'Who takes care of Ramsey's house when he's not here?' she said.

Forbes shrugged. 'Probably a cleaning crew. There is a regular gardening crew, comes here Tuesday and I think Saturday.' Forbes touched an eyelash, scratched the side of his nose. 'Ramsey's also got a gofer, comes up to check out the house. I ran into him on patrol a couple of days ago.'

'Greg Balch?' said Petra.

'Yeah, that's the one.'

The other deputy had turned his back to the cruiser. Shorter, darker than Forbes, thick arms crossing a barrel chest. Another buffboy. Department must have a good gym.

'Switching cars,' said Petra.

'Yeah, a Lexus. Still parked behind the house. At first it looked funny, but he had the keys, a letter from Ramsey authorizing him to drive all his cars.'

Thumping noises sounded from the patrol car. Dr Boehlinger, kicking the window.

'Why don't you let him out?' said Petra.

'You wanna take custody of him?'

'I want to talk to him.'

It took a long time to calm Boehlinger down. He was wearing a gray Washington U sweatshirt, baggy gray tweed wool trousers, probably from an old suit, and white sneakers. Flecks of spit whitened the corners of his mouth, wisps of hair flew at random angles and his goatee looked grizzled.

Finally, thirty seconds of silence earned him unlocked cuffs. The moment his hands were free he brandished fists at the deputies. 'You stupid fucking imbeciles!'

Forbes and the shorter man – Beckel – ignored him. Before uncuffing him, they'd held the little man at arm's length as he shouted and kicked – a cartoon situation. Now they headed back to their cruiser, conferring with Ron, as Petra ushered Boehlinger to her car.

'Idiots!' Boehlinger shouted. He coughed, spit phlegm into the dirt, started to rant again. Petra tightened her grip on his shoulder. He was shaking like a lapdog, still frothing at the mouth. 'Brain-damaged idio—'

'Please, Doctor!'

'Don't please *me*, young la—'

Propelling him faster, Petra talked into his ear. 'Dr Boehlinger, I know you've been through hell, but if you don't settle down, we'll be forced to let them arrest you.'

Boehlinger said, '*You're* an idiot, too! That butcher walks free, bodies pile up, and you threaten me! Goddamn all of you, I'll have you all collecting Welfare—'

'Bodies where?' said Petra.

'In there!' Boehlinger jabbed toward the gate. 'Behind the pond – there must be a God! I came to get into the house, go through the butcher's papers, some evidence of what he did to Lisa, but I saw a helluva lot more than I bargained for—'

'What kind of evidence were you looking for, Doctor?'

'Anything,' Boehlinger said, quickly.

'What made you think Ramsey'd left any evidence behind?'

'I didn't *think*! I *hoped*! Lord knows *you* people haven't done a *damn* thing! I dip into my own pocket and you don't have the brains and the decency to follow—'

'Dr Boehlinger,' Petra said firmly, 'what evidence were you hoping to find here?'

Silence. Boehlinger's watery blue eyes lowered. 'I didn't have a . . . clear concept. But what could it hurt? This is the place he beat my Lisa. What's to say he didn't write notes to himself – or something Lisa wrote – stop interrupting my train of thought, young lady, the point is, I went to find something to break the window—'

'The shovel.'

'No, no, no! I chose the shovel *after* I saw it! I was looking for a *chisel* to pry the lock. I'm good with tools.'

The last sentence a pathetic boast. *Look, Mom, I'm useful.* Sulfurous breath blew out from between Boehlinger's lips. His eyes were frightened. Maybe he hadn't been the best father in the world but Lisa's death had ripped him up. Such a small man.

Petra said, 'You switched from the chisel to the shovel after . . .'

'After I saw the grave. Behind that pond of his.'

'A grave? How can you be—'

'Put your money on it,' said Boehlinger. 'Fresh excavation, about six feet long. Far side of the pond. Plants trampled, plants missing. I've been here before. After the wedding, the bastard was trying to impress me. I have an eye for detail, saw the difference right away.'

'Is the pond plumbed?' said Petra. 'Maybe there'd been a repair—'

'And maybe Charles Manson's the Pope-designate. Don't be *stupid*, young lady! I've assisted at autopsies, seen my share of crime-scene photos. I know what a *grave* looks like.'

Ron came back, saying, 'Looks like you're off the hook for now, Doctor.' Boehlinger huffed.

Forbes waved from the cruiser and Petra went over.

'OK, he's yours. Hope you're taking him straight back to LA.'

'We will eventually,' said Petra.

'Eventually?'

'We're in a bit of a bind, Deputy. He claims he saw a fresh grave on the Ramsey property but we have no jurisdiction, can't step onto the property to check.'

'A grave? You're taking his bull *seriously*?'

'Given the details of our case, we can't afford to ignore it.'

'Oh, come on. Burying someone right here?'

Petra shrugged.

'Oh, man.' Forbes turned and said 'Gary?' to Beckel, who was sitting in the car, writing an incident report. The shorter deputy had a broad, stoic face and a meaty chin. Forbes filled him in. Beckel said, 'What, some kind of serial killer or something?'

'It'll probably turn out to be nothing,' said Petra. 'On the other hand, if something did occur, it's your jurisdiction.'

'We can't just go in there,' said Forbes. 'No warrant.'

'You've already *been* in there. Because of Dr Boehlinger's trespassing – obvious criminal behavior gave you clear grounds for entry. Once on the premises you apprehended a suspect, then noticed something amiss. Fresh excavation.'

'Oh, come on,' said Forbes. 'You're putting our nu— putting us in a position.'

'OK,' said Petra. 'But I'll have to write this up for my boss and you can bet the first thing Boehlinger's going to do when he gets back is contact the media. He's already played that game.'

Forbes cursed under his breath.

Beckel said, 'Let's call it in, Chick.'

'Yeah,' said Forbes. 'I'm calling my boss.'

When Petra returned to the car, Dr Boehlinger was sitting in the back seat with Ron, talking animatedly. Dry-eyed, still tense, but conversing at normal volume. Ron listened intensely, nodding. Boehlinger smiled. Ron smiled back, said, 'Interesting.'

'Extremely interesting,' said Boehlinger.

Petra got in the driver's seat.

'So?' said Boehlinger.

'I told them I thought they should take you seriously, Doctor. They're notifying their superiors.'

'In their case,' said Boehlinger, 'that encompasses most of the world.'

Petra couldn't help herself; she laughed.

Ron said, 'Doctor?' in a prompting tone.

Boehlinger cleared his throat. 'I apologize for everything I said before, Detective Connor.'

'Not necessary, Doctor.'

'Yes, it is. I've been a rude lout . . . but you have no idea what it's like to lose everything.'

'True,' said Petra. Suddenly, she pictured Kathy Bishop under the knife. It was almost noon, Kathy was probably out of surgery, chest stitched. How much had been taken from her? Petra resolved to call the hospital soon.

'So tell me, Doctor,' said Ron, 'those autopsies you mentioned, were they part of your duties as ER chief, or special consultations?'

'That was years ago, Ron,' said Boehlinger wistfully. *Ron?* 'Back when I was Chief Resident. I actually deliberated going into pathology, spent some time with the St Louis coroner's. Back in those days, the place was a regular—'

New man. Dr Banks, master psychologist.

Shuffling sounds drew Petra's eyes to the side window. Forbes's big feet scraping asphalt. 'OK,' he said, looking at Petra, avoiding Boehlinger, 'the boss is coming. Then we'll have a look at this so-called grave.'

Captain Sepulveda was a blocky, silver-haired man around forty-five with brown-suede skin and an impeccable uniform. He arrived in an unmarked with a third deputy, went onto Ramsey's property alone and emerged moments later, ordering all three officers inside.

Petra and Ron and Boehlinger waited in the car as Boehlinger rambled on about medical school, graduating top of his class, multiple triumphs as an ER doctor.

Twenty minutes later, Sepulveda appeared, dirt streaks on his shirt, rubbing his palms together. A few athletic steps brought him to Petra's side. His eyes were slits, so compressed Petra wondered how he could see.

'Looks like we have a body. Female, buried four feet down. Maggots, some deterioration, but plenty of tissue still on it, so it's been days not weeks.'

'Maybe two days,' said Petra, thinking: Had the car-exchange been just a cover for Balch's trip? 'Older Hispanic female? Approximately five two, one forty?'

The razor-cut eyes dipped at the outer corners. 'You know her?'

'I believe I do. You might also want to have a look at that black Lexus.'

'Look for what?'

'Blood.'

54

SLEEPING INDOORS is great. At first I woke up every hour, but then I was OK.

The brown blankets Sam brought me are rough, but warm. The sheet and pillows smell of old guy. Before I turned out the lights I lay there looking up at the *shul*'s ceiling, the red bulb in the silver holder hanging in front of that ark. Sam said it was OK to sleep in the *shul*, but I figured it wouldn't be respectful so I set myself on the floor near the back door, next to the bathrooms. Every so often I could hear a car drive through the alley and once I heard someone's feet shuffling outside, probably someone dumpster-diving and it made me lose breath for a few seconds, but I was OK.

I think I fell asleep watching the red bulb. Sam told me it wouldn't go off, was something called an eternal light to remind the Jews of God. Then he laughed and said, 'Wishful thinking, eh, Bill? The bulb dies every couple of months, I get up on a ladder, take my life in my hands.'

He tossed me a bagel, left, and locked the door.

It's 5:49 and I've been up ten minutes. I can see the colored glass windows in front of the *shul* get brighter. I want to go outside and have a look at the ocean but I don't have the key to the front door. Shaking out and folding the blankets and sheets, I wash off in what Sam calls The Gents, and finish the rest of last night's bagel. Then, opening the back door an inch, I look through.

The air's cool – cold, even – with tons of salt in it. The alley is empty. I step outside, make my way around the side of the *shul* to the front of the walkway. No one's out, just gulls and pigeons. The ocean's dark gray with spots of light in a few places, like orange-pink freckles. The tide's coming in very softly, then rolling back out like someone tilted the earth, back and forth, this whoosh-whoosh rhythm. I think of something I once saw on TV: Panning for gold. God's tilting the whole planet, looking for something valuable.

I stand there, watching and listening. Then I think of that woman in the park and how she'll never see the ocean again.

I shut my eyes tight and blow out those thoughts.

Thinking of the ocean, the air, how salty it smells, how I like that smell. How this is the end of the earth, this is as far as you can run. There's some litter on the walkway – papers and beer bottles and soda cans – but everything still looks beautiful. Quiet and empty and beautiful. Not a single other person.

I will always love being alone.

Now the sky behind me starts to brighten up more and the skin of my arm turns gold and I spot the sun, rising, humongous and egg-yolk yellow. I can't feel any heat yet but with a sun that big I know it will be coming.

Now I'm not alone anymore: From the south, maybe a block away, I see a guy coming toward me on roller skates,

446

wearing nothing but a bathing suit, holding his hands out like he's trying to take off and fly.

The picture is ruined. I go back to the *shul*.

Sam's Lincoln is there, parked crazy as usual, and I find him in the *shul*, looking at a book.

'Good morning,' I say.

He turns around fast, closing the book. He doesn't look happy. 'Where were you?'

'Outside.'

'Outside?'

'To see the ocean.'

'The ocean.' Why is he repeating everything I say? He puts the book down, walks toward me and for a second I think he's going to hit me and I'm ready to defend myself but he goes past me and checks the back door to make sure it's locked, stands with his back to the door, definitely unhappy.

'Do you want me to leave?' I said. 'Did I do something wrong?'

He blows out air and rubs his neck. 'We got a problem, Bill.' He takes something out of his pocket. A piece of newspaper. 'This is yesterday's edition,' he says. 'Dealing with you kept me busy, I didn't get to it until this morning.'

He unfolds it and shows it to me. I see the word *murder*. Then a drawing of a kid.

Me.

I try to read the article but the words are jumping up and down. So is my stomach. My heart starts pushing against my chest, I feel cold, and my mouth is dry.

I keep struggling to read but nothing makes sense, it's

447

like a foreign language. Blinking, I clear my eyes but the words are still weird and jumping. I grab the paper from him and hold it close, finally start to understand.

The woman who got killed in the park has a name. Lisa. I have to think of her as Lisa now.

Lisa Boehlinger Ramsey. Her ex-husband's an actor, Cart Ramsey. A show called *The Adjustor*. I've heard of it, I think Moron used to watch it.

Someone's offering $25,000.00 to find me.

I run for the back door. Sam doesn't try to stop me.

As I reach for the knob, my feet freeze.

Where can I go?

It's going to be a hot, bright day full of people out for that money, the sunlight will uncover me, someone, maybe a bunch of them, will grab me and tie me up and turn me in.

Sam's still standing there. 'You can stay here all day, but remember, tonight's Friday services, thirty, forty *alter kocker* – worshippers showing up a half hour before dark, nothing I can do about it.'

I'm not breathing great and my chest feels tight; I open my mouth wide to capture some air but not much comes in. My stomach hurts worse than it ever did and my heart's still bumping against my chest – *chuck chuck*, just like what happened to . . . Lisa.

'One thing you might consider, Bill: Twenty-five thousand's a lot of money. If you do know something about this, why not be a good citizen and help yourself in the bargain?'

'I don't know anything.'

He shrugs. 'Fine. I accept that. It's not you, just some kid who looks like you. But with the resemblance, how are you gonna traipse around?'

448

I slept so well last night but now I'm tired, just want to lie down.

I sit down on a *shul* bench and close my eyes.

'To see something like that, Bill, of course you're scared. I know. I saw terrible things, too.'

I keep my eyes glued shut.

'You see things like that, you wish you didn't, because you know it'll change you. That's the big difference in this world, Bill. People who're forced to see terrible things, and everyone else, getting away with the easy life. I won't tell you it's good to see. It stinks, no one would choose it. The only good thing is, you can get strong from it – I don't have to tell you that, you already got strong. Being out there, taking care of yourself, you did a good job. Considering what you been through, you did great. It's true, Bill. You're handling things great.'

He's saying nice things, trying to make me feel better. Why does it feel like a punch in the stomach?

'One part of my brain,' he goes on, 'is saying call the cops, protect him – no, no, don't worry, I'm not gonna do it, I'm just telling you what's going on in my brain. The other part – must be the strong part – is reminding me of what happened to me when I wasn't much older than you. Remember those Nazis I told you about? Some of *them* were cops – the bastards who came and took my family *away* were cops – devils in uniform. So it's not always simple, is it? A guy wants to do the right thing, not break the law, but it's just not that simple, is it?'

He reaches out and touches my shoulders. 'Don't worry, you're safe with me.'

He means it. It makes me feel good.

Why does it also make me bend over, so low my forehead's almost touching the floor? And now my eyes hurt, too, and I can't stop myself from rocking back and forth and my body's shaking and I'm crying.

Like a damned baby, I just can't stop it!

With everything that's happened, why cry *now*?

55

WIL FOURNIER returned from Schoelkopf's office, thinking, 'Could have been worse.'

The captain had been irritable but distracted, a meeting this afternoon with Deputy Chief Lazara. 'Including your case, which I assume is stagnating.' Schoelkopf's face started to redden.

Wil headed him off by volunteering the Russian's tip.

'When did this come in?'

'Late last night. The guy's a lowlife, I figured I'd do some checking on him first—'

'Check later, it's a solid tip and I want you back in Venice, searching for the kid. Where's Barbie?'

Wil wondered about that himself. 'Don't know.'

Schoelkopf glared at him. 'Tight team you guys are running. How's Ken's wife?'

'I imagine she's being operated on right now, sir.'

'She'll probably be OK, young woman like that – OK, back to the beach, Fournier. If the kid's there, I want him found.' Schoelkopf picked up his phone.

Straight to the media; no one could see him, but he'd put on a media smile.

Before leaving for Venice, Fournier followed up on the two tips from Watson. Nothing new from one old woman, but the second, a Mrs Kraft, said she was pretty sure the boy lived in a trailer park on the south end of town.

'Low-class place,' she said. 'They started it years ago for retired people, but trash moved in.'

'The boy's family is trash?' said Wil.

'If he lives there, they probably are.'

'But you don't know a name?'

'No, sir, I'm just saying I think he lived there because I think I seen him around there. When I was out with my dog. My dog's a sweetie pie, but the boy didn't come near Jet, like he was afraid of animals. This happened twice. I'm not sure it's him, but I think so.'

'OK, thanks, Mrs Kraft,' said Fournier. 'What's the name of the trailer park?'

'Sleepy Hollow,' she said. 'Like that book, the ghost story.'

He called the Watson sheriff and got a busy signal. Could you believe that? Just as he tried again, Brian Olson, the D at the next desk, waved at him. 'Someone for you on my line.'

Fournier went over to Olson's desk and Olson used the break to get coffee.

'Fournier.'

'Detective? This is Sheriff Albert McCauley from Watson, California. Woulda got back to you sooner but I was attending a firearms conference up in Sacramento. Ever been to one of those? Very educational.' Low, drawling voice. Plenty of free time.

'Not yet,' said Wil.

'Educational,' McCauley repeated. 'So. What can I do for you?'

Fournier had left detailed messages. What was this,

452

Mayberry RFD? He told McCauley about the boy and the trailer park.

'Runaway, huh?' said the sheriff. 'Yeah, the Hollow's a scruffy place. Not much crime, though. Anywhere in Watson, for that matter. Quiet here. Only real problems we get is when the migrants blow in and hit the tequila.'

The kid had run from something, thought Fournier. 'If you could check, Sheriff—'

'Sure, no problem. Got some things to catch up on first, then I'll go over talk to the Hollow manager, see if he can ID this boy. You say it was in the LA paper?'

'Two days ago.'

'Don't usually read the LA papers. Not too friendly to law enforcement, are they?'

'Depends,' said Wil, noncommital. 'I can fax you the drawing.'

'Sure. Do that.'

Wil thanked him again and hung up, resolving to call the Sleepy Hollow manager himself if he didn't hear back from McCauley by late afternoon.

He spent another two hours following up with shelters and social workers, and headed west, having lunch at an Italian place on the Third Street Mall in Santa Monica, then drove to Venice.

A beautiful afternoon at the beach was wasted talking to shopkeepers, restaurant managers, old folks, bodybuilders, rollerbladers. Tourists who looked at him like he was crazy. Some people were scared of him, despite the suit and a flip of the badge. Black skin, maybe one day he'd get used to the reaction, but probably not.

Sleazeball Zhukanov was back behind his souvenir counter

and the first time Wil passed the stand he ignored the Russian's hostile stare. On the way back, he stopped, asked Zhukanov if he'd seen anything.

The Russian shook his head and pushed stringy hair out of his face. Greasy face full of pits. Pus pimple in the fold of his left nostril. Zhukanov's beard was a poor excuse for facial hair, unevenly trimmed, a blemish, not an adornment. The guy didn't believe in deodorant, either. Who'd buy toys from him?

Zhukanov's eyelids drooped. In contradiction, he said, 'Not yet but I keep eyes open.'

'Do that.' Wil started to walk away.

Zhukanov said, 'How can I call you without number?'

Wil fished out a business card and placed it on the counter, ignoring Zhukanov's outstretched palm. Hatred filled the Russian's eyes. He picked a troll doll off the rack and put the tiny figure's neck between two fingers. Wil left, wondering if he'd decapitate the thing.

It was already 6:30 P.M. and he was due at The Cave by eight, ready for Val Vronek to signal the fat biker's arrival. Though the value of that seemed less than iffy, probably just another fool out for the twenty-five thou, but digging dry wells was part of the job.

He called into the station. Nothing from Sheriff McCauley, so either the Watson lawman had checked out Sleepy Hollow and located the kid in question, or hadn't bothered yet. Either way, Wil was annoyed.

The only call was from Petra, 818 area code. He returned it. *The mobile customer you are trying to reach is either away from the vehicle or . . .*

Obtaining a number for the Sleepy Hollow RV Park and

Recreational Facility, he phoned, got another taped message, another drawling voice.

Quiet place, McCauley had said. More like Zombie-Town.

He called Leanna, asked her phone machine whether she was free for a late dinner tonight, let's say nine thirty, ten. Another try at Petra's 818 cell phone, same outcome. It was nearly seven and he was ready to kill the first machine he met. He walked along the beach, found a quiet bench and sat down to enjoy the ocean for a while, watching the seagulls and the pelicans. He loved those pelicans, the way they just cut through the air, no effort, very cool birds. God, it was gorgeous here, if you concentrated on the water, forgot about the people.

Then he found himself turning around. Scanning the walkway. Just in case the kid happened by. Wouldn't *that* be something, a precious accident. Unable to relax now, he found another bench, one that put his back to the water and his eyes on business.

At 7:45 he was on Hollywood Boulevard, drinking an Orange Whip at a snack-stand a few storefronts down from The Cave. The nightcrawlers were already out. Punks, dopers, he-she's, she-he's, all kinds of its, more dumb tourists, small groups of marines on leave – those kids always got into trouble. With their shaved heads, they looked just like skinners, maybe some of them were. As he sucked down the sweet, freezing drink, he saw something that really cracked him up: Pudgy girl around nineteen, shaved head except for one of those rooster-comb deals, leading a guy of the same age around on a leash. Saying, 'Get going, get going.' The guy was skinny, pale, mute, had a romantic smile on his face.

Fournier sipped a little more Whip, tossed the cup and ambled by The Cave. Harleys were lined up in front of the bar. Even from here you could hear the music, some kind of country rock, way too much bass.

A half-open door offered a glimpse of dark room. Wil kept walking, made it to the corner, pretended to examine the cheesy clothes in a store window, turned around. When he reached the bar the second time, Val Vronek was coming out, all leathered and chained, looking almost as greasy as the Russian.

The undercover man paused just left of the doorway, lit up a cigarette, caught Wil's eye for a half-second. His left cheek twitched and he gave his head a very small shake.

No Fatboy.

Wil took a stroll. Fifteen minutes later, V communicated the same thing, made sure no one was watching, flashed ten fingers three times. See you in thirty.

Half hour later, still no sign of the guy. Val lit up a cigarette, walked to one of the Harleys, checked the chain-lock, loped down the street to the corner. A few minutes later, Wil followed. He found the undercover D in the darkened doorway of an apartment building just off the Boulevard. Black windows, city condemnation notice on the door.

'Sorry. Guy was probably full of shit,' said V. 'Or maybe he watches TV.'

'What was on TV?'

'Your kid, didn't you see it?'

'Haven't been sitting in a bar all day.'

V smiled. 'Six o'clock news, Dubba. Some tipster put him in Venice. Maybe Fatboy decided I wasn't worth dealing with and went there straight.'

'Just came from Venice,' said Wil. And the tipster. Had any of the bikers on the walkway matched Fatboy's description? No, he would have noticed that. He hoped.

V said, 'If he shows up, I'll call you. Gotta get back to scroteville.' His white face was glassy with sweat.

'Hot gig?' said Wil.

'Hell would be a vacation, Dubba. And the smell's something else. Not that you'll ever get a chance to know, being dusky.'

Wil chuckled. 'Hey, membership has its privileges.'

Leaving Vronek his beeper number in case Fatboy showed up, he drove home, wondering if Leanna had called back. Maybe she'd tried his apartment, thinking him back already. Logical, it was nearly 9:30 – he'd sure given the citizens full service today.

The beep came just as he pulled into his driveway.

He read the number. Sheriff McCauley. Gee thanks, pard, finally moseyed on down to the ol' Holler, didja?

Collecting his mail, he entered his ground-floor flat, checked the phone. No Leanna. Uncapping a bottle of Heineken, he called McCauley.

'Complications,' said the sheriff. No more drawl, none of that country-bumpkin friendliness. 'Got a tentative ID on your kid. The manager ID'd him. Name's Billy Straight. William Bradley Straight, twelve years old, approximately five feet, seventy-five, eighty pounds. No one's seen him for months. The mother was unemployed, living on Welfare, always months behind on the rent. No father that anyone's ever seen. Not a good situation but the boy never gave any trouble.'

Gone for months but no one in peaceful quiet Zombieville

had thought to report it, thought Wil. Even country lanes could be mean streets.

'What did the mother say about his disappearance, Sheriff?'

'That's the complication. When I went over to talk to her I found her dead in the trailer, looks like a couple of days or so. Contusions to the occipital portion of the skull, some lividity, beginnings of rigor, some blowfly maggots. The trailer was hot, probably hastened the process, but neighbors saw her two mornings ago, so that helps fix the TOD.'

Bye bye Andy Griffith, hello Quincy.

'. . . there was blood on the edge of a dresser, so it looks like she fell backwards and hit her head on the counter. Or was pushed, she's got some old bruises on her, too. There was a boyfriend living with her for a while and all of a sudden he's gone. Biker type, loser with a petty record – we got an ID on him, too, from fellows at the local bar. Buell Erville Moran, white male, thirty years old, six one, two ninety—'

'Brown hair, blue eyes, reddish muttonchop sideburns,' said Wil.

'You've got him?'

'No, but we want him.'

458

56

THERE WAS enough skin on Estrella Flores's face for Petra to make the ID. The maid's throat had been slashed ear to ear but no other wounds were evident. None of the overkill butchery visited upon Lisa.

Made sense, she supposed: Lisa was passion, this was snipping loose ends.

Balch or Ramsey? Or both? *Neither* was no longer a viable choice.

Dr Boehlinger wanted to stay but Sepulveda had Deputy Forbes drive him back to LA, a match made in hell that caused Petra to grin inwardly despite the horror of the situation.

Poor Estrella, talk about wrong place, wrong time. Still wearing her pink uniform. She'd probably been taken care of on Tuesday, or Wednesday, driven up here on Wednesday.

Had to be late Wednesday or Thursday morning, the day Balch had been spotted leaving, because she'd interviewed him Wednesday evening and the Lexus had been parked in front of the Players building. Empty. Clean. In contrast with the mess in the office. Had the deed already been done — *had Estrella been lying in that trunk during the interview?*

She and Ron stood back as the local techs worked, hustling to finish up before darkness changed the game. Ramsey's Montecito spread was huge, the house old and stately, cream stucco and red tile, real Spanish, no bell tower, none of the crazy angles of the Calabasas castle. Giant oaks shaded the acre closest to the building. The landscaping took the shade into account: Ferns, clivia, camellia, azalea. Lovely pathways of degraded granite had been laid out expertly.

The property dipped, leading the eye down to the pond, a hundred-foot disc of green water set out in full light. White and pink lilies claimed half the surface, flame-colored dragonflies zoomed past like tiny aircraft, a bronze heron stooped to drink. Cattails and more lilies in the background, yellow, white with amethyst centers. Petra could see the missing foliage that had tipped Dr B to the grave.

Precise eyes, indeed.

The techs were concentrating on the black Lexus. The interior was onyx leather, black carpeting covered the trunk. Not the easiest surfaces for spotting bloodstains, but one of the criminalists thought he saw a patch the size of a dime on the inner side of the trunk door and Luminol confirmed it. Nothing on the car-seats, but the test brought up Rorschach-like blots of blood all over the carpet.

'I'd say about a pint,' said Captain Sepulveda. 'If that. Meaning he killed her somewhere else, wrapped her in something, and it leaked out. Then he shampooed the trunk – I could smell it. Figured if it looked clean it was.'

Talking softly. Unhappy about being drawn in. Petra wondered if he'd ever been a homicide D.

He said, 'We better get some warrants for the house and the grounds, who knows what else is out here.' He turned to face Petra and his slit eyes must have focused on her, though she couldn't see enough iris to tell. 'I'm going to talk to a judge, right now. What's next for you?'

'Balch drove the car up here, so he's obviously a suspect,' she said. 'I'm calling this in to my captain, asking to put out a warrant. Whether or not Balch was working for Ramsey remains to be seen, but I don't doubt this murder's related to ours. I need Balch and Ramsey located ASAP.'

Telling, not asking.

'Fine,' said Sepulveda. 'I should be back within the hour, any questions talk to Sergeant Grafton.' He indicated a slim, attractive dark-haired woman in plainclothes taking notes by the side of the pond.

He left and Ron handed Petra the cell phone. She phoned Wil Fournier first. Away from his desk, she left the number. Schoelkopf was out, too, meetings all afternoon, but she convinced a clerk to track him down. He called five minutes later.

'I was with Lazara, this better be good.'

'Seems pretty good to me, sir.' She told him.

'Shit – OK, we pick up both of them pronto.'

'Ramsey's hiding behind Lawrence Schick.'

'I know that, so we yank the bastard the hell out behind Schick's skirts. Just to talk, not an arrest. You stay there, be an eagle-eye, don't lose control of the situation. And keep the goddamn phone line open.'

'Balch lives in Rolling Hills Estates,' said Petra. 'His office is in Studio City. I've got both addresses.'

'Go.'

She read off the numbers. Schoelkopf clicked off.

Ron said, 'I should call in too. Hector, and my mom. We're not getting out of here for a while.'

She returned the phone. Nifty little Ericsson. 'Is this private gear or department?'

461

'Private.'

'I'll reimburse you.'

He smiled and punched numbers. The Lexus was being winched to a tow-truck, techs were setting up tape and post perimeters near the burial site, Sergeant Grafton paced off the area, pointing and instructing.

A Santa Barbara County coroner's station wagon drove up and two men in white got out with a folding stretcher. Estrella Flores's corpse was small. Those bowed legs, the gaping throat wound exposing a corrugated flash of trachea.

Ron couldn't find De la Torre but he connected with his mother, and Petra walked away to give him privacy, thinking about the call she'd have to make to Javier Flores. Schoelkopf had ordered her to keep the line open. To hell with him. It was Ron's phone, let the department buy her one.

The tow-truck backed out, manipulating the Lexus around oaks. Moments later, the coroner's guys carried the body to the wagon. The garden looked trampled, fronds and leaves bent over, broken. Petra smelled a hint of ocean. Pacific currents managing to make it this far inland. Lilies swayed. The yellow tape danced.

Ron came back and gave her the phone.

'Well,' she said, 'it started out as a nice day.'

'Still is.' He moved closer to her and his fingers touched hers for a second. Taking hold of her index finger, he squeezed gently and let go. He was staring straight ahead. Drummer's hands tapped a beat on the side of his thighs but his eyes seemed serene.

He loves this, she thought. He'll do Homicide as long as they let him.

The phone beeped. 'Connor.'

462

Schoelkopf said, 'Talked to Attorney Schick. He and Ramsey are on their way up there.'

'What about Balch?'

'Ramsey said he was supposed to be in his office. We called there, got no answer.'

'Same thing happened to me the time I interviewed him,' said Petra. 'He was in, but didn't pick up the phone.'

'Whatever. I've got an officer headed there right now and Rolling Hills has agreed to pay a house call.'

'Why's Ramsey coming here?' she asked.

'It's his house, Barbie. He's very up*set*.'

MOTOR SLEPT lousy and now the headache was a killer.

No blanket, no pillow, just his leather jacket on the warped floor of an abandoned apartment on Edgemont.

Plywood over the windows and some sign about earthquakes on the door told him it was his place for the night. He used his buck-knife to pry the board-up from the back door, rolled his scoot inside and pushed it around from room to room. They were all the same: Tiny, no furniture, light fixtures or plumbing, graffiti all over the walls, linoleum pebbled with mouse shit, cockroach carcasses, oil stains, empty bottles. The room he finally chose was in the back. The whole building smelled of mold and wet dog, insect casts, burnt matches, and the worst thing: A chemical-like stink that made his eyes water.

But it was dark and he was wiped out from riding all day, walking around Hollywood – the place seemed mostly the same – then over to Griffith Park to scope out the rug-rat's territory, but the park ended up being too big to get a handle on, why the hell would the little fuck need such a goddamn big place?

He bought three hotdogs with kraut, washed it down with a chocolate malt and cruised over to The Cave, parking his scoot with all the others in front, hoping no one would look close. Inside, he hoped for brotherhood, had to spend his last dough on beer when no one offered to buy him one. Eating three pickled eggs and stuffing some Slim Jims in his pocket before the bartender evil-eyed him.

No one gave a shit about the picture of the rat. Everyone was watching fuck-films on bigscreen TV; when some chick did something especially nasty up on the screen, a low growl of support rose up from the bar.

Forty, fifty crank-glazed eyes fixed on cumshots, no interest in making twenty-five big ones, except for one dude who didn't really seem that interested either, but said he might know something. Motor arranged to meet with him at eight tomorrow, maybe he'd bother, maybe he wouldn't.

So might as well bunk down. Not exactly the Holiday Inn, but nothing he hadn't seen before. Even though the chemicals gave him a headache, the aloneness turned him on, like the time he was celling with a greaser in Perdido, a DUI rap, three days of inhaling the motherfucker's stale farts, ready to strangle him, and then the fourth day they took the guy away because it turned out he had federal warrants.

Aloneness was like someone massaging your body, only there was no one there, just the feeling.

Now it was Friday morning, ten o'clock, his eyes were swollen and all he wanted to do was cut off this fucking head so he could replace it with one that didn't feel like it was about to explode.

Pissing on the floor of an adjoining room, he spit out morning taste, rubbed his eyes till they focused and wheeled his scoot outside into the sun. *Strong* m.f. sun, that didn't help either. He was hungry, had no money, time to go to work.

It took him two hours to find a Mexican chick walking all alone on a sidestreet, no little gangbangers to protect her honor. He drove past her, stopped, got off, walked toward her and she was scared right away. But he passed her by and she relaxed and that's when he turned around and grabbed her purse and shoved her to the ground.

Telling her, 'Don't fucking move.'

She didn't understand the words, but she got the tone of voice. He kicked her in the ribs just to make sure, walked as fast as his bulk would allow to his scoot and drove a mile away.

Twenty-three bucks in the purse, along with a tin cross and pictures of little Mex kids in some kind of costumes. He took the money, threw the rest of it down a storm drain, drove back to the Boulevard, found the same stand where he'd bought the hot dogs and got two more along with a fried egg on a muffin with hot sauce on the side, extra-large coffee that he drained and refilled, an apple turnover and one of those little containers of milk like he used to get in school and jail. Now he was ready for a day's labor.

He walked the picture up and down the Boulevard again, got nothing but dirty looks, was hungry again by three, forced himself to continue for another couple of hours till he finally couldn't stand it anymore. Figuring he'd earned a real meal, he went over to Go-Ji's and used up most of the Mex chick's money on a corned beef sandwich, fries, onion rings, double banana split, more coffee. Telling the nigger waitress to keep filling his cup till she just left him a pitcher.

Someone had left parta the paper in his booth but it was nothin' but words. The TV over the counter was going – news, sports, weather, dead stuff, then he saw the rat's picture

466

again, stopped eating bananas smothered with whipped cream and paid attention. His heart was zooming away – the coffee – and he was totally awake and ready to do something, anything.

Asshole on TV saying something about the beach – 'reported to have been spotted near Ocean Front Walk in Venice.'

So fuck the dude at The Cave.

Time to putt west – after dark. If the rat saw him it wouldn't be good.

LARRY SCHICK wore a cheap-looking brown suit that probably cost three thousand dollars, all puckered around the lapels and sagging on his meager frame. Instead of a handkerchief in the breast pocket, he carried an ornately carved meerschaum pipe. The bowl hung out like a talisman. Woman's head. Creepy.

The attorney was younger than Petra expected, early to mid-forties, with a very tan pencil-point face, jet-black Prince Valiant do, and pink plastic framed eyeglasses. Snakeskin cowboy boots. Like one of those English rock stars trying to stretch the hip thing into middle age.

He and Ramsey arrived at the Montecito house just after six, Schick behind the wheel of a black Rolls Royce Silver Spur. Malibu Colony sticker on the windshield, a bunch of club emblems fastened to the grille. Another car boy.

Ramsey got out first. He wore a faded denim shirt, black jeans, running shoes, looked even older than the last time she'd seen him. Taking in the scene, he shook his head. Schick came around from the driver's side and touched his elbow. Petra and Ron were with them before they could take another step. Ramsey kept staring at the crime tape.

The estate was quiet now, only a few techs still working. No word from Sepulveda on the warrants yet. Sergeant

Grafton remained stationed near the pond. She'd introduced herself a while back. First name, Anna. Bright, art history degree from UCSB, which gave them something to talk about during the dead time. She was flying to Switzerland next week. 'Major burglary, old masters. We recovered almost all of them. It'll never hit the papers.' No interest in Homicide, no attempt to take over the case.

Now, she watched the arrival of the Rolls, met Petra's eye, studied Ramsey for a while and turned the other way.

Petra said, 'Evening, Mr Ramsey.'

'Larry Schick,' said the lawyer, interposing his arm between them.

Ramsey stepped back. He looked at Ron, then zeroed in on Petra. 'What the hell is going *on*?'

'Estrella Flo—'

'I know, I know, but what was she doing up *here*?'

'We were going to ask you that, sir.'

Ramsey shook his head again and clicked his teeth together. 'Unreal. The world's gone nuts.'

Schick's facial muscles hadn't budged. He said, 'What exactly happened to her, Detective?'

'Too early to give out details, Mr Schick, but I can tell you she was murdered very brutally and buried over there.' She pointed at the pond. The gravesite was marked by a stake.

'My God,' said Ramsey, turning away.

Petra said, 'Mr Ramsey, did Mrs Flores ever work at this house?'

'Sure.'

'Recently?'

'No. Back when Lisa and I were together.' By the end of

469

the sentence, Ramsey's voice had thickened. He glanced at the stake again and winced.

Schick said, 'Detective, why don't we do this a little later—'

'It's OK, Larry,' said Ramsey. 'Lisa and I used to spend weekends here. Sometimes Lisa brought Estrella with us to clean. I don't think Estrella had a key, though. And I can't see why she'd come up here.'

'Who cleans the house now?'

'A cleaning company. Not regularly, maybe once a month. I never use the house anymore.'

'What's the name of the company?'

'I don't know. Greg handles it.'

'Does Mr Balch come up personally to let them in?'

'Sure.' Ramsey studied her.

'Where is Mr Balch, now?'

Ramsey looked at his watch. 'Probably on his way home.'

'He worked today?'

'I assume.' Ramsey's voice had cleared.

'You haven't spoken to him recently?' said Petra.

'The last time I spoke to him was, let's see . . . two days ago. He called to ask if there was anything I needed. I said no. He tried to cheer me up. I've been mostly hanging around the house, trying to avoid the media . . . now *this* insanity.'

Petra said, 'We tried to call Mr Balch at the office and he didn't answer.'

'Maybe he stepped out – what's the big deal?'

'We're talking to everyone with access to this property.'

'Access?' said Ramsey. 'I suppose anyone could climb the gate. Never installed electric gates.'

'No need?'

'Never got around to it. When Lisa and I came up, we used a padlock. The thing that bugs me is how did *Estrella* get up here? She didn't drive.'

'Excellent question,' said Petra.

Schick said, 'Hopefully you people will come up with some answers.' He removed the pipe, inspected the bowl, turned it upside down. Nothing fell out.

Petra said, 'So you haven't asked Mrs Flores to clean this house recently.'

'Never – listen, you have my permission to go over the whole place. House, grounds, anything. Don't bother with warrants—'

'Cart,' said Larry, 'even in the spirit of helpfulness—'

Ramsey said, 'Larry, I want to get to the bottom of this, no point slowing things down.' To Petra: 'Just do whatever the hell it is you do. Tear down the whole goddamn place for all I care.'

He swiped at his eyes, turned his back and walked several steps. Schick followed him and placed a hand on his shoulder. Balch had offered similar comfort that first day and Ramsey's response had been to turn on him. But he accepted the attorney's gesture, nodding as Schick told him something. Petra saw him pinch the top of his nose. He and Schick returned.

'Sorry, Detective Connor. Anything else?'

'Was there any reason for Mr Balch to be up here recently?'

'Like I said, he comes up to fix things, let in workmen. If there was something to fix, he'd have a reason.'

'But you're not aware of anything specific.'

'I *wouldn't* know,' said Ramsey. 'Greg takes care of things.'

'Both houses?'

471

'Absolutely.'

'Does that include exchanging cars?'

'Pardon?'

'Bringing the Jeep to LA for maintenance,' said Petra. 'Leaving his own car here.'

'What are you talking about?'

'Mr Balch did that yesterday, sir. A local deputy saw him exit the property and Mr Balch told him you'd asked him to bring the Jeep down for maintenance. He left his Lexus here.'

'Makes sense,' said Ramsey. 'The Jeep was for weekends here – Lisa liked it. I rarely use it so maybe it seized up.'

'But you don't know that.'

'No, I'm guessing.'

'Where do you take the Jeep for service?'

'Some Jeep dealer in Santa Barbara. I think.'

'Any reason to bring it to LA?'

Ramsey shrugged and stroked his mustache. 'Maybe Greg switched dealers. Maybe he had a problem with the one in Santa Barbara. Why all these——?'

'I just need to get this straight,' said Petra, feigning confusion. 'You never asked him specifically to pick up the Jeep.'

'Not specifically – what are you getting at?'

She pulled out her pad, scrawled. 'Maybe nothing, sir.' After writing, she snuck in a quick cartoon of Schick. The stupid haircut made it easy.

Ramsey was staring at her. 'You think Greg——'

Petra didn't answer. Next to her, Ron was as still as a machine.

'Oh, c'mon,' said Ramsey. 'No way. No, that's absolutely crazy——'

'How did Mr Balch and Estrella Flores get along?'

'They got along fine.' Ramsey laughed. 'This is totally nuts. If Greg says the Jeep needed maintenance, it did. What's going on here is probably some kind of psycho stalker. Someone with a grudge against *me*, so he goes after people . . . close to me.'

'Mrs Flores was close to you?'

'No – I don't know. All I'm saying is these nuts are all over. Look at John Lennon, all the crap people in the industry put up with. Have you checked out anything like that?'

'We're looking at all kinds of things,' said Petra.

Schick said, 'I know someone who can look into it, Cart.'

Ron hadn't said a word. Petra glanced at him, letting him know it was OK. He said, 'In terms of stalkers, do you have anyone in mind, Mr Ramsey?'

'If I did, don't you think I'd tell you?' Harder tone with Ron. 'Jesus.'

Petra closed her pad. 'OK, thanks for giving the OK to search, sir. It will save us time and paperwork. If you don't mind putting it in writing—'

Schick barked on cue: 'Before we go that far, let's pin down the details.'

'Let them do their job, Larry,' said Ramsey. To Petra: 'Whatever turns up, I guarantee you, it will have nothing to do with Greg.'

Schick made his mouth very small and ran a finger under thick black bangs. Why would a grown man opt for a hair-style like that? Something to catch jurors' attention? Maybe the meerschaum was a prop, too.

Reality, fantasy . . .

Petra said, 'I'll get some paper for you to write on, sir.'

Schick said, 'Hold on please, Detective. Cart, you're upset

473

and you're going to get taken advantage of. I've seen the things that occur during searches. Breakage, pilferage. I strongly advise you—'

'Let them break stuff, Larry. I don't give a shit. Like I said, tear the whole place down.' He faced Petra. 'You're just theorizing, right? You can't be seriously thinking Greg had anything to do with this.'

Schick said, 'At the very least, I insist upon being present during any search.'

'Fine,' said Petra. To Ramsey: 'One more thing: Greg Balch's behavior the night of Lisa's murder. When the two of you returned from Reno—'

'Detective,' said Schick, 'there has to be a better time for this.'

Ramsey said, 'What about his behavior?'

'Did he act differently in any way?'

'No. The same old Greg.'

'The day we visited your house your Mercedes was gone. Where was it?'

'What does that have to do with Greg's behavior?' said Ramsey.

'Sir, if you'd just bear with me—'

'The Mercedes was being serviced,' said Ramsey. He'd already told her that, but if the redundant questioning bothered him, he didn't show it. 'Too many toys, there's always something in need of fixing.'

'Did Greg bring the Mercedes in?' said Petra. Ron had turned around, was studying the house.

'Or the dealer picked it up,' said Ramsey.

'What needed to be done to the car?'

'I have no idea.'

'So it was driving OK.'

'Yes, it was fine. Maybe it needed a routine oil change, I don't know.'

'What Mercedes dealer do you use?'

Ramsey put a finger over his mouth. 'Some place nearby – in Agoura, I think.' He laughed harshly. 'As you can see, I'm very in touch with my life.'

Petra smiled at him. 'The second time I came to your house, the Mercedes was back in the garage. Who brought it over?'

'Same answer: Either someone from the dealer or Greg. I think it was Greg – but what's the diff—'

'How did Greg and Lisa get along?' Petra said, talking faster, a little louder. If Schick hadn't been there, she'd have stepped closer to Ramsey, invading his personal space, forcing eye contact. Even with the attorney hovering, it was a silver bullet of a question and Ramsey's head moved back.

'Greg and Lisa? Fine – everyone got along fine.'

'No problem between them?'

'No – I can't believe you're wasting time on – he's my closest friend, Detective Connor. We were kids together. He and Lisa got along fine. Hell, he *introduced* me to Lisa.'

'At the pageant?' said Petra.

'At the pageant, but he knew her before. They—' Ramsey stopped.

'They what, sir?'

'They dated. Nothing serious, just a few times, so don't go construing. It was over by the time Lisa and I started dating. Greg had no problem with it; if he had, would he have introduced us?'

Why, indeed. Suppositions drag-raced through Petra's head.

Beauty queen with sights set on The Industry. Believing, at first, that Balch was a Hollywood heavyweight – maybe Balch had used that as a pickup line. They start dating, he pours on the b.s. but she sees through it, learns where the real clout is.

Throwing the small fish back, she goes for the whopper.

'Everyone got along,' said Ramsey, but his voice had weakened and he was picking at his mustache.

Schick's stick-face was all adrenaline, but he still wasn't moving. Same for Ron. It made Petra feel as if the two of them were fading out of view, bit players, spotlighting her and Ramsey.

She said, 'OK, sir, thanks for your help – do you have a key to the house?'

'Here,' said Schick, taking out a ring and fingering a brass Schlage.

Someone else to answer for Ramsey, take care of him.

Being a star, even a minor one, was a return to childhood.

Drawing Ron fifty feet away, under the largest of the oaks, Petra kicked acorns and said, 'Anything I missed?'

'Not that I see. Be interesting to know if the Mercedes *was* taken in for service. You're thinking it might have been Lisa's murder car?'

Petra nodded.

'Different cars for different kills,' said Ron. 'Keep us guessing.'

'Balch is looking nice and dirty, isn't he?'

'Filthy.'

'Want to try to call some Mercedes dealers?' said Petra. 'Maybe some stay open past six.'

'Will do.' He removed the cell phone from his pocket.

She gazed over at Ramsey and Schick. They'd drifted back to the silver Rolls. Schick was leaning against the front fender, caressing the meerschaum, offering some kind of lawyerly counsel. Ramsey seemed uninterested.

'Cars,' said Petra, 'were also Lisa's preferred venue for sex. The case is pure LA.'

'The Jeep for Lisa would entail driving back and forth from here,' said Ron. 'Balch and Ramsey got back from Reno just a couple of hours before Lisa was abducted. Not enough time, so I bet on the Mercedes or the Lexus or another of Ramsey's wheels – which would be good for Balch if he was trying to shift suspicion. We should also try Burbank airport, that charter company Ramsey uses. Balch has got to have access to the account.'

'Rabbiting by charter?' said Petra.

'Just a possibility.'

Images flashed: Two young bucks head for Hollywood, but only one ends up rich. With the girl, too. Balch had mentioned two failed marriages. Another reason for him to be bitter.

She remembered his remarks about Lisa's temper, her 'going off on Cart.' At the time, it had puzzled Petra, why was good-buddy Greg giving the boss a motive? Now it made perfect sense.

Something else: Balch, a total slob, had been wearing brand-new white tennis shoes.

Because the old ones were soaked with blood?

She said, 'I want to chat more with Mr Adjustor. Thanks for making the calls.'

'Remember the name of the charter company?'

'Westward Charter. The pilot they use is Steve Marionfeldt.' Rattling off facts without consulting her pad. Everything coming together, a new rhythm. She walked back to Ramsey and Schick.

Still by the Rolls, but neither man was talking. Schick studying Ramsey, Ramsey staring at the ground. As Petra got closer, he looked up.

'Mr Ramsey, when you returned from Tahoe, you were extremely tired, went to sleep earlier than usual. Correct?'

'I was bushed. We were going since early morning.'

'Greg Balch drove the two of you from Burbank Airport to your house.'

'Yes.' Mention of Balch's name seemed to weary Ramsey.

'Then you and Mr Balch had dinner at your home and he had you sign some business papers – do you recall the nature of those papers, by the way?'

'Some kind of lease agreement. I own office buildings.'

Petra copied that down. 'All right, please bear with me: Who cooked dinner?'

Ramsey smiled. 'We're talking sandwiches and beer.'

'Who made the sandwiches?'

'Greg.'

'Not Estrella Flores?'

'She went off duty at seven, was already in her room.'

'Doing what, sir?'

'Whatever it is she did in there. I think I heard the TV.'

'Where's the maid's room?'

'In the service wing. Off the kitchen.'

'OK,' said Petra, adding some details to Schick's caricature. Concentration lines on the forehead, pout creases. 'So Greg prepared the sandwiches and poured the beer.'

'Yup. The beer was Grolsch, if it matters.'

Imported lager with a barbiturate chaser? thought Petra. Balch slipping Ramsey a Mickey?

If so, had the underling stopped to deliberate? Wondered about adding a little more powder?

Paying Ramsey back for all those years of friendship.

Some friendship. Not one single acting job, putting Balch down in public, sticking him in that crappy office, a middle-aged errand boy.

The unkindest cut of all: Lisa.

Because *he'd* met Lisa first. Gave her up to Cart. Always Cart.

Petra could almost feel the rage herself.

What had led Balch to stalk Lisa that night? Had she re-ignited their old relationship, then cut it off? Or had Balch just succumbed to his own fantasies?

Petra pictured the blond man, waiting by Lisa's apartment. Watching the Porsche drive out of the subterranean lot. Following.

In one of Cart's cars. He had access to all the cars. All the toys.

Tonight he'd play.

Taking what was his.

The same way he'd taken Ilse Eggermann?

Ilse. Lisa. The names were virtual anagrams.

Patterns. A crazy notion, but when it hit you in the face, you said ouch.

How many other dead blond girls were there? Girls who reminded Balch of Lisa.

Where the hell was Balch?

Or maybe she was all wrong and the lackey would show

up, alibied, a perfect explanation, the case in tatters and some psycho *was* stalking Ramsey.

Or was Ramsey the *stalker*?

The boy in the park might know. Had Wil made any progress? She'd call him again soon as she finished up with Ramsey.

'The beers,' she said. 'Did you drink them from bottles or cans?'

'From a glass,' said Ramsey, as if she'd asked a rude question.

Cans you opened yourself, bottles you could open for someone else . . . 'And right after you drank, did you feel even more tired?'

'No,' he said. 'I told you I was tired all day, I mean the alcohol might've been the topper, but—' the blue eyes widened. 'Oh, c'mon – you've *got* to be kidding.'

'About what, sir?'

'Something in the beer – no, no. No way in hell. I'd know if – no, it didn't feel that way. I was just bushed from overwork and travel. I conked out. We both did.'

'How long did you sleep that night?'

Ramsey stroked his mustache, licked his lips.

Schick said, 'Let's finish up here, Detective.'

'Almost done,' said Petra, smiling. The lawyer didn't smile back.

'I got up around eight, eight thirty,' said Ramsey. 'So eleven hours.'

'Is that your typical sleep pattern?'

'No, usually seven's enough, but – oh, come *on*. I would've felt something. Woozy, whatever. This is James Bond stuff,

Detective Connor. I make movies, I know the difference between fantasy and reality.'

His eyes told her a new, troubling logic had begun to worm its way into his brain.

True confusion or acting?

The difference between fantasy and reality. The phrase seemed to mock Petra.

'I'm sure you're right, Mr Ramsey.' She watched Ron pocket the phone as he returned. Schick was watching her.

She excused herself and met Ron well out of Ramsey and Schick's earshot.

'Only one open Mercedes dealer,' he said. 'Sherman Oaks, never serviced Ramsey's cars. But bingo at Westward Charter. Balch tried to fly out last night. Called around eleven, wanting to book a solo trip to Vegas. Said it was a business trip. Westward doesn't take off past ten and told him to check commercial flights. We'd better start calling airlines.'

'Oh, my,' she said.

'Stupid move,' said Ron. 'Trying to use the charter.'

'Billing it to the boss,' said Petra. Payback.

She noticed Ramsey staring at her. Had she given away something with her body language?

She ignored him. Nice to be able to do that.

59

I JUST GOT out of the bathroom. That's where I ran after I stopped crying. When I came out, I almost hoped Sam wasn't there, but he was shining the silver charity bottle with a corner of his jacket. My eyes were dry. I felt I was walking through a bad dream.

'You got a few hours till they show up to pray tonight,' he said, still polishing.

I sat down again and thought. No ideas came. The walkway, all those people, now it seemed like a haunted place.

I couldn't see any other way out, so I agreed to go to Sam's house. 'But not during the day, I don't want anyone to see me.'

'That's a little difficult, Bill. People start showing up before dark. And I have to be here to run things.'

The way we finally work it out is: At six o'clock, he'll come back with some dinner and sneak me into his car. I'll hide there while the Jews are praying, in the back seat, covered by the blankets.

'How long do you pray?'

'An hour, give or take. I stay late to clean up. When the coast is clear, I'll let you know.'

'Thanks.'

'Don't mention it,' he says. 'Just take care of yourself.' Then he laughs. 'Who am I to tell you that? You been taking care of yourself fine.'

60

NO ANSWER to her second knock and now Mildred Board was worried.

She'd heard the bath filling a full half-hour ago. Had the Missus fallen? Suffered some kind of an attack? Maybe the doctors were wrong and she really was ill.

She turned the doorknob, called out, 'Ma'am?' as she entered the bedroom. Empty.

And the bed was made!

Not Mildred's tight-cornered creation, but a decent tuck. First the bath, now the bed. Why on earth all this independence?

Yesterday, she'd been up extra-early and ready. Hearing footsteps at 6 A.M., she went down to find the Missus in the kitchen, folded newspaper in front of her, next to a cup of something that turned out to be instant tea.

'Are you all right, ma'am?' she'd said.

'Fine, Mildred. And you?' The Missus was smiling but the look in her eyes was . . . distant.

'Ready to greet the day, ma'am.'

'That's the spirit.'

Fighting a frown, Mildred fixed a proper cup of English Breakfast while glancing at the paper.

The Missus smiled. 'I must be developing a belated interest in current events.'

'Yes, ma'am. Up early, too.'

'I seem to be doing that lately, don't I? I suppose it's a change in my biorhythm.'

Later that day, she'd found the Missus out on the patio, her hand on a stone column, as if she needed support. Looking out at . . . what? The ruins of the garden? More like nothing. Her eyes had that blank look again and when Mildred greeted her, they stayed that way for several seconds.

Strange things were happening.

Mildred walked through the bedroom into the first dressing room. No one. The bathroom was empty, too, the tub drained, towels folded.

A long corridor led to the rear walk-in closet. Standing in the doorway, Mildred repeated, 'Ma'am?'

'In here, Mildred. You may come in.'

Mildred hurried through the narrow passage. The rear closet was larger than most rooms, lined with mahogany shelves and racks, built-in drawers. Hand-printed hatboxes, scores of shoes arranged by color. All that was left of the Missus's couture collection were a pair of wool coats, a rain slicker, five suits – black, navy, beige, two grays – and a few casual dresses and cashmere sweaters, all encased in plastic wardrobe bags. The Missus was standing in front of the mirror applying makeup, fully dressed in one of the gray suits, a thirty-year-old Chanel. She wore pearl earrings, the small ones, lovely. Mildred remembered the diamonds Him had showered on the Missus. An annoying little man from San Gabriel had examined them with a loupe and a predatory smile.

The Chanel draped the Missus's figure perfectly. But . . . her feet . . .

White lace-up tennis shoes over bulky white socks.

'I thought I'd go out for a walk, Mildred.' The Missus's thick, wavy hair was brushed and sprayed, chestnut embroidered with gray. Her makeup had been applied expertly except for one stray granule of lipstick near the corner of her beautiful mouth. Mildred restrained the impulse to flick it away, but she did give a pointed look and the Missus caught the hint and dabbed.

'A walk. Lovely idea, ma'am . . .' Mildred's eyes lowered again. Those socks!

The Missus laughed uneasily. 'Not exactly the height of style, I know, but these are easy on the arches. My hamstrings are stiff, Mildred. I tried to stretch them out, but they're still bound up. It's been too long since I walked.'

Drawing back her shoulders and straightening her spine, she started down the corridor.

'Do be careful, ma'am. I watered the orchard just twenty minutes ago and drainage seems to be poor, especially in the rear area, the peach trees. Boggy and slippery, you'd think that gardener's boy would have the sense to——'

The Missus stopped and placed a delicate hand on Mildred's shoulder. 'I'm not walking on the property, dear,' she said. 'I'm going around the block.'

'Oh,' said Mildred. 'I see.' She didn't. 'I'll be happy to come with you——'

'No, thank you, dear. I need to think.'

'With all due——'

'I'll be fine, Mildred.' The Missus's chin began to shake. She drew back her shoulders.

She took another step. Stopped. 'I'm always fine, Mildred. Am I not?'

61

By 6:57 P.M., Captain Sepulveda still hadn't returned and the techs had stopped working. The sun was low and the oaks blocked out straggling daylight. Sergeant Grafton had returned to her car. Petra was finished with Ramsey.

Lawrence Schick escorted his client back to the Rolls, remaining blank-faced as Petra tagged along. Ramsey got in the passenger seat and stared out the open window. He looked ancient.

Petra said, 'If I need to reach you—'

'We're going for dinner,' said the attorney. 'The Biltmore, Santa Barbara.'

'And after dinner?' said Petra.

Schick smoothed his bangs. 'It's not exactly a night for brandy and cigars, is it, Detective, so I guess we'll return to LA. Nice to meet you. Please continue to communicate through me.' Tapping the meerschaum twice, he got into the driver's seat, turned a frail-looking wrist. The car woke up and sailed away, but for the merest spatter of gravel, silently.

A few minutes later, Sepulveda drove up with a handful of warrants, explaining, 'Every judge was playing golf.' He'd changed into sweats, Carpenteria Sheriffs insignia on the shirt.

Despite Ramsey's waiver, no search had begun because Sergeant Grafton had insisted on waiting for Sepulveda.

Petra called Schoelkopf to tell him about Balch's attempted flight to Vegas. No answer and the clerk said he'd signed out for dinner, she didn't know where. No luck with Wil Fournier, either.

She was just about to call Stu when Sepulveda arrived. Ron was using the phone, talking to his kids.

'We'll concentrate on the house for now,' said Sepulveda, waving the warrants. 'Do the grounds tomorrow morning. I've got techs from our station and a fingerprint spec from Ventura used to work for us that I still think is the best. You planning to stick around?'

'For a while,' said Petra.

'You know I can't let you participate in the search. Got to color within the lines.'

'Can we observe?'

Sepulveda considered that. 'Why don't you and your partner make yourself comfortable over there.' He pointed to a wooden bench that curved around the trunk of the biggest oak. Drooping branches afforded semi-privacy.

'No way I can look, Captain?'

'Anything comes up, I'll give a holler.'

Flashing him an ice smile, Petra walked to the bench. Rock-hard and cool. Ron came over, still talking. 'I'm proud of you, Bee. Thanks for listening so well to Grandma. Bye.' He hung up, said, 'We can't go in?'

'Banished to the sidelines,' said Petra. 'Another boss.'

'Too many jurisdictions,' he said. He sat down next to her, grazed her fingertips with his thumb. 'But that's not always bad, is it? Never know who you'll meet.'

She smiled, not minding his touch but unable to think about anything but work, all the things she had to do.

She borrowed the phone, tried Wil again. Still no answer but Schoelkopf picked up.

'Ramsey was just here with Schick,' she said.

'And?'

She summed up the interview, told him about Balch's call to Westward Charter.

'Well that pretty much clinches it, doesn't it? Balch. Shit. And you guys were certain it was Ramsey. Can you imagine the field day the press would've had with that – near prosecution of an innocent man. OK, no release of information till you hear from me, Barbie. Nothing. Understood?'

You're the one with a direct line to Public Information, jerk. 'Of course, sir.'

'I mean it. Tighter than a . . . whatever. I'll handle Vegas for you, I know people in Metro over there. They keep a pretty tight handle on hotels and motels. If he's there, we'll find him. Meanwhile, you call the airlines. Get Fournier on that, too.'

'Haven't been able to reach Fournier,' said Petra.

'I saw him this afternoon. Try his house. What's going on over there, now?'

'They just started to search the house.'

'Keep an eye on those hicks. Flores is clearly the fruit of Lisa's tree so it's our case.'

'What about Flores's son in El Salvador?'

'What about him?'

'He's worried about her. I promised to let him know.'

'I said, keep it all under wraps for now. Another day or

two isn't going to improve his quality of life. They find evidence in the house, let me know right away.'

He clicked off.

Ron remained silent.

Petra said, 'Don't say I never took you anywhere interesting. Your kids OK?'

'Fine.'

'If you want to head back, I'll find a ride somehow.'

'No, I'll stay. Anything to do besides wait?'

'Call the airlines.' She looked at the phone. 'Your bill is going to rival the national debt.'

He laughed. 'You'll get an invoice.'

He'd stuck with her all day, remaining in the background. The guy was a veteran, it had to be hard, and all she did was keep borrowing the damn phone. 'You're sure Alicia and Bee are OK?'

'Mom's taking them out for pizza, she'll sleep over.'

'Nice mom.'

'The best,' he said. 'After my dad died, I thought she'd fall apart. Her whole life seemed wrapped up in his. She was pretty depressed at first but then she came out of it, took up paddle tennis, joined a library group, went on some tours. She misses him, they had a great marriage, but she's doing OK.'

'When did your dad die?'

'Two years ago.'

'Mine, too.'

He reached over, squeezed her hand, let go.

Petra said, 'I have no mother. She died in childbirth.'

Ron said nothing. Smart man. She didn't look at him, didn't want that level of contact right now.

* * *

491

The third try at Fournier's house paid off. He said, 'Been trying that 818 number for a couple hours, where are you?'

She told him everything.

'Unreal,' he said. 'So Balch could be anywhere by now.'

'He was stupid enough to call Westward Charter using his real name so maybe we'll get lucky.'

'How do you want to divide it?'

'Any way you want. Also, S wants a total seal on it.'

'We put a want out on Balch, but don't tell anybody?'

'Not till he hears from upstairs.'

'Great,' said Wil. 'So where does this put the kid?'

'Lower priority.'

He snorted. 'Of course it is, now that I have a name for him. The Watson tips panned out: William Bradley Straight, twelve years old, lived in a lowlife trailer park, missing a few months. If he did see Lisa get murdered, that's not his only problem. Someone killed his mama, push-and-shove case. Got a probable suspect, her boyfriend, some hairbasket named Buell Moran. And guess what: He's been spotted in Hollywood, showing the kid's picture.'

'Oh, no,' said Petra. 'Going after the twenty-five thou.'

'It would motivate me and I don't live in a trailer.'

'Lord,' said Petra. William Bradley Straight. A kid with a survival plan, thinking he had a chance. Pathetic. What had they done to him?

'OK,' said Wil. 'Let's divide up those airlines.'

When she hung up, Ron said, 'What's wrong?'

'Another orphan.'

62

BOUND VOLUMES of *TV Guide*, each with a *No Circulation* tag.

An hour into the surgery, Stu found himself going crazy in the waiting room. Leaving the hospital, he drove to a branch in downtown Burbank, used his badge and good manners, finally convinced the librarian to let him check out a decade's worth.

Now here he was back at St Joe's, waiting with other worried people.

Hundreds of *Adjustor* plot summaries.

Dack Price comes to the aid of a woman harassed by street thugs.

Dack Price helps expose drug dealing at a local high school.

A woman claiming to be Dack's sister, abandoned at birth . . .

Dack Price saves a political reformer's reputation when black-mailers . . .

The same old garbage, over and over.

No mention of any parks, let alone Griffith. Rarely was the setting ever mentioned, except when it was considered exotic: *Dack Price investigates several murders aboard a submarine.*

He kept turning pages, sitting by Kathy's bedside as she slept off the anesthesia.

Snoring. Kathy never snored. A padded dressing was taped to her chest like some bulletproof vest. The IV dripped, a catheter drained, machines graphed and beeped the saga of his wife's physiology. Stu had watched the blood pressure for a while until he was certain it was normal. At the last temperature check, Kathy'd registered a slight fever. Normal reaction, the nurse claimed.

The room was a private with a view, courtesy of Father's clout. Cheerful wallpaper, ten-dollar Tylenols. The nurses seemed smart and efficient.

Drizak had taken Kathy's left breast.

Stu knew the minute the surgeon came out in his greens. Droning on about lymphovascular invasion, nodal status, margins of excision, best efforts at breast conservation.

'So you did a mastectomy.'

'The bottom line is we want to save your wife's life.'

'Did you?'

'Pardon?'

'Did you save her life?'

The surgeon scratched his chin. 'The prognosis is excellent, Mr Bishop, given proper follow-up, radiotherapy. She went through it like a trouper.'

Stu thanked him, pumped his hand and, grateful for the lack of outward anguish, the surgeon walked away with a bounce in his step.

The breast didn't matter to Stu – not as an object – but how would Kathy react to the loss?

What to tell the kids?

Mommy was sick, now she'd be getting better.

No good; when the side effects of radiation showed up, they'd think he lied.

Kathy stirred and moaned. Stu put the book down, leaned over the bed-rails and kissed her forehead lightly. She didn't react. He touched her hand. Cold and limp. Why wasn't the blood circulating to her extremities?

He checked the machines. Normal, everything normal.

Her padded chest proved it, rising and falling.

It was 8 P.M. Surgery had been delayed twice because of emergencies, Kathy wheeled up to the OR, then down, the entire process repeated again. Waiting in the hall on a gurney as the priority patients were rushed through.

A car crash and a shooting.

Stu watched Burbank officers come up to the surgical floor, accompanying the med techs as they wheeled in the shooting victim. Young Hispanic kid, sixteen, seventeen, bad color, vacant eyes. Stu knew DOA when he saw it. Another stupid drive-by.

The cops didn't notice him – just some guy in a sweater reading in the corner of the waiting room.

Youngblood cops, swaggering. Like they knew what they were doing.

Pathetic. No one had a clue. God was a comedian.

Look at Ramsey.

Had a wife but couldn't keep her.

No way was the actor going down for Lisa's murder. Not with what they had so far. No help from *TV Guide*.

He suppressed bitter laughter.

Dack Price butchers a woman. Now a word from our sponsor.

63

I'M TALKING to Mom, trying to explain something important to her but she's not getting it. She's not even listening.

I get mad at her, start to yell, she just stands there, arms at her side, this weird look in her eyes. Like I don't matter.

Then her face starts to melt and blood shoots out of her eyes like red faucets. She cups her hands to catch the blood, splashes it all over her face and then throws some at—

I wake up sweating. My head hurts, my arms hurt, my stomach *kills* worse than ever, I can't breathe.

I'm in a dark box with cold, hard walls. Glass walls. Trapped, like a bug in a jar – I *really* can't breathe – no air holes in the box, no matter how hard I suck in the air it won't feed my lungs – then I see it. Crack at the top of one glass wall. A window left a little open.

Car window.

I'm in Sam's car. The back seat. Must have fallen asleep under the blankets.

It's making me sick being cooped up here, I want to break out but the alley at night, who knows what's out there. At least let me open the window a little wider – nope, electric, they don't budge.

My Casio says 8:19. The Jews have been praying for a while. When they finish, Sam will take me with him. He's a stranger and I don't know anything about his house, but there's no other place to hide, not with that twenty-five-thousand-dollar reward.

Maybe I *should* try to get the money, like Sam suggested . . . no, the police would never give it to a kid. Even if they did, Mom and Moron would find out and take it all and I'd be back in the trailer and they'd have dope money.

I could call the police without telling them who I was, let them know I saw PLYR 1 stab Lisa. But what if they had a way of tracing the phone and PLYR found out and went after me?

Who saw me and gave them my face for that picture?

No, I'll just keep my mouth shut. If I dream about Mom again I'll try to figure out what it is I want to convince her of.

64

LAND OF the free, home of the stupid.

In the cramped storage room behind the souvenir shack, Vladimir Zhukanov finished the vodka and wondered if he'd been an asshole to leave Russia.

At least there he had a uniform, a purpose. There was always someone who needed controlling. Even more now, since capitalism was sinking its claws in. The gangs were taking over and half the gangsters were ex-police. He could've found something.

In America, he had no respect, only stupid dolls. Stupid nigger cop ignoring him, then taking his information to the TV, the black bastard.

Anonymous tip. Meaning they didn't want to pay him.

One thing: It proved he'd been right about the kid. Like there'd been any doubt – that dimple in the chin, just like the drawing. Scratches on his face, what you'd expect on someone hiding in a forest. Zhukanov's father had told him stories about forests, the war. Militia men chasing Yids through clumps of wintering birch. Bare trees, iron sky, the marriage of bayonet and flesh, crimson stains on snow.

Anonymous tip. The TV news meant competition for the twenty-five thousand. Only one competitor, so far, but he was trouble enough. Fat guy in filthy leather, walking up and down the walkway with the kid's picture.

From his station behind the counter, Zhukanov watched the big pig. Up and back, up and back, walking laboriously, breathing hard in the heat. Growing visibly pissed off as the day wore on and he got nothing but headshakes and blank stares.

The first time the guy waddled toward the souvenir shack, Zhukanov made sure to be in the back room, examining the day's receipts, trying to figure out how much he could skim and get away with. The second time, though, he was up front, counting trolls, making sure no one had ripped *him* off.

The big pig said, 'Hey, man,' and shoved the picture in Zhukanov's face. Zhukanov shook his head dismissively, it wasn't even worth talking about, but the guy just stood there.

'You didn't even look at it, man.' Breath like a toilet. Zhukanov refused to dignify the question, picked up a Malibu troll. 'Want to buy something?' His tone making it clear that the guy couldn't afford a lousy toy.

The fat guy tried to give him the evil eye. Zhukanov almost laughed out loud. Big but flabby. Back in Moscow, he'd trampled runny-shit like this half-drunk.

Finally the guy jiggled off. What an imbecile.

Still, it was competition. He'd have to be sharper than ever.

Now it was dark and all the retail shops were closed, the only things open were the cafés on the north end of Ocean Front. And the Yid church a few stores south. Bunch of old Yids in there wailing, plotting, whatever the hell they did when they got together.

He had skim money in his pocket, the vodka had awakened his senses, and he was hungry and horny and getting angrier by the minute at the nigger cop and everyone else who was conspiring to deprive him of what was rightfully his.

Tomorrow, he'd call the newspapers and tell them the truth about the anonymous tip. How stupid cops didn't respect dutiful citizens.

No, no, not yet, that would focus more attention on the walkway, bring in more problems. He'd give the nigger one more chance. What was his name, he had the card, somewhere . . . not in his pockets, maybe he'd left it in the back room.

Slipping behind the curtain, he searched among the clutter but didn't find it. No matter, he'd ask around, a bald nigger detective, someone would know him. Then a man-to-man talk. Maybe offer him a piece of the twenty-five. If that was the only way.

If the nigger *still* didn't cooperate, he'd go to the papers — no, the TV stations. Get in touch with one of those blondies who read the news, tell her the truth. Maybe some bigshot movie producer would be watching and say, 'Hey, this is a good idea for a movie.' Arnold Schwarzenegger as a Russian cop, comes to America to show the stupid Americans how to— did they do that one already? It sounded familiar. No matter. With movies, you had something good, you did it again.

Publicity. That was what he needed.

On top of the money, he'd be the hero, trying to find the kid, solve a crime, but no one listened and—

'Hey, man,' said a voice from up front.

500

Fatso.

How had he gotten in? Then Zhukanov realized he'd forgotten to pull down the shutters and lock up. He took another swallow of vodka.

'*Hey!* You back there, man?'

Stupid asshole. Get rid of him and find some place to eat and drink. Zhukanov put on his Planet Hollywood jacket and tapped his front pockets. Cash in the right front pocket, knife in the left. Cheap Taiwan blade, he carried it with him for the walk from the shack to his car, along with an unlicensed 9mm. Part of the back-room arsenal: Nunchucks, a sawed-off baseball bat, age-blackened brass knuckles he'd inherited from his father. So far, the only thing he'd had to use was the bat, as a warning to kids with itchy fingers, but you never knew. The gun was back home. Cheap junk, it had jammed, and he had it out on the kitchen table, trying to figure out what was wrong with it.

'Hey!'

Zhukanov bolted the rear door before parting the curtains. The fat bastard had his elbows on the counter, scratching a blubbery chin, sweating, eyes raw-looking and swollen. Hulking silhouette against the black beach sky, maybe tough-looking to some tourist, but all Zhukanov saw was a vat of grease.

'Hey, bro, din' you hear me?'

Zhukanov said nothing.

'Listen, man—'

'Can't help you.'

'How can you say that, man, you don't know what I'm asking?'

Zhukanov started to slide down the front shutter. The fat man reached up and stopped it.

Zhukanov pulled. The fat man resisted. Flabby, but his weight gave him strength.

Zhukanov said, 'Move, fatso.'

'Fuck you, shithead!'

That brought the blood to Zhukanov's face. He could feel it, hot as winter soup. His neck veins throbbed. His hands ached from gripping the shutter.

'Go away,' he said.

'Fuck *you*, man. I got a question, you could at least try a fucking answer.'

Zhukanov went silent again.

'No big deal, bro,' said the fat man. 'Maybe you've seen this kid since I was here. You say no, fine. So why you giving me shit?'

The shutter wouldn't budge. The fat guy's resistance enraged Zhukanov. 'Go away,' he said very softly.

The fat guy pushed at the shutter and it shot up. Daring Zhukanov to try closing it. A bully, used to having his way.

Zhukanov remained in place, smelling him. The stench wasn't just his breath, it was all of him. A walking garbage heap.

'Seen him?'

'Go away, asshole.'

Now it was the fat man's turn to go red. Pig-eyes bulged, spittle bubbled at the sides of his mouth. That soothed Zhukanov's anger, turning it warm and smooth. This was starting to get funny. He laughed, said, 'Stupid fat-ass piece of shit.'

The fat guy made a deep, fart-like, rumbling sound and Zhukanov waited for the next insult, ready to throw something back, laugh in the bastard's face again.

But the fat guy didn't say a word, just went for him, faster than he thought possible, one huge hand shooting out and snagging him by the throat, pulling him up so hard against the counter he thought his ribs had broken. The pain nearly blinded him and he thrashed helplessly.

The fat guy's other hand was fisted, zooming at him for a face-pulverizing punch.

Zhukanov managed to jerk his face away from the blow but the hand around his neck kept squeezing and he could feel all the breath go out of him, hear the fat guy snarling and cursing. Ocean Front was dark, abandoned, just the waves, no one around to watch this monster strangle him to death – no one but the Yids, yards away, doing their Christ-killing chants, they wouldn't help him anyway.

He tried to tear at the strangling hand but his hands were sweat-slick, so weak, and the fat man's arm was moist, too, and he couldn't get a purchase. Slipping and flailing as his field of vision funneled to a pinpoint of light, he saw the fat man's enraged face, another fist coming at him.

A spasm of panic saved his face but brought the blow along the side of his head, hard enough to rattle his brainpan. His arms continued to wave around uselessly. He didn't remember the knife until he'd nearly lost consciousness.

Then he remembered: Pocket, front pocket, left side for the quick draw, just like they'd taught him in hand-to-hand. The fat man began shaking him harder, feeding off the pain and terror on Zhukanov's face, not noticing as Zhukanov reached down.

Zhukanov floundered, found it, grabbed too low, cold

metal, a sting, grope-grope, finally he touched the warmth of wood.

He yanked upward. Pushed the blade. No strength, not even a thrust, just a weak, womanish poke and—

Must have missed because the fat man was still choking him, cursing . . . gargling. And now the shaking had stopped.

Now the bastard wasn't making any sounds.

A look of surprise on his face. The blubbery lips formed into a tiny O.

Like saying, 'Oh!'

Where was the knife?

Suddenly, the hand around Zhukanov's throat opened and air rushed into his windpipe and he retched and choked, finally realized he could breathe but his throat felt as if someone had used it for a lye funnel.

The fat man was no longer facing him, he was flopped down on the counter, arms hanging over.

Where was the knife?

Nowhere in sight. Losing everything. Must be the vodka.

Then he saw the slow red leak from under the fat man's shoulder. No gush, no big arterial spurt, just seepage. Like one of those summer tides when the waves got gentle.

He took hold of the fat man's hair and lifted the massive head.

The knife was still embedded in the guy's neck, just offcenter from the Adam's apple, tilting downward. Diagonal slice through jugular, trachea, esophagus, but gravity was pulling the blood back down into the body cavity.

Zhukanov panicked. What if someone *had* seen?

Like the kid in Griffith Park, watching, thinking he was protected by darkness.

But there was no one. Just this fat, dead piece of shit and Zhukanov holding his head up.

A hunter with a trophy. For the first time in a long time, Zhukanov felt strong, territorial, a Siberian wolf.

The only bad thing was the size of the bastard, and now he had to be moved.

Letting the head flop down again, he turned off the lights in the shack, checked the cut on his hand – just a nick – vaulted over the counter and scanned the walkway in all directions just to make sure.

The stained-glass window in the Yid place was a multi-colored patch in the darkness, but no old Yids out in front. Yet.

Removing the knife, he wiped it with his handkerchief, then eased the corpse down to the ground. Wiping blood off the counter, he stuffed the kerchief into the neck wound. Having to roll it up into a tight ball because the slash was only a couple of inches wide.

Small cut but effective. Small blade – it was the angle that had done it, the fat guy leaning forward to strangle him, Zhukanov giving that little girly poke upward and then suddenly the guy's weight had reversed the trajectory, forcing the knife down into his throat, severing everything along the way.

Making sure the handkerchief plug was secure, he inhaled deeply and prepared himself for the tough part. Mother of Christ, his neck hurt, he could feel it starting to swell around the hem of his T-shirt and he yanked down, ripping some elastic. Looser, but he still felt like the fat guy was choking him.

Another look around. Dark, quiet, all he needed was old Yids flooding out.

OK, here goes.

Taking hold of the fat guy's feet, he started to pull the corpse. The damn thing only budged an inch and Zhukanov felt horrid pain in his lower back.

Like dragging an elephant. Bending his knees, he tried again. Another vertebral warning, but he kept going, what was the choice?

It took forever to get the bastard out of view and by then Zhukanov was sweating, out of breath, every muscle in his body aflame.

And now he could hear voices. The Yids coming out.

He yanked, dragged, breathed, yanked, dragged, breathed, frantic to get the corpse well back from the walkway. Had he gotten all the blood off the counter?

He rushed back, found a few stains, used his shirt, turned off the lights and slammed down the shutter.

Now he could hear them louder, old voices jabbering.

He got the corpse halfway to the back of the shack. Stopped when his chest clogged up. Bent his knees again, resumed.

Yank, drag, breathe.

By the time he reached the alley, all he could hear was the ocean, no voices, all the Yids gone home.

He dragged the corpse next to the shack's garbage bins. Not a commercial dumpster because the boss was too cheap. Two wooden shipping cartons that some Mexican illegals emptied every week for ten bucks.

OK . . . now what?

Leave him there, concealed by darkness, fetch the car, load the bastard in it and take him somewhere to dump – where did the West Hollywood guys go for that? – Angeles

Crest Forest. Zhukanov had a vague notion where that was, he'd find it.

Another forest. If the old man could see him now.

David had finished off Goliath and soon Goliath would be rotting in some gulley.

No, wait, before that he had to triple-check for bloodstains. Inside the shack and out, along the side of the shack, where the pig had been dragged.

He'd get the car, load the guy, keep him there while he gave the shack a thorough going-over. Ditch the knife, the clothes he was wearing. The nunchucks and the baseball bat, too? No. No reason to panic, why would anyone connect him to the fat bastard, even if they found the corpse?

Just the blood, the knife, his clothes.

Get it done before sunrise.

The guy would leak all over his trunk but he'd clean it. Running it through again, he decided it was a good plan.

He stretched, fingered the tender, hot flesh of his neck. Slow down, slow everything down, it's over – why had the bastard invited trouble like that?

Zhukanov thanked him for starting up. He hadn't felt this good since leaving Moscow.

OK, time to get the car. He'd taken three steps when light caught his eye.

The back door of the synagogue opening – someone still there!

He pressed himself against one of the wooden bins, tripping over the corpse's legs, nearly falling on his ass.

Forcing himself not to curse aloud, he breathed through

his nose and watched as an old Yid came out of the synagogue, Zhukanov could see him clearly, illuminated by the light inside. Short, thickset, one of those beanies on his head.

The Yid reached in and the blessing of darkness returned. But just for one second because now the guy was opening a car door.

Not the driver's door, the left rear door. Someone in back of the car sat up. Got out. Stretched, just like Zhukanov had done. The Yid talked to him.

Shorter than the Yid – a kid.

Hiding in back – had to be *the* kid, why else would he be hiding?

The right size and he'd been lying low, who else could it be?

The kid got back in the rear seat, lay down, disappeared.

So he'd been here all along. Hidden by the Yids – made sense, twenty-five grand would make them come in their pants.

We'll see about that.

The Yid's car started up and the headlights went on. Staying in the shadows, Zhukanov ran toward it. The Yid started backing out just as Zhukanov got close enough to read the license plate.

Bunch of letters and numbers. Zhukanov mouthed the magic formula soundlessly. At first his brain refused to cooperate.

But the old Yid helped him, taking a long time to back the car out and straighten up and by the time he finished, Zhukanov had it all memorized.

No time to get to his own car to follow. He'd write the

508

number down, call the Department of Motor Vehicles tomorrow. Giving out addresses was illegal but he knew a clerk at the Hollywood branch, wise-ass louse from Odessa, who'd do it for fifty bucks.

Given the payoff, an excellent investment.

65

By 10 p.m. the search of the Montecito house had turned up nothing.

'The place is just about empty,' Sepulveda told Petra. 'A little furniture in the living-room and one bedroom, the rest of the rooms have nothing.'

'Check for secret passages?' she said, only half in jest.

Sepulveda stared at her. 'I'll let you know if the Phantom of the Opera shows up.'

She and Ron headed back to LA. She'd been running up his cell-phone bill, talking to airline supervisors, some of them impressed by her title, others skeptical. So far, no flights under Balch's name had turned up and a 9:50 call from Wil let her know he was meeting with the same results. Thoroughness would demand paperwork, the proper forms. Tomorrow. She was exhausted. Angry at Schoelkopf for keeping the news about Balch under wraps.

The kid he publicizes but this scares him.

She and Ron talked about it till they got to Oxnard. Bosses were always easy targets. When they reached Camarillo, the car turned silent and she saw he had his eyes closed.

He awoke when she stopped the car in front of his house.

'Rise and shine,' she said.

He smiled groggily, apologized, then leaned over to kiss her.

She shifted her hips in the seat and met him halfway. One of his hands passed behind her head, pressing gently. The other found its way to her breast. He was smoother when fatigued.

He squeezed her softly then began to remove his hand. She held it in place. The next kiss lasted a long time. He was the first to pull away and now he looked wide awake.

She said, 'Some first date.'

'Second. The first was the deli.'

'True.' She realized she'd thought of that as getting acquainted.

He said, 'Well, you've got plenty to do, I won't keep you.'

She initiated a third kiss. He didn't try to feel her, kept both hands above the neck. Then he cupped her chin. With Nick she hadn't liked that, too confining. He did it differently. She traveled his mouth with her tongue and he made a small, baritone noise of contentment.

'Oh, man,' he said. 'I really want to see you again – I know it's not a good time to be thinking about going out.'

'Call,' she said. 'If I say I'm too busy it'll be the truth.'

He kissed the tip of her chin. 'You are *so* pretty. The first time I saw you I—' Shaking his head, he got out, groped in his pocket for his keys and waved.

'Wait,' she called out as he turned and started toward his front door.

He stopped.

'Your phone.'

He laughed, returned to the driver's side, took it.

'Make sure you send me the bill,' she said. 'It's going to be huge.'

'Sure,' he said. Then he kissed her again.

* * *

511

Back on the 101, she could barely keep her eyes open. Exhaustion even in the face of all that adrenaline meant she was severely sleep-deprived. She'd go home, take some caffeine, squeeze in another hour or so of phone work, then enough.

By the time she reached her apartment, it was 11:23. One message on her machine. She let it sit there, changed into a flannel nightie and got extra-strong coffee going. Realized she still hadn't called Stu. Too late, now. She felt lousy. One day this case would be over but Kathy's experience would last forever. Would Stu remember her as being neglectful during his crisis?

The message turned out to be him, phoning at 11:09, and asking her to call back up to midnight. The St Joe's operator was reluctant to put her through this late, but finally, she heard Stu say, 'Petra?'

'So sorry for not calling sooner. How's Kathy?'

'Fine,' he said. 'Resting.' Someone who didn't know him would have thought he sounded OK.

'Everything went smoothly?'

'Very smoothly – they did a mastectomy. One breast. The surgeon says she'll have total recovery.'

'That's great.'

'I got through four years of *TV Guide*—'

'Don't worry about that, Stu. How can I help?'

'Thanks but we're OK,' he said.

'You're sure? Do the kids need anything?'

'Just their mom,' he said, and his voice changed. 'They'll get through it, Petra. We'll all get through it.'

'I know you will.' One breast . . .

'Anyway,' said Stu. 'How was *your* day?'

Apart from that, Mrs Lincoln, how was the play? Keeping her at arm's length. He'd cried once in her arms, probably vowed never to lose it again.

'Actually, a huge amount of stuff hit the fan, Stu.' She told him about Estrella Flores, the bloodstained Lexus, Balch's attempt to rabbit by charter. Then, William Bradley Straight, ID'd but still unaccounted for, left without a mother.

'Poor kid,' he said. 'I leave you alone for one day and look at all the trouble you get yourself into.'

Everything coming together and he had nothing to do with it. She wanted to tell him it was OK, but it wasn't.

'Balch,' he said. 'He fits that well?'

'As well as Ramsey does.'

Stu didn't pick up on that. He was the veteran. Maybe she should focus.

'So we track Balch,' she said.

'Any idea where he is?'

'My bet is some other state or out of the country, but S says we can't publicize it, yet. Near prosecution of an innocent man and all that scared the hell out of him. But it's nuts, right? With the Straight kid we go media-wild but on Balch we're gagged, giving him a headstart. Oh, yeah, something else: Karlheinz Lauch died a year ago, but the similarities between Lisa and Ilse Eggermann got me thinking. Eggermann was picked up in Redondo and dumped in the marina. Balch lives in Rolling Hills Estates, right down the coast.'

'A serial?'

'Wouldn't it be weird if he was some bigtime creep and this is just the tip of the iceberg?'

Silence. 'The number two man strikes out to achieve dominance . . . another inadequate psychopath.'

'Exactly.'

'Hold on,' he said and Petra heard him talking to someone. 'That was the night nurse. OK, what can I do to help?'

'Right now? Just stay with Kath—'

'She's sleeping,' he said, sharply. 'I want to work tonight, Petra. What airlines have you checked?'

'Wil and I split them up. We haven't gotten through to some of them, they want paper. I figured—'

'What about international carriers?' he said. 'Does Balch have a passport?'

'Don't know—'

'I've already made contact with the passport office on Eggermann. I'll do international. And the domestic carriers you haven't reached. You sound bushed, get some sleep. I'll talk to you in the A.M.'

66

LET THEM think he'd rabbited to Vegas.

Let them think they were dealing with someone stupid.

It would help him tie everything up. He liked being neat.

Not as bad as Lisa. She was compulsive, wanting everything just so. Irregularities set her off. That vicious mouth . . .

She hated surprises. So he gave her one.

The German girl, too. Little stupid Sally.

One more surprise left, and the stupid cops were making it a little easier, leaking 'anonymous tips.' Venice Beach. Ocean Front Walk. Could the kid still be there? Maybe. Sometimes those runaways bunked down.

How far could a street kid go? If he'd tunneled deep, could he be found?

Should he forget about the kid? Was he over-reacting? Obsessing? Sometimes he did that, like the way he'd worry a hidden pimple till it got infected and festered and he'd have to lance it himself, coat it with Neosporin, live with the pain. No one knew that about him.

Maybe the kid hadn't even been in the park. If he'd seen something, wouldn't he have turned himself in, tried to collect the reward?

But that assumed he read the papers, watched TV, knew

515

what was going on in the world. Some of those kids were so stoned-out or brain-damaged, they didn't have a clue.

Not much of a witness. Should he just let it ride? Live with the uncertainty?

He considered it for a long time. The idea bothered him. *Big* loose end.

He could at least check it out. He thought a long time about how to do it without putting himself in danger, finally came up with the plan.

Perfect. And ironic. The hardest thing to pull off, irony, according to the bullshit-artist acting coaches.

What's my motivation?

Self-preservation.

67

SAM'S HOUSE has a living-room, a kitchen, two bedrooms with a bathroom in between. I got a real bed. The sheets felt new. Sam slept in the other room and I could hear him snoring through the wall.

It's only a few blocks from the *shul*, on what Sam calls a walkstreet. Instead of a road to drive through, there's a sidewalk, maybe twice as wide as a regular one.

'I should walk,' said Sam, driving there. 'But at night there are too many nuts out.' He parks in an alley around the back.

He's got an alarm with panels on the front door and the door to the kitchen. I looked the other way while he punched the code, so he wouldn't think I was up to something. He said, 'I'm ready to hit the hay,' and showed me my room. On the bed were a new toothbrush and toothpaste, and a glass.

'No pajamas, Bill. Didn't know your size.' He looked embarrassed, standing in the doorway, not coming in.

I said, 'Thanks. This is great. I mean it.'

He clicked his teeth together, like his false teeth didn't fit. 'Listen, I want you to know I don't usually have guests – never did before.'

I didn't know what to say.

'What I'm getting at, Bill, is you don't have to worry about something funny going on. I like women. Stick around long enough and you'll see that.'

'I believe you,' I said.

'OK . . . better get some sleep.'

The bedroom is painted light green and has old, dark furniture, a gray carpet and two pictures on the wall hanging crooked. One's a black and white photograph of a woman with her hair tied up and a guy with a long black beard. The other one's a painting of some trees that looks like it was cut out of a magazine. The room has that old-guy smell and it's a little hot.

I brush my teeth and look in the mirror. The scratches on my face aren't too bad, but my chest hurts, my eyes are pink and my hair looks nasty.

I strip down to my underpants, get under the covers and close my eyes. At first it's quiet, then I hear music from Sam's room. Like a guitar, but higher. A mandolin. A blue-grass band at the Sunnyside had one of those.

He plays the same song, over and over, it sounds sad and old.

Then he stops and the snoring begins. I think of Mom. That's all I remember till morning.

Now it's Saturday and I wake up before he does and go into the living-room. The curtains are closed and the house is dark. I pull a living-room curtain aside and see a couple of metal chairs on Sam's front porch, then a low wall, houses across the walkstreet. The sky is getting blue and some gulls are flying. It's weird, but I swear I can smell the salt through the windows.

The living-room has more books than any place I've seen except a library. Three walls are covered with bookshelves and you can barely walk cause of all the magazines on the floor. In one corner's a couch with a knitted blanket thrown over it, a TV, and a music stand holding a song by some guy named Smetana.

I sit down on the couch and dust shoots up. No morning stomach ache. It's the best sleep I've had in my life and I decide to say thank you by making breakfast.

In a box on the kitchen counter I find whole-wheat bread and I toast four slices. There's a coffee machine, but I don't know how to use it, so I just pour milk and orange juice into glasses and set them out on the table, along with paper napkins, forks, spoons, knives. In the refrigerator are fruits and vegetables, butter, some sour cream, eggs, and a big jar of something silvery-looking, like out of a science lab. Pickled herring. I take out the eggs, hoping Sam likes them scrambled.

They're frying up when I hear him coughing. He comes in, wearing this light blue bathrobe, rubs his eyes and pushes at his teeth. 'Thought I heard something – what, you're a gourmet?'

'Is scrambled OK?'

He turns his back on me, puts his hand to his mouth and coughs some more. 'Excuse me. Yeah, scrambled is great. Usually I don't cook Saturday – it's my Sabbath. I'm not that religious, but I usually don't cook. Maybe cause my mother never did.'

'Sorry—'

'No, no, this is good, why should it apply to you?' He comes closer, looks into the pan. 'Smells good, I could use something hot – you know how to make coffee?'

'No.'

He explains how to use the machine and leaves. When he comes back, the coffee's poured and he's dressed in a tan suit and a white shirt with the collar open, his hair's brushed and he's shaved. By now, the eggs are pretty cold.

'OK, let's chow down,' he says, unfolding his napkin and putting it on his lap. '*Bon appétit* – that means eat up in French.' He tastes the eggs. 'Very good. Very gentlemanly of you to do this, Bill. Maybe there's hope for the younger generation.'

He finishes everything on his plate, has two cups of coffee and lets out a big sigh. 'OK, here's my schedule: I go to the *shul* for Saturday services, should be back around eleven, eleven thirty, noon at the latest. You want to leave the house, I'll keep the alarm off.'

'No, I'll stay here.'

'You're sure?'

'Yes.' Suddenly my voice is tight. 'I'll read.'

'Read what?'

'You've got a lot of books.'

He looks over at the living-room. 'You like to read, huh?'

'Very much.'

'You work and you read . . . I'm a reader, too, Bill. Once upon a time I wanted to be a lawyer. Back in Europe. No one in my family was a professional. We were farmers, miners, laborers. My father knew the Bible by heart but they wouldn't let us get an education. I was determined to get one but the war interrupted – enjoy the books. There's nothing in there a guy your age shouldn't see.'

He wipes his hands, carries his plate to the sink and checks himself in a little mirror over the faucet. 'Sure you want me to leave the alarm on?'

'Yes.'

'I just didn't want you to feel like you were in prison.' He touches his shirt collar, smooths it out, pats his hair. 'Here I go, ready for God, hope He's ready for me. If you get hungry, eat. I'll bring something back, too. See you eleven, eleven thirty.'

He's back at 11:27, pulling the Lincoln behind the house and getting out in a hurry, carrying something wrapped in aluminum foil. He opens the passenger door and a skinny old woman with red hair gets out. The two of them talk for a while and then they disappear.

He comes through the front door fifteen minutes later. 'Escorted a friend home.' He puts the foil thing on the table and unwraps it. Cookies with colored sprinkles on them. 'Here you go.'

I nibble one. 'Thanks.'

'You're welcome – listen, I appreciate manners but you don't have to thank me for every little thing. Otherwise we'll be standing around here like Alphonse and Gaston – two very polite French guys.' He puts one hand behind his back, the other over his stomach and bows.

'*You* first – no, *you* first. It's an old joke, they're so polite, they stand there all day, never cross the street.'

I smile.

He says, 'So what'd you end up reading?'

'Magazines.'

Most of his books turned out to be fiction, the real stuff I found was mostly catalogues of sinks and toilets. The magazines were interesting, though, really old, from the fifties and sixties. *Life, Look, Saturday Evening Post, Time, Popular*

Mechanics. Presidents back to Eisenhower, stories about the Korean War, movie stars, animals in the zoo, families looking happy, weird ads.

'You hungry?'

'No, thanks.'

'What'd you eat?'

'The cookie.'

'Don't be a wise guy.'

'I had some milk.'

'That's it?' He goes to the refrigerator and takes out the jar of herring. Pieces of fish are swimming around in this cloudy-looking juice. 'This is protein, Bill.'

I shake my head.

'It's fish. Don't like fish?'

'Not very much.'

He opens the jar, takes out a piece, eats it, opens the refrigerator again and looks inside. 'How about some salad?'

'I'm fine, Mr Ganzer. Really.'

He puts the herring back and takes off his jacket. 'I'll go out later, get us a couple of steaks – you're not one of those vegetarians, are you?'

'Meat's fine.'

'What an agreeable fellow – you play chess?'

'No.'

'So learn.'

It's basically war and I like it. After six games I beat him and he says, 'Very good,' but I'm not sure he's happy.

'Another one, Mr Ganzer?'

'No, I'm gonna take a nap.' He reaches out to touch my head but stops himself. 'You've got a good brain, Bill.'

I read while he sleeps, getting comfortable on the dusty couch with the knitted blanket over my legs. A few times I get up, look outside, see a beautiful sky. But I don't mind being inside.

He wakes up, takes a shower. When he comes out of his bedroom, he's wearing another suit, brown, a blue shirt, tan shoes.

'I'll go get the steaks,' he says. 'No, wait a second—' Opening the freezer compartment above the fridge, he pulls out a package of chicken. 'This OK?'

'It's fine, Mr Ganzer, but I'm not really hungry.'

'How could you not be hungry?'

'I'm just not.'

'You don't usually eat much, do you?'

'I do fine.'

'How long you been on your own?'

'A while.'

'OK, OK, I won't pry – I'll defrost it and broil it, it's healthy that way.'

By 7:20 the chicken's done, and I'm eating more than I thought I would. Then I noticed Sam has barely touched the drumstick he put on his plate.

'You need protein, Mr Ganzer.'

'Very funny,' he says. But he smiles. 'I'm taken care of in the cuisine department. Got an appointment tonight for dinner – you going to be OK alone here?'

'Sure. I'm used to it.'

He frowns, puts the drumstick on my plate, gets up. 'I don't know when I'll be back. Probably ten, ten-thirty. Normally, I might entertain here but I didn't figure you'd want to meet anyone. Right?'

'It's your house. I could stay in the bedroom.'

'What? Hide like some . . . no, I'll go over there. If you need me, it's six houses down, the white house with the blue trim. The party's name is Kleinman. Mrs Kleinman.'

'Have a nice time,' I say.

He turns pink. 'Yeah . . . listen, Bill, I been thinking. That twenty-five thousand. If it's rightfully yours, you should claim it. That's a lot of money for anyone. I could make sure no one swindles it from under you – there's a fellow across the street, used to be a lawyer. A communist, but smart, knows the angles. He wouldn't take a penny from you, could make sure you're protected—'

'No one can protect me.'

'Why do you say that?'

'Because no one ever did.'

'But look—'

'No,' I say. 'There's no way they'd let a kid keep all that money. And I can't help them anyway, I didn't see the guy's face, all I saw is a license plate—'

'A license plate? Bill, that could be very helpful. They've got ways of tracing license plates—'

'No!' I shout. 'No one ever did anything for me and I don't care about any of it – and if you think that makes me a bad citizen and you don't want me around, fine, I'll leave!'

I get up and run for the door. He grabs my arm. 'OK, OK, calm down, take it easy—'

'Let me go!'

He does. I reach the door, see the alarm's red eye, stop. Here comes a stomach ache.

'Please, Bill, relax.'

'I am relaxed.' But it's a lie. I'm breathing fast and my chest is really, really tight.

'Look, I'm sorry,' he says. 'Forget it, I just thought . . . you're obviously a good guy and sometimes when good guys don't do the right thing, they feel – ah! Who the hell am *I* to tell *you*? You know what to do.'

'I don't know anything,' I mutter.

'What's that?'

'Every time I try to learn, something gets in the way – like with you and the war.'

'But look, you're making it. Like I made it.'

I want to cry again, but no way, no damn way! Words start pouring out of me: 'I don't know what I'm doing, Mr Ganzer. Maybe I *should* call the police – maybe I'll do it from a pay phone. Tell them the license plate and then hang up.'

'If you do it that way, how do you collect the money?'

'Forget the money, they'll never give me the money. Even if they do, my mom will find out and then Moron – he's the guy she lives with. He's the reason I left. He'll end up with it, believe me, there's no way I'm going to get a penny and I'll be right where I started from.'

'Moron, huh? A dim bulb?' He taps his head.

I laugh. 'Yeah.'

He laughs. I laugh harder. I'm not really happy, but it's a way to get out the feelings.

'A smart guy like you and a dim bulb,' he says. 'I can see why there'd be problems – OK, I'm gonna give you the alarm code. Just in case you want a breath of fresh air. One one twenty-five. Think of January first, 1925. My birthday, I'm a New Year's baby.'

'I'm not going out.'

'Just in case.' He punches the numbers, the light goes green, and he opens the door. 'Relax, take it easy – try the herring.'

'Not a chance,' I say and he leaves smiling.

The chessboard is still out on the kitchen counter. I think I'll experiment with different moves. See things from both sides.

68

SATURDAY MORNING at 6:46, the phone woke Petra. Schoelkopf's voice played havoc with her brain waves.

'Got comprehensive warrants on Balch's office and home. You and Fournier go over both with a fine tooth before we put a bulletin out on him. I've messengered the paper and keys to you, should be there any minute. Get it all done today so we can cast the net on the bastard.'

'Why do we have to wait to cast?'

'Because that's the way Upstairs *wants* it, Barbie. The fact that we came so close to tunnel-visioning on Ramsey scares them shitless. No more questions, get moving.'

'Does Fournier know about the assignment?'

'You tell him.'

The doorbell rang just as she was stepping out of the shower. Drying off frantically, she wrapped herself in a bathsheet, ran to the door, saw a patrolman through the peephole and stuck her hand out through a crack in the door for the manila envelope containing the warrants and the keys. The uniform, a tall guy, grinned, checked her out, and said she'd have to sign a form.

'Slide it under the door.' After I slam it in your face.

She roused Wil at 7:15. He sounded half-dead and she thought she heard a woman in the background.

'All right,' he said. 'Where first?'

'Up to you.'

'Balch's office is closer. How about . . . nine? Make that nine thirty.'

'Want me to pick you up?'

He didn't answer immediately. There was definitely a woman there, talking low and rhythmically, almost singing. 'No,' he said, 'I'll meet you.'

With no traffic, the drive to Studio City was fifteen minutes of morning breeze and she had time to stop at DuPars near Laurel for takeout coffee and an apple cruller. In the lot fronting the brown building was a gray Acura but no signs of the driver. The license plate said SHERRI. She pulled up next to it and was eating in the car when Wil arrived in his civvy wheels – a black Toyota Supra. He wore an off-white linen suit, black polo shirt, perforated black shoes, looked ready for a Palm Springs weekend; she'd put on the usual pant suit.

He looked at the building. 'What a dump.'

'Ramsey lives like a king but treated him like a serf. Maybe the guy finally exploded.'

'Didn't know you were a shrink,' he said. 'Actually, that makes sense.'

'Want more? This occurred to me last night: The way Lisa's body was left out in the open, no attempt at all to conceal. Same with Ilse Eggermann. It's as if he's boasting – look what I can get away with. All his life, Balch is subservient to Ramsey, eating dirt, taking verbal abuse. What better way to undo that psychologically than by taking Ramsey's woman then discarding her and announcing it to the world?'

'*Taking* her,' said Wil. 'You think Balch and Lisa were making it?'

'I think Balch wanted to. He's no Adonis but she dated him once and we know she likes older men. Whether or not she agreed to start up again, only Balch knows. Unless we find something in there.'

They had their guns in their hands as they approached the door. Basic procedure: Detectives did little shooting but a good deal of it took place while serving warrants.

Petra unlocked the door and went in first. Someone was sitting at the desk in the front room and she brandished her 9mm.

A young woman in a budget power-suit working the morning crossword. The sight of the gun painted her face with terror. Pretty brunette, very short hair, dark eyes, maybe Hispanic.

'Who are you?' said Petra. Wil was behind her. She could hear him breathing.

The woman's voice dribbled out, nearly inaudible. 'Sherri Amerian – I'm an attorney.'

The Acura in the lot.

'Mr Balch's attorney?'

'No,' said Amerian. 'I work for Lawrence Schick.' Stronger voice now, a little brassy with resentment, and the eyes had turned chilly. 'Am I allowed to show you my ID? It's in the purse over there. I mean, I don't want to get shot in the process.'

'Go ahead,' said Petra.

Amerian produced a driver's license and her business card from Schick and Associates. The license made her twenty-seven years old. Fresh out of law school. Doing Schick's scutwork on a Saturday.

'OK?' she said imperiously. Junior associate, but to look at her body language, she was arguing before the Supreme Court. Didn't take long to get that lawyer 'tude going. 'Will you please put those *guns* away?'

Not waiting for a reply, she came around from behind the desk. Great figure.

Wil holstered his piece. 'What are you doing here?'

'Representing Mr H. Cart Ramsey's interests, Officer . . .'

'Detective Fournier. This is Detective Connor.'

Amerian's shrug said their names didn't matter. 'Our firm was informed that you intended to conduct a search of these premises related to possible evidence pertaining to Mr Gregory Balch. May I see the warrant?'

'Why?' said Wil.

'Because the premises are owned by Mr Ramsey and we represent his—'

'Here.' Petra slipped her gun back into her purse and gave her the Studio City paper.

The young lawyer studied it. 'Exactly right: Material pertaining to Mr Balch. Not Mr Ramsey. This office contains numerous documents of a confidential nature pertaining to Mr Ramsey's finances and we insist that they not be tampered with. As such, I'll be remaining here while you conduct your search. In order to accomplish that, our suggestion is that we set up a procedure in which you indicate a given drawer and/or shelf and I review the contents beforehand—'

'If I have to blow my nose,' said Wil, 'are you going to review the tissue?'

Amerian frowned. 'I really don't see the point of—'

'Fine,' said Wil. 'Cut to the chase. The top drawer of this

desk first. And no chit-chat or coffee-breaks. Fold your puzzle and put it away.'

They took three hours to search every inch of the suite. After the first hour, Amerian got bored with her role as gate-keeper and started to say, 'Sure, sure,' when Wil or Petra pointed out a book on a shelf or a box on the floor. Short attention span, the *Sesame Street* generation.

The only remnants of Balch's presence were fastfood cartons, takeout menus from local restaurants and a top drawer full of office supply flotsam. No family photos – Petra supposed that made sense, Balch was a two-time marital loser.

Man with no attachments? Something about him that got in the way of relationships? So what? The same could be said for millions of people who didn't kill.

She kept going. All the papers were Ramsey's. Now Amerian was paying attention again. Rent books, tax returns, folders listing deductions, business contracts. Documents Petra would have loved to see a few days ago. Balch had worked here for years but left nothing of himself behind.

Did that say something about the way he viewed his job?

She removed a *California Tax Code* from the shelf, flipped pages, turned it upside down. Nothing. Same for the next ten books. The place was even messier than when she'd interviewed Balch. For a guy with such a disorganized mind, he'd proved a canny killer, so many steps, carefully laid out.

Then why had he been sloppy enough to call Westward Charter and alert them to the rabbit?

The usual psychopath's self-destructive behavior? Or a ruse . . . where *was* he!

* * *

They left at 1 P.M., stopped for lunch at a seafood place on Ventura. Not much conversation. Wil had started off grumpy and four hours of futility hadn't improved his disposition. He ate his sand dabs slowly, drank a lot of iced tea, looked out the window. Petra's crabcakes went down like deep-fried hockey pucks, and by 3 P.M. they were in separate cars on the 101 headed for the 405 interchange and the one-hour ride to Rolling Hills Estates and Balch's home on Saddlewax Road.

He got ahead of her at Imperial Highway and she'd lost sight of him when she thought of something. Speeding up, she managed to spot the Supra just past Hermosa Beach and waved him off at the Redondo Beach exit. They both pulled onto the shoulder. Petra jogged to his car.

'Humor me,' she said, 'but I want to take a look at the place on the pier where Ilse Eggermann was last seen, then go to Balch's.'

'Fine,' he said. 'Good idea. I'll stick with you.'

A fifteen-minute westerly cruise down Redondo Beach Boulevard took them to the former site of Antoine's, now a Dudley Jones Steak House franchise with a harbor view. Deep red room full of weekend brunchers and noise, blond surfer/waiters sailing past with platters of rare flesh and melon-sized baked potatoes.

Petra allowed herself a second to visualize Ilse Eggermann feuding with Lauch. Leaving the restaurant, descending wooden steps off the pier, just as she and Wil were doing now. Continuing down to the parking lot. Late at night, deserted, the place would be spooky.

The drive to Rolling Hills Estates chilled her.

Six-mile straightaway on Hawthorne Boulevard, it began

as a swath through the usual mash of car dealers, malls and office-supply barns then narrowed just before Palos Verdes Drive where a median strip appeared, planted with eucalyptus and pine and black-trunked shaggy trees that resembled willows. A white wooden sign welcomed her to Rolling Hills Estates and low white corral fencing appeared along both sides of the road.

Ten minutes from Redondo, driving leisurely. This was Balch's turf.

She pictured him coming home from a long day as Ramsey's slave, stopping off for a drink, noticing Ilse and Lauch fighting. He follows them out, sees Lauch drive off, picks up Ilse, promising to drive her to her hotel near the Marina, but they never get there.

Open dump in a parking lot.

Look what I can get away with!

Then back home. So simple.

A day at the beach.

69

BEAUTIFUL OCEAN, but too many people.

He wore a top-quality, real-hair, false beard, similar to the one he'd used for the German girl, a wide-brimmed straw hat, a long brown ratty raincoat over a frayed white shirt and cheap gray cotton pants. Running shoes, relatively new, but dirtied up to stay in character.

The gait he adopted was a clumsy, stiff-legged shuffle. When he walked, he pretended to stare at the ground but was able to sight upward without being obvious, because the hat did a good job of concealing his eyes. If someone made eye contact, he could half-lower the lids and focus on nothing.

Mr Mentally Disordered Homeless. Ocean Front Walk was full of them, sitting on benches, lurching along with the crowd, staring at the sand or the palm trees or the ocean, as if something important were happening out there. What? Imaginary whales? Mermaids with big tits flapping around on the beach?

His mother had gone crazy when he was fourteen. He'd never wondered what she thought about. Just stayed away, as if she were contagious.

He walked up and down Ocean Front very slowly. Every so often, he'd sit, make like he was dozing off, while examining passersby.

No one paid attention to him. The bicycle cops were on the lookout for violence, so if you kept to yourself they were happy to ignore you. Same with the tourists, anything to avoid being panhandled.

The problem was the quantity of people. Nice, warm Saturday, everyone flocking to the beach, the slow-cruising walkathon along Ocean Front so dense you could barely make out individuals.

Plenty of kids, but not *the* kid. After an hour, he was able to classify them into two groups: The well-scrubbed spawn of the tourists and clots of dark-skinned, big-mouthed local brats weaving in and out of the pedestrian stream, probably looking for pockets to pick.

Why would *the* kid be out in broad daylight?

Why would he be here, period, after the 'anonymous tip'?

Waste of time, but considering all he'd accomplished, he didn't feel that bad.

Beautiful day, go with it. Long time since he'd been here and the walkway had gotten more commercial, lined with shops, snack-stands, restaurants, even a synagogue – that was odd. Some of the buildings ran through to the alley and, beyond it, the Speedway. Others occupied the ground floors of multi-story prewar apartment buildings. The boy could be in one of those buildings and how could you find him?

The boy could be anywhere.

He'd give it a few more hours. The beard and hat and coat were heating him up, a cold drink would be nice and he had ten bucks in his pocket, more back in the car, parked six blocks away. But a crazy bum fishing out money might attract attention so he decided to settle for water from a fountain.

There was one down at the other end, near the synagogue. He'd shuffle clear to the northernmost end of Ocean Front, turn around, come back, drink, repeat it a few times, take a pseudo-nap on a bench, call it a day.

Forget about the kid. He told himself it was OK but it stuck in his throat. Big, hot pimple full of pus, just itching to be squeezed.

He preferred to give in to his compulsions. Avoiding them built up tension.

His mother had been unbelievably compulsive before going completely bonkers. Smoking five packs a day, picking at her face, rocking when she sewed, going on food binges, then starving herself for days. When they put her in the hospital, she began to bang her head against the wall, like one of those autistic kids, and they forced her to wear a football helmet. Flowered dress and a helmet – what position do you play, Ma? She looked ridiculous and he did everything he could to avoid visiting her.

She'd died ten years ago and he was sole surviving kin. Through a local attorney, he'd instructed the hospital to cremate her and bury her ashes on the grounds.

Thinking about her evoked no emotion. He was hot, discouraged, not happy about abandoning the loose end. Mostly the heat, right now. That was the biggest part of what he felt.

He took an hour to cover the walkway two more times, getting more and more uptight about not succeeding.

No kid who looked anything like the picture. He reached the water fountain, filled his belly with water, wiped the beard. A tourist about to drink changed his mind. Talk about a convincing performance.

The nearest bench was occupied by a young couple in spandex. He stumbled over, muttering, perched his butt on a corner and the couple got up and left.

This was good!

The synagogue must have just let out because he saw old people milling around outside the front door, then dispersing. He had nothing against any group, even Jews, just wished those who couldn't take care of themselves would die and make room for everyone else.

Someone else didn't like the Jews, though.

Guy working the souvenir stand a couple of stores down. Look at how he stared at them, real hostility.

Ugly guy, mid-forties, long greasy-looking blond hair, probably tinted. Bad skin, skinny arms sticking out of the sleeves of a really hideous purple *California Here I Come* T-shirt.

The stand stocked similar shirts, hats, sunglasses, toys and banners and postcards, a tiny little place crammed with junk. No one was buying, probably because the proprietor was about as welcoming as a piranha.

Hostile *and* jumpy. Looking up and down Ocean Front, too.

Interesting.

A pair of cops walked their bicycles past the stand and the ugly guy's eyes widened and his body shot forward, almost throwing himself over the counter.

Wanting to tell them something?

But he stopped himself, picked up some kind of doll, pretended to be checking the price.

Strange . . .

The cops must have thought so, too, because they stopped

and talked to the ugly guy. He produced a sick-looking smile and shook his head. The cops didn't leave right away. Something about the guy was making them wonder. The guy kept smiling, fingering the doll, and finally they did leave.

The guy stood there for a long time watching them before returning to his old routine: Looking north, then south, north, then south. Not a glance at the beach.

Looking for something in particular. Some*one*?

Anonymous tip. Could it be? Was God that good?

He studied the souvenir vendor for another twenty minutes and the pattern never altered: Pace, check out the walkway, take a doll down, squeeze it, put it back, pace . . . Suddenly, the guy altered his routine, going behind the cheap chintz curtains that backed the souvenir stand. Probably a rear stockroom, maybe a bathroom break.

For five minutes, the stand was left unattended and some local kids cruised by and pulled postcards from the rack. When the long-haired guy came out, he was wiping his lips.

A drink break. Here he goes again: Up and down, up and down. Definitely on the prowl.

Could it really be? Maybe he was waiting for a dope deal.

Then again, the tip had come from somewhere.

To a loser like this, selling crap no one bought, twenty-five thou would be a helluva lot of Saturdays. Good reason to be jumpy.

He observed the guy some more. Same routine, one more booze break. The guy was robotic, on auto-pilot, just like the nuts he used to see when he visited his mother.

Definitely worth looking into, what did he have to lose?

He got up, walked a hundred yards south, reversed direction and shifted closer to the storefronts, passing close to the stand and looking for posted hours. There it was: *Summer hours: 11 to 5 M-F, Weekends, 11 to 8.*

He'd leave, come back close to eight, hopefully the crowds would be gone. Hopefully the guy wouldn't close up early or go off-shift, if he did there was always another day.

Given no other leads, it was all he had and he decided to be hopeful.

Optimism, that was the key. Long as you didn't lose the irony.

SADDLEWAX ROAD was a quarter mile in from the Palos Verdes turnoff. Along the way, Petra saw two little girls in full equestrian dress riding gorgeous brown horses. A woman on a black steed trailed them, scrutinizing their posture or the horses', or both.

Balch's house was three-quarters up the shady street, a one-story, apricot stucco ranch atop a high bed of devil ivy. That same white, corral fencing cordoned the property and all its neighbors. Boys shot baskets, a man in a bright green polo shirt hosed down a vintage Corvette, the neighborhood had that aura of families with bright futures.

Strange place for a man living alone. Maybe the remnant of one of the marriages.

There was a basketball hoop atop Balch's garage, too. No cars parked outside. The few roses planted next to the house were leggy and browning and the roof shakes were warped. Bound stacks of mail – four days' worth – sat in front of the screen door. A very small notice stapled to the screen said the local sheriffs had assumed jurisdiction over the property, no one was to trespass. The locals hadn't taken in the mail.

Wil phoned them and they said it was OK to enter – if he and Petra removed anything, make a list and send a copy.

He got evidence bags and recording forms from the trunk of his car, Petra picked up the mail and they went in.

The living room was dark, rancid, littered with unfolded newspapers, dirty clothes, empty cans of beer and Pepsi, bottles of orange juice and vodka. A screwdriver man.

A sty, just like the office. Unlike the Lexus. As Petra read the mail, Wil got to work on the sofas, removing cushions, unzipping them, yanking out the foam.

Four days of post yielded utility bills, junk ads, coupons. Three days ago, he'd been spotted at Montecito switching cars, after burying Estrella Flores. Where had he cut the maid's throat? Probably somewhere in the hills above RanchHaven. Petra's best guess was he'd over-powered Flores in the house, drove her out through the fire road, found some nice quiet kill-spot. Then wrapping the body in plastic, stashing her in the trunk, he made the forty-five-minute drive to Montecito, entombed the body, left the Lexus behind because he thought it was clean and why would the cops check out Ramsey's weekend house?

Picking up the Jeep because that had been Lisa's murder vehicle and he wanted to make sure *it* was clean?

She recalled his demeanor during the interview. A little downbeat, self-effacing. No edginess, but if he was that psychopathic, why would there be?

Slipping in Lisa's bad temper, how she took it out on Cart. Brand-new running shoes. A clever bastard, Mr Gregory Balch. So why had he stayed a lackey all his life?

Embezzling cash from the boss, waiting for the right moment to bolt? Original plans to do it with Lisa, but some-thing had gone wrong . . . was Balch somewhere in Brazil with suitcases of cash, the satisfaction of having destroyed Ramsey's life in more ways than one?

She went into the kitchen. The food in the fridge was sad-bachelor fare: Beer, wine, more orange juice and Smirnoff, more takeout cartons. Beef lo-mein and ribs from a Chinese place on Hawthorne Boulevard, KFC crispy chicken bucket, no address, but she'd seen an outlet along the way. On Hawthorne. Half a gigantic pizza from a place called DeMona's in Studio City. Ventura Boulevard, just a few blocks from the office. All the food was long past edibility. The pizza looked petrified.

In the living-room, Wil worked grimly and silently, upending couches, slitting burlap bottoms, pulling a clock off the wall and shaking it hard enough to do serious damage, peering up the fireplace.

She decided to get an overview of the house, found three bedrooms, two bone-empty, one a disgusting mess, a pair of bathrooms, a dining area off the kitchen and, next to the living-room, a paneled den that looked out to the back yard, nothing in it but a brown leather recliner and a sixty-inch TV. An illegal black box sat atop the television. Petra switched on the set and was assaulted by five feet of penis entering vagina, a lazy synthesizer score, moans and grunts.

'Oh, those men,' said Wil, laughing.

She turned off the TV, opened the curtains. The yard was nice-sized, with several mature trees and an oval swimming pool, but the grass was ten inches of hay, the pool a sump of algae-streaked soup. High block walls and shrubbery blocked the neighbors' views. Lucky for the neighbors.

Light years from Ramsey's princely lifestyle. All those years of being nothing like Ramsey.

She decided to tackle the disgusting bedroom first. It smelled like the bottom of a laundry basket. King-sized bed, cheap headboard, black sheets and pillowcases flecked with oily gray stains. Gloving up, she bagged the linens. The mattress was a mildewed ruin. Even protected by surgical rubber, she found handling Balch's linens repulsive.

Facing the bed was another TV, same size, and a second black box. Same porn station. Wadded tissues and stroke books in a nightstand added to the picture of Balch's solitary sexual life. She flipped through the magazines, hoping for some really nasty S & M to build up the bad-guy psyche, but most of it was straight hetero male fantasy, the worst, some lightweight bondage.

The porn went into a bag, duly noted.

Piles of dirty underwear and socks created a lumpy rug between the wall and the left side of the bed. Balch probably slept on the right side, tossed his junk across. The closet was crammed with sweatsuits in varying colors, drawstring lounging pants, jeans, shirts, all with Macy's labels. A plastic bag with a ticket from a dry-cleaner – on Hawthorne Boulevard – contained two pairs of pants and three shirts, including the bright blue silk he'd been wearing the day of the notification call.

She removed the plastic-wrapped garments. He leaves dirty laundry on the floor for days but chooses to clean these.

Probably the stuff he'd worn while murdering Lisa. Two pants, three shirts.

If they were bloodstained, why hadn't the cleaner noticed? She tagged and bagged, moved on to the shelf above the closet. Thirteen file boxes up there. Balch's tax records. She took her time with them.

His salary from Ramsey was his sole income. Ramsey'd started him off twenty-five years ago at twenty-five thousand. Regular raises had brought him to a hundred and sixty thousand. Nice, but nothing compared to the boss's millions.

The forms listed little by way of investment. He'd deducted depreciation on the Saddlewax house, which had been purchased fourteen years ago, and his car leases – Buicks, then Caddies, now the Lexus, but no other real estate. For thirteen years, alimony had been paid monthly to Helen Balch, of Duluth, Minnesota. For the last nine, he'd also divvied up to Amber Leigh Balch.

Helen's name conjured up a middle-aged woman, the dutiful first wife. The house bought fourteen years ago – right after the marriage? If so, dissolution had taken place one year later.

Amber Leigh sounded like an Industry pseudonym. Petra saw a home-wrecker with big hair, long legs, probably blond because Lisa and Ilse said he liked blondes. Big-chested bimbo, a face not quite pretty enough. That hadn't lasted long, either.

Two thousand a month to Helen, fifteen hundred to Amber.

His take-home was a little over eight thou a month. Lease payments on the Lexus were six hundred. Take away that and spousal support and he cleared thirty-nine hundred a month. For the last few years, he'd received tax refunds of twenty grand or so. Not poverty, but chicken feed by Industry standards. By Ramsey standards.

No obvious signs of big-ticket hobbies or conspicuous expenditures. Did he play the track? Sniff coke? Had he accumulated a money stash? Augmented it with skim?

She searched every corner of the room, found no bank books or investment material. Unlike Lisa, no plans. Had *she* been his launderer?

Then she'd demanded more. Or tried to blackmail Balch. Money and passion; had to be.

A door slammed. She looked out the window and saw Wil heading for the garage. He pushed a remote and the door slid open. No car that she could see. She returned to the tax files, labeling each carton. Onward.

The first of the empty bedrooms was just that. In the second, though, she found more booty on the closet shelf: Three shoeboxes of loose photos. First came thirty-year-old professional shots of football teams, high school and college, the faces too small to make out, then home-camera jobs showing Ramsey and Balch in full athletic gear, giant, padded shoulders, tight waists.

Tall, Dark, and Handsome and his flaxen-haired buddy, both grinning, cocky, ready to take on the world.

After that came wedding snaps, Balch still lean and tan, wearing a powder-blue tux, ruffled shirt, and an unsure expression. Helen turned out to be slender, attractive, with short dark hair and a prim mouth. Later photos showed her aging well, staying slim, sometimes wearing glasses. Holding a baby.

Wrapped in pink. A daughter. Balch had never mentioned a child during the interview, but why would he, they'd been focusing on other people's lives. Petra remembered how he punted away personal questions. At the time, it had seemed aw shucks. Now she understood.

Twenty or so pictures of the child, no name on the backs of any of the pictures. A pretty dark-haired girl who favored her mother. Snapshots up till age eight or so, then nothing.

The divorce, or had it been worse – a death? Yet another loss in Balch's miserable life?

Box number two contained smaller versions of the celeb shots Petra had seen on Balch's office wall. Mostly Ramsey, a few of Balch. Various photographers, Hollywood and the Valley.

The last box was nearly empty. Just a wedding portrait, photographer's stamp from Las Vegas – a Vegas connection. Balch in a dark suit and white, banded-collar shirt, pink-faced, puffy, slightly off-kilter, towering over Amber Leigh, who was tiny and Asian with incredible cheekbones and breasts that screamed augmentation. Not what Petra had pictured, but definitely bimboistic.

He married dark-haired women but killed blondes.

Beneath the photo was an envelope dated three years ago. Loopy childish handwriting addressed to *Mr G. Balch* at the Saddlewax address. On the return side, *Caitlin Balch*, no address, Duluth, Minnesota postmark.

The same handwriting on a single sheet of lined notepaper.

Dear Dad,

Well, Im graduating from Junior High and I won an award for band, but I don't think you care about that. You never call or come here anymore and you never send the alemoney on time and with Mom being sick that makes it really hard for us. Im only writing this because Mom said I should, you should know when your daughter graduates.

You don't care. Right?

Your daughter (I guess)
Caitlin Lauren Balch

Pathetic. Had he ever answered? No further correspondence said probably not.

No shots of Lisa. Or Ilse Eggermann, that would have been too much to hope for.

If he'd been obsessed with either of the dead women, he'd probably destroyed the evidence. Or taken it with him to play with.

Petra bound all the shoeboxes with rubber bands, and was carrying them out when she heard Wil shout.

He'd laid it all out on the floor of the garage.

Six handguns – two revolvers and four automatics, three rifles, two shotguns, one an expensive Mossler. Boxes of ammo for everything. The garage smelled of gun oil.

Toolrack on a wall above an empty workbench, two large toolboxes full of assorted gizmos, a pair of fishing tackle boxes, six fishing rods, seven reels.

'Deep sea and lake,' said Wil appreciatively. 'Good lures, too. Hand-tied. And look at this.'

Knives. Petra counted thirty-two.

Bucks, fighting daggers, long-bladed boning knives Wil said he'd taken from the tackle boxes.

'The man likes to shoot and cut, Petra. There's blood on the boning blade. Might be trout – then again, maybe not.'

'Fishing and hunting,' said Petra. 'Maybe he's got himself a little cabin up in the woods.'

'That's all we need, one of those Nature Boy-survivalist deals. Better take our time with all this. I'm gonna put on fresh gloves, get my video-cam.'

* * *

It was 8:14 when they finished, the house had grown almost unbearably hot, and Petra's nose had gotten accustomed to the smell.

Wil said, 'We earned our keep,' and clicked the TV on again, switching channels from an oral-sex pretzel to local news. 'Just in case something broke. It seems to be the way we find out anything.'

The news was all crime — a nine-year-old girl abducted in Willow Glen, a drive-by in Florence, and a DB out in Angeles Crest, but nothing on Lisa or William Bradley Straight.

'Work, work, work,' said Wil, yawning and rolling down his sleeves. He'd folded his linen jacket and placed it on the mantel, over a protective layer of LAPD plastic. He looked as tired as Petra felt.

He yawned again and she said, 'I know we're supposed to start casting the net on Balch, but I for one need some food—'

He held up a silencing finger. Something on the TV had turned him wide awake.

'. . . white male,' the reporter was saying. 'No name has been released yet, but sheriff deputies have described the victim as unusually large, over six feet and three hundred pounds or more. The body parts were separated, but hadn't yet been scattered in this remote area of the forest. The boyscouts who may have disturbed the killer report seeing a car drive off quickly, with its lights off. That's it for now, Chuck, we'll keep you posted.'

Fournier gunned the remote, speeding through channels. Three other news-shows, but either the dismemberment had already been covered or only one station had the story so far.

'What?' said Petra.

'Six feet, three hundred,' he said. 'Maybe it's a coincidence but that's real damn close to the size of Buell Moran, the fool who was looking for the Straight kid. The one who probably killed the kid's mother. I mean I know this country's got an obesity problem, but . . . We were figuring he'd heard about the beach tip and headed west. If he did, maybe he met someone he thought could help him but didn't. I'm not saying it *is* him, lots of bikers get dumped in Angeles Crest, plenty of them are big, but it's too cute to ignore.'

'Much too cute,' said Petra. 'Enter it in a baby contest.'

'And here's another thing, Petra: Dismemberment and Angeles Crest reminds me of something I dealt with years ago, working on those Russian cases. Russians loved to cut up the bodies. We walked in on one of them doing it. They concentrate on the head and the fingertips, think it screws up ID's. And they were using Angeles Crest, had just discovered it. The guy who gave me the tip on the kid is Russian. First time I met him I had a feeling about him. Con eyes.'

'Why would he kill Moran?'

'How about competition for the twenty-five? Let's say both of them got a serious case of The Greeds, both are lowlifes, no impulse control. The Russian – Zhukanov's his name – sees Moran showing the kid's picture around, gets worried. Or maybe Moran approaches him, tells Zhukanov he's the kid's father, has some rights here. Zhukanov says enough of this noise. Those Russians are mean, Petra. The guy we caught playing human jigsaw had been paid two hundred bucks. Imagine what twenty-five thou would motivate.'

'If Zhukanov was threatened enough to kill Moran,' said

Petra, 'it might mean he learned something new about the Straight boy's whereabouts. More than he told you. Let me phone in to see if any new messages came in on that.'

The clerk said, 'You've got messages but it's crazy, can't go up to check.' No one answered in the squad room. She hung up and Wil took his jacket off the mantel. His forehead was as dark and slick as licorice and he wiped it and dialed the phone. A number she recognized: Downtown Sheriffs. Ron's HQ.

'Good old tans again,' he said, 'their solve rate's about twice ours but they don't have to deal with the gangbanger-no-witness bullshi— Hello, this is Detective Fournier, Hollywood LAPD. Could you please—'

Petra took the shoeboxes out to her car. In the dark, Balch's street was silent and peaceful, happy families cozy in front of the big-screen. If they only knew. She filled her nose with warm, piney air. What was the weather like in Duluth, Minnesota? What would Helen Balch think when the ex's face was all over the tube?

When she got back, Wil was smiling.

'No ID on the body, but they've got the head – thank you boyscouts – and the description fits Moran to a T. I know we've been cranking up the overtime and I was looking forward to some shuteye, Petra, but I think we need at least to check this Russian out. Maybe we can't solve Lisa right away, but wouldn't it be nice to solve something?'

'It would be loverly,' said Petra. 'Do you mind if we stop on the way for some grub? There's a Chinese place on Hawthorne that Mr Balch patronized. I doubt he's got good taste, but who knows?'

KATHY BISHOP awoke at nine, sweating, chilled, in terrible pain. Stu punched the call button and held her hand. She looked at him but from her face he couldn't tell what she saw. Where the hell were the nurses – he wanted to run over to the station but didn't want to leave Kathy.

Finally they came, and he had to control himself from screaming at them.

Now Kathy was sedated, back asleep and he realized it hadn't taken that long after all.

Get a grip.

The room felt like a cell; he'd only left for an hour, when Mother had vanned all the kids over at five thirty and they'd gone for burgers and fries at a local McDonald's. All six were quieter than usual, even the baby. He assured them they could see Mommy soon, played around, told jokes, thought they were buying the Daddy-as-usual bit, but wasn't sure. He felt out of it, some impostor inhabiting Daddy's body.

The kids started acting up and Mother said, 'Let's go, troops.'

On the way out, Stu noticed other diners staring and he filled with anger.

What's wrong, turkeys, never seen a big family before?

He stayed hot all the way to St Joe's. Weird, he'd never had a short fuse before.

Meanwhile, Petra and Wil were chasing what looked to be a multiple killer and he was calling airlines, catching guff and bureaucratese, turning up empty, no record of Balch booking any flights, but with all the turn-downs he'd received, who knew?

He used to be able to worm stuff out of bureaucrats. Mormon charm, Kathy called it. Kissing his forehead and favoring him with her come-hither wink. He loved that wink.

Not an ounce of charm in him tonight. He held Kathy's hand. Limp, lifeless. But for the warmth of her skin he might have panicked.

Breathing evenly. The machines said she was fine.

No more airlines to call, not a damn thing to do but wait. For what? More pain?

Too wound up to sleep, he got up and paced the room. He needed to sleep, needed to be together for Kathy . . . the stack of *TV Guides* sat on an end table. Maybe stupid, derivative Dack Price plot-lines would get him drowsy.

He was into the second volume when he felt his posture slacken and his eyelids droop. The third made the room grow dim.

Then something filtered through the fatigue.

Words, sentences – something a little different.

Now he was sitting up. Wide awake.

Re-reading . . . wondering . . . should he call Petra?

Strange – maybe nothing. But . . .

He didn't even know where Petra was. So out of touch. Could his judgment be trusted?

He'd try to find her. Worst came to worst, he'd have wasted some time.

Wasting time was his new hobby, anyway.

72

THE WHITE cop was taking him seriously.

Finally. Which is what Zhukanov told him when the guy appeared at the counter, just before closing time, showing his badge and the picture of the kid.

'Finally.'

'Pardon, sir?'

'I talk to one of you but he don't call back. A black guy.'

The white cop stared. 'Yes, sir, I know.'

'What do you want?' demanded Zhukanov.

'Double-checking on the identification, sir.' The cop leaned his elbows on the counter and put the newspaper clipping down. Big guy, blond, ruddy, dark suit, dark tie. He reminded Zhukanov of a colonel he'd worked with on crowd control back home, a real sadist, loved to twist limbs, knew how to do maximal damage with just a flick of a wrist... Borokovsky. This guy looked a lot like Borokovsky. Was he of Russian descent? His card said Detective DA Price, but everyone changed their names.

'Double-checking? I already tell you he been here, no one calls me, it's on the TV.'

'It's a homicide investigation, sir, we have to be careful,' said the blond cop, looking over Zhukanov's shoulder at the shelves of toys.

554

Calling me 'sir' but probably thinking I'm some kind of joke, a clown. The fat guy thought so, too, and look where he was.

Having had several hours to think about it, Zhukanov felt good about killing the fat guy – great, even, the Siberian wolf dispatches its prey, paints its muzzle with blood, howls at the moon. While cutting the guy up, Zhukanov had *felt* like howling.

Moving him into the car, then dragging him out, had been torture, Zhukanov's back and shoulders and arms still throbbed. Getting the bastard into pieces turned out to be not so easy, either. He should've sharpened the kitchen knives better, that cleaver should've gone right through the joints, not stuck like that.

The head, though, had been less of a problem than he expected. Rolling away, like a soccer ball, eyes open. That was funny. He felt like kicking it, but you had to get rid of the head, and the fingers, let the cops have the rest of the carcass. His plan had been to take the head somewhere it would never be found, but the boyscouts had ruined it, hiking through the forest, yelling like drunks. So now the cops had the head, maybe they'd learn who the fat guy was. Big deal. No connection to him, he'd cleaned all the blood. And here was a cop leaning over the very same counter, no clue.

Zhukanov fought not to smile. He'd tossed the knives into five separate storm drains from Valencia to Van Nuys. The fat man's clothing and billfold ended up in dumpsters near Fairfax and Melrose, let the Yids get blamed.

No bills in the billfold, just a driver's license and a nice picture of a naked girl with her legs spread that Zhukanov pocketed. The license he slipped down another drain. The fat man's name was Moran. So what.

When he got home he washed his bloody clothes, took a shower, had something to eat, worked with the broken gun for a while, still couldn't figure out what was wrong with it. Then a few glasses of vodka and he was out like a light by three.

And now look how calm he was, facing the white cop. Though if the guy had just showed the badge, no picture of the kid, he might've figured it had something to do with Moran – what the hell would he have done then?

'I tell the black guy,' he said. 'He never call me back.'

'I'm sorry, sir. We've been quite busy—'

'You busy looking for the kid,' said Zhukanov, 'but I see him.'

'You saw him several days ago, sir.'

'Maybe,' said Zhukanov, smiling.

'Maybe?'

'Maybe I see him again.'

The blond cop pulled out a little notepad. 'When, sir?'

'I tell your black buddy the first time, he never call me back.'

The blond cop frowned, leaned a little closer. 'Sir, if you have information—'

'I don't know,' said Zhukanov, shrugging. 'Maybe I forget. The way the black guy forget to call me.'

The pad shut. The cop was annoyed but he smiled. 'Sir, I understand your frustration. Sometimes things get busy and we don't dot every *i*. If that happened to you, I'm—'

'Dot every *i* is important,' said Zhukanov, not sure what that meant. 'But also money.'

556

'Money?' said the cop.

'Twenty-five thousand.'

'That,' said the cop. 'Sure. If we find the boy and he helps us, it's yours. At least that's what I was told.'

'No one tell *me*.'

'I've seen the forms, sir. My captain signed them. If you'd like to call him—'

'No, no,' said Zhukanov. 'I just wanna get it square, you know? Maybe I know something more than I told the black guy, but what if kid runs, you don't find him? What happens?'

'If your information's solid, you'll get partial payment,' said the cop. 'Part of the twenty-five thousand. That's the way we always do it. I'm not saying you could get all of it, but—'

'How much part of it?'

'I don't know, sir, but generally in these situations it's around a third to a half – I'd guess ten, twelve thousand. And if the boy is there, you'd get all twenty-five – why don't you speak to my captain—'

'No, no,' said Zhukanov, thinking: If the old Yid did take the kid home with him, the kid could still run, better not dawdle anymore. 'I want you should write it down.'

'Write what?'

'What you say. Twelve, fifteen to Zhukanov just for telling, all twenty-five if kid show up.'

'Sir,' said the blond cop, sighing, 'I'm not in a position – oh, all right, here you go.'

Ripping a sheet out of his pad, he said, 'How do you spell your name?'

557

Zhukanov told him.

The blond cop printed neatly:

This stipulates that to the best of my knowledge, Mr V. Zhukanov is due $12,000.00 because of information he has offered about a missing boy, unknown identity, related to L. Ramsey, PC 187. Should Mr V. Zhukanov's information lead directly to this boy and this boy's information lead to apprehension of a suspect, he would be due $25,000.00.

    Det. DA Price, Badge # 19823

'Here,' said the cop, 'but to be honest, I can't promise you this means much—'

Zhukanov snatched the paper, read it, and stuffed it down his pants pocket. Now he had a contract. If the bastards gave him trouble, he'd hire Johnnie Cochran, sue the hell out of them.

'I know where he is,' he said. 'Enough for the twenty-five.'

The blond cop waited, pen poised.

'The Yids – the Jews, from over there, got him.' Zhukanov pointed south. 'They got a church, the old Jew hid him in there, took him home last night.'

Not quite accurate. He'd paid his fifty to the DMV thief, gotten the address, drove over to check it out, found the old Yid's car parked in the alley behind the house.

'You have an address, sir?' said the cop. He straightened and his shoulders spread.

'You bet.'

'Good detective work, Mr Zhukanov.'

'In Russia, I was policeman.'

'Really – well it paid off, sir. Thank you. And believe me I'll do everything I can to make sure you get every penny of that twenty-five thousand.'

'You bet,' said Zhukanov. The wolf triumphs!

The blond cop said, 'What's the address?'

'Twenty-three Sunrise Court.' Twenty-five-thousand-dollar address.

'That's here in Venice?'

'Yeah, yeah, right here.' Idiot, didn't know his own city. Zhukanov hooked a thumb. 'From alley, you go to Speedway, then to Pacific, then five blocks over.'

'Great,' said the cop, closing the pad. 'You've been a tremendous help, sir – when you say the alley, you mean the one back there?'

'Yeah, yeah – I show you.'

Vaulting over the counter – adrenaline-charged, despite his aching limbs, Zhukanov led the blond cop around the side of the shack, past the shipping-carton trash boxes. If the guy only knew what had been in there yesterday.

'Over there,' he pointed, 'is Jew church, where I see car. OK?'

'By the way, what kind of car is it, sir?'

'Lincoln. White, brown roof.'

'Year?'

'You want, you can find out.' Grinning, Zhukanov recited the license number. The cop scrawled in the darkness. 'Other way is where he went.'

'North,' said the cop.

'Yeah, yeah, right up to Speedway and then Pacific, five blocks.'

559

The cop repeated the instructions, a real dummy.

'That's it,' said Zhukanov. Go find him, you stupid bastard, I'm giving him to you on a platter!

The cop put his pad away and shot out a hand. 'Thank you, sir.'

They shook. Firm, manly shake. If the cop only knew the hand he was grasping had been bloody up to the elbow a few hours ago. Zhukanov tried to break the clasp, get the guy moving, but he couldn't pull away – the cop was holding on to him, yanking him close – what the hell was this? – the cop was grinning, like he was going to kiss him, this wasn't right, this was wrong.

Zhukanov struggled, struck out.

A hand grabbed his wrist, twisted it, something broke and pain devoured him from fingertip to the bottom of his ear. One quick move, just like Colonel Borokovsky. He cried out involuntarily and something big and meaty exploded in the middle of his face and he went down.

Then more pain, even worse, burning, searing, like a fire igniting his bowels.

Starting right under his navel then spreading upward, like a burning rope. Then he felt cold, a strange cold – cold air blowing . . . inside him, *deep* inside, and knew he'd been split open, filleted – the way he'd split the fat bastard and now it had happened to him and he couldn't do a damn thing, just lie there and take it.

The last thing he felt was a hand going through his pocket.

Fishing out the contract. Liar! Cheater! The money was hi—

BEING ALONE here is different from the park. Different from Watson.

I've got all these rooms, these books, someone who trusts me. Once in a while I hear footsteps out on the sidewalk, or someone talking or laughing, a car driving by. But they don't bother me, I'm here, locked in. I can sleep without waking up to see what's around. I can read without a flashlight.

I've thought about it a lot and Sam's right. Tomorrow I'll find a phone and call the police, tell them about PLYR 1. Maybe I can call Mom, too. Tell her I'm OK, not to worry, I'm doing just fine, one day I'll come back, be able to support her.

What would she do? Cry? Get mad? Beg me to come back?

Or worse: *Not* beg me? She must miss me a little.

I stop thinking about it, stretch my feet out on the couch, pull the knit blanket up over my knees, start in on the next *Life* magazine. The main article's all about John Kennedy and his family, happy and handsome on the beach.

California beach, same sand that's just a little way up. I could walk over, look at it, pretend to be John Kennedy, come back. But I told Sam I'd stay here and he gave me the alarm code.

1 1 2 5. I get up and try it. Green light.

Red light, green light, red light.

Green light. I open the door, smell the salt, that beach smell, no one's out, most of the houses are dark.

I go out to the porch. Feel cold, scared.

Back in the house. Why does just going outside scare me?

I'll try again later. Back to the Kennedys.

THE OWNER of the Chinese restaurant had no memory of Balch. Petra and Wil ordered some spring rolls to go, ate them in her car, agreed to drive separately to Venice, meet on Pacific and Rose, walk to Zhukanov's stand together.

Petra was back at Redondo Beach Boulevard when the desk at Hollywood station called her.

'Detective Bishop for you half an hour ago,' said the clerk. Had Stu gotten hold of flight information on Balch?

The hospital operator refused to put Petra through. 'No calls to surgical patients past nine, ma'am.'

'I'm a police detective returning another detective's call. Stuart Bishop.'

'Is Mr Bishop the patient?'

'No, his wife is.'

'Then I'm sorry, ma'am, I can't put you through.'

'Let me speak to your supervisor, please.'

'I am the supervisor. The rules are for our patients' welfare and comfort. If you'd like, I can have a message slip sent up to the room telling him you called.'

'Fine, I'll wait.'

'Can't do that, ma'am. It'll take time, we're understaffed and I need to keep all the lines open. If it's important, I'm sure he'll call back.'

'Sure,' said Petra. 'Have a nice night.'

She drove on, hoping it wasn't that important. Even if they found a flight reservation, she had doubts Balch had actually shown up. The call to Westward Charter had to be a fake-out. Balch had been too careful about everything else to slip up like that.

Meaning what?

He was anywhere *but* Las Vegas. Site of his second wedding. Tomorrow, she'd try to get hold of Amber Leigh. And Helen. Find out why they'd divorced the guy. His kinks, bad habits, what might lead him to murder blondes.

Anywhere but . . . the cabin in the woods? Homicidal Thoreau? If no leads showed up soon, Schoelkopf would probably go straight to *America's Most Wanted*. Maybe that was the best way to handle it. Take the heat off her and Wil. Off William Bradley Straight, now motherless, poor, poor kid.

And now the guy who'd probably turned him into an orphan had been butchered like the squalid ton of pork he was.

One less felon heard from. Petra felt grim satisfaction about that.

Not that it would stop her from going after the butcher.

DINKY LITTLE house. Light on in the front room, but dim. The Lincoln parked in back.

So the old man was home with the kid. Was he married? Zhukanov hadn't mentioned anything about seeing a wife, but that didn't mean anything, the old guy could've gone to temple, left her behind. Maybe she was sick, an invalid.

Easy.

On balance, the walkstreet was probably an advantage. No cars to hide behind but no drivers interrupting. No pedestrians, either, during the half-hour he'd watched the house from three different spots.

He tried the back alley again, rubber soles swallowing his footsteps. New running shoes, he'd walked around in them, made sure there was no squeak.

Out of the cheap-suit cop-getup and into black sweats and a black windbreaker with pockets. The van, rented from a fly-by-night place down near the airport, a perfect dressing room. He'd paid cash, used no ID, leaving the guy who ran the rental lot five hundred in cash as collateral. Five hundred he'd never see again. Worth it. The van was parked four blocks away, east of Main, on a residential street.

Pleasant stroll to Sunrise Court, the beach air was tangy, invigorating. He'd never lived on the beach. Maybe one day . . .

From the back he could see that the kitchen light was still on. 10:38. Someone up, or just a security measure? Probably the latter, he'd seen no trace of any movement.

Why had the old guy taken the kid in? A relative? The drawing didn't show a Jewish-looking kid, but you could never tell. No, if it was a family thing, wouldn't they be pushing the kid to collect the money?

A good samaritan? Religious convictions? Giving the kid sanctuary in the temple? Did Jews believe in that? He had no idea. Returning to the front, he hid behind a clump of shrubbery, continued to watch the house.

How to do it?

The only way was a blitz. Home invasion. Gangbangers were getting into that, especially the Asians. A small place like this, how many rooms could there be?

A knife would be best because of the sound factor, but running from room to room, stabbing, was risky; even with weak prey, there was the risk of escape.

The alternative was the Glock, but that meant noise. Venice was high-crime, he'd heard about gangs on Ocean Front, had seen gang-types during today's surveillance. So the neighbors were probably used to hearing gunshots at night. But a street like this, the houses close together, bursting in, doing it, ditching the gun, taking the escape route he'd plotted back to the van . . .

Risky.

But fun, admit it. The risk was *part* of the fun. That and simply being able to do it.

A zapperoo commando blitz then, one hand on the knife, the other on the gun. If it was just the kid and the old man and they were close together, the knife would probably work.

So he'd start with the knife, have the gun ready for complications.

One thing he'd decided for sure: Rear entry was best. Ha ha.

Another advantage of the walkstreet: Everyone parked in back, so walking through the alley wouldn't be viewed as deviant. If he was spotted, he'd affect a relaxed stroll, pretend to belong, jangle his keys and head for one of the cars. The way he looked – white male, sweats – wouldn't be threatening, he hoped.

His knees hurt. Too much squatting, the percs were no longer doing the trick. Lisa had claimed coke was a good anesthetic, dentists used to smear it on gums. Always wanting him to try it. Screw that. He bought it for her, *spooned* it up her cute little nose, tried to get some satisfaction from her body while she was high, but no way would he do it, percs were as far as he went.

Maintain the upper edge.

He waited. Nothing. OK, back again, ready to blitz.

He was just about to leave when the front door opened and someone came out.

On the patio, looking around.

The kid!

Perfect! He'd sprint across the sidewalk, grab him, cut his throat, be off – God *was* good!

But just as he got ready to spring, the kid ran back inside.

Scared?

You've got good reason, sonny.

76

'THAT'S THE place,' said Wil, waiting, the phone to his ear.

Ocean Front Walk was dark and deserted and Petra could barely make out the souvenir stand. As they got closer she saw it was a tiny, ramshackle thing, roll-down shutter over the front.

'OK,' Wil said to the phone. To Petra: 'Got a home address for him. West Hollywood. Of course.'

They were twenty feet away from the shack. No one on the walkway for at least a hundred yards. They'd passed one homeless guy at the corner of Paloma and Speedway and Petra saw another sitting on a bench to the north but he got up and shuffled away. The tide whispered secrets and the beach looked like ice.

They were about to turn around when she noticed something. Two inches of space beneath the shutter. Closed but not locked?

Gun out, she hurried over, Wil following. Loops for a lock were welded to the lower-right-hand corner of the steel roll and a ring was bolted to the counter. But no lock in sight. She peered through the two inches. Dark, but she could make out stuff wrapped in plastic hanging from racks . . . postcards. Hats. Just like the kind William Straight wore.

She backed clear across Ocean Front, watched the stand while talking to Wil in a low voice: 'Clear sign of illegal entry, our duty to investigate.'

'Absolutely,' he said. 'But what if the guy's some nut and he's lurking inside there – let's check the back first.'

Whipping out penlights, they snaked along the north side of the stand. Too damn dark, too damn quiet. Petra liked using her brains, psyching out bad guys. She could do without this TV cop stuff.

Behind the building were two huge wooden packing crates, slats over plank sides. Her penlight said they came from the docks at Long Beach.

The stand's back door was bolted, a nice big padlock in place. Off, definitely off. Unless it hadn't been a thought-out burglary, just something impulsive . . . the packing crates stank of garbage. The neighboring buildings all utilized commercial dumpsters. City regulations – the Russian saving money?

One good thing about the crates, though, the slats offered an easy foothold. She got a toe in, hoisted herself up the first one, looked inside. Nothing.

She found Zhukanov in the second crate, lying on his back atop a heap of trash, mouth open in the dead-man's stupid gape, one arm spread, the other pinioned under his head in an angle that would have been excruciatingly painful had he been alive.

Bisected, disemboweled. The penlight turned his intestines into overfed eels.

Same killing wound as Lisa.

Balch had never left town at all, the charter call a fake-out just as she'd suspected – so what had *Stu* phoned about?

No time to think about that. She ran the light over the trash, saw the blood now, a huge, crimson oblong, spattered on paper refuse.

Wil had found blood, too. Specks and drips on the front of the crate, another large stain on the ground. She'd been standing right in it, dammit! How could she have missed it?

They phoned it in to Pacific Division, were told to safeguard the scene, it might be a while before anyone showed up because a shooting had just gone down in Oakwood and some of those victims were still breathing.

Inside the stand, they found no evidence of break-in, just crappy toys, a rear stockroom with a chair and a card table full of receipts and sales slips, no apparent system. A Planet Hollywood jacket hung from a nail in the wall. On adjoining nails were nunchucks, half a baseball bat with a leather thong, tarnished brass knuckles.

The Russian, equipped for battle. Someone had taken him by surprise.

Several bottles in the corner might explain it. Cheap-looking Russian labels, cloudy vodka. One of the bottles was nearly empty. Zhukanov drunk, his defenses down? Bolstered by booze when he killed Moran?

If he *had* killed Moran. Maybe he'd been Moran's crime buddy, a drug connection, whatever, and the two had colluded to collect the twenty-five thousand.

Somehow, Balch had figured it out and finished them both off.

But then why bother taking Moran to Angeles Crest while leaving Zhukanov right here where he was sure to be found?

Look what I can do!

Zhukanov's gut wound matched Lisa's. And Ilse's. But

Moran didn't fit. So the Russian probably *had* dispatched Moran. And Balch had finished off Zhukanov.

There could only be one reason: The Russian knew something vital about William Bradley Straight.

All Zhukanov had told Wil was that the boy had bought a hat from him.

Not enough to kill for.

Had the Russian held back? Did he know more?

She shot her theories at Wil, who was up in front, examining the inside wall beneath the counter, looking for more bloodstains.

She was talking at manic speed, couldn't believe the edge in her voice. Wil listened, said, 'You think Zhukanov saw the boy again? Got a fix on his location? But how would Balch find out?'

'I don't know – but if it was him, he took Zhukanov by surprise. Maybe force. Or Zhukanov was plastered. Or he pulled some kind of scam on Zhukanov. The guy was crazy for the reward. It could have clouded his judgment.'

'A scam,' said Wil. 'Someone who'd be legit asking about the boy?'

'Yes,' said Petra. 'A social worker – a cop. Maybe Balch impersonated a cop.'

Wil thought about that. 'A suit and a fake badge is all it'd take. Yeah, Zhukanov's greed would do the rest. But for Balch to risk killing him now, when he knows we're going to be looking for him?'

'We haven't caught him, he may not even know we're on to him,' said Petra. 'And if it leads to the boy, it could seem worth it. That tells me Zhukanov may very well have learned something more about the boy.'

She returned to the stockroom, searching nervously, frantically. Toys, stupid toys — imagine a hairbasket like Zhukanov peddling playthings to little kids . . . nothing in the pocket of the Planet Hollywood jacket . . . the card table, the receipts — she grabbed them all up, started scanning.

Ten slips in, she found an invoice form, no sale marked, no date. Just a single line of shaky printing.

2RTRM34

License number? Had the Russian seen William Straight in a car and copied down the plate? Everyone knew you could bribe info out of DMV. The papers had covered a big bribery scandal a few months ago. A street guy like Zhukanov would know his way around that kind of thing. Pay up, get the address.

She looked for a phone in the shack. None in either room. What a hovel. Fournier was still looking for blood. She borrowed his phone — what was the night number for DMV traces . . . yeah, yeah, she remembered it. When the clerk came on, she had to fight from barking orders at the woman. This one was another stickler for regulations.

Lord save me from rule-books.

But a little assertiveness finally made her cooperate and, a few computer clicks later, Petra had it: Samuel Morris Ganzer, 23 Sunrise Court, Venice, California.

Birthdate in 1925.

An old man.

Had William found himself a protector?

THE LINCOLN was parked inches from the back of the house and its front bumper gave him a great boost to the window.

Drapes on this one, too, but not drawn tightly, he had a perfect view of the kitchen, helped along by a small light over the stove. The living-room, too, separated only by a waist-high counter. A floor lamp there cast charcoal shadows on gray carpet. Enough light to see the front door. Red glow off to the right side. Alarm. Too bad. But better to know, up front.

Three doors to the left, probably bedrooms and bathroom. Not much space between them. Small rooms, better for stabbing.

And that was the entire layout. Excellent.

No sign of the boy since he'd first ventured out onto the porch. The old guy, either. Both bedroom doors closed. The boy and the old man — with or without wife — fast asleep? Or maybe the old guy was a queer and the boy was sleeping with him.

That would sure explain taking him home.

Sleep made it a helluva lot easier: Burst in, throw the bedroom doors open, boom boom boom, gone even before the time-delay kicked in on the alarm.

Knock stuff over on the way out, maybe steal something, to make it look like a gang thing.

He got down from the car, checked the alley for intruders, examined the house's rear door. Two deadbolts. Bad. But putting a little weight on the wood, he felt some give. One or two good shoves would take it off the hinges. Probably ruin his shoulder, but he was used to pushing his way through obstacles. The door was nothing compared to a defensive line.

OK, then. Here come da blitz. The knife if it worked, the gun ready for backup. Either way, he could do it in seconds, run out the back, fade into the night.

One last look through the kitchen window.

He was scared, had to admit it. This was different, not like Lisa, the German girl, Sally, the stupid Russian. All those times, he'd set up the scenes.

But there were times you had to improvise.

He climbed up on the Lincoln's bumper again. Nothing different, but still he hesitated. Up again, down again. Compulsive. When his anxiety rose, he handled it with repetition. Like his mother's head-banging. The stupid bitch. She deserved to die in that stupid helmet.

OK, one last look – this time, he saw the boy – see, it pays to be thorough!

Coming out of the middle door to the left. A bathroom, just as he'd guessed.

Skinny little thing, light enough to drop-kick. He watched him emerge, go into the kitchen, open the refrigerator, take something out – a carrot.

Would he wash it? The sink was right below the window. *Duck*.

Crouched next to the outer wall, he heard plumbing kick in. Hygienic little sucker.

The water stopped. He waited, finally raised his head, peeked in again. The kid was standing in the living-room, back to the kitchen window, eating the carrot. Finishing half of it, he walked to the front door, punched the alarm panel – damn, too far to make out the code.

Opening the door, the kid stepped out again. But only for a few seconds and here he was again, back inside, closing the door, turning, about to face the window.

Could he see anything out here in the darkness? Probably not unless it was right up against the glass, but be extra-careful, duck again.

Another thirty seconds passed before he dared another look. The kid was still standing in the living-room, munching on the carrot, visible in profile.

Just another face.

The kid finished the carrot, bent and picked something up. A magazine. He eats healthy, washes, reads. Such a good little citizen.

But not careful. Because the light on the front alarm panel was green.

He'd forgotten to trigger the goddamn alarm!

God was *wonderful*!

The blitz was on!

'SUNRISE COURT,' said Petra, thumbing through her *Thomas Guide*.

Wil took his penlight out of his mouth. 'I know it, one of the walkstreets.' He was outside the stand, recording the details of the Zhukanov crime scene.

'Which direction?' she said.

'North, five, six blocks.'

The license number and Samuel Ganzer's name hadn't impressed him. 'Could be Zhukanov's boss, a customer. Zhukanov could've recorded the license for a check authorization.'

'Could be,' said Petra, having only instinct to back her up. She closed the map book. 'So you'll stay here, keep Zhukanov company?'

'Sure. Maybe he'll teach me Russian.'

IT'S ALMOST eleven. Sam should be back soon. I thought I'd stay up till he got here, but now I'm tired, guess I'll go to sleep.

He's probably having a good time with Mrs Kleinman. I could eat another carrot but I'm not really hungry . . . maybe I'll take another shower. No, I already had one, don't want to use up too much of Sam's water.

I go to turn off the living-room lamp — maybe I'll take some magazines to bed — uh-oh, I forgot to switch the alarm back on.

I head for the panel, reach out for the buttons and from behind me comes an explosion, then a crash — from the back of the house. *Oh no, did I leave the stove on or something?*

But I don't smell gas or anything burning and when I turn I see a big black space where the kitchen door was and the door's down on the floor and a guy's coming through the space, he's in the house, now, seeing me, throwing open the door to Sam's room, looking in, coming out—

Coming at me.

Dressed all in black.

Weird orange-pink skin and yellow hair.

Big.

He looks right at me. I don't know him but he knows me!

PLYR 1!

How?

Oh God, no oh no – he's coming right at me and he's got a knife – a big pink man with a knife I want to scream but my mouth is frozen. I reach for the doorknob, touch only air and he's coming faster, closer, such a big knife – I run to the left, but that just puts me in a corner, nowhere to go, bookshelves behind me, I have to do something – *throw* something, that worked before – books.

I start pulling them off the shelves and heaving them at him as hard as I can. A few hit him but he keeps coming, walking slower, smiling, taking his time, holding the knife out in front of him, waving it back and forth.

I keep pulling out books and throwing them, they hit him in the face, the chest, the stomach, he laughs, pushes them away, keeps coming, the room's dark, but he can see me, he keeps coming straight at me.

I try to shove the dusty couch at him but it's too heavy. He laughs.

I pick up the music stand and throw *it*.

That surprises him. He loses his balance and I run around him into the kitchen, toward the back door.

Suddenly I'm down on the floor.

Something around my leg.

He's pulling me by the ankle, I see his knees bend, see the bottom of his chin, his arm, the knife's coming down—

I twist around like a snake, just keep moving, moving, maybe if I move he'll miss and I can get out through the back door. He's squeezing my ankle, hurting it, I punch at him, keep twisting, get close enough to the arm that's holding my ankle and bite it, bite it hard Billy Snake Billy Viper.

He shouts and lets go and I want to run out the back but he's blocking the way – where where where – the only choice is fake him out, move to the left then the right, into the bathroom, next best thing get in there, lock myself in.

I jump up run faster than I've ever run before across the kitchen he's running too breathing hard I make it into the bathroom slam the door lock it squeeze in between the toilet and the bathtub cold floor breathing fast my chest hurts so bad—

No sound.

Then he laughs again. I hear footsteps. Slow footsteps, he's relaxed. I'm trying to breathe slower but every breath makes a squeaky sound.

Through the door I hear: 'Stupid little shit. You cornered yourself.'

He's right.

The bathroom has no window.

Now he's kicking the door it shakes the wood swells like a balloon that cracks right in the middle I jump up open the medicine cabinet feel in the darkness for something sharp a razor blade scissors anything no razor blade no scissors here's something pointy a nail file I think it's not sharp but I grab it he kicks part of his leg comes through black sweats black tennis shoes I stab down at the pants the nail file hits bone but it slides off doesn't go in he yells calls me a little bastard—

Another explosion much louder.

Something comes through the door flying by me the mirror on the medicine-cabinet door shatters I feel pain in the back of my head put my hand there warm and sticky needles glass needles.

A gun – he's got a gun, too.

I throw myself into the tub he shoots again now the door is full of holes splintering and now I can see part of him on the other side his legs and shoes and the drawstring on his pants he's still shooting I'm lying face down in the tub as low as I can go but a bullet hits the tub and the porcelain shatters and part of the wall falls off this is it I'm trapped finished I did my best it wasn't good enough another explosion the bullet goes into something above my head stuff falls down on me dust tiles I'm getting buried.

Now there's no door just him big huge the knife in one hand the gun in another.

He turns on the light.

I've still got the nail file. He sees it and laughs.

Puts the gun in his pocket.

Oh no the knife.

I curl up don't want to see it just don't let me feel it.

He takes hold of my hair pulls me up so I'm on my knees pulls my head back.

I piss my pants and shit slides out of me running down my leg thank you God for nothing you don't exist you liar—

Another explosion.

More and moreandmoreandmore I can't stand the noise I don't get it what's he doing—

He drops me and I fall into the tub hard.

A woman's voice says, 'My God!'

Then: 'It's OK, honey.'

A hand touches the back of my neck.

I scream.

RED PUFFS sparked from Balch's back, neck, posterior skull. Later, Petra learned she'd shot him nine times within a two-foot diameter, each bullet lethal, a tight little circle of death.

He fell on his face next to the bathtub, stayed there, the gun tangled in his fingers. She freed the weapon, kicked it across the floor. Kicked him to make sure he was dead though maybe that wasn't the only reason. The knife had fallen to one side. Big ugly commando thing with a black hard-rubber handle. She kicked it away, too, stepped over the black, sweat-suited corpse. Bits of blood-pinkened bone gritted the tile floor. The bathroom door was a splinter of frame barely hanging from one hinge.

The boy was huddled fetally in the tub.

What was left of the tub; ragged chunks of porcelain had been torn loose, glass shards and dust and broken tiles were everywhere. Blood had flowed over Balch's back and wormed onto the floor. The place looked as if it had been through a war – how could the idiot think he'd get away with this?

He'd come close.

She'd had trouble finding a space within eyeshot of the house, and even though she saw no sign of intrusion, something pinged in her gut and she double-parked.

She got out of the car, smelling sea air, expecting another dead end.

Then gunshots raped the silence and she pulled out her gun and ran around to the back, found the door kicked in, a dimly lit kitchen beyond the threshold, off to the left another ravaged door, black sweat-suited bulk nearly filling the opening – an upraised knife, a child's limp legs.

'Stop!' she screamed, but it was no warning, she was already shooting.

When she got to the boy, he refused to uncurl, whimpered when she talked to him, screamed when she touched him. Such a skinny little thing! His long hair was blood-stained, porcupined with glass fragments. Twelve, but the size of a ten year old. A yellow pool had spread underneath him. She smelled feces, saw the stain covering the seat of his jeans.

The urge to pick him up, hold him, rock him in her arms was so strong it made her palate ache. She got down on the floor, talked to him, finally managed to stroke his hair without repulsing him.

He stopped shaking, went rigid, then limp. She cradled his head and now he let her. She knew how to comfort. At that moment she thought, crazily, of Nick. You were wrong, you prick.

When the boy was breathing regularly, she laid him down gently in the tub and called for an ambulance and uniformed backup, Code Three. Returning, she stayed with him, picking glass out of his scalp, getting splinters in her finger, it didn't matter, it felt OK. Calling him William, using a soothing tone, not really knowing what she was saying, wanting to calm him down but how could you comfort a kid who'd been through this?

She heard sirens. Pacific Division cops burst in, then came the paramedics. Only when the boy was up on a stretcher did she allow herself to leave him. Fetal again, so small under the shock blanket. An old man rushed in looking stunned. The paramedics seemed pained as they carried the boy out.

She watched them carry him away, ignored the old man's questions. The uniforms' too. Walking straight to Balch's body, she turned it over.

Not Balch. A stranger.

The shock punched her in the heart and she broke out into a sweat.

A second jolt hit her, even stronger. Recognition.

Ramsey.

His mustache was gone and his skin was different — some kind of salmon-pink theatrical makeup was smeared all over his face and down his neck, flaking around his nostrils. Dark shadows around his eyes — gray makeup. The bushy blond wig had been jarred loose, revealing a crescent of black curls. Blond tint in the eyebrows, he'd even done the eyebrows.

Blue eyes, dull as sewer water.

Mouth open, the same old death-gape. She looked down his mouth, saw the tongue curled back, blood collecting at the bottom of his throat.

Thinking about what he'd put the boy through, Lisa, Ilse, the Flores woman, she would have welcomed the chance to kill him again.

81

THEY FOUND Gregory Balch's body the next day, buried under dirt, hay, and horse manure in the barn behind the Calabasas house, his throat cut, just like Estrella Flores.

Entombed in dung. You didn't need to be a shrink to interpret.

After tearing the pink palace apart, the closest they got to a motive was a single piece of notepaper in Ramsey's bedroom rolltop. One of those *From the desk of* things. In the center, he'd written:

L and G?

Lisa and Greg. A sweat stain beneath the inscription indicated stress, according to a department shrink. Very profound. The psychologist was light on facts, heavy on pomposity, suggested he be the one to see Billy Straight for 'debriefing.'

Petra had other ideas and she stood her ground.

Stu's find clinched it: Ten-year-old *Adjustor* plot out of *TV Guide*.

A football player attempts to frame his best friend for murder and Dack Price investigates.

Maybe eventually it would help Stu feel he'd played a

part. Right now he had Kathy's recuperation to deal with, she'd finally gotten realistic, agreed to his thirty-day compassionate leave.

L and G? Had Lisa and Balch tumbled? Or was it all in Ramsey's paranoid mind? Or maybe it was money, Lisa and Balch conspiring to skim. No way to know till all the financial records were pried loose from Larry Schick. Maybe never. Petra really didn't care.

Same for the specifics of Lisa's murder, just paperwork now. Her best guess was the original scenario: Ramsey had doped up Balch on Sunday night, snuck out, followed Lisa, abducted her. Using the Mercedes, not the Jeep. Because Billy had seen the plates. PLYR 1.

Turned out that's *all* he'd seen. Not enough to point a finger at anyone, the boy had been turned into quarry for nothing.

Or maybe Ramsey had switched plates, used the Jeep after all. Or some other set of wheels, he had so many, let the techs logic it out.

Killing Estrella Flores up in the hills because she'd seen him sneak out. Or might've. Borrowing Balch's Lexus for the Flores kill. Or maybe Balch had been in on it, after all, friend to the end. Whatever, Ramsey had used him, tossed him away.

A football player attempts to frame his best friend ... pilfering from a script that hadn't been very good in the first place. No imagination. The Industry.

Industry bigshots called themselves players.

Ramsey styling himself a player, knowing he really wasn't one. Because his ratings were low, his acting was a joke and his penis wouldn't harden.

To hell with him. Billy was her concern.

The boy was beginning his sixth day at Western Pediatric Hospital, where he'd proved a difficult patient, at first. Petra neglected her paperwork, ignored Schoelkopf's calls, spent most of her time at his bedside. When she left, a hospital play therapist filled in. At first, Billy ignored both of them. By the third day, he was accepting the books and magazines that Petra brought him. On the fourth day, Ron came and took her to dinner at the Biltmore downtown.

Nice dinner — great dinner. She found her hand seeking his. The way he listened to her turned her on. Till then she'd wondered if what had happened between them was due to the tension of the case.

To her great pleasure, now that things were calming down, she wanted to be with him more. Maybe soon she'd get to meet his girls.

Sweet fantasies . . . She harbored no illusions of healing the boy's emotional wounds, had called Alex Delaware, a psychologist she'd worked with and trusted, friend of Sturgis, a man who'd been willing to go undercover for something he believed in. But he was out of town with his girlfriend, would be returning today.

Meanwhile, Billy stayed in the hospital for antibiotic treatment and nutrition, a police guard sitting ten feet down the hall. No reason Petra could see for that, but Schoelkopf had ordered it, maybe he was feeling guilty, so why not?

The cop had been called into action only once, dealing with Sam Ganzer, who insisted on visiting. Feisty old guy, standing on his tiptoes, facing up to the uniform, fingers pointing, things getting loud until Petra interceded, said

Ganzer could see Billy, took him for coffee in the family lounge first, to calm him down.

He wanted to know what would happen after Billy left the hospital. Telling Petra she was brave, a 'real hero,' but no way would he allow her or anyone else to send the boy to some 'stupid juvenile hall, I can tell you about institutions – hell, I'll adopt him myself before I let you get away with that.'

Petra promised she'd take care of Billy. Adoption fantasies had filled her head, too.

Billy needed to be hospitalized for at least three weeks. He'd emerged from the nightmare encounter with only superficial scratches, but medical tests revealed a low-grade bacterial infection in his lungs, foot fungus, slightly elevated blood pressure and a pre-ulcerous stomach. The doctors pronounced the last two symptoms as probable stress reactions. No kidding. The infection was their main concern and they had him on IV antibiotics. No one had told him about his mother, yet. Delaware said he'd handle it and Petra was grateful it wouldn't be her.

Ilse Eggermann would never be solved officially, but Petra was sure Ramsey had done her, too. How close she'd come to being fooled – OK, humility was good for the soul. Good for the career, too. In the future, she'd be careful about assuming anything.

She thought about how Ramsey and Ilse could have gone down: Ramsey visiting Balch in Rolling Hills Estates, couple of beers between friends, then on the way home, nice, easy drive up Hawthorne, he decides on a stopover at the pier. Had he used a disguise that night, too? Had he been planning something all along? Or had Ilse's foreigner status

587

protected him from recognition – *The Adjustor* had never made it over to Europe?

That kind of MO indicated he might've killed other women. She'd beg off that part of it, let the Feds have their fun, anyone else who wanted the glory. Schoelkopf was already holding press conferences, talking about *his* investigation.

No news on the reward, yet. Dr and Mrs Boehlinger had returned to Ohio to finalize Lisa's funeral arrangements and they hadn't returned Petra's calls. Whether or not Billy deserved the reward legally, he was certainly the moral recipient. Boehlinger would probably try to avoid paying. After what he'd put Billy through, Petra wanted to lean on him, but what could she do? Maybe an anonymous leak to the papers. Or perhaps Mrs B would come through.

All secondary. For now, Billy slept, helped along by a big dinner and sedation.

Angel face, white and smooth, so peaceful.

She bent down, kissed his forehead, left the room, went to get the play therapist.

On her way out of the hospital, one of the administrators, a middle-aged suit named Bancroft, snagged her.

'How's our little hero, Detective Connor?'

'Fine.'

Bancroft caught her arm, let go quickly when she stared at his hand. 'If you have a moment, Detective, I have someone who'd like to speak with you.'

'Who?'

'In my office, please.'

* * *

His office was big, done up in blue tweed and fake Colonial. Two women in their sixties sat in overstuffed chairs. One was chunky, broad-shouldered, with wiry gray hair uncoiling under a small, charcoal pillbox hat, an ancient, no-nonsense tweed suit, a melt-the-glacier stare. The other was very thin with coiffed hair the color of brandy, no jewelry, light makeup. Navy suit that looked like Chanel, matching shoes. Her face was longish, painfully angular. She'd probably been beautiful, once. She looked frightened. Petra was baffled.

'Detective,' said Bancroft, 'this is Mrs Adamson, she and the late Mr Adamson were among our most generous benefactors.'

Slight inflection on the past tense. Bancroft winced. The thin woman smiled. Her hands were white, blue-veined, slightly liver-spotted. Petra noticed one index finger making tiny circles atop her purse. Gorgeous shoes, gorgeous suit, but like the stocky woman's getup, the outfit looked old, gave off a clear sense of history.

No introduction of the other woman. She was examining Petra like a fishwife rating mullet.

'Well, I'll leave you to talk,' said Bancroft. He left.

The chunky woman got up, too, looking none too happy.

'Thank you, Mildred,' Mrs Adamson told her. Mildred nodded grimly before closing the door.

Mrs Adamson turned to Petra. Her mouth worked. Finally, she said, 'Please call me Cora. I'm so sorry to take your time but . . .' Instead of continuing, she removed something from her purse and held it out.

Color snapshot of Billy. A little younger – maybe eleven. He stood on a boat dock, waving.

'How did you get this, ma'am?'

'It's mine. I snapped the picture.'

'You know Billy Straight?'

The bottom half of the woman's mouth trembled and her eyes pooled with tears. 'This isn't Billy Straight, Detective Connor. It's Billy Adamson. William Bradley Adamson, Jr My son. My late son.'

Petra examined the back of the photo. A handwritten inscription said: *Billy, Arrowhead, 1971.* The colors were a little faded, she should have noticed. Some detective.

The boy was smiling but something was off – the smile required effort.

A handkerchief had flown to Cora Adamson's face. She said, 'Perhaps there are things I could've done differently, but I wasn't – how could I know for sure?'

'Know what, Mrs Adamson?'

'Forgive me, I'm not making sense, let me organize my thoughts . . . Billy – *my* Billy – was an only child. Brilliant, he taught himself to read at four. He graduated from Cal law school thirteen years ago, immediately began doing legal work for the Farm Workers' Union. My late husband was convinced it was a stage, rebellion, getting back at the corporate world. But I knew better: Billy had always been caring, kind, even as a small boy, he refused to hurt anything – he wouldn't fish. Bill Senior loved to fish but Billy refused. The day I shot that picture, he and Bill had had a tiff about that. Bill insisted he was going to show Billy how to fish, once and for all. Billy cried and insisted he wouldn't get in the boat, refused to kill anything. Finally, Bill told him if he couldn't be a man, just to stay behind with his mother. Which he did. But he was upset – he loved his father. I took the picture to cheer him up.'

Petra stared at the photo. Same eyes, same hair. Same cleft chin. Jesus, even the expression was a clone.

'At twelve he became a vegetarian,' said Cora Adamson. 'Again, Bill thought it was a phase, but Billy never touched meat or fish again – I'm wandering, forgive me – where was I – the farm workers. Billy could have gotten a job with any firm in the country but he chose to travel around the state with the farm workers, looking for violations, living the way they lived. He seemed happy, then suddenly he showed up at home and announced he'd quit, gotten a job with the public defender's office. But he wasn't happy there, either, and left soon after.

'After that, he started to drift, driving around the state in an old car, growing his hair long, a long beard, doing legal work for various free clinics, never settling down. I knew something was bothering him but he wouldn't tell me what it was. He wasn't around long enough to tell me. His father was so angry at him . . . he just kept wandering, leaving me no phone number, no address – I knew he was lost but he refused to be found.'

Sitting up straighter, she twisted the handkerchief. 'Then one weekend, he showed up at our place in Arrowhead. We had guests – business associates of his father – and Bill was embarrassed about the way Billy looked. Billy didn't care, it was me he wanted to talk to. He came to my room late at night, brought a candle and lit it. He said it was confession time. Then he told me he'd had an affair with a girl in Delano, one of the migrant girls, a young girl, under-age. And she became pregnant. Or claimed to. Billy never saw a child because he panicked when she told him, being a lawyer, her age, statutory rape. He was also worried some grower would find out and use it against the union. Instead of shouldering his responsibility, he gave the girl every dollar he had with him and left town. That's when he joined the public defender's office. But it never stopped bothering him and he began driving around California, trying to find her – he said her name was Sharla and that she wasn't sophisticated but she had a good heart. He never found her.

'"But let's face it, Mom," he told me, "if I'd wanted to badly enough, I would've, right? I'm not sure I want to know – Father's right, I am a coward, spineless, no use to anyone." I told him the fact that he was telling me now showed he was extremely courageous, he still had a chance to buck up. I promised to do everything I could to help him find the girl, make financial arrangements for the child. If there *was* one – because I was skeptical, thought the girl was out for money. That infuriated him. He began pounding the bed, shouting that I was just like all the others, everything was money, money, money. Then he blew out the candle and stomped out. I'd never seen him like that and it shocked me. I thought I would let him cool down. The next morning, he was found floating in Lake Arrowhead. They said it was an accident. I never looked for the girl. I was never sure it was true. I did wonder from time to time . . . and then I saw the picture in the paper. And I knew. And now you've found him, Detective Connor.'

Petra took another look at the photo and handed it back. Too close to be anything but righteous, and the time-line was right. William Bradley Adamson. William Bradley Straight.

'What is it you want me to do for you, Mrs Adamson?'

'Detective, I know I have no right to – maybe legal rights,

but morally . . . but this child. He must be my grandson. There's no other rational explanation. I'm sure we can prove it. With genetic tests, but not now, not with all he's been through – I want to . . . help him.'

Suddenly, she looked down at her lap.

'I don't have the resources I used to have. My husband ran into some . . . misfortune before he passed away.'

Petra found herself giving a sympathetic nod.

'The truth is,' said Cora Adamson, still averting her eyes, 'I've been living off savings for several years, but I know how to budget and I'm by no means penniless. Learning about Billy – this Billy – has crystallized my plans. I live in a grotesquely oversized house that I've been thinking of selling for some time. Until now, I lacked the incentive – and the will – to make the change. Now, it's clear. There's no mortgage on the house. Once I sell it, even after taxes, I should have enough to support myself and my grandson in a reasonable manner.'

A pleading note had entered the woman's voice. Here she was, Chanel suit and all, applying for parental rights to Petra. What do you say to that?

Cora Adamson's head rose. 'Perhaps it's all for the best. Too much privilege can create its own difficulties.'

Petra wanted to say, I wouldn't know. Instead, she nodded.

'I love children, Detective Connor. Before I was married, I taught school. I always wanted *lots* of children but Billy's birth was difficult and the doctors forbade it. Other than the loss of Billy and Bill and my parents, learning I couldn't have more children was the saddest moment of my life.'

A thin white hand clutched Petra's sleeve. 'What I'm saying is I sincerely believe I have something to offer. I make

593

no excuses for the lack of— Detective Connor, can you see it within yourself to help me?'

The woman's eyes locked into Petra. Hungry, desperate.

Delaware was flying into town tonight. Why couldn't he be here *now*?

'Please,' said Cora Adamson.

Petra said, 'Let's talk about it.'

YESTERDAY, DR Delaware told me about Mom. My stomach caught fire and I wanted to rip the IV line out and punch him in the face.

He sat there looking sad. What right did *he* have to be sad?

I rolled over and ignored him. No way would I let him see me cry but the minute he left I started crying and I went on crying all day and all night. Except when someone came into the room and then I pretended to sleep.

Sometimes, when they thought I was sleeping, they'd discuss me, nurses, interns.

Poor kid.

He's been through so much.

Tough little bugger.

I am *not* tough. I'm here because what's my choice?

Thinking about Mom made me want to be dead, too, but then I thought what good would that do? There probably is no God so I wouldn't get to see her anyway.

That first night I dug my nails into my hands, made them bleed. A little extra pain felt right.

It's the next day and I still can't believe it, I keep thinking she's going to walk through the door, I'll say I'm sorry for running away, she'll apologize, too, we'll hug – then it hits me. She's gone. That's it. Never again. *Never! This hurts so much!*

I cry a lot, fall asleep, wake up, cry some more.

Haven't cried for an hour. Maybe I'm all dried up, no more tears.

Hey, Doc, put some tears in the IV.

I spit on the floor. If I could empty my mind the way the orderlies empty my trash can. Out with all the garbage.

When I'm alone I think of her. Even though it hurts. I *want* to hurt.

Being alone is what I'm used to, I don't get enough of it. With all the doctors and interns and the nurses, sometimes I can't stand all the noise and the sympathy, want to punch all of them.

Not Sam. He comes every morning, brings me candy and magazines, pats my hand and talks about how we're two peas in a pod, tough, survivors. How he won't let anyone 'mess' with me, don't worry, he's got connections. He repeats things and sometimes his voice puts me to sleep. I fight to stay awake, don't want to make him feel bad. He was my friend when no one else was. One time he came with Mrs Kleinman but she annoyed me, touching my cheek, bringing food I didn't want to eat, trying to feed it to me. I was polite to her but maybe Sam could tell because he never brought her again.

Petra brings me books. She's very pretty, not married, not a mom, and I think maybe she likes me because it gives her mom-practice. Or it's a vacation from being a detective.

She killed him. She's a serious person, doesn't tell jokes, doesn't try to cheer me up when I don't want it. Even when she smiles, she's serious.

Even if I'm totally exhausted, I can't be anything but nice to her.

She's about Mom's age – why'd Mom have to take that idiot Moron in, let him run her life, let him put a split in our family?

Why couldn't Mom learn to be *alone*?

Dr Delaware said it was probably an accident, he pushed her and she fell, but that doesn't make her any more alive.

I keep thinking: If I'd been there I could've saved her.

Dr Delaware talked to me about guilt, how it was normal but it would pass. How it was the parents' job to take care of children, not the other way around. He said Mom did love me, she meant well, but she'd hit some bad luck. He also said what happened to her was terrible, no way would he try to tell me everything was OK because it wasn't.

He was certain, though, that Mom would be proud of how well I'd done on my own.

Maybe.

He considers me very 'impressive.'

At first I thought he was full of it, the way he'd just sit, not saying much. At first I thought he didn't care. Now I think he probably does. He shows up every day at 6 P.M., stays with me for two hours, sometimes more, doesn't mind if we don't do anything.

Before he left, he noticed the chessboard that Sam left and asked if I wanted to play. He's about as good as Sam and I beat him two out of three. He said, 'OK, next time,' and I said, 'Prepare to lose.' He laughed and I asked him who's paying him to play games and he said the police, don't worry, he'd collect, he always does.

Sometimes he tells jokes. Some of them are funny.

The nurses seem to like him. I heard one nurse ask another if he was married and the other one said she wasn't sure, she didn't think so.

He and Petra would make a good couple.

I can imagine the two of them in a nice house, a good car, some kids, a dog. Or even one kid, so he could get all their attention.

Nice happy family, taking trips, going to restaurants.

Maybe it happens. I don't know. I'll never stop thinking about Mom – the door's opening and for a moment I think it's her.

It's Petra and she's wearing a red suit.

That's different, she always wears black. She's carrying a bag and she gives it to me.

Inside is a book.

The Presidents book. Not the one from the library. A brand-new one, clean cover, crisp white pages. It has that new-book smell. The colors in the illustrations are very bright. This is very cool.

'Thanks,' I say. 'Thanks a lot.'

She shrugs. 'Enjoy. Who knows, Billy, some day you might be in there.'

'Yeah, right.' It's a crazy idea. But an interesting one.

Bad Love

Jonathan Kellerman

AN ALEX DELAWARE NOVEL

No good will come.

It starts with a tape delivered to psychologist Alex Delaware's house – a recording of a soul-sickening scream followed by a twisted, childlike voice chanting 'Bad love. Bad love. Don't give me the bad love . . .' Alex heard that phrase a decade ago, at a symposium for Dr Andres de Bosch and his work with troubled teens; why is he hearing it now?

Then there are strange phone calls, a horrific act of vandalism and the discovery that other symposium delegates have been murdered. Unless Alex can make sense of the mind games being played he will be next . . .

Praise for Jonathan Kellerman

'Convincing psychiatrics; stylish, solidly character-ised and salted, as usual, with Kellerman's distaste for the LA landscape' *Literary Review*

'His portrait of lotus land under siege, with its underclass of sickos, addicts and no-hopers, is precise and convincing' *Observer*

978 0 7553 4292 1

headline

Devil's Waltz

Jonathan Kellerman

AN ALEX DELAWARE NOVEL

It's a living hell

Twenty-one-month-old Cassie Jones has spent most of her short life in and out of Western Paediatrics Hospital. Cassie is persistently, seriously, ill and when no amount of testing can identify the cause, her doctor is led to a disturbing diagnosis – Cassie's mother could be making her daughter deliberately sick.

Child psychologist Alex Delaware is brought in to make an independent assessment of the Jones family. But Alex's attempts to find the answers and save a young girl's life will reveal a terrifying circle of corruption, abuse and murderous hatred.

Praise for Jonathan Kellerman

'Has vampiric grip' *Guardian*

'Sophisticated, cleverly plotted and satisfying psycho-drama' *Sunday Telegraph*

978 0 7553 4291 4

headline

Now you can buy any of these other bestselling
books by **Jonathan Kellerman** from your bookshop
or *direct from his publisher*.

FREE P&P AND UK DELIVERY
(Overseas and Ireland £3.50 per book)

When the Bough Breaks	£7.99
Blood Test	£7.99
Over the Edge	£7.99
The Butcher's Theatre	£7.99
Silent Partner	£7.99
Time Bomb	£7.99
Private Eyes	£7.99
Devil's Waltz	£7.99
Bad Love	£7.99
Self-Defence	£7.99
The Web	£7.99
The Clinic	£7.99
Survival of the Fittest	£7.99

TO ORDER SIMPLY CALL THIS NUMBER

01235 400 414

or visit our website: www.headline.co.uk

Prices and availability subject to change without notice.